n the distance a siren wailed and died. He shifted in his seat. Porch lights were winking out and the breeze carried the velvety scent of pink and lavender night-blooming stock. Suddenly Jackie's porch window was bright.

Craning his neck, he followed the progression of lights— front hallway up the oak staircase to the landing, onward to the second floor. As the upstairs fixture flashed on, he pictured her slipping off her clothes in the bedroom and padding naked to the bathroom at the rear of the house. First a shower, then towel dry her hair. . . .

The light in the hallway flicked off and he imagined her walking down the stairs in her robe, coppery hair damp and loose around her shoulders. When he saw her shadow cross the window in the front room he knew she was in her study.

He climbed out of his car, closing the door with a soft thunk. Ducking his head, he crossed the street with a loose-limbed gait that said he had nothing to hide. When he reached the sidewalk he slipped into Jackie's yard. . . .

BANTAM BOOKS

New York | Toronto | London | Sydney | Auckland

BLIND

Stephanie Kane

SPOT

Stephanie Kane

BLIND SPOT

A Bantam Book / October 2000

ISBN 0-553-58175-9

Published simultaneously in the United States and Canada

Bantam Books are published by Bantam Books, a division of Random
House, Inc. Its trademark, consisting of the words "Bantam Books" and
the portrayal of a rooster, is Registered in U.S. Patent and Trademark
Office and in other countries. Marca Registrada. Bantam Books,
1540 Broadway, New York, New York 10036.

PRINTED IN THE UNITED STATES OF AMERICA

OPM 10 9 8 7 6 5 4 3 2 1

For John

Acknowledgments

I am grateful to my editor, Kate Miciak, for her guidance and wisdom; to my agent, Angela Rinaldi, for her persistence and patience; and to those souls who were generous enough to read and brave enough to comment on the manuscript. To Leslie Hoffman, Alan Shafer, Judith Shafer, Mary Ann Kane, Mark Shafer, Harry Shafer, Bob Kane, Harry MacLean, Stephen White, Joseph McNamara, Mike Gray, Dirk Eldredge, Rose Lassus, Herb Cohen and Dr. Alvin B. Reing, thanks. And to Bob Gorski, for a contribution only he could make.

Author's Note

The Cherry Creek Arts Festival is held in Denver on the Fourth of July weekend. Liberties taken with that event and certain locations were my own.

BLIND SPOT

Clumsy with anticipation, his fingers roam his prize. He listens for the spirit waiting to be freed. As with all art, he knows that this, his creation, will be an illusion—a replica born from nature. The air is green and wet, and in the fading light he is humbled by the grace with which this object surrenders its warmth. Its surface is satin but porous, a collage of minute pocks sublime in their imperfection. He traces the asymmetrical ridges and depressions, his thumbs probing the rounded contours that so allured him. But mind, eye, and hand must be in harmony to create a form that inspires the viewer, and all will be lost if he surrenders to the impulse to stare.

With his eyes closed he grazes the form one last time, committing its proportions to memory before discarding the surplus. He turns from the stone bench to his instruments. Though of the highest quality and honed and oiled with his customary precision, he takes pride in the fact that they are simple hand tools. Reaching for the powerful curved blade, he makes the decisive cut. Clean and smooth. Now he can give full rein to his artistry and skill. Enrapt, he snips and trims until the last light flees the room. Only then does he lift his creation by the hair to gaze into its sightless eyes.

Chapter One

No more date rapes, Jackie Flowers swore as she flung her bomber jacket over a chair and kicked her brief-case under her desk. No matter who called or how big the retainer.

Slipping off her hiking boots, she closed her eyes and tried to block out everything but the sound of the copy machine down the hall. When all extraneous stimuli had been reduced to a rhythmic whoosh and thump, the image behind her eyelids began to take form and she switched on her microcassette to record her impressions of the witnesses she'd interviewed in Boulder. Having found the missing piece to her client's defense, she wasn't about to lose it.

"Courtney Briggs, eighteen, freshman from Grand Junction . . ."

Elfin face and ragged cuticles, the little match girl staring through the window as the banker carved the Christmas goose. But the setting was an ivy-covered sorority house on the University of Colorado campus and not a fairy tale. . . . The phone rang two doors down and a burst of laughter from the estate planner across the hall sent the match girl scurrying back into the cold.

Concentration shot, Jackie padded across the floor to the window. Her second-floor office was one of the smaller units in the converted mansion of a silver baron who'd gone bust a century before. The suites on the first floor had bars on the glass, and when you looked out you were as likely to catch a man urinating against the Dumpster in the parking lot as a whiff of lilac and forsythia. The mansion on Denver's Capitol Hill was now home to a band of solo practitioners who enjoyed an easy camaraderie no downtown sweatshop could match. And far fewer financial entanglements.

Gazing across the street at the egg-carton high-rise that partially obstructed her view of the mountains, Jackie spotted one of the few reliable signs of spring: dusty ficuses and elephant ferns crowding the screened balconies, hauled outside to bask in the sun. But the brilliant rays masked a nip to the air and the trees couldn't decide whether to trust the calendar. Three inches of wet snow had fallen earlier in the week, and the cherry blossoms outside the window had turned to wax. In her own yard the dwarf irises had come and gone, the crocuses that pushed through the earth in March like grape and lemon lollipops were but a memory, and now the daffodils were struggling to . . . With a sigh she realized she was projecting her own ambivalence about the date-rape case onto the weather. Spring storms always threw her.

Back at her desk, she unsnapped the waistband of her stone-washed designer jeans and flexed her toes in the Ragg socks she hadn't worn since college. Regression had paid off; Courtney Briggs's sorority sisters had told her everything she needed to know. Or, more accurately, *shown* her. Prom queens though they may have been in high school, these children with their professional manicures and cover-girl smiles were nonetheless novices at the art of deception. A dip of the chin and sudden hesitation, the momentary drop in pitch—Jackie caught it all and was about to memorialize every gesture and phrase to use against them if any of them pulled a one-eighty on the stand. Freeing her honey-colored mane from its leopard-print scrunchie, she punched the rewind button and started over.

"Courtney Briggs, a *very young* eighteen, at the Delta Kappa—"

"Cute outfit. Takes me back to a place I never was." The smell of freshly brewed coffee hit Jackie before she looked up. Pilar Perez, built like a desktop computer but four times more efficient, gazed enviously at the getup that made her boss appear no older than the girls half her age she'd gone to Boulder to meet. "Figure out your opening statement yet?"

"Peer pressure." The coffee's earthy scent dispelled the vision of bloodred nails and perfect teeth. "Too bad they can't charge Courtney's sorority sisters."

As Jackie gratefully sipped her coffee, the afternoon sun embraced her wall of books in its mandarin glow. *AmJur* legal treatises with pebbled covers the color of jade, maroon Colorado statutes with gold lettering across fat spines, an entire set of calfskin *Colorado Reporter*s she'd bought at auction from a law firm that rode the energy boom of the early '80s to crash just as spectacularly a decade later. A fitting library for the long-dead silver baron. Like her own immaculate desk, those rows of books provided a queer comfort.

"Gonna knock off a bank with Vinnie and the boys?" Jackie asked Pilar. In her man-tailored pinstriped suit and snap-brim hat, her fifty-five-year-old investigator resembled a Mafia don.

"Just drinks with that silver fox from Dispatch," Pilar replied. "Maybe place a couple bets at the dog track. He got paid today, sky's the limit."

"I thought he was history."

"Springtime in the Rockies." Pilar treated Jackie to a lewd wink. "Speaking of which, when's the last time you had a date?"

"Longer ago than either of us can remember."

They both laughed, and Pilar switched on the television set on the shelf behind Jackie's desk. The Channel 9 logo flashed across the screen, quickly replaced by the five-o'clock anchorwoman. The generic blonde who'd almost been canned the year before for pronouncing "Deutschemark" as if it were a feminine hygiene product.

"I hate to be rude," Jackie began, "but I've got to dictate my—"

"Haven't you heard?"

"Heard what? I've been in Boulder all day, squeezing blood from adolescent barracudas—"

"Shush!" Pilar turned up the volume. "They found the body of that woman from Castle Pines. You know, the divorcée . . ."

The story had made every edition of the papers and each nightly broadcast for the better part of a week. It had all the right ingredients: ex-wife of a wealthy developer, abducted without a trace from her home off the fifth hole of the most exclusive golf course in the state. Nothing stolen, no enemies or ransom note. Every clerk at the supermarket checkout stands had a theory, and there was nothing Pilar relished more than sinking her teeth into a juicy murder.

The camera moved in for a close-up of three squad cars beetled nose-in by the railroad tracks, then cut to a cluster of uniformed men kneeling over something in a slushy patch between two fences a hundred yards away.

"—Rae Malone," the man in the Channel 9 windbreaker was saying, "missing since last Friday from her exclusive estate in Douglas County. For complete coverage of this breaking story, we now return to—"

"My money's on the ex," Jackie said. "With a spread in Castle Pines, he must be paying alimony up the wazoo."

"What's a million here or there?" Pilar parked her square butt on the arm of Jackie's chair. "But my source says it's a sex crime. The bedroom was a mess and they found blood in the drive—"

"—eminent forensic psychiatrist," the anchorwoman intoned, "Dr. Richard Hanna, Jr." To her right sat a man in his mid-forties with pale skin and a shock of black hair. "As some of you may recall, Dr. Hanna testified in the case of convicted killer—"

"A hunk." Pilar sighed with the resignation of a woman never too old to look. "Of course, he only bats for the prosecution. . . ."

The camera zeroed in on the psychiatrist. Hanna's aquiline features and startlingly blue eyes would have qualified him for a GQ cover, and the conservative cut of his suit seemed calculated to mute an attractiveness of which he was surely aware. The camera moved to a close-up of his left hand to capitalize on the Channel 9 logo on his coffee mug. No ring.

"—suspects in the most heinous crimes in recent memory." The anchor ended her fifteen-second recap of a two-decade career with a smile that was positively kittenish. "Working with these people must be *fascinating*. Tell me, doctor, have you ever felt in danger?"

"My job tends to be more frustrating than dangerous." Hanna shrugged with an appealing modesty and Jackie leaned forward. "Modern psychiatry and the legal system are frequently at odds. Courts are geared toward absolutes, yes-or-no answers to questions that are inherently uncertain, whereas psychiatry is ambivalent. We're more concerned with internal motivation, emotional truth—"

"I'm sure you're very good at what you do." The anchor licked her whiskers. "Now, what can you tell us about the man who killed Rae Malone?"

"Not much, I'm afraid. It would be unethical to provide a real diagnosis for someone I've never met." His voice was low, almost intimate, the diction curiously without inflection, and Jackie wondered where he was from. Was it that soft-spoken tentativeness or Hanna's unwillingness to allow himself to be reduced to sound bites that made you not want to miss a word? "But I will say this. Whoever killed Ms. Malone is almost certainly a psychopath."

"Does that mean he's insane?"

"Not necessarily. Psychopaths mimic sanity." His eyes were close-set but they drew you. *Trust me,* they said, *I'm here to listen.* "They construct a mask of self-control, live a life of deceit while acting out fantasies to deal with a sense of impotence and need for revenge originating in childhood. But inside they're hollow." His tapered fingers spread as if to pluck an image from the air. "You might call them empty suits."

"Speaking of suits," Pilar whispered, "he must have a hell of a practice to afford threads like those. And I'd give anything for that head of hair."

But Jackie was mesmerized by the vision he had conjured. A walking husk. A hollow man . . . Her gaze wandered to the neat row of *AmJur*s across from her desk. What would the good doctor say about her if he knew those spines had never been cracked?

"Will he strike again?" The anchorwoman leaned forward expectantly. Thirty seconds to kill and the ratings signs in her eyes were dimming.

"Who knows?" Hanna shrugged again with mute eloquence. Not too slick or folksy, a nice note to end on— "But I'd venture a guess Ms. Malone wasn't his first victim."

The anchor pounced.

"Why do you say that?"

"I—well, violent patterns are often established early in life. From what I've been told of Ms. Malone's death—"

"The decapitation?" she asked sweetly, and Hanna gave a start. She'd sandbagged him; he walked right into it. "We have it from an inside source that body parts were left at two locations north of Coors Field. . . ."

"*Jeez*-us!" Pilar exclaimed.

"I'm afraid I can't go into detail," Hanna replied. But his failure to deny that Rae Malone had been beheaded had given the anchor her lead for that night's broadcast, and Jackie couldn't help feeling sorry for him.

"Tune in at ten for the latest," the woman purred.

Pilar switched off the TV and Jackie settled back in her chair. As she reached for her dictaphone she was still picturing a husk in shiny black wingtips.

"The barracudas bite?" Pilar asked sympathetically, but her boss was lost in thought. "In Boulder," she prompted.

"We have a solid consent defense. Courtney Briggs bragged to half the sorority the next morning that she had sex with our guy. When he didn't call that weekend, she had to cry rape."

"She told you that?"

"Didn't have to. She comes from Grand Junction and still wears a training bra, for God's sake! Of course she wants their approval."

"But why did her sorority sisters turn on her?" Pilar persisted.

"It was a one-night stand. When those girls bag a tight end on the football team, they make sure he's good for a couple of dates. Blaming our guy was the only way for Courtney to save face."

"Great!"

"Yeah." A guilty victim and a semi-innocent client . . . Richard Hanna had it right. In the courtroom there were no shades of gray, and no place for an attorney who was ambivalent about her work. Jackie stuffed the recorder in her briefcase and reached for the clunky boots.

"I thought you were going to stay and dictate your interviews," Pilar said.

"Have to stop at the dry cleaner's before it closes." A white lie, but Pilar wouldn't hold it against her. She'd been claiming she was thirty-nine years old since the day Jackie met her.

"Nothing wrong with Lily, is there?" Pilar demanded.

On target as usual, but there was no sense worrying her.

"Of course not," Jackie replied.

"Know what you need?"

"Besides getting laid?"

"A nice, clean murder. Maybe when they bust that guy—"

"The Hollow Man?"

"Yeah, the Hollow Man." Pilar patted Jackie's arm reassuringly. "Maybe he'll call."

"His brand of deceit would be refreshing," Jackie said, and meant it.

Chapter | Two

Just up the hill from the gold-domed state capitol on Colfax stretched a strip of pawnshops and liquor stores, tattoo parlors, and motels with hourly rates, and the surrounding streets were a collage of halfway houses and turn-of-the-century mansions gone to seed. Neighborhood merchants tried to spiff up the boulevard by chasing off dealers and prostitutes with wrought-iron benches and flowerpots, but the establishments that thrived appreciated Colfax for what it was *not*: neither destined to return to the glory of yesteryear nor a competitor to the affluent shops a mile to the south. As Jackie drove, she had no doubt what Lily would make of the reformers' pretensions.

Even at four Lily had lacked the round-faced sweetness associated with Chinese girls; when Jackie's next-door neighbors adopted her, she'd been all sharp angles and harsh planes, and she'd lost most of her baby teeth to malnutrition. All Britt and Randy were told was the child had been found on the steps of a seamen's club up north near Shanghai. For that reason, and because Lily was so scrawny and tall for her age, it was assumed her father was a sailor.

That first evening Jackie saw her watching from Britt and Randy's porch. The next night Lily appeared at her window, but when Jackie invited her in, she ran off. Three days later she was waiting when Jackie came home. In a desperate attempt to look like the doll her adoptive parents had given her on the plane, the four-year-old hacked off the front part of her hair to make bangs. Jackie trimmed them straight and made a friend for life. Four years later they still kept their fingers crossed that Lily's bottom teeth would grow in, but it would take a great deal more than incisors to make her belong. She'd outgrown the spitting and scratching but had started kindergarten late and been held back in first grade, and Britt told Jackie that Lily still refused to read.

Twenty blocks east of Colorado Boulevard Jackie spotted the forest green awning of Dog Day Afternoons. When she'd stumbled across the shop six months before, it was that rounded canopy that caught her eye. Jaunty and inviting, an emerald in a pile of glass. Pilar's affinity for dogs—of the human and canine variety—was legendary, and Jackie had been looking for a gift for the latest addition to her menagerie. From the sign she'd assumed it was a pet store, and she parked around the corner and walked in. Immediately she realized her mistake.

If she'd closed her eyes, she would have known it by the smell: the vanilla scent of yellowing paper, the deeper note of dusty leather, a ticklish must saturating the air. Books. Lots of them. Walls packed, more volumes stacked on the counter and tables. Like a library but worse; here you *breathed* print. And they were used, every one of these books had been owned and read. The knowing look from the wirehaired terrier in a fleece-lined vest perched in the armchair beneath a two-hundred-and-fifty-pound stuffed mountain lion added to her betrayal. Jackie backed out, drove to the PetsMart on Colorado, and loaded her cart with dried pigs' ears and rubber chew toys.

Spotting that canopy now, Jackie was reminded how out of place it seemed on this rundown stretch. Lesser of the evils, she thought as she parked and, brushing aside a twinge of resentment at the misleading name, entered. The counter was unattended, but from the voices in the rear she knew the establishment doubled back on itself on the other side of the wall. She tried to get her bearings. Two walls of hardcovers towered over the front of the shop, whose easy chairs and small table gave the space a cozy feel. For an instant she was transported to the lap of her aunt, enfolded in her arms with one hand slowly turning the page.

Would you like to hear a story?

But cozy was a short step from claustrophobic, and the comforting image vanished as abruptly as it came. Now those shelves yawned like rows of teeth, and the sheer volume of colors and variety of lettering on the spines made her head swim. Breathing hard, she turned to the counter. To its right lay a labyrinth of chest-high shelves. On one of them stood the mountain lion.

Four feet tall at the shoulder and six feet long from nose to tail, he was mounted on a wooden base whose surface was textured with sand. She touched the leather knobs at his heels. They were black and smooth as river stones and his pelt had the silky coarseness of an animal brought down in his prime. Block out all but one tawny patch of fur, and take another deep breath—

"Can I help you find something?"

A tiny woman had emerged from the back and was looking at her with a friendly expression.

Tell her why you're here.

"I was just admiring your cougar," Jackie replied, relieved when her voice came out normal. "Where on earth did you find him?"

"An estate sale in Longmont. We couldn't resist."

Jackie slowly let out her breath. She could handle this, all she needed was *one*. "Do you carry children's books?"

The woman led her past the lion to a wall of gaily colored spines.

"What did you have in mind?" she asked.

Pulling a book from the shelf, Jackie pretended to skim the first few pages. "Something with illustrations."

"Are you interested in fairy tales? Andrew Lang's a classic." The woman handed her a fat volume with gothic script on the cover and distressingly small print. Inside, princes knelt at the feet of their betrotheds, as feckless and stagy as the figures in a deck of tarot cards. "Is it for a girl?"

"Not exactly the princess type."

"Of course . . ."

Jackie's eyes flitted across the shelf in search of an uncluttered spine. They stopped at an oversized volume whose title was chiseled like Roman numerals in stone. *Myths and Legends.* On the cover a winged creature with the head of a woman and talons for feet swooped down on a figure in a Greek helmet with an upraised sword. Turning to the table of contents, she began skimming.

Twenty stories divided into manageable blocks with subheadings in the same Roman style as the cover. Short paragraphs, dark print, most of the words two syllables or less. Vibrant drawings spilled across each page, bold images that dwarfed the text and left the imagination free to roam.

"Not just Greeks and Romans," the woman added helpfully, "but Beowulf, and Roland at the Battle of Roncevaux."

With gashes for features the narrow faces defied ethnicity, and there was an appealing universality to the tapered limbs and fingers that stabbed like tines. The monsters' anguished eyes cried, *why me*? and conventions of color had been tossed to the winds: skin tones of man and beast ranged from olive to charcoal to magenta. The flanks of one steed were a magnificent grape.

Lily would love it.

Chapter | Three

As Jackie drove home under a slate-colored sky, the wind rocked her ten-year-old Corolla. A bank of clouds scaffolded the Front Range all the way south to Pikes Peak. Winter was gearing up for one final blast, and she zipped up her bomber jacket and pictured a large can of chunky chicken soup.

The trip to Boulder that morning had taken more out of her than she'd realized. It wasn't the first time she'd stuck her hands in muck to find an unpalatable truth she had to exploit to win; that was the job description of a criminal defense lawyer. But the price of an acquittal would be the destruction of a mere child whose true failing was caring more about what her friends thought than what her accusation would do to Jackie's client. Pilar joked about jumping at a chance to represent the Hollow Man, but she'd come closer to the truth than Jackie liked to admit. Murderers *were* easier to defend. Their victims could no longer speak.

Jackie turned into the alley behind her house two blocks east of Cheesman Park and made the sharp left into her garage. The sky was already starting to spit and, tucking the mythology book into her jacket and her briefcase under her arm, she darted through the back gate and entered by the kitchen door.

The boxy two-story brick with hipped roof and attic

dormer was a Denver Square, built in 1911 when plans could be purchased from the Sears catalogue. The upstairs windows were widely spaced and of different sizes, which gave the facade an astigmatic, half-witted look. Later versions corrected the squint by moving the windows closer together or adding a third eye, decorative brick, or terra-cotta ornamentation in the center. But Jackie's only major improvements had been to install an attic fan and insulate the interior walls the previous fall.

Now she walked through the downstairs, flicking on lights, signaling Lily she was home. Britt sold real estate and Randy was an investment adviser; both worked irregular hours that left their adopted daughter a great deal of independence. It wasn't that they weren't *concerned*, Britt would explain, it was just that Lily expressed a preference not to be smothered. And since they were now responsible for her future, it was all the more *important* that she and Randy accommodate their clients' busy schedules. . . . What it boiled down to was Lily's new parents were delighted Jackie showed an interest in their daughter. Lily was so much more than they'd bargained for.

After her soup and crackers, Jackie settled in the room just off the front hall. The previous owner claimed the house was built for a doctor who used the paneled space with sliding doors as a waiting room and the balance of the downstairs as a surgery. Upon seeing the room the first time, Jackie immediately designated it her study.

Two walls of the chamber were windows; the east faced the wooden porch and the south was a tall pane of glass overlooking a garden just wide enough for a flagstone path. The wall facing the garden held a large mineral collection Jackie had started when she was sixteen. The only furniture was a narrow desk and an overstuffed armchair in brocaded silk that had belonged to her aunt.

Settling in her chair, Jackie fastened on a fluorite with sharp geometric lines. It was too dark to see the mauve and violet shapes inside the crystal, but as the minutes passed, the stone silhouette absorbed the tensions of the day and she was at last able to focus. Flicking on the microcassette, she resumed recording her impressions of the witnesses in

Boulder. Details tumbled back, a flood of gestures and expressions and peculiar turns of phrase, and she recounted them all without regard to whether they made sense. It wasn't as if these notes would be transcribed; she recorded them only to refresh her memory on the eve of trial.

When the phone shrilled at a quarter past eight, she was tempted not to answer. Her home number was unlisted; evening calls were inevitably solicitations for the mayoral campaign or a useless subscription to the *Denver Post*.

"Miss Flowers?"

The voice was vaguely familiar, an easy masculine beat that wasn't trying to sell. He sounded like he was at a pay phone at the end of a long corridor.

"Yes?"

"I—I don't know whether you remember—" The rest of the sentence was lost to background noise, muted shouts with a repetitive quality Jackie thought she should recognize. "—last September."

Best Energy, the "green energy" company that insulated her house the previous fall. Two men had come—one clean-shaven, in a neatly pressed sport shirt and chinos, the other in tight Levis, with a handlebar mustache and dishwater hair. They'd used fire-resistant cellulose made from shredded newsprint; was this call to warn her of a problem?

"Is something wrong?" she asked.

"Well, that's the thing." Metal clanged. "You're the only lawyer I know. . . ."

The county jail. And his diffidence identified him all but by name—Aaron Best, the Levi-clad owner of the company.

"What happened?"

"You know that woman out in Castle Pines? The one they found today? Guess who they busted."

Now his face zoomed into focus—Aaron Best had an unfinished look, as if someone had sketched him in outline and left the details for later. The mustache was too aggressive for the softness of his mouth, the Levis more self-conscious than bold. He'd brought his son along to inspect the job one weekend, and Jackie remembered the way he kept his arm around the boy, his watchfulness as his son climbed the ladder to her attic.

"Did you know her?" she asked. "The murdered woman?"

"Not really." That meant *yes*. "We did an energy audit of her home back in January. A real lady." He waited, but Jackie resisted the impulse to prompt. Clients were never more suggestible than in these first moments, and if she wanted the truth, it would have to come from his lips and not hers. "But you know me, I couldn't hurt a fly."

The immediate question was not whether Aaron did it but whether Jackie was willing to get involved. Which meant the odds of mounting a successful defense. She raced through the little she knew. Divorcée abducted from fancy home, head and body found behind Coors Field . . . There must be physical evidence linking him to the crime; the case was too high-profile for the cops to make a hasty arrest.

"Would you at least see me?" he continued, his voice rising on the last two words. Guilty or not, like any client, he'd been thrust headfirst into a world where everything was upside down. Jackie didn't have to wonder how *that* felt.

"—nightmare, I could lose everything . . ."

An irrelevant snippet popped into her head. When Aaron presented his bill, it had seemed a bit light. The job came in under bid, he explained; he charged only for work done. Ten minutes of her time, didn't she owe him that?

"I'll be there tomorrow," she replied. "In the meantime, keep your mouth shut. Don't trust *anyone*."

Chapter | Four

As Jackie settled in the back row of Courtroom 16 of the City and County Building at half past eight the following morning, Duncan Pratt's baritone rang from the well of the court to the polished oak bench, bouncing off the faux columns to the gold filigreed ceiling. She'd known he'd be at this arraignment of four gang members charged with last week's drive-by shooting on Colfax. No one was more conscious of the weight of his office than the district attorney, and never did he wear its dignity more splendidly than when he stood before a courtroom packed with reporters to bring down the bar of justice on a manacled man's head.

Someone had left that morning's *Rocky Mountain News* on the bench beside Jackie. Beneath the tabloid headline "Millionaire's Ex Murdered" was a large color photo of Rae Malone and her husband apparently lifted from the society pages. A statuesque redhead in a strapless satin gown, Rae had yards of hair pulled back from her face in an Alice-in-Wonderland look. In his custom-made tuxedo Rodger Malone was squat and toadlike, an impression enhanced by the glare on the flash on his balding pate and the arm cinched protectively about his wife's waist. At Rae's elbow stood the newly elected governor of the state of Colorado.

Pratt's rhetoric was winding down and Jackie tossed the newspaper aside. Flanked by public defenders, the men in jailhouse greens with chains about their waists mumbled not-guilty pleas. This would be Duncan Pratt's last appearance in the case; the DA was there for the media in the front row, not the dirty work of a trial. As the defendants were shuffled off by potbellied deputies, Pratt scoured the prosecution table for stray paper clips and pens, gathered his manila folders, and left the less weighty matters to his subordinates. Leaning over the rail to chat up a fellow from the *News*, he straightened his tie in anticipation of a photo op. Jackie waited until he'd cleared the reporters, then followed him out.

"Dunc—"

"Jackie!"

Pratt's rabbity eyes lit with pleasure, or what might have been pleasure were he capable of sincerity. Even in law school he'd been glad-handing for office. An earnest if unremarkable student, he'd sat in the precise center of every class, ensuring he would be neither the first nor the last called upon in the canny way of cattle assessing their prospects of slaughter. But despite his political cunning Pratt was a far better DA than his predecessors—neither a rabid proponent of the death penalty nor a dupe of defense counsel, in favor of gun control so long as it didn't jeopardize the suburban vote. Jackie had cast her ballot for him and would do so again. In the days when he was still trying cases, she'd wiped up the courtroom with him more than once.

"Didn't see your name on this morning's docket," he continued.

"I was hoping to run into you." Nonresponsive of her, but Pratt appreciated flattery. "I understand you made an arrest in the Castle Pines case."

The boyish grin tightened. Pratt didn't like surprises, and Jackie on the other side of a case was a bad surprise.

"Aaron Best moves fast, but his case is open and shut. We've got him dead to rights."

"Then you won't mind telling me what you've got."

"A body and a head. One under the viaduct, the other by the railroad tracks." Pratt pressed the button for the elevator. The half dozen people waiting were an excuse not to talk, and Jackie took his arm and steered him toward the steps. He moved gracefully for his bulk; guiding him was like being at the helm of a-dirigible. "Your boy's going down."

"Come on, Dunc." She wasn't about to admit she had not yet been retained. "You'll have to tell me sooner or later. . . ."

"Off the record?" As if there were such a thing.

"Sure."

"We go back a long way, Jackie." From study group the first semester of law school to whipping him at moot court finals just before graduation. If he fed her any more of these lines, she would make him buy her lunch. "I'm no bullshitter, you know that."

"And?"

"DNA." Pratt gazed at his old classmate with regret; Jackie kept her face blank. "Best's biting the big one."

"I'm famished," she announced.

It was barely nine in the morning, and as she propelled him through the lobby and down the granite steps, she kept her eye out for the hot dog vendor. He was at the corner of Fourteenth and Bannock, setting up his steam cart. It was too early for a beer and anyway, with Pratt, food worked better.

"I'm due back—" he protested.

"Just a second." The man in the apron flashed her a broad smile. His first customers, at this hour a sign of luck. "Two Polish," she told him, "smothered with green."

"Too early for me," Pratt replied, licking his lips.

"Who said anything about you?" She turned back to the hot dog man. "He'll have the same."

Jackie fumbled in her briefcase and came up with a twenty, knowing the vendor wouldn't have change and Pratt would pay with the gallantry of one who enjoyed having his adversaries in his debt. Dunc fell for it every time. Briefcase under her arm, she held one dog in each hand as they crossed to Civic Center Park and found an empty bench.

"So, what's this about DNA?" She swallowed a third of her first dog in one bite, expertly intercepting a dollop of chili destined for her silk blouse. In law school they said she ate like a bird, meaning she consumed three times her weight each day to keep going. But eating was disarming; like a parlor trick, she could turn it on or off. And men loved to watch her do it.

"Semen on Malone's sheet." Pratt seemed heedless of green sauce dribbling down his chin. For a man to whom trial prep meant alphabetizing and arranging his notes in accordion files for his associates to carry to court, he could be surprisingly sloppy. "We've got Best cold."

Energy audit, my ass, Jackie thought, remembering Aaron's words.

"That's it?" she said.

Pratt stopped mid-bite, instantly suspicious. Most lawyers would be cozying up for a plea. "Jackie, the coroner said she was screwing just before—"

"The last time I had sex, it didn't kill me."

"No, I can't imagine any guy making you lose your head."

What was that supposed to mean?

"All these years, Dunc, and I never knew you cared." Come to think of it, she'd never seen her old classmate with a woman. But Pratt prided himself on keeping it professional; that crack must mean he really wanted a plea. "How many killers do you know who voluntarily give DNA samples? Don't tell me that's *all* you have."

He chewed slowly and took his time swallowing.

"What about blood?" she pressed.

"No one twisted Best's arm, Jackie. He gave us that sample entirely of his own—"

"I mean hers. At the scene."

Pratt blinked twice, meaning he was pissed. "Who told you about that?"

"The drops in the driveway? Common knowledge." Not as far as she knew, but Jackie wasn't about to toss Pilar's contact to the wolves. "I mean on the bed."

Pratt wiped his fingers on his handkerchief and she let silence do its work.

"No blood," he finally replied. "Just semen."

"But it wasn't only on the *sheet* . . ."

"Matter of fact, it was." She leaned forward, forcing Pratt to meet her eyes. For a prosecutor, he was a lousy liar.

Even in moot court he folded. "Her body was washed clean," he admitted.

"No hair, no fibers? Nothing under the nails?"

"Nope." He rose, knowing he'd just paid far more than the price of a couple of chili dogs. "Now, if you'll excuse me—"

"Where was Rodger Malone while his wife was getting whacked?"

"At the Governor's Economic Summit in Snowmass!"

The best alibi money could buy.

"Let me get this straight. You're charging Aaron Best with first-degree murder just because he picked the wrong time to have sex?"

"I've won convictions on far less."

"Not against me, Duncan."

His teeth flashed. "This is one slimeball you ain't gonna walk."

As Jackie drove east on I-70 toward the county jail, her elation dimmed. As a defense attorney, she was trained to treat everything a client said with healthy skepticism. But here the honeymoon was already over. At best, she had a prospective client who'd lied to her in the first thirty seconds of their relationship; at worst, Aaron was a killer who'd had sex with his victim before decapitating her. A proponent of the half-full glass, Pilar would say she was crazy not to jump at the chance: her upside was a high-profile case she might win; the downside, a client who could pay the freight. But if she couldn't trust Aaron to level about the most easily proven facts, defending him would be like playing hacky-sack with a live grenade.

Just south of the Rocky Mountain Arsenal, once given the distinction of being labeled the most polluted acreage on earth, the jail had a timeless brand of institutional malevolency. Which did it resemble more—a nineteenth-century insane asylum or a stronghold from another millennium? Surrounded by rolled razor wire and a twenty-foot chain-link fence, the vertical slits for windows were too narrow for a head to slip through but ideal for shooting arrows at Huns. The eighty-foot guard tower was an anachronism too, relegated to a grim reminder of the days of the ball and chain, sundown parole, where no charges were filed if your client left town by twilight, and the option of joining the military.

Sliding her driver's license and attorney registration card through the slit in the bulletproof glass at the information booth, Jackie said she wanted to see Aaron Best. The deputy exhibited no surprise at her empty briefcase and promptly buzzed her into the sallyport leading to the interview rooms. As the door slammed shut behind her, she stared at the walls and breathed through her mouth.

Some claimed it was the constant noise, others the total loss of freedom that made being imprisoned so unbearable. To the old-timers at the public defender's office where Jackie learned the ropes, the worst thing about the jail was the odor. Before smoking was banned, visiting a client was like being trapped inside a spittoon. The jail was no longer a cuspidor, but it still reeked of too many bodies pressed together, men who never brushed their teeth or used deodorant. But to Jackie the noise and stench paled beside the claustrophobia of the sallyport.

The rock-walled enclosure was coated with a glossy substance that conjured the slow drip of water. Like the Bermuda Triangle, the portals unlocked in a precise sequence. Only one door opened at a time, and if the deputy at the front desk was otherwise engaged or pushed the wrong button, you could be stuck forever. The opposite wall finally swung open, and Jackie offered up a silent thanks before entering the limbo of the jail itself.

As she waited for Aaron in a cubicle barely large enough to accommodate a metal table and two chairs, Jackie glanced behind her at the information booth. Lined up like rooms in a railroad flat and divided by chest-to-ceiling glass, each cubbyhole was visible at all times to the deputy in the booth. If he happened to be looking. Given the antipathy toward lawyers, the administrators who approved the prison's construction plans would not have been dismayed to learn a female colleague of hers had been dragged to that shiny yellow linoleum and raped before anyone knew something was wrong. Nor had the red panic button beside the table stopped another lawyer from having his ear bitten off before a deputy could respond. Prisoners shuffled into court in leg irons and shock belts surrounded by six armed guards, but was it any coincidence the cuffs came off before they entered that five-by-five-foot cubicle?

The door suddenly opened and Aaron filled the threshold. When it clicked shut and he saw Jackie's expression, his smile faded.

"You lied to me," she said.

His eyes were greener than she remembered and his hair two shades darker, a contrast reinforced by an ashy pallor that showed he hadn't slept. Settling in the opposite chair, Aaron massaged his wrists to restore their circulation.

"I'm sorry," he replied.

No denial, not even a what-the-hell-are-you-talking-about. Good.

"Try it again and I'm out of here. Now, tell me what happened and skip the crap."

He ducked his head but his eyes remained watchful. "Like I said last night, I did an audit at her home in January." As he leaned forward and hitched his sleeves over his forearms, Jackie saw the tattoo. It looked adult, not adolescent—certainly not military. "A real showplace out in Castle Pines . . ."

If she didn't break him of depersonalizing the victim now, the DA would.

"Use her name."

"Rae. Rae Malone."

"And?"

"We hit it off." His fingers were scarred, the nails bitten to the quick. "She was lonely and I was going through a rough patch with my wife."

"How many times did the two of you have sex?"

"Half a dozen, no big thing. She liked me and I liked her." He gave a little laugh. "Guys like me don't often meet a goddess on the job."

"Goddess?"

"That's what we called her. The Goddess of Castle Pines."

"We?"

"Me and the guys on the crew that did the energy audit." He smiled at a private memory, and Jackie wondered what the men who'd insulated her home last winter had said about *her*. "She kind of made a play for me."

"Why'd you give the cops a sample of your blood?"

"Someone must've said I was balling her"—was he evening the score with crudity because she'd cut his preening short?— "and they asked if I'd cooperate. I had no reason not to."

"Did they tell you what evidence they had?"

"I didn't ask." Aaron leaned forward again, spreading his hands in the time-honored pose of innocence, and Jackie's irritation grew. She had to push him, get under his skin; it was the only way to know if she could help him. "Like I said, I've got nothing to hide."

"So why lie to me?"

"My wife booted me out six months ago. She wants custody of my boy."

"Have either of you filed for divorce?"

"I want to patch things up, but she—"

"Has your wife filed for divorce?"

He looked away. "Yeah."

"Any incidents I should know about between the two of you?"

"No."

"Is there a custody action pending?"

"Nobody's taking my son!" Aaron's eyes blazed, and in them Jackie read his first unguarded emotion. Her key to making him real for the jury. "Trevor means everything to me. You think I'd be stupid enough to do something that could hurt him?"

"When's the last time you saw Rae Malone?"

"A week ago Thursday." The day before she disappeared.

"The two of you fight?"

"No."

"Did you have sex?"

"Yeah."

"Where?"

"Her house. The master bedroom."

"Did you wear a condom?"

A startled grin. Half-sheepish, half-proud. Did he think she was getting off on these questions?

"I like to ride bareback," he replied.

"She shower afterward?"

"I don't know, I just left."

"The DA's going to come at you swinging with both fists, and I don't like surprises. Anything else I should know?"

He looked confused. "No."

Jackie pushed back her chair.

"That all?" he asked.

"For now."

"Will you take my case?"

"If you're willing to pay my retainer." She waited for him to ask how much.

"Money's no problem."

She reached for her briefcase, still unopened on that gleaming lemon floor.

"One more thing," she said. "No more free samples. No talking to cell mates, friends, or relatives. Anything you say or do goes through me."

"When can you get me out of here?"

Usually the first question, not the last.

"Right now, Aaron, I'm more concerned with *keeping* you out."

W hen the tap at her window came, Jackie was in her study, reviewing what she knew of the case. While Pratt processed Jackie's formal request for the file, Pilar had retrieved the press reports, including the front-page shot of the spread at Castle Pines in the *Rocky*'s late edition and a grainy aerial view of the viaduct and railroad tracks from the *Post*. On the legal pad in her lap she'd blocked out the evidence: a castle with turrets in the upper right corner of the page, a penciled squiggle on the pennant over the battlement for semen, two dots of red ink leading away from the moat. A bold black arrow pointed to the lower left corner of the page, with a crosshatch and a circle with hair beside it. She just had time to tear off the sheet and stuff it in the wastebasket before Lily was at her door.

"Can I come in?"

"Of course."

They always observed the ritual of permission asked and granted.

Unzipping her parka, Lily settled on the rug and folded her long legs beneath her.

"Are you working?" she asked, and Jackie wondered whether she'd been peeking in the window. Lily claimed to have forgotten every word of Chinese, and her vocabulary was much better than her diction, especially since she'd lost her bottom teeth, but she was as watchful now as the day she'd arrived.

"Why don't we hang up your parka?" Jackie offered. The afternoon had been too warm for goose down, but red was Lily's favorite color and Britt insisted she bundle up regardless of the weather.

"That's okay, I'm not staying."

When Lily was adopted, she was the most fastidious child Jackie had ever seen. Potty trained and neat as a pin, she would accept nothing but egg drop soup and steamed rice. She ate only with chopsticks and not so much as a grain dropped to the plate; for two full years she resisted the lure of chicken tenders. Though she still drew the line at potatoes and manipulated Britt and Randy by demanding rice, with Jackie she scarfed down everything from hot dogs to sushi to macaroni and cheese. More American every day, she'd gone from perfecting a Doppler-registering belch and the armpit fart to an infatuation with toenail polish, reserving good manners for the few people she couldn't afford to alienate and moments when she felt she had something to gain. Now she wriggled out of her parka and meticulously compressed the entire affair into one pocket.

"How was school today?" Jackie asked.

Lily's face went dead. If you overlooked the fact that such an expression had no place in the repertoire of an eight-year-old girl, it was comical, the way she slackened her jaw and made her eyes go blank. When Jackie said nothing, Lily amplified her response with an elaborate one-shoulder shrug. Spotting the leopard-skin hair ornament, she slid it over her wrist. "This is better than school."

Lily was the only Chinese at the private academy where she was enrolled, and Britt said there was talk about holding her back once again. Her problems were both academic and social; Lily held her classmates and the curriculum in equal contempt. As Lily's gaze turned to the shelf of minerals, Jackie watched her slip the scrunchie into her back pocket. She reached for a fluorite, then turned to Jackie.

"Can I play with the rocks?"

"Sure."

Standing on her toes, she chose a specimen from Tennessee, freckled cubes extruding from a mountain of glistening sphalerite. Holding it to the light, she peered at the violet and gold-rimmed squares embedded in the crystal.

"Why do you have rocks on your shelves instead of books?"

"They tell stories."

"How?"

"If you look at them long enough, you'll see what I mean."

Lily stared at the fluorite, then set it down and chose a bronze-colored specimen the size of a baseball.

"This weighs a ton!" The dense cluster of sharp-edged cubes had a rounded underside that glittered like metallic sand. "Is it real gold?"

"Pyrite," Jackie replied.

Fool's gold. Her first rock.

"What story does it tell?"

"Maybe you'll be the one to discover it."

Lily reluctantly set down the pyrite. "Which one is your favorite?"

Jackie reached for a fluorite just large enough to enfold in her palm. An aqua crystal with striking inclusions on a wavy base, its surface as satiny as worry beads. "Look closely and tell me what you see."

Lily frowned at the cube under the light.

"Try it the other way," Jackie suggested. "Upside down."

Lily turned the fluorite on its head and shook it in frustration. Suddenly she stopped and lifted it to eye level. "Is that a boat?"

"Yes." Together they examined it. A shaft of light splintered one corner, illuminating a mast and twin sails tossed on a silvery sea. "See the sail?"

"Yes! Are there people?"

"Inside the boat."

"Are they on their way home?" Handing back the fluorite as if she didn't want to know the answer, Lily boosted herself onto the desk. "I hate school."

Hate was not a word Britt and Randy permitted in their home, and Lily used it as often as she dared when she was with Jackie.

"How come?"

"The kids make fun of me."

"Maybe if you got to know them better—"

"They call me a retard."

Jackie, spell cat!

"Why do they do that?" she carefully asked.

The two-shouldered shrug tore her heart.

"The teacher makes us read aloud. I hate her."

Nightmares about standing in front of the class, stomach-aches that sent her to the school nurse, feigning laryngitis . . . all to escape the stigma of being labeled handicapped. But Lily had no organic—

"Don't you like to read?" Jackie asked.

"I hate books!"

Not the fear of books, but the prospect of failure they represent.

"But you like stories, don't you?"

"Sure."

"Would you like me to read you one?"

Lily looked at her with suspicion. "From a book?"

Reaching in the shelf under her desk, Jackie withdrew *Myths and Legends*.

"I'll let you pick it out."

Lily climbed down from the desk and came to the chair. Jackie watched as she flipped through the pages. "This one."

It was the story about the winged creature with snakes for hair, whose glance turned men to stone. Jackie could understand the attraction: the monster's expression mirrored the storm-cloud face that kept Lily's own antagonists at bay. It was several pages long and divided into four sections. She looked up and saw Lily watching her. "I'll read out loud," she said, "and you can follow along."

"Can we do the whole thing?"

"Let's see how it goes."

Lily climbed in her lap and Jackie slowly began.

"Acresius, King of Argos, came home from Delphi with a heavy heart, for he had received a dreadful oracle. 'No sons shall be born to you,' the priestess had told him. 'But you shall have a grandson, and by his hand you shall die. . . .' "

Chapter | Five

Aaron Best's brick bungalow north of Washington Park seemed identical to the dozen others on his block. All looked like nothing so much as an army of mushrooms that sprang up in the lawn after a week of rain. What distinguished Aaron's house from its neighbors was how little effort had been invested in maintenance and landscaping; the yard sloped steeply to the sidewalk, with four cracked cement steps cut into the turf, and the flower beds that rimmed the porch were plugged with crabgrass.

A humble abode for the proprietor of an alternative heating business, but as Jackie mounted those steps she recalled Aaron had built his firm from a much smaller plumbing company he'd inherited from his father. A monument to his origins? The thought gave her the boost she need to face a dicey interview. She was there to speak with his wife, Wendy, because Duncan Pratt was endorsing her as a witness.

Pratt had complied with Jackie's request for the investigative file with unsettling speed. When she dropped by his office to pick it up, he stuck out his head and casually announced he would oppose bail under any circumstances and that her client had a history of domestic abuse: Aaron had assaulted his wife twelve months before Rae Malone was murdered.

Nodding as if that were old news, Jackie accepted the file and reviewed it with Pilar when she returned to the office.

Even with the details of the domestic assault and the pathologist's report, the DA's case was comfortingly slim. Now, as she waited for Wendy Best to answer the door, Jackie ran through the contents of the file in her head.

Rae Malone had been abducted on a Friday afternoon and her body dumped within twenty-four hours of the time it was found the following Wednesday; the snow had kept insects and predators away and retarded decomposition. Although she'd been decapitated, the cause of death was manual strangulation. That sequence was determined on the basis of four factors: edema fluid in her nostrils, hemorrhaging into the muscles of her neck, congestion and cyanosis in her face, and petechiae—minute dots of blood in the whites of her eyes. Jackie had skipped the photos; at this stage they would only distract her. The wino who found Rae's head when he left his cardboard packing case by the tracks shortly after eight Wednesday morning to take a leak had been so sickened by the sight, he tossed up the previous night's Thunderbird.

There were signs of recent sexual activity, but the coroner would not opine as to whether that had occured before or after death. Rae's body had been bathed with a commercial grade of antibacterial soap, which meant the killer was either savvy in investigatory techniques or had reason to believe he'd left identifiable evidence. In a crude, sawing fashion she was beheaded with a sharp blade.

Though the decapitation could have occurred at any time between Friday and Tuesday, the pathologist believed Rae was killed closer to the time of her disappearance, four to six hours after she last ate. Her stomach and small intestine contained traces of lettuce and a partially digested olive, suggesting a salad, and her best friend said they'd met for lunch that day at Park Meadows Mall. The probable scenario was abduction and strangulation within hours after that meal on Friday, washing of the body Friday night or Saturday morning, and beheading shortly before it was dumped on Tuesday night or early Wednesday. And God only knew what occurred in between.

Jackie rang the bell once more, then peeked in a window. The shades were drawn and the house seemed to be holding its breath, waiting for her to give up and leave. She walked around back. The yard was fenced with six-foot grape

stake, but a freshly painted garage stood at the alley entrance.
A motion-activated security light was mounted on the pad-
locked garage door. Standing on tiptoe to peek in the window, she saw an immaculate floor and an extraordinarily neat
workbench. Aaron obviously placed a high priority on his tools
and vehicles. Rae Malone should have been half as careful.

The last people who'd seen her alive were a neighbor
who waved as Rae got into her silver Lexus shortly before
noon on Friday and the friend she'd met for lunch. When
her maid came at two o'clock, the Lexus was in the driveway
but Rae was gone. The bedroom was in disarray but the rest
of the house was relatively neat, and droplets of blood near
the driver's side of the Lexus were identified as Rae's. "Disarray" was cop talk for pigsty: clothes and shoes strewn around,
bedspread and sheets balled up at the foot of the bed, and
water slopped from the sink to the tile floor in the master bath. Nothing was missing except the designer sweats
she'd last been seen wearing and her purse. There was no
sign of forced entry. But Rae's absence alarmed the maid.
Rather than cleaning up, she contacted the victim's former
husband.

As Jackie turned from the garage, she saw movement in
a window at the back of the house. Was Aaron's wife avoiding her, or did the doorbell not work? Under no obligation to
talk, Wendy Best had ducked her calls until Jackie finally
caught her at the number Aaron had given for her mother in
Pueblo. Wendy had said she'd be in Denver that afternoon,
packing.

"Mrs. Best?" Jackie knocked at the back door once, then
again. Still no answer.

In deference to Rodger Malone, the cops had waived
the customary forty-eight-hour waiting period for missing per-
sons and immediately began processing the house in Castle
Pines as a crime scene. When they found dried semen on a
sheet, they sent it to the lab for analysis and questioned
friends and neighbors about Rae's love life. Both her maid
and her closest friend said she'd been having an affair with
Aaron for approximately three months.

That the lovers made no effort to hide their involvement
was a definite plus, one of the few bright spots at this stage
in the case, but Jackie had put off questioning Aaron about

an alibi until she knew the time of death. The four-day window between the abduction and dumping would make a complete accounting of his whereabouts difficult, and her client's line of work compounded the problem: a booming construction business offered no end of sites where a body could have been stashed for that length of time.

"Mrs. Best?" Leaning over the railing of the back porch, Jackie tried to look in the window. Suddenly the door opened.

"So you're his lawyer."

Wendy Best stood at the threshold with no apology. Pretty once, she'd retained the mannerisms. As she tucked a lackluster strand of blond hair behind one ear, she cocked her head at a forty-five-degree angle to hide a discolored front tooth.

"I appreciate your agreeing to see me," Jackie replied.

For an awkward moment she thought she wouldn't be invited in, but then the door swung open and Aaron's wife stepped back. Coffee and ammonia hit Jackie at the same instant; the linoleum gleamed and by the stove a percolator chugged. As Wendy led her through the kitchen, she noted the outdated appliances. Her client had no trouble arranging to pay the first half of her retainer but obviously ran his house on a tight budget. Frugality, or had success taken him by surprise?

Jackie settled on the couch and Wendy stationed herself near the front door with a steaming mug; she hadn't offered her visitor refreshment. Calculated rudeness? A screen for fear? Jackie leaned back to signal she was staying. Two large cartons half-filled with clothing and toys rested on the braided rug before the fireplace. Had Wendy seen her on the porch and retreated to the kitchen hoping she'd leave?

"I've caught you at an awkward time," Jackie began.

"I know why you're here."

Wendy set her coffee on the windowsill. Lighting a cigarette, she took a drag and leaned against the wall with her arms folded. She was wearing terry-cloth shorts and a sleeveless blouse—Target or T.J. Maxx, a step down from the malls—and her wiry physique radiated tension. As she took another drag, the vertical grooves above her lips deepened and Jackie decided she must be at least ten years older than Aaron—in her late forties. Or was she witnessing the domestic equivalent of the picture of Dorian Gray?

"You filed a police report against Aaron last year. Why?"

"He broke my arm, that good enough for you?"

"What happened?"

"He was out drinking with that brother of his, and he slammed me into the wall."

"What were you fighting about?"

Wendy shrugged, an up-and-down jerk that said it was no one's business but her own. But the woman was held together with Scotch tape, and Jackie wondered again whether the emotion roiling her was anger or fear.

"Was that the only time he shoved you?" A push was considerably better than a slap or a punch. Guy comes home drunk, gets in a quarrel with his wife, maybe stumbles . . .

"Look, it wasn't my idea to testify against Aaron."

Jackie didn't believe that for a moment. Call Wendy's bluff by telling her the DA couldn't force her to take the stand? Or play it out?

"Did you know he was seeing Rae Malone?"

"It didn't surprise me, if that's what you mean."

It wasn't. "Why not?"

"She wasn't Aaron's first and she won't be his last."

His wife expected him to be acquitted.

"Women mean nothing to Aaron," Wendy continued, ashes spilling down the front of her blouse. "Rae Malone was no different from the others."

"How many others?"

"He's been having flings on the job for years. Wham, bam, thank you, ma'am. That's Aaron's motto."

The crudity was intended to shock—was she still in love with him?

"So you finally had enough."

"I don't need Aaron."

Not, *I'm afraid* of him.

Jackie heaved an inward sigh of relief. Anger was easier than fear. It didn't matter which had been more difficult to put up with—Aaron's chintziness or his philandering—jurors distrusted witnesses with an ax to grind. Stack the panel with women. . . . Rising, she turned to the mantel, which was covered with pictures of a towheaded kid about Lily's age. The photos were of the boy alone, or with one parent or the other. Never the three of them together.

"Is this your son?"

"Trevor."

"Handsome boy." She tacked on a year. "Second grade?"

"I'm home-schooling him the rest of the term. Down in Pueblo. Aaron's arrest made it impossible—"

So she wasn't afraid to let their son be around him either.

"This must be very difficult for both of you."

"The one thing I'll never forgive that son of a bitch is what it's done to Trevor. That kid worships—" Abruptly Wendy stopped.

Jealousy and rage. If the DA twisted her arm to testify, it hadn't been very hard. Having gotten what she came for, Jackie now had to put distance on it before the woman realized she had just handed Jackie a blueprint for cross.

"You mentioned Aaron's brother. Are they the only children?"

"Mark's eight years older. Their parents are dead."

Evasion was Wendy's style; at trial, Jackie would have her pick of targets. "Do they own the company together?"

"No, it's Aaron's free and clear." Had their parents left it to one son and disinherited the other, or did Aaron buy his brother out? "Mark's his right hand, foreman of the crew."

The clean-shaven man at her house that day—could he have been Aaron's brother? Now that she thought of it, there *was* a resemblance. "Sounds like they're pretty close."

Wendy snorted. "Monkey see, monkey do." Leaving it to the imagination which monkey was which, she headed for the door. Taking the hint, Jackie rose. She extended her hand: Aaron's wife ignored the gesture.

"I appreciate your time, Mrs.—"

The door closed before the name left her mouth. But the interview had been worth the price of admission, because Jackie now knew two things.

Wendy Best hated her husband and she didn't believe he killed Rae Malone.

Chapter | Six

In the domain of the Honorable Bertram J. Worrell, the twenty-foot molded ceilings muted the din of the masses to a genteel murmur and the chairs in the jury box were leather with brass tacks instead of the molded plastic of county court. District court was serious business: pilasters sprang from pink marble baseboard to be capped by gilded Ionic scrolls and the belts of the brawny deputies stationed at the door were so loaded with paraphernalia, the men looked like human bombs. All talk came to a halt when the bailiff rapped his gavel and the judge mounted the bench, but once he was seated, the undertone resumed like a low-grade fever.

With appointed counsel roving the aisles, calling out names of clients they had not yet met, and prosecutors and defense attorneys negotiating last-minute concessions, the ambiance on days in which no trial was scheduled was more commercial than adversarial—a bazaar, if not a flea market. As the judge handled bond matters and pleas with the ruthless efficiency of an auctioneer, the courtroom emptied and refilled in a parade of jailhouse green and anxious-looking relatives. From the second row behind the swinging gate Jackie waited. Aaron's bail hearing was the last item on the morning docket, but she had no doubt Worrell would get to it long before any thought of a solitary sandwich in chambers entered his mind.

Bertram Worrell was a stickler for punctuality. Because

his internal clock was set five minutes faster than Mountain Time, lawyers were well advised to advance their watches accordingly. The judge opened his own mail, had no use for law clerks or computer research, and wrote his decisions in longhand. Though his rulings were seldom appealed and almost never reversed, Worrell liked to say the only time he was certain he'd been right was when a higher power disagreed with him. When Jackie learned Aaron's case had been assigned to him, she'd told Pilar to break out the champagne.

Pratt was presenting a plea bargain for a drunk driver who'd killed a patrolman in an accident on Speer Boulevard. Worrell nodded impatiently, his round head bobbing on his reedy neck. His eyes were fixed but glazed, as if he were speed-reading the DA's statement somewhere on the rear wall of the chamber and was three lines ahead of him. This impression was confirmed when he cut Pratt off in midsentence and began questioning the defendant himself. As a flush crept from Pratt's collar to his ears, Jackie prayed the DA wouldn't delegate Aaron's case to one of his subordinates. Bail was only the first hand in the high-stakes poker game that would culminate in Aaron's trial.

At twenty minutes past eleven the doors swung open again and there was a sudden hush. A steady stream of reporters had filled the courtroom, and now they leaned forward as one. The steam radiators made the room unbearably stuffy and, sensing the barometric shift, the spectators roused themselves from their torpor. The sheriff's deputy escorting the single prisoner gave a self-conscious cough.

Catching Jackie's eye, Aaron raised his manacled wrists in acknowledgment and took his seat with the remaining men in the dock while two deputies stationed themselves at either end. As Jackie watched his gaze roam the courtroom, her misgivings about seeking her client's release returned. Denying bail would be more than a moral victory for the prosecution: at trial a jailhouse pallor spoke louder than words, inviting the jury to send the prisoner back to the hole. Moreover, keeping Aaron in custody would have enabled her to force Pratt's hand by seeking an early trial, and Jackie had the nagging sense that her client was better off where she could keep her eye on him.

But seeking bail provided at least one advantage besides the freedom upon which Aaron insisted: to deny bail, the DA had to establish that the proof was evident and the presumption great that Aaron murdered Rae Malone. That meant a free peek at the prosecution's case—warts and all. Not a bad trade-off. In fact, a win-win situation for the defense no matter which way it came out.

Now, peering out over the gallery, the judge posed a rare rhetorical question.

"Are there any other matters to be heard before People vs. Best?"

Warfare in Worrell's court was nothing if not civilized.

The public defenders gathered their files and, comrades in arms, yielded the defense table to Jackie. Pratt's two assistants remained where they were, clearing the center of the prosecution table for their boss. Were all three planning to try Aaron, or had Pratt divided the work for the purpose of pretrial motions? Settling in the chair closest to the lectern, Jackie opened her briefcase and withdrew a yellow pad. As a deputy escorted Aaron to her side and unlocked his cuffs, she squeezed her client's arm. The gesture would not be lost on the reporters sitting directly behind them.

"Very well, then." Worrell scrutinized the file as if seeing it for the first time, but Jackie knew he read the day's briefs when he arrived at his chambers two hours before the bailiffs punched in. "Ms. Flowers, I believe you filed this motion for—what is it?" He pretended to examine Pilar's paperwork more closely. "Ah, yes. *Bail.*"

Jackie rose but remained at her table. "That's correct, your honor." The burden was on the DA, and she wasn't about to let herself be suckered into counterpunching before her opponent entered the ring.

The judge fixed his beady eyes on Pratt.

"You're versed in the statutes, Mr. Pratt. I don't have to tell you" —but he would anyway, for the benefit of the stringers in the front row— "that Colorado law requires me to release Mr. Best on a suitable bond unless you convince me the proof is evident and the presumption great that he indeed committed the offense for which he is charged."

Pratt rose and strode confidently to the lectern.

"Yes, your honor. The abduction, murder, and decapitation of Rae Malone was a *heinous* crime, and we are quite satisfied—"

"Save the bombast for your opening statement—*if* the case gets that far. Proof, Mr. Pratt?"

"We have physical evidence linking Aaron Best to the crime scene. Specifically, a sheet from the room from which Ms. Malone was abducted, bearing DNA evidence establishing the defendant's presence."

"Which is evidence of what?"

"A sexual assault we believe occurred just prior to the abduction."

The courtroom was silent as Worrell took in this revelation with a slight frown.

"No eyewitnesses?" he asked.

"Well—of course not." Pratt turned slightly, playing to the crowd. His gaze lingered in one spot. Glancing over her shoulder, for the first time Jackie noticed Rae's husband, Rodger Malone. "In my experience, rapists and murderers restrict their audience to their victims. And physical evidence never lies."

"I see. How about the weapon, then?"

"Our investigation is ongoing. . . ."

"Do I take it all you have at this point is a *bedsheet*?"

Pratt clasped his hands behind his back. He'd gambled by calling the sexual encounter rape and upped the ante: with reporters—or was it Malone?—hanging on every word, the DA was trying to pressure the judge into denying bail by turning Aaron into Jack the Ripper. But Worrell wasn't buying, and now Dunc would have to play another card.

"And Mr. Best's history of violence against women," Pratt replied.

A nice fat headline for the early editions.

Jackie glanced at Aaron, who was doodling impassively on her yellow pad. Unless it established motive or some other element of the crime, his record was irrelevant both to the bail hearing and at trial. But she had to draw Pratt out.

"Mr. Pratt is referring to a scuffle in Mr. Best's home more than a year ago," Jackie replied, "a matter resolved by private counseling. It has no relevance to this case, and if the prosecution insists on making an issue of it, I will move to have it suppressed. If that and the bedsheet are Mr. Pratt's *entire case*—"

"Not by a long shot! In addition to his record for domestic assault, Ms. Flowers's client almost killed a man in an unprovoked attack for which he *was* charged. This man is a threat to the public—"

What else hadn't Aaron told her?

Aaron had stopped doodling, but his eyes were glued to the pad. No matter what he was concealing, she had to act fast.

"And we will certainly move to suppress that incident as well!" Jackie strode to the lectern, giving Pratt no choice but to move aside. "Dirty linen, your honor, nothing more. A bedsheet showing evidence of a consensual sexual act" —let the *Rocky* and the *Post* print that tomorrow!— "establishes neither proof nor presumption of abduction and murder. As for prior *alleged* altercations in which my client may or may not have been involved, the sole purpose of bail is to ensure Mr. Best's presence at trial, and not punish him before conviction, either here or *in the press*—"

"I am quite aware of the law, Ms. Flowers. . . ."

"He's a flight risk, your honor," Pratt broke in, "especially with a charge of this magnitude hanging over his head. Aaron Best—"

"—owns a business that's been in his family for two generations," Jackie smoothly continued. Because Aaron's family circumstances were relevant only to type and amount of bail, Pratt must be conceding he hadn't met his burden of proof on denial. "Mr. Best recently received the Entrepreneur of the Year Award from the Coalition for the Environment, runs his company with the assistance of his brother, lives with his wife and son in a bungalow near Washington Park—"

"He's separated from his wife," Pratt bellowed. "He isn't even in contact with his son!"

"That's quite enough from you both," the judge decided. "Ms. Flowers, when do you intend to file that motion to suppress?"

"As soon as I return to my office, your honor."

"I'm setting your motion to be heard in two weeks. What

do you think would be the appropriate amount of bond?" He directed the question to her, ignoring Pratt.

Jackie skipped through the alternatives. Worrell would never release Aaron on personal recognizance, but if she started low, he'd bring it way down—"PR, your honor. Despite his awards, Mr. Best runs a modest—"

"One million dollars!" Pratt shot back.

"A hundred thousand," Worrell ruled. "Property or cash."

"But, your honor—" Pratt blustered.

"Court adjourned."

Turning, Jackie saw Rodger Malone push his way through the crowd and out the door.

"—fantastic job." Aaron gripped her arm in excitement, grinning as if they'd just won the lottery. "Mark thought I should hire a guy to defend me, but I wanted you. I *knew* you could pull it off—"

Jackie heard a reporter call her name. For the first time since the hearing began, she looked her client square in the face. What did that artless front conceal? And if she was such a hero, why did she feel like she'd just been had? She detached herself from her client's grasp.

"Don't kid yourself, Aaron. Duncan Pratt's just warming up."

Chapter | Seven

Pulling into the two-car parking area adjacent to All-Star Cleaners, he set the automatic lock and climbed out of his vehicle. As he stepped through the doorway he wondered at the revolving rack that stretched from the front of the shop forty feet back. Always filled, but he was invariably the only customer. The Korean girl looked up as he approached the counter, pretending she'd just caught sight of him.

"How are you today?" he asked. He treated her to an extra-special smile, his gaze lingering on her hair. A swath of midnight silk, it twisted and gleamed like a river under the fluorescent light.

"Very fine, thank you." Her chin dipped modestly, but the pulse in her throat throbbed with a rosy glow. "I have your shirts."

She threw a switch, and the rack came to life like a beast emerging from hibernation. Why was it she never consulted the computer to locate his clothes? The metal apparatus groaned to a halt, and she began counting his hangers. He eyed her round bottom in the tight jeans.

"Light starch," she confirmed over her shoulder, "collar only. Hand-pressed the way you like." She turned to him with an armful of shirts, almost catching him staring. He never let them put his shirts in a box; he loathed creases. As his smile broadened, her lips surrendered and crooked teeth flashed. It had taken less time than usual to overcome her resistance. "I mend trousers myself."

As she began bagging the shirts, he examined the place he'd snagged, just below the left knee of his navy blue slacks. The repair was almost undetectable, neat stitches running in tandem with the flat weave. As he leaned closer, acid tickled his nostrils. They'd dry-cleaned his trousers despite his explicit instructions to launder them. Had the spots required special treatment, or did she think she was doing him a favor?

"A beautiful job," he replied. The flush spread to her flat cheeks and she looked away. Her eyes were extraordinarily guileless and her isolation emanated from her in waves, like the chemicals filling his mouth. He placed one hand on the counter, testing how close she would let him come. "Big plans for the weekend?" he asked.

"He makes me work." Her chin jerked toward the back of the shop, where a small man in black waiter's pants and starched white shirt bent over the presser. The man had waited on him once when the girl was absent. At least twenty years older than her, his English not as good. At the time he'd wondered whether the man was her father. "Do you think I'm ugly?"

"No, of course not." He kept his eyes on her mouth to reassure her, his nostrils still smarting from the solvent. He would have to throw out the trousers. "You're very pretty. Who said you're ugly?"

She gestured again to the back. Not her father after all.

"He doesn't know what he's talking about," he promised. She was waiting for him to say more and he remembered their conversation about coffee shops in Korea. She'd lamented the fact that there was nowhere in Denver to sit with friends, though there was a café just down the street. He handed her his MasterCard, holding on to it an extra beat. "Maybe someday . . ."

"Someday what?" His remark had emboldened her, and when she made no move to ring up the charges, he saw the man in the back scowl.

"I'll show you he's wrong."

That should last her until next time.

Conscious again of her teeth, she ducked her chin once

more and swiped his card through the magnetic reader. He reached for the hangers, silently counting to make sure she hadn't lost one of his shirts. Pity about the trousers . . . She looked up, desperate to prolong their encounter.

"Have a nice—"

"—weekend." With a wave he left.

At the corner he stopped at a box for the *News*. The banner at the bottom of the front page caught his eye and he fed a quarter to the slot. Carefully hanging his shirts on the hook in the backseat of his car, he settled behind the wheel with the tabloid.

DA LOSES ON BAIL—*Right Man Behind Bars?*

He tasted metal deep in his throat.

Turning to page 4A, he skimmed the story. Rae's autopsy report had been leaked and they made it sound like a sex crime. Inept, positively inept. The arrest had been amusing at first but was rapidly wearing thin. The accompanying photo showed Duncan Pratt elbowing his way out the courtroom, grimacing in a parody of the rock-jawed-prosecutor pose. Was *he* going to turn unpredictable on him? He closed his eyes and saw the Korean girl's crooked teeth. Let him rot, let them all—

Rolling up the newspaper, he thrust it under his seat. Be damned if he let this spoil his evening. Friday, wasn't it? He'd have a drink, unwind, put all this nonsense out of his head. He backed out of the parking space, merging effortlessly with the traffic heading toward the chic shopping district of Cherry Creek.

He turned south on University, left at Third. Mama Sam's, the new in spot. Happy hour was just beginning, and it was still early enough to get a table on the sidewalk. A drink and dinner, nothing more. He remembered the last time he'd driven past, the two women at the table by the entrance who looked like they were waiting for dates. What they wanted you to believe, but on the next pass he saw the waiter serve a second round. . . . They had it all wrong. It had nothing to do with sex. Would he have to *make* them understand?

He was approaching the restaurant now and the mock Oriental lettering on the canopy reminded him of the Korean girl. No challenge, and decidedly not his type. If he'd known his last foray would be such a waste, he might have chosen her instead. Maybe he could have salvaged his trousers. . . . In an hour it would be dark. This latest development had complicated everything; in another life he would be cruising and not pondering where to eat his dinner. As he imagined the crisp skin of an egg roll exploding under his teeth, he tasted cleaning solvent. Gunning his engine, he turned north. For him it had never been about *sex*.

There was nothing to fear. He was in control, could stop whenever he liked. The sleek vehicle with tinted glass glided away from Cherry Creek toward Colfax.

The wild card was the lawyer.

Chapter | Eight

want to be fair to *both* sides," claimed the brunette in the cropped coral tank top as she dumped a third packet of artificial sweetener in her iced tea.

Whenever Jackie heard that line she patted her wallet. Not only was it seldom the case—and never less so than when pitched to a lawyer—but here it made absolutely no sense. Why should Sunny Abbott care about being fair to the man accused of killing her best friend, Rae Malone?

At Sunny's suggestion, they'd met for an early lunch at Park Meadows Mall. The French restaurant proved to be bright, airy, and generic, but Jackie was coming to realize that the barrier with Rae's friend was not merely language. With the hearing on her motion to suppress Aaron's priors a week away, she was in no mood to be blindsided, but that appeared to be the least of it. If not for the DNA he'd so obligingly left in Rae's bed, Sunny's take would have been impossible to square with what Jackie knew of her client.

"I certainly appreciate your meeting with me, Ms. Abbott. I wanted to find out just a few—"

"Rae was a sucker for a certain type of man. You know, the guys who strut around like they've got rocks the size of grapefruit in their pants?"

Jackie's tea went down the wrong pipe.

"I'm sure Mrs. Malone—" she began, but Sunny was off and running.

"One thing she knew was how to have a good time. Not that Rae ever confused fun with marriage," Sunny hastened to add. "She knew exactly where to draw the line."

A waitress in a black skirt the size of a dime was poised to take their orders, and Jackie handed her menu back without looking at it. She'd finagled her way out of French in high school—as if the same alphabet were any help!—and made up for it by painting scenery for a production of Molière. Even if she could decipher the offerings, ordering whatever Sunny did created the possibility of rapport.

"Salade niçoise," Sunny said, dragging out the "z" in a drawl somewhere between Commerce City and Texas.

"I'll have the same," Jackie said, trying to think of an appropriate follow-up to her last response. Sunny was as slippery as a raw egg. "Was Rae married before?"

"Her first husband was to get herself established, the second to provide a cushion."

"Any kids?"

"You kidding? Both times she signed prenups, and those guys knew to the penny what they were paying for. She took care of herself first, and they just kept coming back for more."

"What exactly was her relationship with Rodger Malone?"

Sunny took her time selecting a baguette and broke off a morsel before carefully placing it in her mouth. Except for a pair of elderly ladies by the window, the bistro was empty. Jackie wondered whether it was the time of day or the food.

"Like I said, Rod went into it with his exit strategy mapped out. With her looks, Rae could've had any guy she wanted. Not that she had an enemy in the world."

One non sequitur too many.

In court there were two types of witnesses: yours and theirs. *Yours* fell into two camps—the ones you *had* to call and the ones you hoped no one would find. With Sunny, Jackie never got to the second stage; as soon as Sunny asked if Aaron planned to take the stand, Jackie had known she was a shill for the DA and the most she was likely to get out of this lunch was a preview of the spin Pratt would put on Rae's character at trial. But Jackie had to understand Rae's relationship with her client before she next argued for him in court.

The waitress served their salads, a mound of water-packed tuna on a bed of iceberg fenced in by cucumber spears, hard-boiled egg, and canned asparagus. As two black olives peeped up at Jackie from the center of the fish, she was uncomfortably reminded that this had probably been Rae Malone's last meal. But Rodger Malone was a powerful man, and regardless of their marital status, Rae's affair with Aaron would have been humiliating. *If* he'd known about it . . .

"Did the marriage end amicably?" Jackie asked.

"Let's put it this way, not even Viagra could have saved it." Sunny stared at her plate with regret, either in memory of her friend's failed marriage or reaction to the salad. "Like me, Rae had healthy appetites" —the salad aside, was she now suggesting something kinky? "—and Rod golfed. But they got along beautifully."

"Then why the divorce?"

Sunny shrugged. "Three years were up and she'd vested in his pension."

Certainly an unappealing view of the victim. Jackie felt a twinge of sympathy for Pratt, stuck with having to make plausible a passionate affair with Aaron and a tempestuous breakup. Not to mention that Rae was the ex-wife of one of Colorado's wealthiest men. But the spin didn't quite add up.

"You were the last person to see Rae alive," Jackie began.

"We had lunch right here." Sunny speared a wedge of egg. "At this very table."

"What did you talk about?"

"Aaron Best. Rae was tired of him and planning to break it off."

Motive. The ace up Pratt's sleeve.

"Did she tell Aaron that?"

"She saw him Thursday night, and—" Sunny tried to cover by sipping her tea.

Ambiguous, but Jackie liked it just the way it was left. An admission that Rae saw Aaron the night before she was killed, just as he'd said, at which point she either told him to take a hike or she didn't. If she did and that sent Aaron over the edge, why not kill her then? And if she didn't, motive went out the window. But that wasn't the only value to Sunny's slip.

The linchpin of Pratt's case was Aaron's semen on Rae's

sheet, which he claimed was the product of a sexual assault at the time of the abduction. Under the Brady rule, the DA was required to give Jackie any evidence negating Aaron's guilt, and if Sunny had told Pratt that Rae admitted to sex with Aaron the night *before* she was killed, it certainly wasn't in the material Pratt provided. Given Aaron's visit the night before, it made no sense for him to return to Castle Pines on Friday. . . .

"Was Rae a neat person?" Jackie was picturing the video the police had shot when Rae was reported missing.

"Rae had a housekeeper," Sunny carefully replied, "if that's what you mean."

"How often did she come in?" She or Pilar could interview the maid, but it was always nice to co-opt a prosecution witness. Particularly when the witness was the victim's best friend.

"Twice a week."

If it were possible for a sunken great room with nothing but sectional pieces, abstract paintings, and a knee-high glass table to look messy, Rae's did, and the video technician had faithfully documented every detail that was out of place—ashes ground in the plush ivory carpet, fashion magazines strewn across the table, pillows on the couch and floor. The camera obsessively followed the disorder upstairs, where Rae's king-sized water bed and walk-in closets would have made a bag lady cringe. The Goddess of Castle Pines had needed a retinue of footmen to pick up after her.

"Which days?" Jackie continued.

"Tuesday and Friday."

There was no way Pratt could establish Aaron hadn't visited Rae Thursday night.

Chapter | Nine

Blinking in the sunlight, Rodger Malone emerged from the recessed entrance to the Varsity Club. Jackie watched as he shook hands with his companions, who briskly headed off in the direction of the State Capitol. In his tan gabardine suit and emerald-and-gold rep tie, Malone didn't look like a man in mourning, although lunch at the V Club should have been enough to depress anyone.

Located at almost the precise spot where the financial district and silk-stocking law firms gave way to liquor stores and cut-rate parking lots, the V Club catered to Denver's moneyed elite. Jackie had eaten there once, at the invitation of the recruitment partner in one of the large law firms after she'd won back-to-back murder cases at the public defender's office. Silent waiters clad in red vests and bow ties, dim lighting and walls that exuded the confidences of generations of powerful men—the V Club was precisely the sort of spot where she'd expected to find Rodger Malone, even if his secretary hadn't been so unwittingly obliging.

Jackie quickly crossed the street and approached with her hand extended. Still distracted by the good-byes and thinking he should recognize her, Malone clasped her fingers and smiled back. Up close his upper body seemed disproportionately large—he had the physique of a weight lifter, not a golfer.

"Mr. Malone? I'm Jackie Flowers."

Rodger Malone's lips tightened and he dropped her hand. He wasn't bald, as she'd thought from the *News* photo, but had thinning blond hair brushed straight back from his brow, and his face was as pink and shiny as a shrimp. As he quickly recovered from the surprise of being accosted by Aaron Best's defense attorney, Jackie saw that above all else he wanted to avoid a scene.

"I'm on my way to a meeting," he blandly replied.

"I'm sorry to inconvenience you, especially at a time like this." As if he hadn't been ducking her for the better part of a week. "But—"

"I've already spoken to the police."

"You want to see the man who killed your wife brought to justice."

"Ms. Flowers, I have nothing more to say."

She might have expected any number of reactions—grief at his loss, anger at her intrusion, refusal to help the man charged with killing his ex-wife, or a righteous reminder that how he felt was none of her damned business. But Rodger Malone's indifference was truly a surprise. He reached into his breast pocket for his sunglasses and turned to walk away.

"Did you know Rae was seeing Aaron Best?"

Malone froze. When he turned back to Jackie, she would have given anything to see behind those mirrored lenses. "My wife was in a class all by herself."

Admiration or contempt?

"Did you tell her to break off the affair?" she pressed.

"I had no control over Rae."

Bitterness, wounded pride? Or was it simply irony?

"You never wanted the divorce. . . ."

He was so close, she could smell the baron of beef on his breath.

"That house in Castle Pines, did you know I built every fucking brick of it for her?"

As he turned on his heel and strode off, Jackie wondered who Rodger Malone had hated more—the wife who'd made a mockery of his devotion or the man with whom she'd humiliated him?

Chapter | Ten

The red Viper glided to a stop at Seventeenth and Park like the Castle Pines pro sinking a ten-foot putt. Glancing to his right as he waited for the signal to change, he saw the coupe was this year's model. At the wheel lounged a sporty blonde with a ponytail like corn silk flowing from the hole in the back of her visored cap. She caught his look of admiration and gunned her engine. A beat before the light turned green she was off. Halfway through the intersection she cut in front of him, only to be stopped by the light at the next block. With all the time in the world, she reached into the passenger seat and rummaged through her purse.

He switched to the left lane and pulled up to within a hairbreadth of her rear bumper, but she didn't budge. Instead she dipped her chin to the rearview mirror with the clinical self-absorption of a fashion model on a shoot, a golden tube in her right hand. How many times had he watched the women in his life do just that?

With a jerk the Viper entered the crosswalk, the blonde shrugging winsomely at the wino with the shopping cart she sent scooting back to the curb. Payback for forcing her to abandon her touch-up? Anticipating the green arrow, she barreled west, all for nothing because she couldn't beat the next light. He pulled up on her right and looked through the open window on the passenger side of the Viper just as she twisted the bottom of her lipstick and a flamingo shaft emerged. Tantalized, he watched her spread her lips and hold them taut. And he was sitting on the quilted bench at his mother's vanity again.

With her hair bound in a terry-cloth turban she would examine her face as if it belonged to an exotic stranger. Tilting her chin this way and that for the benefit of every exposure in the three-paneled glass, she searched for minute imperfections. She reached for the tube of concealer. He tapped his toe against the leg of the table. Her hand froze in mid-air and in the mirror her eyes blazed. He stopped. Peering again at her reflection, she squeezed a dot of concealer on the web between her left thumb and forefinger, and blotted twice with her right pinkie before dabbing it on the fragile tissue where her eye socket met the bridge of her nose. Leaning closer, she inspected her work. Beside her on that quilted bench he was once again invisible.

Her left hand reached for the tortoiseshell compact with the golden crest. She flipped it open, swiped the pad across the cake of powder, and patted it gently on her smooth skin. Smiling tightly to reveal the apples of her cheeks, she used them as a guide to sweep rose-colored dust from the outer corner of her eye to her hairline, blending and fading as she went. . . .

The girl in the Viper caught him staring but pretended not to notice. She was putting on a show for him, but *he* wasn't fooled. Moistening her lips with her tongue, she turned back to the mirror and he swallowed deeply.

Now his mother reached for her pencil and inscribed a pouty bow across her upper lip. She glanced at him in the mirror to assess the effect. Satisfied, she resumed. Her fingers hovered over a score of tubes ridged like golden bullets. Burgundy or plum? With a tap of her manicured nail she chose. The darker shade, always the darker. As she stroked in the buttery pigment, she peeled back her lips to make the surface smooth and shiny, embracing the full intensity of the color. For him, her private audience, all for him . . .

Bee-eep!

The BMW behind the Viper blasted to signal the light was green. When the blonde ignored him, the driver honked again, and the Viper lurched through the intersection just as the signal turned yellow. She coasted, oblivious to the fact that her tardiness meant she would miss the next light. No, not oblivious, but glorying in her self-absorption as she held up two lanes of westbound traffic. He gripped his steering wheel, powerless to tear his eyes from her. Smoothing back her brows with a tapered forefinger, she flicked her lashes to check the condition of her mascara.

How dare she ignore him?

In the mirror his mother blinked. At first he feared he'd displeased her by sitting too close, but there was plenty of room on the bench and she had no care but for her own reflection. Her eyes were her best feature, his father claimed, as self-possessed and golden as a cougar's. At twenty paces they appeared unfocused, but the closer he drew the more piercing they became. She had mastered the effect of shadow—teal or plum to enhance the green, olive or jade to bring out the gold in her eyes. Reaching for another brush, she lined her top and bottom lashes with teal from inside edge to outer corner, then applied a petal tint from upper lid to brow and a smokier shade between the lash line and the crease. The effect was utter transformation: this goddess bore no resemblance to the one whose flashing eyes signaled omniscience or disapproval.

Last came her hair. Sometimes she would let him dry it with the Turkish towel and comb and plait the silky ropes before bed, but if the occasion were very special, she might wear one of her wigs. His favorite had shoulder-length waves that glistened like garter snakes. He was so entranced with it that she finally gave it to him to keep beside his bed so he would never be alone. . . .

Beeeeep!

As the BMW's horn blasted, the blonde in the Viper jerked her wheel to the left and sped south, abandoning him in the westbound lane. Lurching through the intersection, he roared down Eighteenth under the lowering sky.

Chapter | Eleven

Tell me about that bar fight," Jackie began.

Aaron leaned back in the chair across from her desk.

"I thought the DA wasn't allowed to bring that up."

"The guys on the cell block tell you that?" Like predators on a starvation diet, the scraps of knowledge jailhouse lawyers survived on only made them hungry and mean. And they could afford to misinform the unwitting; at the end of the day, it wasn't *them* holding the bag.

"I saw Wendy," he replied.

"When?"

"She said the DA talked to her."

Jackie let the evasion pass. It was Friday afternoon and the hearing on the motion to suppress his priors was Monday. Whether Aaron was embarrassed about his past or stupid enough to believe she wouldn't find it out, she hadn't yet decided. The third possibility—that he was a pathological liar—she was not willing to entertain. Yet.

"And?" she prodded.

"He's going to make her testify about that hassle we got into a year ago."

"What's she planning to say?"

"That it was an accident, I didn't mean to hurt her." Certainly not what Wendy had told her. Had they worked that out in advance? Or was Aaron's estranged wife scamming him—

or Jackie? "—going through a rough patch now, but we had some good times together. It's tough building a business."

Obviously more to the story.

"Tell me what happened that night," Jackie said.

"She hates it when I come home loaded." Present tense; did he think his wife would give him another chance? "It's a bad influence on Trevor."

"Did you often come home loaded?"

"That was the only time Wendy got hurt. She was ragging me about missing parent-teacher night at Trevor's school, and I guess I pushed her. I never meant—"

"Did she go to the hospital?"

"Hairline fracture. A bone in her wrist."

Conversing with Aaron was like the overlapping monologues they called Socratic dialogue in law school. Professor poses one question, student answers another, and before you know it, they're on nonintersecting trajectories. Jackie rephrased.

"When did Wendy see the doctor?"

"I took her to the ER myself."

That she could work with: if Aaron drove Wendy to the hospital, how drunk or uncaring could he have been? She made a mental note to have Pilar get the police report.

"What was the charge—assault?"

"The complaint was withdrawn."

"Why?"

He grinned like a boy who made it to second base on his first date. "We reconciled."

"And now she wants custody. . . ."

He looked away. "She'll come around."

Jackie could hear Pratt's opening statement.

The wife Aaron Best abused in the past had left him and he vented his frustrations on the most convenient target: Rae Malone, the woman with whom he was having an affair. What better way to prove he was a real *man?*

"What happened eight years ago?" she continued.

"Mark saw this fox in a bar and bought her a drink." Aaron's brother was surfacing in the strangest places. "She was a tease, we could tell she was playing with him, so we went to the pool table. Then her boyfriend comes over and throws a punch at Mark. Big guy, really loaded. I tried to get between them and he ended up getting hit with the cue."

"Where?"

"In the bar."

Aaron's minimization of his problems was getting on Jackie's nerves, and his flashes of intelligence made her wonder whether the obtuse responses were a product of craft. She tried once more.

"Where was he *hit*?"

"In the gut. His spleen was ruptured."

"Did he die?"

"Hell, no. But he won't be eating barbecued ribs anytime soon."

"What did they bust you for?"

"Aggravated assault."

"Did you enter a plea?"

"Deferred prosecution. They said if I kept my nose clean for five years, it'd be wiped off my record. The DA can't—"

"Was Mark charged?"

"Never even had to throw a punch." A touch of bravado—pleasure at having one-upped big brother? Of course Wendy resented Mark; he'd caused the fight and walked away. "But you can keep it out, can't you?"

"Probably. It was eight years ago, you met all the terms of the deferral" —or Duncan Pratt would have cheerfully flung it in her face— "and the circumstances bear no similarity to the offense with which you're charged."

"What about the fight with Wendy?"

So now it was a *fight*.

"The timing and the victims' sex make that a closer legal question, but the DA still has to show the incident has some logical connection to the abduction and decapitation of Rae Malone." She didn't tell him that for some judges, ruling on motions was like officiating at a tennis match—one for the prosecution, one for the defense. Out with the eight-year-old bar fight, in with the domestic assault.

"No matter what, we can still call Wendy. Right?"

"Why would we want to do that?" Jackie shot back.

"Because she wants to help me, she said—"

"If she's sincere, she should steer clear of the DA." His eyes narrowed and she wondered how much he'd already told his wife. "Look, Aaron, if we put Wendy on the stand, they can hit her with the assault on cross. I'd just as soon you didn't talk with her again before trial."

"What if she needs to reach me about Trevor?"

"Have her call me. Do you have any other priors?"

"Like what?" His eyes widened with indignation. "You want to know every parking—"

"Skip the moving violations and spitting on the sidewalk. But I need to know up front if you so much as gave a kid a nosebleed while you were in cub scouts. I mean it, Aaron: scam me one more time and I'm gone."

He was silent for three full beats.

"I'm clean."

Enough for the moment.

"Now walk me through everything you did from the last time you saw Rae to the day you were arrested."

"I left her house before midnight on Thursday. I had—"

"That's the last time the two of you had sex?"

"Last time I saw her, period. As I was saying, I left early because I was bidding a job at eight the next morning. After that we left for Dinosaur in Mark's SUV—"

"Dinosaur?"

"National Monument. Over by the Utah border." Three hundred miles northwest of Denver. "We go camping this time every year."

"And you went with your brother?"

"Yeah. When he dropped me off at my place Monday morning, the cops were waiting."

"What did they say?"

"Asked if they could come in and look around."

"Did they tell you why?"

"They said Rae was missing. I said sure, look all you want. They went through my house and garage, even crawled under my truck and stuck their nose up the exhaust pipe." He was enjoying the memory. "All for nothing, but what did they care?"

"Did they question you?"

"They asked if I knew where Rae was. I said I hadn't seen her since Thursday, when I dropped off some stuff about the energy audit."

So he'd lied to them too. "Did they ask where you were that weekend?"

"Nope." Good, at least until she had a chance to check it out. "Just would I come to the station and give samples of hair and blood, which I did. I didn't hear another word till they hauled me in thirty-six hours later. That's when I called you."

"Just you and Mark on the camping trip?"

"Yeah, I wanted to bring Trevor, but Wendy pitched a fit."

"Was she down in Pueblo that weekend?"

He nodded. "She had Trevor with her. You know what they say, possession is nine-tenths of the law. . . ."

"Anyone see you up in Dinosaur?"

"It was too cold for camping, there weren't many folks about."

"What time did you arrive?"

"Around three P.M."

Six-hour drive from Denver, which meant the brothers left by nine. Hours before Rae's neighbor saw her in her driveway.

"Did you stop for gas, get any receipts?"

"When Mark filled the tank in Craig, he might have paid with a credit card. You'll have to ask him."

Family alibis stank, and Pratt would howl when he heard this one. Before Jackie gave him that chance, she would have to be damn sure Aaron could take the heat.

"I don't believe you," she said.

His shock seemed real.

"You think I'd lie about a thing like that?"

"I think you'd do what most people faced with a first-degree murder charge would do, which is just about anything to get themselves off. The jury will laugh in your face if we tell them your alibi is your brother. As for me, even if I were inclined to believe you, I'd have to wonder why you didn't mention it sooner. Like the first time you called me."

"Because I didn't want to get Mark—" He stopped.

"Get Mark what?" This had better be good.

"Look, it's off season up there. We did a little hunting."

"So what?" Gaming violations were peanuts.

"Well, it wasn't just antelope. Friday night we got pretty loaded, and by Saturday we were looking for fun."

"And?"

"We packed a couple six-packs and our rifles and went

hiking. After an hour we came to a ridge that looked down on a little canyon. One end was kind of boxed off. And then we saw the horses."

"Horses?"

"Mustangs. You know, wild ponies. And before you could blink, one of us just picked up his rifle and started shooting."

Jackie willed her eyes to remain on his. "Did you hit any?"

"Two or three. They had nowhere to go, and once we started firing, they really freaked."

"Are you telling me you and your brother shot wild horses on BLM land? Don't you realize that's a federal—"

"—crime. Yeah, I know." Not to mention the most disgusting alibi she'd ever heard. "If we hadn't been drunk . . ."

"And that's why you didn't tell me, because you didn't want to get *Mark* in trouble?"

"I know it sounds crazy, Jackie, but it's the truth. I swear to God."

How would a jury react to the argument that Aaron couldn't have decapitated Rae Malone because he was slaughtering horses trapped in a canyon? Feeling sick at heart, she tried to assess it rationally. The alibi more than stank—it smelled so bad, it had to be true. The real problem was it raised more questions than it answered, and the biggest one was Aaron's brother. Would he be one of those witnesses she hoped no one would find?

"Tell me about Mark," she said.

"What do you want to know?"

Sell him to me, like I have to do to the jury for you.

"Everything."

"Well, you met him." So he *was* the other guy at her house that day. Clean-shaven, with the clipboard— "Couple inches taller and eight years older than me. Went to Colorado School of Mines and graduated with an engineering degree."

"Start earlier. What was Mark like as a kid?"

"Read a lot. I liked doing things with my hands, like my dad."

"But he ended up working for you?"

"Mark's kind of the brains behind our operation. I'm more the builder."

"It can be tough, following a brother to high school. Especially if he's a good student."

"I didn't follow Mark anywhere." Aaron's reply was strained. "Dad sent him to a private school out of state. He was slated for better things than plumbing."

That explained how little brother ended up on top but not how the son with the real future fizzled out. "And?"

"Nothing. End of story."

"Is he married?"

"No, the lucky dog." This topic was safer. "Said I was nuts to tie the knot. He couldn't stand Wendy, but it was more than that. He's too independent for most women."

"Would he testify about Dinosaur? If he comes forward, you can count on the DA making a criminal referral to the U.S. Attorney."

"We've always stood up for each other."

"Whether he's willing to back you or not, have him call me." Aaron nodded and Jackie sighed with relief. This view of the world from inside her client's head had been unusually exhausting, and she yearned to climb out. But there was one more topic to cover. "Did Rae tell you she was planning to break it off?"

"That's a lie!"

"Not according to her best friend."

"Sunny didn't know shit."

But Aaron knew her well enough to know who Jackie meant, and the thought of putting him on the stand made her stomach pitch. Whether her client was trying to con her or his own perceptions were out of whack wasn't the issue; unless she got to the bottom of his story, Pratt would eat him for breakfast. The possibility that Aaron might be telling the truth about his relationships with the opposite sex was becoming increasingly slim. But the next hurdle was the motion to suppress.

"I still want to push for an early trial date. Having you out on bail has cost us some leverage, but it is *absolutely critical* that you keep your nose clean."

"Keep my nose . . . ?"

"Stay away from anyone who might be a witness in the case. That includes Wendy and Sunny and anyone else connected with Rae. Stay busy with your work—be able to account for your whereabouts at all times. There's nothing Duncan Pratt wants more than to throw you back in the slammer. Don't give him an excuse."

When the call came, Jackie was in her den, roughing out a time line.

She'd divided the top sheet of her yellow pad into seven columns, one for each of the days of the week from the Thursday when Aaron last saw Rae to the Wednesday her body was found. First she entered the physical evidence: a rumpled square with a stain for Thursday night, an olive and squiggle of lettuce for Friday noon. As she doodled, her mind saw other images—the Goddess of Castle Pines waving good-bye in her Lexus, the water on the tile in the master bath. In the last column on the right she drew a stick with arms and legs an inch away from what might have been a hockey puck. Railroad tracks and a drunk tossing up cheap wine . . . She'd just sketched a cart with wheels and a gun rack underscored by a bold arrow pointing to the weekend, when the phone shrilled.

"Ms. Flowers?"

"Speaking."

"I'm sorry to bother you at home."

If the death penalty were reserved for callers who rang after ten at night and failed to identify themselves, Jackie would have been a proponent of capital punishment. That this man was soft-spoken and sounded reasonably intelligent were not mitigating factors.

"Then call me tomorrow at the office," she replied.

"I would have phoned sooner, but I've had my hands full for the last two weeks."

"Look, *whoever* you are—"

"Mark Best. Aaron's brother . . . The company's been a madhouse since he was busted, and we have jobs from Glenwood Springs clear up to the Nebraska border. Aaron said we needed to talk."

Phone interviews were a poor substitute for face time. Deprived of demeanor and body language, she would be forced to rely on timing and tone. And Mark was clearly sophisticated; he'd thrown the ball in her court by forcing her to set the agenda. The only way to tell whether Aaron's alibi was real was to toss it back to him.

"I understand the two of you spent that weekend together," she began.

"Camping up in Dinosaur."

"How long were you gone?" Keep the questions vague, let him supply the details.

"We met with a client in Lakewood at eight on Friday morning." Just west of Denver. "The appointment lasted less than an hour, and we came home first thing Monday."

"What client was that?"

"I'll call you with her name when I'm back at the office."

"How did you get to Dinosaur?"

"I-70 to Dillon and Highway 40 the rest of the way. It took about six hours." Mark's voice was deeper than Aaron's, more confident of the facts; at least he gave direct answers. "Could have made it sooner, but we ran into snow."

"Any stops?"

"Lunch at a burger stand in Craig. Probably the last time I sat down to a meal." On her notepad, Jackie penciled in a squeeze bottle with a rubber nipple and a salt shaker an inch below Rae's scrap of lettuce on Friday afternoon. Mark really did sound exhausted. "Oh, and I guess we gassed up at a Chevron before hitting the road again."

A tombstone with a nozzle for an arm joined the condiments.

"How did you pay?"

"Cash. Both times. I keep plastic for emergencies." He waited for the next question as she smudged the gas pump and ketchup bottle with her eraser. So far the alibi was uncomfortably soft, like the rest of Aaron's story.

"Would anyone remember seeing you?"

"Gal at the burger stand, maybe. Big blue eyes and a ponytail. Pulled tight and tied at the crown with a scarf."

"What'd you do when you hit Dinosaur?"

"Drank a little beer, camped out in the SUV."

Jackie extended the arrow under the box with wheels into Saturday and darkened it. Would Mark bring up the horses or make her do it? "Sounds a little cold for camping. What'd you do all weekend?"

"Didn't Aaron tell you?"

"I need to hear it from you."

The pause was long and heavy.

"You know about the mustangs." A statement, not a question.

"Aaron said something about it. . . ."

"I don't know what got into us."

Us. Did big brother fire too?

"Neither of us did anything like that before." He sounded numb.

"How many horses did you shoot?"

"When the second one stumbled, he stopped."

He?

"All of a sudden it hit."

The droplets she'd been doodling in Saturday's column could have been snow or blood, but Mark's remorse sounded real. Jackie penciled them in as tears.

"Did you tell anyone what you did?" she asked. His chance to confirm it was Aaron and not him. True or not, that would really stick the knife—

"You kidding? We run a green energy company, Ms. Flowers, we've built our reputation on saving the environment. It would destroy us if this got out!"

Mark spoke as if the company wasn't just Aaron's, but *his too*, and her concern that he might sabotage his younger brother began to fade.

"Were there witnesses to the shooting?"

"We didn't see anyone. It was so cold, we were probably the only campers."

"Anything in the papers about it?"

"I'd be surprised if it made the local press; wild horses are a nuisance to ranchers up there." Unlike Aaron, he hadn't tried to blame it on the beer. Were they so different, or did Mark not realize just how much he'd risked for a little target practice?

"You understand you could be prosecuted for shooting horses on a government preserve," she began.

"We weren't actually in Dinosaur at the time, it was closer to Rangely—"

"Federal land is federal land. The BLM owns most of it thereabouts."

"What's the penalty?"

"Under the mandatory sentencing guidelines"—as oxymoronic as the concept of a mandatory guideline was—"the least you could get is eighteen months. And a stiff fine."

"Probation?"

"Prison." She relented. "Maybe an honor camp if the pre-sentence report is favorable. If it were bald eagles, you'd be looking at three years."

A shocked silence. She'd blindsided Mark and he was trying not to panic. Would he let his brother hang? Her pencil inscribed a large question mark over the arrow linking Friday to Saturday.

"What do you want me to do?" he finally said.

"Are you willing to testify to Aaron's alibi?"

"Can I just say we went camping?"

"It's not that simple." No matter how helpful he wanted to be, Jackie wasn't about to put a liar on the stand. "If you testify, you'll have to tell the truth."

"Do I have to decide now?"

"Not tonight, but I need to know soon." Her thoughts were racing ahead. If she wanted to introduce an alibi, she had to tell Pratt where Aaron was and give him Mark's name thirty days before trial. But timing was the least of her concerns. An alibi would move the defense from punching holes in Pratt's case to assuming the burden of proving Aaron's whereabouts. And as grisly as the mustang slaughter was, it still seemed too good to be true. "When the DA finds out, he'll want to interview you."

"Do I have to talk to him?"

"If you don't cooperate, he'll use that at trial. Of course, we can always decide at the last minute not to call you." And with an alibi like this, she'd do everything she could to avoid putting him on the stand.

Mark heaved a sigh. When he spoke again, his voice was resigned.

"I'll do anything to help Aaron, Ms. Flowers. If that means facing prison—"

"We'll need to meet in person before I file that notice." Despite herself, Jackie was moved. How many men in his position would risk their neck to save their brother? "I want to be sure you understand what you're getting into."

"As soon as I can make the time, I'll come down."

No reason not to believe him, and chances were a jury would too. But Jackie had one last question. One test of Mark's honesty, or perhaps his self-interest.

"Who fired the shots that brought those mustangs down?"

"What difference does that make?"

Loyalty—or pragmatism?

"Eighteen months, maybe hard time . . ."

"If I was with Aaron, it might as well have been me. I learned that lesson early."

As Jackie hung up the phone, she tore the sheet from her pad. Crumpling it, she lobbed it in the direction of her wastebasket. There was plenty of time to decide whether to use him. Her last thought before she fell asleep that night was to have Pilar perform a background check on Mark Best.

Chapter Twelve

Who is ready to proceed?"

Before Jackie could respond, Duncan Pratt leaped to his feet.

"The People, your honor."

Worrell's rubbery lips twisted in an ironic smile, and Jackie could almost hear him murmur, "Unrepresented, as usual . . ." She'd been in this courtroom years ago when a prosecutor asked to approach the bench and Worrell leaned forward and muttered into the newly installed mike, *Wonder what that stupid sumbitch wants this time.* . . . In the old days lawyers never had to guess what was on the judge's mind.

"Any objection, Ms. Flowers?"

This round Pratt had to win. It was Monday morning and he'd loaded up the prosecution table with his two as- sistants and more law books than there were in Jackie's li- brary. Decked out in his trial suit, a double-breasted navy pinstripe with a white shirt and rep tie, he looked every inch the champion of justice. His motion to admit Aaron's prior offenses had landed on Worrell's desk the same day as Jackie's motion to exclude them. If Pratt wanted to assume the psy- chological if not legal burden of carrying the motion, more power to him. With an adversary who telegraphed his punches, it was easier to bob and weave.

"No, your honor," she replied.

"Very well, then, Mr. Pratt."

"As to the matter of the defendant's prior crimes—"

"Objection," Jackie interceded mildly. "The DA is well aware that in one of the incidents in question the complaint was withdrawn, and the other resulted in a deferred prosecution with no conviction."

"Save the bombast for the jury, Mr. Pratt." Worrell seemed to be stifling a yawn.

"As I was saying"—the DA cast an injured glance in Jackie's direction—"the defendant has a prior record, and we believe its relevancy outweighs any conceivable prejudice from admitting it at trial. The first incident occurred in 1992 in a bar in Sedalia."

Lead with the worst and exaggerate; as Jackie's aunt always said, you get only one chance to make a first impression. Worrell's pumpkin head tilted dangerously. He would give Pratt thirty seconds to state his case and no more.

"The victim was brutally beaten with a pool cue," the DA continued, "which ruptured his spleen and left him near death. According to witnesses, the assault was entirely unprovoked—"

"Whatever could *that* prosecutor have been thinking?" Worrell mused, tapping his lower lip. Sometimes even thirty seconds was too long.

"Beg pardon?" Pratt asked.

"Unprovoked aggravated assault, victim well on the way to his eternal reward. Had *your* office been prosecuting Mr. Best for this heinous crime, surely you would have demanded jail time. Which leads me to wonder whether you're being altogether candid with this court."

"Well, I—*we* have the police report and medical records right here. . . ." Pratt gestured to his first assistant, an earnest young man with large ears who was digging through a file. "The connection to our case is the sheer brutality—"

Worrell's eyes gleamed and one hand hovered near the mike. Jackie recalled a warning never to use "we" or "our" in his court. *That a turd in your pocket, counselor?* he'd asked one rookie who insisted on using the plural possessive while arguing his case.

"Eight years ago, eh?" the judge asked. "Does this alleged offense, for which Mr. Best was never convicted, establish a motive for killing Rae Malone?"

"No, but we—"

"Plan, knowledge, or opportunity?"

"No, but—"

"Accident or absence of mistake?"

Had she been the sort to revel in easy victories, Jackie would have been elated. But Worrell was giving Pratt an unnecessarily hard time—it was too early in the game to demonstrate antipathy for one side. The judge didn't give a damn about the press, but his evenhandedness reflected a refined sense of aesthetics. In a multi-issue hearing, that could only mean he was going to slam the defense on the domestic violence report. Could she reverse her momentum without jeopardizing her client?

"—denied," the judge was saying. "I hope your argument on the domestic assault is better, Mr. Pratt. Make Ms. Flowers *earn* her retainer."

Now she understood. Worrell sensed a larger strategy afoot; he was planning to make her fight for every yard no matter how he ruled on the incident at Aaron's home.

"Twelve months before Rae Malone was murdered," Pratt continued, "Aaron Best viciously beat his wife. Like the prior attack in Sedalia, this assault was unprovoked and landed his victim in the hospital."

Worrell pretended to sift through the voluminous attachments to the DA's motion. "I don't believe I saw evidence of criminal charges—"

"The rule speaks to other wrongs and acts," Pratt interjected, "not full-fledged crimes."

"Quite so," the judge replied, "but they're still inadmissible to prove Mr. Best's character. Unless you can show—"

"—motive, your honor." That the DA was rattled enough to interrupt Worrell, much less finish his sentences, told Jackie the testimony of Aaron's wife was more important than she'd imagined. What else was Wendy Best prepared to say? "We believe—"

"*Believe?*"

"Have evidence to show that Aaron Best murdered Rae Malone to prevent her from exposing their affair to his wife." Jackie resisted the impulse to glance at her client. Announcing his theory of motive in open court, in full hearing of the press and the judge who would be trying the case, showed just how far Pratt was willing to go to put Aaron's wife in front of the jury. Was he trying it on for size, or had she misjudged Wendy's vindictiveness? "—custody dispute," Pratt was saying, "originating the very night he assaulted his wife and put her in the hospital. As such, it falls squarely within the rule."

"Ms. Flowers?" The round head bobbed in her direction.

"Pure fantasy, you honor. The DA wants the jury to believe that if Aaron Best got into a fight with his wife, he is equally capable of decapitating another woman twelve months later." Abandoning the pretense of her yellow pad, she stepped to the lectern swinging. "No matter how thin the DA slices the baloney, unless he has some witness who's prepared to testify to direct knowledge of such a motive, he has no business serving it to this court. And if there is such a witness, I'd like his or her name right now."

"Mr. Pratt?" Worrell was enjoying the spirited response, even if the conclusion was foregone.

At Pratt's hesitation, Jackie's ears pricked up. For a man who placed such a high premium on organization, it could only mean he was withholding something important. Or one of his witnesses was waffling.

"Your honor, the list of witnesses will be provided as soon as we've completed interviews."

"Based on your representation that Mrs. Best's testimony about the altercation is integral to the motive for the Malone slaying, I'll admit it. Subject, of course, to cross-examination." Worrell nodded to himself. "Any other matters before we adjourn?"

"One thing more, your honor," Jackie said.

"Yes, Ms. Flowers?" His impatient tone warned her not to upset the cart.

"I would like the DA to go on record as to whether he has provided the defense with all Brady materials." An insulting request, given the prosecution's absolute and ongoing obligation to turn over exculpatory material, including that in the hands of his investigators or staff. But both sides were playing for keeps, and inconvenient evidence had a way of getting lost.

"Is Ms. Flowers impugning the integrity of my office?" Pratt blustered. He was furious, Jackie saw. Genuinely furious. Why did this case mean so much—"I have never, in all my *fifteen years*—"

"And now wouldn't be the time to start," Worrell interrupted bluntly. "It's a straightforward request, Mr. Pratt. Have you provided the defense with all Brady materials in your possession or control?"

"We most certainly have."

"See that you continue to do so." The judge rose. Like puppets on a string, the gallery jerked to its feet. "Court adjourned."

Jackie watched Pratt storm out of the courtroom, leaving his associates to retrieve his papers. Gathering her pencil and pad, she stooped for her briefcase.

"Did she make you crazy?"

The voice was soft, almost friendly. Meant for one person's ears.

"Crazy?" Aaron replied and Jackie resisted the impulse to turn.

"You know what I mean." Louder now, the insistence colored by familiarity. "Did she tease you?"

Aaron gave a nervous chuckle. "Hey, now . . ."

Rising, Jackie saw Rodger Malone. He was smiling but his pupils were pinpricks. She scoured the courtroom for a bailiff, but it had emptied before anyone smelled blood.

"Did she treat you like some kind of *toy*?" Malone continued.

Jackie took a step forward but both men ignored her. Aaron was hyped, defiant. Relishing the encounter.

"Your ex-wife wrote the book."

A vein in Malone's neck bulged and Jackie grabbed Aaron's arm. His muscles were taut. "Come on. Let's go."

"Every page but the last," Malone replied, and as the smirk slowly faded from her client's face, Jackie suddenly sensed she was the odd man out. Without another word, Rae's ex-husband turned and exited through the wooden gate.

Chapter Thirteen

Where's your reader?" Pilar asked.

Lily blew a Bronx cheer. Sprawled on the floor of Jackie's office, she reached into her backpack and pulled out a coloring book and a box of crayons. Her parents had dropped her off while they attended an end-of-year conference at her academy, and homework was to do at *home*. "Can I have a pop?"

Jackie was putting the finishing touches on her strategy for dealing with Pratt's chronology: she would bait the trap with another request for Brady materials, elicit the maid's schedule from Sunny at trial while the DA's star still shone brightly, and then hit her with the slip about Thursday night. Even if Sunny denied it, the implausibility of the DA's time line would have been firmly planted, and the right judge would go ballistic over the Brady blunder. She scrawled her signature at the bottom of the new Brady demand and handed it to Pilar, who disappeared down the hall.

"Can I use the electric sharpener?"

Lily held a sorry-looking black Crayola, worn to a greasy stub.

"You know it'll melt," Jackie replied.

"But it would be fun to try." Leaning over Jackie's shoulder, she pointed to a photograph of Rae Malone sitting on the hood of her Lexus. "Who's she?"

"Someone in a case."

"Why are you looking at her picture?"

"I'm trying to fit some pieces together."

"Like a puzzle?"

"Sort of . . ."

Pilar returned with two cans of real Coke. No diet soda on her watch; when the temperature of aspartame exceeded eighty-six degrees, it converted to formaldehyde and the poison found in fire ants. Using the distraction, Jackie gathered up the photos of the viaduct behind Coors Field and slipped them in her top drawer. Lily's next questions would be what kind of case was it and why she was looking at pictures instead of meeting with the woman in person.

"What's on your schedule this afternoon?" Pilar asked Lily.

"It's too *hot* to go outside." Lily was adept at ringing Pilar's bells—they were two of a kind. "Can we go to a horror movie?"

"Not till you do your homework," Jackie replied absently. She was trying to picture the Goddess of Castle Pines with Aaron Best, and the image kept flickering in and out.

Lily appealed to Pilar and Jackie tuned them out. An alibi would add weight to their defense, but its credibility hinged on Mark. Had he conducted the audit at Rae's house too? She'd told Aaron she needed to meet with his brother face-to-face, but so far—

"Ms. Flowers?"

The man on the threshold was taller and more muscular than Aaron.

"There was no one at the front desk, so I wandered back. . . ."

Mark, the mold from which his younger brother had been stamped. Even his features seemed more defined—the weakness of Aaron's chin squared off, the softness of his mouth firmed, and the eyes unblinking. How was it she'd remembered only his neatly pressed trousers and shaven cheeks?

"I hope I'm not inconveniencing you." Where Aaron's pitch slid up an octave of uncertainty, Mark spoke clearly and with confidence. There was something presumptuous about his failure to introduce himself, but two could play that game.

"Thanks for dropping by," Jackie replied.

He glanced at Lily, who'd stopped swinging her legs on the credenza, where she was perched beside Pilar, and then at Jackie's investigator. Pilar continued to sip her soda, but Jackie knew from her casual posture that she'd shifted into her role as second pair of ears.

"If I'm interrupting—" he continued.

"We were taking a break," Jackie told him. The last thing she wanted was to question Mark about Aaron's alibi in front of Lily. "My colleagues were just about to leave."

Neither took the hint. Unsure who Mark was, Pilar stood her ground. Lily was capable of filling in the blanks in any number of combinations, none of which she was about to miss.

"I knew you wanted to meet me in person and the sooner the better. I've been up to my ears with work, and this was the first afternoon I could break free."

"We'll have time to go over certain details of the alibi closer to the trial." Jackie shot a meaningful glance in Lily's direction and was relieved when Mark gave a nod of acknowledgment. "For now I just need to know whether you were able to corroborate your trip to Dinosaur."

"I found that receipt for the gas we bought in Craig." Reaching in his hip pocket for his billfold, he handed Jackie a fuzzy yellow MasterCard slip. She didn't even try to make out the date. "I guess I charged it after all."

"Was that on Friday?"

"No." The full lips curved in a rueful grin. "I was wrong about when we stopped. It was Saturday."

Not a total disaster, but nowhere near as helpful as evidence that the brothers had been three hundred miles from Denver the day Rae Malone was abducted. "What about lunch?" Jackie continued. "You said you stopped at a burger stand."

"McDonald's, I can tell you that much. But I must have tossed the receipt."

"Were you able to recall whether you ran into anyone in Dinosaur?"

"Couple of older guys with fishing gear, they might remember us. I'll have to ask Aaron what kind of truck they were in—he picks up on that sort of thing."

At least they had the gas receipt. And now it was time to pose the big question.

"Have you thought through the personal risks of taking the stand?"

Mark's eyes swept from the gold-embossed treatises on Jackie's shelves to the paperless surface of her desk before fastening on her own. He smiled as if he thought she already knew the answer.

"I told you, there's nothing I wouldn't do for my brother."

"You may want to consult your own—"

"I don't need a lawyer. I understand the ramifications."

"Then I'll need some information about your background. Aaron said you graduated from the Colorado School of Mines. . . ."

"My undergraduate degree was in geochemistry, but I got my master's in petroleum engineering. Would've completed the doctorate if the oil boom hadn't gone bust."

That explained why he worked for the family business but not why Aaron had inherited it. With degrees from Mines— "Have you ever been in trouble with the law?"

Behind her, Lily was suspiciously quiet. The second time Jackie mentioned Dinosaur she'd set down her soda, and now she made not a sound.

"Don't you know my alma mater's song?" With a wink at Lily, Mark began to sing in a surprisingly melodic tone.

"Now here we have the mining man, in either hand a gun.
He is not afraid of anything, and he's never known to run,
He dearly loves his whiskey, and he dearly loves his beer.
He's a shooting, fighting, dynamiting, mining engineer. . . ."

"Very nice," Jackie said. If not for the image of Mark gunning down a defenseless horse, his attempt to charm might have succeeded. "Which attributes apply to you?"

"Since I favor neither whiskey nor beer and the only gun I've owned is a hunting rifle, I plead guilty to being a mining engineer. And that, I regret to say, is in the past."

"Is that a yes or a no?" she persisted.

"To which question?"

"Whether you have a record."

"No." He glanced at Pilar. "And you can underline that twice."

"If I notify the DA you might testify on Aaron's behalf, he'll want an interview. That's entirely up to you—"

"I'd feel more comfortable if we could meet again before then. I don't know when I'll be able to grab another afternoon off, but maybe some evening after work . . ."

With a promise that he would call when the DA contacted him, Mark took his leave.

"Whew," Pilar said as his footsteps descended the stairs.

"He's a creep," Lily declared. "If he wants a date, why doesn't he just *ask?*"

"Because that isn't what he was doing," Jackie protested. But Mark's physical intensity was difficult to reconcile with her memory of the man who'd examined every inch of her house the previous September, tapping her walls and making careful notations on his clipboard. Other workmen resented it when you asked them to take off their boots before going upstairs, but he'd done so without protest or surprise. . . .

Pilar shook her head in disgust. "Crude but effective."

"I don't date witnesses!" Jackie insisted, shrugging off Pilar's ironic look. Not since that disaster with the DNA expert two years back. "And if you find Mark Best so distasteful, whatever happened to that background check you were going to run?"

"It just moved to the top of my list."

Pilar's response was unaccountably peeving.

"Weren't you two going to a movie?" Jackie demanded.

Lily flashed Pilar the thumbs-up and scooted down the stairs before Jackie could change her mind. Still shaking her head, Pilar gathered up the pop cans and slowly followed.

The first mistake Jackie made when she left her office that afternoon was turning a block short, which put her in the direction opposite from home. Not an uncommon occurence on a day like this, but then, sirens and a fire truck disoriented her even more and she found herself heading north to get out of their way instead of hanging in an extra block so she could loop back to her office to start all over again. It would have been amusing if she hadn't been so tired; and as she approached downtown, she got caught in the rush-hour exodus from the skyscrapers on Seventeenth.

Now she was heading for I-25, where she certainly didn't want to be, and it wasn't until she was finally able to make a left that she realized she was almost at Coors Field. Just over the viaduct lay the broad plain of the South Platte valley, where farmers used to sell fruit and vegetables wholesale.

Northwest on the viaduct, past the spruce stands and redbrick walls of Coors Field—unless she turned soon she would be heading to Boulder in bumper-to-bumper traffic. Left or right, flip a coin . . . To her right lay the road to the old Denargo market, to her left the stadium and a return to the skyline shimmering in the late-day sun.

The left on Wewatta was Jackie's second mistake. Now she was rapidly descending into the deserted bowl of the Burlington Northern railroad yard. Passing from asphalt to dirt to gravel strewn with broken glass, she headed for the broad strip in the shadow of the ramp to make a U-turn and retrace her course. As she pulled up between a mound of riprap and a pile of railroad ties, she suddenly realized where she was. Directly ahead of her, propped against a concrete pillar, had sat the headless body of Rae Malone.

Backing up in deep gravel, she heard a beer bottle crunch, slammed on the brakes, and got out to examine her rear tires. On the siding to her left stood rusted tank cars covered with graffiti, to the right a mountain of plywood pallets and tin barrels of the sort winos used for fires. Coal dust and creosote permeated the air. So this was where Rae's body had been found. *Why here?*

Between the viaduct and the stadium lay railroad tracks. The Burlington Northern's property was bounded by no-trespassing signs on chain link, separated from Coors Field by a narrow strip of weeds and the stadium's wrought-iron fence. In the middle lay a no-man's land. Tossed onto that hell strip like an opening pitch, Rae's head with its flowing red hair had landed facing the fuchsia tent of the beer garden behind center field.

Chapter | Fourteen

An ozone advisory was in effect until four o'clock. The red alert triggered by sweltering sun and windless skies was accompanied by a recommendation that Denver residents delay mowing lawns and filling gas tanks until after dusk, but the throngs at the Cherry Creek Arts Festival couldn't have cared less. Three days of record heat had dampened only the spirits of the artists who came from as far away as Europe expecting cool mountain air and brisk sales of pricey art. For the glitterati, this was a chance to see and be seen, to much spinach-cheese wontons with raspberry wasabi and catfish in green curry over jasmine rice while being entertained by roving bands of mutant puppeteers.

He had arrived before the official starting time. He enjoyed seeing who came first, watching them peck around the edges and form groups that eddied and coalesced in a rising tide. Patterns of movement fascinated him—the mindless surge to a particular booth like a swarm of ants to a half-eaten jelly doughnut. As the temperature rose, the Brownian motion accelerated until the random swirling throbbed like a giant pulse. The scents of garlic and roasting meat rose above the crowd, and he felt the first pangs of hunger.

At a booth featuring life-sized oil paintings of fleshy matrons at the beach he paused. These were *fun*. The women were Junoesque and jolly, on the wrong side of fifty, and not the least self-conscious about cellulite or wrinkles, with their hair stuffed into bright-hued rubber bathing caps whose bitter odor he remembered from youth. Why did aging pose such dread? When one considered the alternative . . . A woman in white jersey shorts and matching T-shirt elbowed her way to the paintings. Stepping back, he let her through.

The left side of her costume was a river of red and white, with a patch of navy embroidered with mirrors meant to resemble stars. Fort Worth or Kansas City, he thought as his eyes traveled from her jeweled sun visor to lacquered toenails in red patent leather sandals. Celebrating the Fourth of July four weeks early. Her upper arms were smooth and firm and her breasts taut, a fiction maintained to the hem of her shorts. Legs were the giveaway; her brown thighs were as wrinkled as crepe and the knees like apples baked too long in the oven. Closer to the subjects in the paintings than the image her face-lift and designer ensemble projected, a spoiled suburban matron. With an admiring look to assure her the charade succeeded, he melted back in the crowd.

Each year he eagerly anticipated the arts festival because the human traffic represented a true cross-section of the community. Three distinct classes of women: those who had arrived, the wanna-bes, and the ones who lived their lives oblivious to fat, cholesterol, and exercise. The first wore hats— elegant straw with bands of silk—and gleaming platinum at wrist and throat, and the understated extravagance of rayon swathed their asexual torsos like cocoons. Except for the rare indiscretion of the woman decked out like the star-spangled banner, their age was always difficult to determine. The third wore whatever was comfortable without regard to whether it was becoming or not; flaunting the cooked flesh that was the norm for Colorado from June on, they cooled themselves with paddle fans bearing the logo of Metro Taxi and gravitated to booths featuring earrings and miniatures under the misimpression that volume meant bargains. It was the second group that interested him—the wanna-bes who thought their problems would be solved if they were rich and stylish. Their desperation made them vulnerable.

He smelled Cajun sausage around the corner and began making his way toward the culinary tents. A tiny woman in a floral frock with a child-sized dummy clinging to her leg blocked his way. Accompanying them was a man in a bee-keeper's mask and black nylon flight suit holding a six-foot puppet with green skin and molelike features.

Mole Man was evidently hungry, because he wrapped his rubbery arms around a large-breasted woman in the crowd, dipped his rodentlike snout to her chest, and noisily began to slurp. "*I'm* your mama," the tiny woman wailed, "Papa and lunch are waiting in the car!" Her right foot kicked, as if trying to dislodge the parasitic rubber creature on her leg, and she pursued Mole Man into the crowd in a parody of maternal devotion. Mothers. All the same . . . The onlookers applauded, and the woman who'd been assaulted gave a laugh that fell short of being good-natured.

After a five-minute wait at the Cajun food stand he bought a crispy lobster tail over sweet jalapeño cornbread and devoured it in three quick bites. Hunger temporarily abated, he strolled past booths at a more leisurely pace.

Porcelain teapots with matte glazes, booth after booth of beaten silver, hand-tinted photographs, and bowls carved from exotic woods. Primitives had made a strong showing this year, and as he passed an acrylic of horses grazing in a meadow oblivious to flames licking over the next hill, he wondered how the jury had been selected. One booth was devoted entirely to studies of birds, which he loathed, and another to prints of insects that were appealingly lifelike. As the gimmicky nature of the art began to pall, he turned his attention to the spectators.

The next tent was an island of calm, a death knell for the artist perched forlornly on a canvas director's chair at the rear. A slender, silver-haired man in a maroon polo shirt and neatly pressed khakis was gazing at an oil of a sun-drenched wall in an unidentified Mediterranean village. The Rolex on his left arm and rail-thin woman on his right screamed money.

"Nice use of shading," the man murmured to his companion just loud enough for the painter to overhear. The woman nodded noncommittally and the artist turned away to signify indifference to the prospect of a sale. Swallowing the bait, Polo Shirt stepped forward and the mating dance began. Had artistic technique matched ability to size up patrons, this booth would have been mobbed. Always something to learn . . .

The noon sun chased the shade clear into the buildings and still the crowds kept coming. Damp flesh pressed against his own, French perfume intermingled with rank sweat. Just ahead the fountain and wading pool was filled with children. A young boy squealed and the man saw one of the wandering entertainers clad in Grim Reaper garb. The performer's head, chalky and bullet-shaped as Uncle Fester's, sat in a bird cage on his shoulders. As he watched, the Reaper reached up and whipped off his head.

The boy screamed again, this time in unmistakable terror. The severed head was clearly papier-mâché and not real, and for a moment the man was perplexed at his reaction. There was no blood, no . . . Then he realized it was the suddenness of the movement, the shock of it coming off, that had unnerved the child. Wondering how the boy would sleep that night, he slipped back into the throng.

He'd dressed for the weather, but the army of sweating faces and sunburned flesh was turning what had been so eagerly anticipated into an exercise in tolerance. Just as he was deciding which escape route would be shortest, he spotted the woman decked out like the Fourth of July. What made her think those legs fooled anyone? Discomfort forgotten, he followed her.

She threaded her way through the crowd with surprising nimbleness, as if she knew she was not alone. Six booths away she stopped. Attracted by the knot of spectators, or was this her destination all along? She elbowed her way to the front. Without thinking, he followed. When he could at last see what the booth offered, the world came to a halt.

A gallery of clay monsters jeered from the canvas tent. They were everywhere, perched on shelves and prancing on pedestals, and every one of them was staring at *him*. Their leader crouched at eye level, knees bent and splayed to reveal her pubis. Ropes writhed at her crown and she was tattooed head to toe with black and ochre and the brown of dried blood. Breasts embellished with concentric rings, the nipples bull's-eyes, larger circles culminating in the hood of a cobra in the precise center of her swollen abdomen. Her elbows rested on her knees and her hands, oversized and clownish like her feet, beckoned him in a mocking gesture. . . . And he was back in the game. Playing statues with his mother.

The game began even before his father left for Korea, the special times he and his mother shared. A secret—she made him promise, and that compounded the excitement as she must have intended. At first it was the grooming of her hair. The ritual opened with her emergence from her bath on Friday evening. Modestly draped in a towel, she would sit at the edge of the tub. With a wide-toothed tortoiseshell comb he untangled the snarls in the thick tresses, then plaited them in gleaming braids she coiled and pinned on top of her head. It was a privilege to be permitted to do that, a reward for his obedience and attentiveness during the preceding week. She was training him to be her little man, his father's replacement, and a good husband to the woman he would one day marry. Once his old man shipped out, the game entered a new phase.

After he combed her hair, if he had been *very* good, his mother would climb onto the bed she'd shared with his father. As she leaned back against the headboard, she would allow the towel to slip from her shoulders, exposing her breasts. His role was to remain in the doorway as still as a statue, until she beckoned. If she so much as caught him blinking, the game was off and he would not be given another chance for an entire week. Slowly, she would motion him forward, two paces at a time, and the towel would gradually fall to the floor. With each step she would change her pose, pulling her knees to her chest and then dropping them to the sides, revealing herself with greater and greater intimacy as she tested his discipline. Watching him become aroused, pretending not to see, she beckoned him closer and then with a glance turned him to stone. If he made it all the way to the bed without any untoward motion, she would reach for the lotion she kept in her night table and allow him to massage her.

Finally freeing him from her gaze, facedown on the comforter she lay. As he straddled her back and his fingers kneaded the oil into her shoulders and down the delicate knobs in her spine to the rounded firmness below, he could feel his excitement mount until it was almost unbearable. Would she give him release or send him to bed? He continued stroking the slick lotion into her skin, knowing that an instant's hesitation could result in his banishment. When she was ready she signaled with a deep sigh and he dismounted to allow her to turn. Through half-closed eyes she would inspect the state of his arousal before allowing him to massage her stomach and breasts. Guiding his fingers lower and deeper, until he felt her tremble. As she began to throb she cried out once, sharply. *His* reward. Because in making him her tool, for one unforgettable moment *she was entirely under his control*.

Afterward she might stroke him but never to the point of release. That could be accomplished only if she wasn't looking, and her eyes were everywhere. Only she determined if and when. Even before she painted the stars on his ceiling to wink him to sleep, the last thing he saw before he closed his eyes each night was her wig, perched on the stand beside his bed. . . .

"Don't you just *love* her?" A woman with hair like cotton wool had risen from the camp chair at the rear of the tent. The crowd had cleared and the Fourth of July harlot was nowhere to be seen. "I call her my goddess. She's been with me so long, I dread the thought of selling her."

"I can see why." Was the bitch teasing him? "Your technique's fantastic."

Her smile broadened and all he saw were teeth. And that mass of writhing hair. Not snakes but worms, tiny little—

"Some men find her disturbing," she continued coyly.

Her throat was very slender and his fingers tightened. But there was so much at stake: he had to be patient.

"I can't imagine why."

"I'll tell you something if you promise not to laugh." As her voice dropped to a throaty whisper, her breasts tightened against her blouse. "Sometimes I think she's me. Of course, we *look* nothing alike."

Two could play.

"Where do you get your inspiration?"

She shrugged modestly, but he wasn't fooled, not for an instant. They were all the same, *all* of them. . . .

"The goddess calls to me."

"And you've come here all the way from"—he glanced at the sign above her credit card machine—"Indiana?"

"I consider it a privilege to have been selected. Of course, I donate a portion of my proceeds to environmental causes."

"If you're free after the show tonight, perhaps you'll let me take you to dinner."

What was he saying? She was testing him to see whether he would lose control. That's why Fourth of July led him to this booth, wasn't it?

"—have to be here till eight, but by then I'll be *famished*."

Voracious, like them all. Dare he risk . . .

"I'll meet you here at a quarter past, how's that?"

"Better make it eight-thirty. The guy in the next booth is going to help me load my stuff for the night. It'll take at least that long."

He grinned in anticipation, but inside he was relieved. Fate had saved him from acting on impulse—he could not afford to be seen and remembered. The balance of risk had shifted from marginal to unacceptable and he would leave the festival now and not return. Standing the bitch up was the mildest form of discipline he could impose, but it would have to suffice.

"I can hardly wait," he promised.

Her smile widened until her teeth seemed to swallow her face. "I'll just bet you can't."

Chapter | Fifteen

Jackie stared at the ink on the yellow slip. The date was right and the credit card receipt looked legit, but anyone could have signed it. For that matter, even if Mark had been behind the wheel in Craig, how did she know Aaron was with him?

"Feel like a trip to Dinosaur?" she asked Pilar.

"Not gonna take Mark's word for it?" her investigator replied. "Can't say I blame you."

"I hate to send you all that way, especially on a holiday weekend. If the weather up there was as bad as they said, chances are no one will remember seeing them. But you never—"

"—know unless you *look*," Pilar finished, and glanced at her watch. She would gas the Spider tonight and leave first thing in the morning.

"What time is it?"

"Quarter till six."

Jackie jumped out of her chair. "Got to go, I promised Britt and Randy I'd take Lily for the night."

"Is Britt still complaining about Lily putting gunk in her hair?"

Being placed in detention for making faces at her classmates was nothing new, but as the school year drew to a close, Lily had taken to twisting her hair in coils and molding them with Vaseline. At wit's end, Britt was threatening to give her a crew cut when Jackie suggested a time-out that weekend.

"Maybe I'll get to the bottom of it tonight," Jackie replied. "Want to come over for dinner?"

"And a movie? *The Maltese Falcon*'s on at eight."

Jackie shook her head. "Tonight is story time."

"Gonna toast marshmallows and try to scare the bejesus out of that poor little—"

"Actually, we've become quite involved with a book."

"You're kidding!" Pilar's eyes narrowed. "She still won't read?"

"Been pinched and poked like a lab rat, and there's nothing organically out of whack."

"Trust Britt and Randy to cover all the bases."

"They mean well, Pilar, they just—"

"—haven't got a clue. They still going to that nitwit the school recommended?"

"Not since Lily stopped saying she was a boy."

"Sounded pretty healthy to me," Pilar sniffed. "Who *wouldn't* want to play with Power Rangers?"

They smiled at the memory of Britt and Randy's consternation when Lily insisted not that she wanted to be a boy, but in fact *was* one, and the school psychologist who claimed it was because Lily knew girls were unwanted in China. At his urging, Lily's parents had embarked on a rigorous course of reassurance, which only made Lily regret she'd brought it up in the first place. As soon as she outgrew that phase she started putting Vaseline in her hair. The parent-teacher conference the week before had been a disaster.

"The immediate concern," Jackie continued, "is her refusal to read in class."

"It's that private school, they don't know what to do because they've never seen anyone like her." Pilar shook her head in admiration, then hesitated. "Do you think she can read?"

"I don't know. But if she doesn't start proving it soon, they'll hold her back again. And you know what that means. . . ."

"You bet I do." Pilar gave a mock shudder. "Three inches taller and four times as smart as any boy in her class."

.

On the way home Jackie stopped for a large pizza with pepperoni, onions, and anchovies and a veggie chef's salad. If Lily palmed the anchovies and discarded them in a napkin, what did Jackie care? She never knew whether Lily actually enjoyed hot stuff or was emulating Pilar, whom she regarded as the height of cool. Lily was below the legal age and too short to buy cigarillos, but if she talked about packing a gun, it would *really* be time to worry.

When Jackie mounted Britt and Randy's front steps, the girl stood waiting at the door. She was clad in black leggings and the ruby sequined slippers Pilar had bought her at Target, with dark sunglasses halfway down her nose, and her hair was skinned straight back in a ponytail with an elastic so tight, it looked like she'd had a face-lift. In her red nylon backpack were a nightgown and fresh underwear for the morning. Nobody ever said Lily lacked style.

"She's all shampooed and ready for bed," Britt said as she planted a kiss on Lily's forehead and Lily rolled her eyes at Jackie. "I don't know *what* we'd do without you. . . ."

Safely ensconced in Jackie's kitchen ten minutes later, Lily opened the pizza box while Jackie got the plates. "Did you get extra sauce?" she asked, peering under the robe of cheese.

"For you, always."

Jackie divided the salad and put half on each plate. With a table knife, Lily meticulously cut the pie to free two perfect wedges. Not so much as a thread of mozzarella hung off the sides when she was through. She took a careful bite, avoiding a salty creature. "Fan*tas*tic!"

They clicked their Coke cans and dug in.

"So, what's with the hair?" Jackie asked when they were midway through their second slices.

"What hair?"

"The Vaseline."

"Just thought it'd be cool to try it." Removing a shred of Calamata olive from her salad, Lily deposited it at the edge of her plate. "Can we play Go Fish after dinner?"

When they'd had their fill, Lily put the leftovers in the refrigerator while Jackie went to the den for the cards. She was about to set up a table in the living room, when Lily appeared in the doorway.

"Can we play in here?" she asked.

"How come?"

"It's quiet." Reaching for the cube of Chinese fluorite, Lily held it to the light. "I see the boat. Can we do a story later?"

"Let's see what time it is after we're done playing."

They settled on the floor and Lily kicked off her ruby slippers. Her toes were as long and tapered as an adult's, with chipped metallic polish on the nails. Jackie passed her the deck to shuffle. Unable to do a bridge without scattering the cards, Lily laid them out in small piles and meticulously mixed each one. When the deck had been shuffled to her satisfaction, she passed it to Jackie to cut and deal.

"You go first," Lily said as she scrutinized her hand, slowly shifting the same cards back and forth. Her brow furrowed and the elastic securing her ponytail seemed to grow tighter. She freed her hair from the rubber band and a silky hank fell over her eyes. Absently, she brushed it away.

"Want a scrunchie?" Jackie asked.

"Shh! I'm thinking. . . . Got any eights?"

"Go fish."

Lily drew a card.

"Sixes?" Jackie asked.

"Fish." So much for the report that Lily couldn't count. "Queens?"

"Unh-uh."

Groping in her backpack, Lily emerged with the leopard-print ornament she'd filched from Jackie weeks before. In a fluid motion, she twisted it around her hair.

"Nice scrunchie," Jackie remarked.

"I borrowed it from you. Your turn."

"You can keep it, but next time ask first."

Lily's impassive gaze marked the subject closed. "Deuces."

"Go fish."

"That Vaseline must have been tough to wash out."

"Almost impossible!"

"Who were you trying to look like?"

Lily grinned mysteriously. "You'll see. . . . Any Ks?"

"Ks?"

"*Kings.*"

So she knew the alphabet too. Jackie handed over a king. "I thought it was my turn."

"Too slow," Lily replied, "you lost it. Sixes?"

"What's your least favorite thing about school?"

Lily studied her hand. "When the teacher makes us stand in front of everyone and read. . . ."

Jackie's heart skipped a beat.

Nowhere is the establishment of the pecking order more brutal or swift than in first grade. As a child, Jackie had always been uncoordinated; it wasn't just that she couldn't skip rope and chew gum at the same time, she had trouble learning to use zippers and tying her shoes. Worst of all, letters and numbers blurred and vanished or simply would not hold still. A "b" could be a "d" or a "p," and sixes had a way of turning into nines. And how could she read from left to right when she couldn't even *tell* left from right? She learned to make a joke of her clumsiness and confusion, using her alertness to the reactions of others to convert her gaffes to pratfalls and quips that won her the reputation of class clown. She might even have gotten away with it had she never been asked to read aloud.

The hell began in early August between first and second grade. Nightmares about standing in front of a room full of jeering faces who corrected her in unison were followed by strategic visits to the school nurse throughout September for stomachaches of unexplained origin. Protracted bouts of laryngitis carried her until Christmas and into the next semester. When she couldn't escape, she would listen carefully to the other children and memorize the material until she could recite it, pretending to follow the lines and praying she would turn the page in the right place. If memory failed her, she would improvise, supplying a word she thought might fit. On a sunny spring morning near the end of second grade her world shattered to pieces.

The material was from a book that had recently been assigned, something about a little girl who lived in an old house in Paris with a nun. There were lovely pictures on each page and the verses rhymed, so Jackie knew she would have no trouble memorizing it after hearing it once or twice. Two students in her row had already recited that day and she thought she was home free. It had been weeks since she'd complained of a stomachache, and when her turn to read came the next day she could make a trip to the nurse. Disengaged, she allowed her mind to wander into a familiar daydream. She was a ballerina, floating across the stage to the applause of thousands of adoring fans. . . . Just before recess the teacher called her name.

With book in hand Jackie reluctantly rose. Staring at the page, she took a deep breath and tried to orient herself. The illustration was of a white truck with a red cross racing off into the night in the direction of a metal tower. Placing her left index finger at the beginning of the first sentence, she began to read.

" 'In a . . .' " It looked like *cat*, but that couldn't be. Maybe it was *car*.

" '—car,' " she continued.

Glancing up at the teacher, Jackie received an encouraging nod. When she looked down again, the next word had vanished. Just like that. Trying desperately to divine the context, she flipped back to the previous page. A man in a long black coat and a funny hat was carrying the heroine downstairs, bundled in a blanket. She must be sick. . . . And suddenly the truck with the cross clicked. An ambulance, but the words had to rhyme.

"Come on, Jackie," the teacher coaxed, "you know these words." To help her along she added, " 'In a car *with a* . . .' "

" '. . . girl . . .' "

Someone behind her giggled.

"You know very well that isn't what it says," the teacher scolded. "The word is *red*, not girl."

" 'In a car with a red . . .' " She recognized the first two letters but the rest were a gray blur. Li—life? That didn't make sense. It must be—"line. In a car with a red line . . ."

"*Line?*" The teacher had lost all patience. "What's the matter with you? That doesn't make any sense at all! The word is *light*. 'In a car with a *red light!*' "

The whole class was laughing and Jackie's cheeks burned. In her worst nightmares nothing had been as bad as this. Now everyone knew she was stupid. And she would fail the class, they'd say she was retarded, and she would have to repeat the grade. . . . The teacher left the blackboard and came down the aisle to where Jackie stood. Snatching the book from her hands, she turned it upside down.

"You might as well be reading it like this!" The laughter was louder and louder and—

"Your turn, Jackie." Lily was staring at her curiously. "I just fished, remember?"

"Yeah, okay." Jackie looked at her hand and the queen of hearts undulated before coming into focus. "Queens . . ."

"Go fish," Lily replied. "You still want to play?"

"How about dessert? It's ice cream."

"Rocky Road?"

"But of course."

Lily gathered up the cards and Jackie went to the kitchen for two heaping bowls. When she returned to the den, Lily had pulled the mythology book from its shelf. "Now can we read?"

Perched on the arm of the overstuffed chair, Lily flipped through the pages. When she came to her favorite story, she handed the book to Jackie.

"This one."

"Again?" It was the myth of Medusa, the golden-scaled monster with bronze claws. What was it about her that so entranced Lily—the fact that Perseus and his mother had been set adrift on the sea in a chest, or the deadly gaze that turned men to stone? "Where shall we start this time?"

"When he's flying over the island."

They found the place by the picture at the top of the page. Three blind women were passing around the single eye the hero had stolen to force them to tell him where to get the paraphernalia he needed to slay the beast and escape unharmed. Winged shoes that enabled him to fly, a helmet that conferred invisibility, and a magic wallet that shrank or stretched to fit whatever Perseus wanted to carry. With her bowl of ice cream melting on the floor, Lily moved closer and Jackie began to read.

"*Perseus lightly sped through the air over land and sea to the fearful island of the Gorgons.*" Lily's index finger followed hers across the page. "*As he approached, he could see, scattered in the fields and along the roads, statues of men and beasts whom the sight of the Gorgons had turned to stone.*"

Stealing a glance at Lily, she saw her lips moving. She was reciting the words under her breath, in time with Jackie's slow and careful intonation. *"And, at last, from high above, he beheld the monsters themselves reflected in his shield. Their scale-covered bodies glistened in the sun, their great wings were folded, the snakes that were their hair . . ."*

Jackie stopped.

"Is that what the Vaseline was for?" she asked.

With a pleased smile, Lily nodded. "When I tried to turn them to stone with my eyes, it didn't work. But *girls* are scared of snakes."

Lily trying to hold her tormentors at bay with that storm-cloud glare. "Why do—"

"Keep going, we're getting to the best part!"

"—the snakes that were their hair lay hideously coiled and intertwined. The Gorgons were asleep. . . ." She looked at Lily again, and this time saw her finger was moving but her eyes weren't tracking the text. She was faking. Just as Jackie used to. *"Perseus swept down, and still gazing into the shield, boldly swung his blade. With one stroke he cut off the grisly head. Then, springing into the air, he thrust his prize, all writhing and hissing, into the magic wallet. . . .* You don't have to pretend," Jackie said.

"Pretend what?"

"That you can read. There's no reason to be ashamed—"

"What do *you* know?" Lily demanded.

"When I was your age, I had problems too—"

"I can do it," Lily insisted. "I just don't want to."

"Why not?"

"Because they want to make me. I won't do *anything* they try to *make* me do."

"Would you do it for me?" Jackie asked. "I can help."

"Maybe."

"What would it take?"

The girl's eyes fastened on the shipwreck fluorite, still on the floor where she'd left it after picking up the cards. "That rock."

"It's a deal."

Chapter | Sixteen

With the good-natured insistence of a hooker in Hamburg, a parking attendant in black shorts and red polo shirt motioned him to the Mardi Gras casino lot. Honky-tonk music rattled the air like a merry-go-round gone mad as a trolley filled with rollicking passengers tooted past. Black Hawk a century after the gold boom went bust.

Ignoring the attendant, the man finally found a parking spot. As he strolled down the winding street that Saturday night, he let the lawlessness of this historic town soak into his pores. Hundred-year-old buildings with carnival lights that flashed "Have a *Lucky* Day!" signs advertising five-cent slots—all they needed were busty broads standing on the corners in satin garters and extravagant décolletage. Black Hawk had been raped by its city fathers: what difference would one more assault make?

At the south end of Main Street the Gold Coast promised a tropical escape smack into the face of a mountain. Would she be there, drinking a mai-tai at Bimini Café or plugging quarters in the Double Wild Cherry? Perhaps at Shannon's, with its boast of the loosest slots . . . Surveying his choices, he knew he would not find her there either. He gazed past the towering cranes. When indigo turned to black, would the stars still wink?

The Painted Lady.

From across the street he watched her enter with two

women. Hair glossy and thick, parted slightly to the side with soft curls gathered at her shoulders. Tight black top emphasizing full breasts and white skin shielded by day from the sun. Protecting her investment . . . Brows expertly arched to highlight limpid eyes intriguingly off kilter in the almost perfect oval of her face. Enjoyed her meals; if not for those magnificent breasts, she could never have gotten away with that top. Yes, it was *her*. He gave the three women a moment to buy drinks from the bar and settle at their favorite games.

From a Top Dog slot across the aisle he watched her take a seat at an Elvis machine while she sipped from a cloudy drink with a maraschino cherry. Whiskey sour. Balancing a container of coins on the shelf above the machine, she fed it her first quarter. Elvis gyrated on the display and she leaned in for a better view. Perfect. Grasping the shaft with a two-handed grip, she gave it a firm pull. The slot whirred and a kaleidoscope flashed across her chest.

Lunar eclipse. A broad-shouldered figure had planted herself between him and his prize and was leaning over her in a proprietary fashion with a can of Colt. He tensed. All he needed was some *butch* moving in. . . . At that moment she turned and he recognized the newcomer as one of the friends with whom the woman had arrived. He let out his breath. A small reminder that he would have to peel her away from her companions and be patient.

All the time in the world.

The interloper moved off with her beer and he came one machine closer. Ideal entertainment—mindless, hypnotic, no talent required. Defeats that fed the hunger to win, small victories that made you *believe*. The pathetic hope that drew her to him.

She plugged one quarter more and rose. Still invisible, he followed her to the bar for another whiskey sour and then to a Sphinx. The skill was entering her orbit gradually, timing his moves to her mood. Once she registered his presence, she would do the rest.

She stopped to chat with her friend who'd moved to a Ten Times Pay, and then the other who was playing Crazy Eights. He tapped his finger on his watch. Twenty-five minutes since the last check-in. He would give them one more chance. The next round would make her careless and she would visit the lounge on the second floor. . . . She brushed past his chair, but he didn't look up. Settling down with a fresh supply of coins, she began feeding them to the Sphinx.

With Elvis she'd gone slow. She'd played each quarter carefully and pulled the handle with a decisive jerk. Now she was plunking in the coins faster and jiggling the lever, as if she could shock the Sphinx into paying off. Three slots away, he glanced at her face in the flashing lights. Isolation, loneliness, a hint of desperation . . . Her transparency made him feel tender toward her, but the machine was impervious to her pain.

Frustrated, she rose and came toward him. This time he met her gaze with an ironic smile. Her eyes widened in a calculated show of interest, and she pulled back her shoulders. As brazen as the goddess at the arts festival the night before. If not for Rae, he might have gone *months* . . . As she glided past with an insouciant roll of the hips, he turned and calmly inserted another quarter. When she returned, he was gone.

Ten minutes later he let her find him three rows away at a keno machine. Pretending not to notice him, she stationed herself at the edge of his vision. They played that way for a while, and just as she was about to turn in his direction, he left. From the balcony on the second floor by the blackjack machines he monitored her search. Three whiskey sours was all it had taken—he knew her so well he could have placed money on it. She joked with her friends and then slowly mounted the stairs.

He watched as she made her way to the ladies' lounge, wobbling ever so slightly in her platform sandals. From one flight above came the smell of burgers and fries, cheap steaks and cheaper beer. The music was a raucous blend of Vegas and jazz. As he waited for her to emerge, he kept her friends in sight. The big one was going for another beer, which meant a good fifteen minutes before she too would feel the call of nature.

"Oh, it's *you!*" she said with a giggle. "I wasn't sure. . . ."

She'd freshened her lipstick and mascara, but the pulse at her throat was all hers. Eyes impossibly bright. For him.

"I saw you downstairs," he answered.

So delicate, making them feel in control but keeping

them just a shade off balance. They liked that, the excitement. He would show them how it was done.

"It hasn't been a lucky night." Her lower lip drooped in exaggerated disappointment.

Breath mints.

Had she guessed he'd be waiting? Stepping away from the light, he began moving toward the blackjack tables. Not too fast. It wouldn't do for her friends to see them now. When they were a safe distance from the stairs, he turned.

"Luck can change," he said.

"Do you really think so?"

"The first step is another drink."

"My friends are downstairs."

"Not here. I know a place."

"I don't want them to worry. . . ."

He steered her to the elevators at the end of the floor. Slow *down*.

"They'll never miss you," he promised.

They exited the Painted Lady and with one hand at her elbow, he guided her across the street to the narrow sidewalk. He glanced up at the sky. No stars watching.

"Where are we going?" she asked.

"Not far."

As they stepped onto the threshold of a casino to let another couple pass, she leaned against him and he slipped his arm around her. She pressed the length of her torso to his. Soft belly, hard breasts. Almost the size of Tabitha Kaminski . . . and what a fiasco that had been.

He'd dispensed with the cord but Tabitha had awakened too soon, and when she began clawing at his arm, he'd had no choice but to strike her. As he broke her nose the screams subsided but those eyes kept staring. He'd sped down I-70 toward Golden and at the first turnoff bludgeoned her until they rolled in their sockets and she slumped forward in the seat. He'd broken every rule, his car was a bloody mess, and he'd almost lost control. Worst of all, she'd *seen* him, the dilating drops had failed. . . .

"—sure my girlfriends won't miss me?"

He gave her shoulder a tender squeeze. Softer than those cones on her chest. And he'd thought he knew *all* her secrets.

"I'll have you back before you know it."

"That fast?" she pouted. Teasing him, *teasing* . . .

He was parked just ahead, this was no time for a scene. He let his fingers caress her bare arm while he reached in his pocket with his other hand.

"You don't want them to worry," he reminded her, drawing her closer. She rested her head on his chest and he feared she could feel his heart slamming against his ribs.

"Am I really safe?"

Flirting to the last.

He turned so they were face-to-face. Gently, he tilted back her chin.

"Don't peek. . . ."

He thrust the stun gun to her breast and pulled the trigger.

Chapter Seventeen

No snow," Pilar said.

It was Monday morning and she was reporting back on her trip.

"Are you sure?" Jackie asked. "The last week in April was a blizzard—"

"—in Denver, but up in Dinosaur it was dry as a bone." Rolling her newspaper, Pilar began fanning herself with it. "In fact, the woods were packed."

Pilar always found what she was after. Her wallet bulged with snapshots of kids who could be daughters, nieces, or grandchildren, depending on the age and sex of her target, and she was as tenacious interviewing runaways at a crack house as sitting at a computer screen or sweet-talking courtroom clerks to move Jackie's cases up on the docket. She'd spent ten years in the DA's office before jumping ship.

"Campers?" Jackie asked hopefully.

"More nuts than a jumbo can of goobers. A 'We the People' caravan, cattlemen protesting the expansion of the national monument, everything but a boy scout jamboree."

Jackie slumped at her desk. "Maybe I misunderstood Mark."

They both knew she hadn't.

"The good news," Pilar reminded her, "is Pratt can't prove our boys *weren't* there that weekend. By the way, I meant to show you this." She unfurled her paper. "Gal got snatched from one of those casinos up in Black Hawk." She shrugged. "I've never cared for those mining towns."

"Where else can you get prime rib for $1.99 at ten in the morning?"

"If you're willing to step on a tour bus with fifty little old blue-haired ladies whose husbands' Keogh distributions are burning a hole in their polyester pantsuits."

Jackie glanced at the photo accompanying the brief article. Mass of dark hair and an eager, wide-eyed look. Starla McBride was certainly striking, though the plunging neckline identified the shot as a studio portrait. "How long has she been missing?"

"Since Saturday night. Last time her friends saw her she was on her way to the john."

Jackie switched on her microcassette recorder. When Pilar came in, she'd been in the middle of dictating a motion on the date-rape case in Boulder. The preliminary hearing was two weeks off, and she wanted to rattle the prosecutor's cage. "Maybe she found Mr. Right."

"I doubt it," Pilar replied. "Something tells me Starla's joined the cosmos." She stared wistfully at the photo. "I never looked that good when I was thirty, much less forty-one."

"Cheer up, it's probably ten years old."

"Have you ever seen brows that arched? She must have had a face-lift."

"Shameless," Jackie agreed.

"And a boob job. Maybe she lost her balance and drowned in the sink. It's so dark in those damn casinos. . . ."

Three days later Starla McBride's headless body was found in Roxborough Park, a rugged recreation area southwest of Denver. Pilar pounced as soon as Jackie returned from court.

"What'd I tell you?" Positively triumphant, she switched on the TV at the tail end of the morning news. The screen swelled with a view of a massive ridge of sandstone, and the camera panned to a ruddy monolith that dwarfed the knot of uniformed men at its base. The closing shot was of an ambulance with its lights forlornly spinning.

"He stuffed her in the crack," Pilar explained.

"I beg your pardon?"

"You can't see it now, but there's a crevice in the rock. That's where he dumped her."

"He?" Jackie dropped her briefcase under the desk and switched off the TV as the closing music came on. "Don't tell me they caught the killer so soon."

"Of course not. But get this, she was found nude and they still don't have the head. Too many rattlers—"

"*What?*"

"My contact in the JeffCo Sheriff's Department says the body was clean. No semen or trace evidence, but it looks like she was raped. Sound familiar?"

Jackie closed her eyes. She should have trusted her instincts on bail, not given in to Aaron. "Get our boy on the phone," she told Pilar. And what if it *wasn't* just a coincidence, what if—She couldn't afford to go there, not yet.

Pilar was dialing Best Energy. "You'd better collect the rest of that retainer while you still can."

"Don't worry, I will." A copycat, maybe it was a copycat. . . . "What's that about snakes?"

"Hiking trails out there are full of them, especially this time of year. The mild weather in February and all that snow in April produced a bumper crop of rattlers. They're not done looking for the head, but they need to take precautions—" She passed the phone to Jackie.

"Where were you Saturday night?" Jackie demanded when Aaron came on the line.

"Saturday? Working, like you said." He seemed unsurprised by the question. "A meeting at the Tech Center. We won the insulating bid on Crestwood Park, a residential project out in—"

"What time?"

"We met at—oh, around six o'clock. Went over plans for a couple hours, had a bite to eat. Came back at nine and kept at it till after midnight. When we were done we had a few drinks."

Neat—a little *too* neat?

"You often conduct business on Saturday night?"

"Depends how busy I am during the week. This time of year, construction—"

"Who else was there?"

"The developer and a couple guys from his outfit."

"I need names." She made a scribbling motion, signaling Pilar to pick up the extension and grab a pad.

"I thought you trusted me," he said.

"Names . . ."

"Tom Morrissey. Morrissey Construction—that's where we met. Tom's second-in-command is Gene Davis. They called the third guy Skip. . . . What's going on?" he finally asked.

"Another woman was abducted and killed." Jackie made a dialing gesture, but Pilar was already pulling out the business directory. "Unless your alibi's airtight this time, Pratt's going to move to revoke your bail."

"But it happened in another county. . . ."

So he *did* know.

". . . Can he do that?" Aaron continued.

"Just you watch."

Hanging up, she turned to Pilar.

"Call those guys at Morrissey ASAP and find out who the third one was. I don't want Aaron or anyone else getting to them first. This time I want the straight story."

Chapter | Eighteen

The next morning Jackie was on her way back to Worrell's court. Pilar had interviewed Aaron's alibi witnesses and confirmed his whereabouts, but Duncan Pratt's forth-with motion had netted a call from the judge's clerk requesting the presence of Jackie and her client at ten sharp. As she waited in the corridor outside the courtroom for Pratt to appear, she wondered if he'd had half as much trouble falling asleep the night before as she did. When he finally rounded the corner five minutes before the hearing, she grabbed him by the arm and steered him into an empty jury room.

"Jackie! We're due—"

"Worrell can wait. We need to talk. You know Aaron had nothing to do with the McBride murder."

"Jeez, Jackie, two decapitations in the metro area in the course of a month. . . ." The jocularity rang as false as the grin on Pratt's face. "When's the last time we had one of those?"

"He's got an alibi."

"Oh, yeah?"

"Three guys. And I think you'll find them credible."

"They're not my concern. Right now Worrell's kicking himself for letting Best out in the first place. Don't count on being lucky with him twice."

Pratt should have been coming from a position of strength, but Jackie's instincts told her otherwise. The district attorney's office wasn't the final stop on Dunc's campaign trail—did political ambition drive this case, or was it something else?

"When is Douglas County filing charges?" she asked.

"Douglas County?"

"Isn't that where Starla McBride's body was found?"

"I—I'm not sure."

What did Pratt know that she didn't?

"Not sure that's where Roxborough Park is, or not certain your buddy plans to charge Aaron?" Pratt reached for the door to the courtroom, but she blocked his way. "There isn't a shred of evidence connecting him to Starla's murder, is there?"

"We're late for court."

Pratt wanted this conviction so badly, she could taste it.

Waiting in the corridor for her client, Jackie saw Rodger Malone by the elevators. Details of his encounter with Aaron after the suppression hearing came flooding back. The threat was not so much in what Malone said, but what he *hadn't*. The fact that she couldn't read him was an uncomfortable reminder that the real enigma was her client.

For an instant her confidence in Aaron's latest alibi wavered. No matter what was going on between him and Rae's ex, Malone wouldn't be here now unless Pratt had tipped him off. Increased pressure on the judge, the newspapers would pounce. . . .

Pratt was at his table and the bailiff was pacing the well of the court. Where the hell was Aaron? Retreating, she spotted him halfway down the hall with his back to her. He was talking to a taller man and she frantically waved, hoping one of them would see her. His companion was clasping Aaron's shoulder and as she drew closer she saw it was his brother Mark.

"Hey," she called. "We're late!"

As Mark glanced up, his knuckles went white. Tension, anger? "I'm here for you, Aaron," he said. Turning to Jackie, he pretended to notice her for the first time.

Aaron swung around with a cocky grin. "Just like always, huh?"

"Wipe that smirk off your face," she warned him.

"You're five minutes late and Worrell's the wrong judge to keep waiting."

"Where would I be without my big brother?" His insolent tone belied the words, but Jackie was in no mood to screw around.

"Forget the cakewalk. Pratt wants your ass."

Seeing Jackie and her client at last, the bailiff scurried off to the judge's chambers, and a moment later Worrell mounted the bench. The hearing began with no comment about tardiness, which Jackie took as a bad sign.

"Mr. Pratt?" Worrell inquired.

"The People move to revoke Aaron Best's bail."

"On what grounds?"

"The recent murder of Starla McBride."

As Pratt began describing the similarities between the crimes, Jackie could see that however reluctant Worrell was to reverse his earlier decision, the judge's mind was already made up. The parallels were unmistakable. By the time it was Jackie's turn, she was prepared for the inevitable but determined to score a couple of points.

"The one argument Mr. Pratt has *not* made," she began, "is that there's anything linking Aaron Best to the McBride murder. Perhaps that's why the Douglas County district attorney is in no rush to file charges."

"Is that a fact?" Worrell turned to Pratt. "I assume you've been in contact with Douglas County?"

"Of course, your honor. We've discussed the matter at some length."

"And do you have any reason to believe the DA plans to *charge* Mr. Best in Ms. McBride's death?"

"Well, I—The matter's still under investigation."

"That wasn't my question, Mr. Pratt."

"I—I'm not at liberty to divulge a confidence, your honor."

Something was clearly wrong. Pratt had gone out on a limb in this case with a zealousness foreign to his character but hadn't so much as blinked when Jackie told him about Aaron's alibi. The similarities practically compelled the conclusion that the two women were killed by the same man, but Pratt *knew* Aaron had nothing to do with Starla McBride.

What did he know that she didn't?

Aaron was tugging at her sleeve. "Do something," he hissed. "Don't just sit there and let them send me back!"

"—one thing I *do* know," Pratt was saying, "is that when Aaron Best's in jail, we don't have other women getting their heads cut off."

Maybe they would be better off with Aaron back in the can, but not for the reason Pratt was suggesting. . . . With a shock Jackie realized this was the first time she truly believed her client could be innocent. And if that were the case—

"Why aren't you doing anything?" Aaron snarled.

The wrong guy in the wrong place, or the victim of a frame? Was the weakness in Pratt's case the *similarity* of the crimes? Should they be looking for others?

"Ms. Flowers . . . ?" Worrell said.

Jackie rose.

"We protest the patent unfairness of revoking bail on the basis of a crime for which no one intends to charge Mr. Best. That said, in the event bail is revoked, we demand the earliest possible trial date."

"In that case, bail is revoked." The judge turned to Pratt. "How many days will you need to present your case?"

"A minimum of two weeks. Perhaps three—"

Worrell pulled out his calendar.

"Two weeks, then. My first available date is—July nineteen."

Six weeks from today, and just two and a half months since Aaron's arrest. Worrell had cut the prosecution's trial prep time in half. And with Aaron back in the slammer, the balance had suddenly tipped in Jackie's favor.

Pratt was on his feet. "My office has three major trials between now and the middle of July!"

"How many of those will you personally try?" Worrell asked.

"I have supervisory responsibility—"

"July nineteenth, counselors. Court is adjourned." Worrell waved as if swatting a fly.

Turning from her in disgust, Aaron extended his wrists for the deputy to snap on the cuffs. As she watched them lead her client away, Jackie knew it was time to widen the net.

Chapter | Nineteen

The walnut table was littered with manila folders, newspaper clippings and colored pens, three days' worth of coffee cups, stale danish and pizza crusts, and two ashtrays overflowing with cigarillo butts. The former dining room in Jackie's office, used for negotiations and depositions, was the only place with a surface large enough to accommodate the files Pilar had amassed. On this Monday morning five weeks before Aaron's trial was to begin, a decision had to be made.

"I say go with them all."

Jackie shook her head. "Too many and we come across as desperate, not to mention assuming a burden of proof on crimes Pratt hasn't even charged."

"So what do we do," Pilar challenged, "go with the gals who were stabbed in the throat? Or can we stick in a couple of strangulations?"

Jackie rubbed her eyes and sighed. "Let's run through them one last time."

"Chronological order?"

"Yeah."

"First the overview. Our boy's gone full circle, starting and ending in Gilpin County. The first dump was fifteen years ago—near some mine tailings off Russell Gulch—and then he moved to Grand Lake and Weld County. Over the years he's grown bolder, leaving them in places where they'll be quickly found. Sometimes he rapes, sometimes he doesn't. And he's gone from manual strangulation to slashing throats to full-fledged decapitation."

"What makes you so sure it's the same man?"

"Patience . . ." Pilar dug through the folders until she located one an inch thick, crammed with notes in violet ink. "His first victim was Louisa May, an understudy at the Central City Opera. She went missing in August of 'eighty-five after the final rehearsal of *Kiss Me Kate*."

Just up the road from Black Hawk.

Opening the file, Pilar passed Jackie a copy of a playbill. Twenty cast members posed in costume and full makeup on the cover. A purple arrow pointed to a woman wearing a ruffled taffeta gown, but the picture was too blurry to see anything but a squinting smile.

"Suspects?" Jackie asked, studying the photo of Louisa May.

"She was dating a stagehand and another member of the troupe, but the investigation focused initially on a college kid who worked as a night auditor that summer at the Teller House next door. The cast stayed in cottages and he'd been seen escorting her home. A May-December kind of thing—no pun intended—but you know how horny college boys can be. He had some pretty raunchy photos pinned to his—"

"How old was she?"

"Mid-thirties, what used to be considered long in the tooth. In our more enlightened times—"

"Where was she found?"

"Off Highway 119, strangled and nude."

"Raped?"

"Yeah, but no physical evidence was recovered. The forensic work back then was shabby and the locals weren't about to call the CBI."

"Was the student the only suspect?"

"Cleared along with her other boyfriends. Case is officially still open, but according to my contact with the Gilpin County sheriff, the file went inactive because it could have been any one of thousands of tourists who flocked to Central City that summer."

Jackie handed back the playbill. "Who's next?"

"Fast-forward three years." Pilar's maroon nails hovered near a stack of folders at one end of the table, then moved to two thicker ones. "Grand Lake. Two skeletons were found a mile from each other. One was identified from dental records, the other had her teeth knocked out. But get this, they were killed in 'eighty-eight and 'eighty-nine—a year apart."

"If they don't know who the second victim was, how could they tell when she was killed?"

"Because they searched the area when they found the first and the other wasn't there. And they *did* identify the second one."

She passed Jackie a snapshot of two women in hiking boots and shorts, sitting on a boulder with their arms about each other's waists. One appeared slightly older than the other, in her early forties, and her skin had the leathery look of a marathoner. Her head was thrown back with a delight that suggested her companion had just told a joke.

"Members of a CSU alumni group who'd gone hiking at Grand Lake every summer for the past twenty years," Pilar told her. "The younger one, Holly Sellers, disappeared from the campfire when she wandered off to take a squat. Her friend Mary DiManna was snatched almost exactly a year later."

"You'd think she'd have the sense not to go back."

"Mary told her sister she felt she owed it to Holly to continue the tradition. Needless to say, 'eighty-nine was the last hike."

"You said Mary's teeth were knocked out. Were those women beaten to death?"

Pilar shook her head. "Strangled, hyoid cartilage fractured. My man in Grand County thinks he knocked out Mary's teeth to screw up identification of the body."

"With two women missing from the same group in consecutive years, the killer must have known they'd figure it out." Jackie stared at the photo. The pose felt intimate; the two women were obviously unaware of the camera. Could the killer have been watching them, biding his time after Holly? If so, it suggested not just cruelty but design—a *game*? "I'd say he was thumbing his nose at the cops."

"He had every reason to—they found nothing but bones. By then they couldn't even tell whether either woman was sexually assaulted. In November 1990 he shifted to Weld County." She slid another photograph across the table. "Elaine Sherman, mother of three, snatched on her way back from King Soopers. Her Subaru wagon was found with keys in the ignition two blocks from home, ground chuck still frozen in the backseat."

"Suspects?" Elaine looked like the kind of woman who baked cookies and planted pansies in her kitchen window.

"Her ex was at work when she disappeared. Friction over visitation rights but no history of violence. And the attack was way out of scale for a squabble over what time to bring the kids back Sunday night."

"What did the killer do?"

"After raping her he stabbed her in the throat. Like the Subaru, he left the body where it would easily be found: in the pit for the foundation of a new housing development being built three miles from where she lived. In 1991—"

They'd been going at this for three days and Jackie had a crashing headache. The sheer volume of names and dates was sending her brain into toxic shock. With Aaron's trial just weeks away and an alibi that was distressingly soft, the last thing she needed was the stress of proving her client wasn't a serial killer.

"Look, Pilar, it's not like I don't feel for these women. But the only common denominator is the sex angle. The victims had different interests, they were killed across the Front Range, even the dump sites have nothing—"

"You forgot one thing: they're all unsolved."

"That's great! Now I'm supposed to argue not just that Duncan Pratt runs a sloppy operation but law enforcement in Gilpin, Grand, Weld, and God knows where else—"

"Which is precisely the point." Pilar broke off a piece of pizza crust and popped it in her mouth. "This guy is clever enough to know about linkage blindness," she mumbled.

"Since he isn't here, maybe you'll be good enough to fill me in. . . ."

"The number-one reason serial killers aren't caught is because local cops don't share information. You've seen it on the prosecutor's end: Duncan Pratt doesn't give a damn what happens in a Douglas County case and vice versa. Detectives always assume the first body found in their jurisdiction must be the first in the series, and if the killer's savvy enough to switch counties, they may never catch him. Their other mistake," Pilar continued, "is to think the MO has to be an exact match for the crimes to be connected, when just the opposite is true: they should be looking for *changes* because these guys *evolve*. Like cons in prison, these monsters hone their skills on experience. And when they finally break out—"

"If what you're saying is true, he could have started anytime, anyplace, with an MO that bears no resemblance—I have an easier explanation."

"What's that?"

"These murders were committed by different men. Your theory wouldn't even pass Lily's smell test."

Pilar's face fell, and Jackie regretted her lack of tact.

She remembered the day Pilar walked up to her at the public defender's office with only her freedom left to lose. Jackie's first case, and she had nothing going for her but her client's trust. Pilar could have stuck with the story the beat cops told her to give, but when Jackie said she'd represent her only if she leveled, Pilar gave it to her straight. She'd plugged her husband, a plainclothes detective on the DA's staff, three times in the back and he'd had it coming. Jackie won her an acquittal on self-defense and Pilar surrendered her gun. She still played poker with the boys in blue on Thursday nights and on Christmas brought them a pot of posole stew. Loyalty was a two-way street and Jackie owed her a fair hearing.

"Go ahead," she continued in a softer tone, "I'm just being cranky."

"In 1991 Bonnie Masters was last seen before the factory outlet stores closed in Silverthorne, in—"

"Summit County—"

"—with her throat slit ear to ear. See what I mean by working his way up?"

"Where was she left?"

"Dumped off the road on the way to Keystone. They found her the next day. With the next two he struck closer to home. Denver, in fact."

Jackie reached for the next clipping. A shot of the Auraria campus in lower downtown; a cluster of commuter colleges with the historic Tivoli Brewery on the right. She didn't need to be told the victim was another woman seeking a second chance.

"Meg Anthony," Pilar continued. "Single mom hoping to get into med school, last seen at the Tivoli having a beer with classmates after their chemistry final. Throat slit, raped, and dumped in the foothills west of Golden. And that brings us to the most interesting victim of all. Tabitha Kaminski."

Tabitha had curly hair and the ruddy cheeks of a child who'd just come in from a snowball fight. "What's so special about her?" Jackie asked.

"She was snatched from a country-western bar and bludgeoned to death. *Not* raped."

"Then she doesn't fit the pattern at all."

"But she's the bridge to his next victim, and *she's* the link to Rae Malone and Starla McBride."

"They weren't bludgeoned, they were decap—"

"Like he was planning to do to Tabitha, but he panicked. That's why he beat her. The others were practice."

"What are you—clairvoyant?"

"I'm telling you, Jackie, this guy's a perfectionist. He likes being in control. After screwing up with Tabitha he had to get it right before taking the final step. Enter Becky Cox." Pilar reached for the final stack of files. Carefully arranging them before her, she opened the one on her left. "LoDo, July of 1996."

"That was three years—"

"—later. He went underground and reassessed his MO." She handed Jackie a photo of a good-looking blonde with windswept hair and designer sunglasses. "A legal secretary snatched from O'Dell's before a Rockies game, beheaded, and dumped two days later in the Garden of the Gods."

Closing her eyes, Jackie pictured the park at the base of Pikes Peak renowned for its sandstone formations. Linear logic was not her forte, but Pilar was starting to make sense. Could the Hollow Man really exist?

"Raped, but wiped clean. El Paso County's forensics in 'ninety-six were more sophisticated than Gilpin's a decade earlier. If they say the killer left no DNA, I believe them. One year later Carole Wade disappeared from the parking lot of her son's middle school. She was found stuffed in a cave at

Red Rocks amphitheater three days later." The eight-by-ten glossy showed a brunette with strikingly pale eyes.

"Raped—"

"—wiped, and beheaded. The whole nine yards."

Jackie pointed to the last folder. "Who's that?"

"Fern Kaplan, his final victim before Rae Malone. Valentine's Day 'ninety-eight." Pilar slid another studio portrait across the table. Fern's silver hair made her flawless complexion all the more youthful, a contrast played up by the half-glasses suspended from her neck on a jeweled chain. "Last seen at the Rubio Melendez salon in Cherry Creek, body dumped at Pioneer Cemetery four days later, on the Denver side of the border with Adams County. A minor error because it meant the Denver detectives couldn't pass the buck. Not that they solved—"

"He's keeping them longer each time," Jackie murmured.

"Hmnn?"

She hadn't realized she'd said it aloud.

"He keeps each woman a day longer. Becky two days, Carole three. Almost a week with Starla and Rae. What does he do with them?"

Knowing she'd at last hooked her boss, Pilar was smart enough not to reply.

Jackie thoughtfully chewed her stale pizza. Facts were her anchor, the building blocks of the story she would spin for Aaron's jury. But her job was to present the smallest possible target, and there was a perilously fine line between suggesting the Hollow Man murdered Rae Malone and assuming the burden of proving who and why. A line she could not afford to cross.

"So what do we really have?" she asked. "Women in their thirties or early forties who may or may not have been looking for a man. This guy they meet not only melts into the woodwork but is comfortable in a wide range of settings. He likes to play games with his victims and the cops."

"His technique evolves—"

"—and he's savvy enough not to leave DNA or physical evidence. Comfortable outdoors, a hands-on guy in the worst kind of way, but we still don't know why he picked them. . . . Let's go with the last three. Kaplan, Wade, and Cox."

"Besides being the magic number, why?"

"The forensics will be better and more witnesses will be available. If your theory's correct, he took a few years off and modified his MO before he killed Becky Cox. And the bottom line is, it'll be easier to sell the jury if we stick with victims he beheaded."

Pilar sat back with a satisfied grin. "Exactly what I knew you'd say. Where do we start?"

Jackie closed her eyes. What was she getting her client into?

"Find out as much as you can about those three women: Fern Kaplan, Carole Wade, and Becky Cox. And I want pictures. The more the better."

"Of what?"

"The dump sites. And their faces."

If she was to convince a jury Aaron was innocent because the Hollow Man existed, she would first have to believe it herself. And with stakes as high as these, no one would take *her* word for it. She needed an expert.

Chapter Twenty

At first glance all that distinguished the two-story brick from its neighbors on this comfortable street was its white picket fence. Denver was not a picket fence sort of town, and it was only when Jackie let herself in the gate that she saw the peonies. Their blossoms were six inches across, raspberry and peach and a magnificent coral with golden stamens. With upright heads on three-foot stems flanking the flagstone path, they would have been the envy of her aunt, who'd won ribbons for her hybrid teas. Dr. Richard Hanna, Jr., must pay a small fortune for his gardener.

Jackie had been trying to arrange to see him for the better part of a week. When Hanna did not return her messages, she'd considered waylaying him at his seminar in forensic psychiatry at the medical school. Pilar thought it was crazy even to try; he'd made no public statements about the case since the Channel 9 interview the day Rae Malone's body was found *six* weeks earlier, but her sources confirmed two factors that made Hanna the kiss of death for any criminal defense lawyer—not only did he never testify for their side, he also served on the boards of several victim-advocacy groups. Neither factor deterred Jackie. No matter what his record, Richard Hanna didn't sound like the typical prosecution whore.

The psychiatrist's comments during the interview had stuck with her—or, more accurately, the picture he'd painted of the psychopath who murdered Rae Malone. Pilar had teased her about the image of a Hollow Man, but the vividness of the likeness was precisely what Jackie needed to impress on the jury to convince them Aaron was not Rae's killer. And his remarks about the ambivalence of psychiatry pitted against the black-and-white absolutes of the legal system intrigued her. But there was only one way to find out. To approach him on his own turf, at a time and place when he felt the least defensive, she'd had Pilar call and make the appointment in her name.

Despite the charming garden and impressive facade, Hanna's building projected a distinctly nonresidential austerity. There was neither a mailbox nor doorbell, nor even a number designating the address; she knew it was the right place only by process of elimination—the lot was four in from the corner. A discreet hand-lettered sign directed her to the side entrance, but she continued on back to where the garage should have been. In its place stood a black-topped space for three cars, occupied by a slightly battered green Volvo. In all this time she saw and heard no one.

The side entrance had two names and opened into a waiting room empty of all but a leather banquette and a glass table with neat stacks of *National Geographic* and *Nature*. A narrow staircase had a sign that read "Dr. Margolies" with an arrow pointing up, as if the good doctor had ascended to a higher reward. The door opposite the bench bore no sign. She didn't need a watch to confirm she was early.

It had taken Jackie ten minutes to walk there from her office; the tailored slacks and low-heeled shoes she wore on days when no court appearances were scheduled would have cut the time in half, but wanting Hanna to feel deferred to entailed additional sacrifices. Skipping past the dresses and suits that were her trademark at trial, she chose a fawn-colored gabardine skirt that skimmed her knees, a silk blouse in a subdued salmon and gold that warmed her skin and made her copper eyes gleam, and her sheerest pair of hose. The final touch was letting the full weight of her hair fall to her shoulders. Settling on Hanna's couch, she hitched down her skirt and demurely crossed her legs.

Reaching for a *National Geographic,* Jackie scanned a photo essay of whales in the North Atlantic before flipping to a multicolored schematic of coca processing in Colombia. The minutes stretched and she strained her ears for sounds on the other side of the wall. For a while she heard nothing, then a low monotone. Magazine in hand, she rose and stood directly outside the door. The sound stopped and footsteps approached. A radio, or had his last patient left through another door? She just made it to the side table, where she began shuffling through issues of *Nature*.

"Ms. Perez?" he asked.

Hanna was dressed in a sport shirt the color of ashes and dark corduroys that made his hair very black. In person he seemed younger than he had onscreen, the boyish intensity of his expression underscored by his relaxed stance and casual attire.

Jackie gave a warm smile in response to his quizzical look. He was thrown by her name, which hardly went with her coloring and hair. Fingers crossed that he would be flattered and not offended by her duplicity, she stepped past him into his office. Once she was in, his only choices would be to toss her out or let her stay; having booked his next fifty minutes, she knew she wouldn't be keeping him from a patient.

"Have a seat." He gestured to a pair of Eames chairs, waited for Jackie to choose, then settled in the other as she took in her surroundings.

The large square space must have been the living room before the house was converted to offices. The ceiling was molded and the walls papered in a watered silk the same pale green as the thin slotted blinds, and on a marble-topped table stood a grouping of a dozen bonsai trees in a shallow ceramic tray. The display was so captivating that she rose impulsively for a closer look.

The focal point was a tree almost two feet tall, its trunk just inches in diameter, whose upper reaches were dotted with tiny cones perched in the branches like a flock of sparrows. The remaining trees were arranged in an asymmetrical pattern that drew the eye to the one in the center.

"This is spectacular," she said, turning back to Hanna. "How long have you had it?"

"Twenty years, but the trees themselves are older than that." His gaze was warm and penetrating. "They were about eight years old when I harvested them."

"How did you get the cones to grow?"

"Fertilizer. Ms. Perez, why don't we start—"

"Flowers," she said, suddenly ill at ease. "My name isn't Perez, it's Jackie Flowers."

"I don't understand."

"You wouldn't return my calls, so I had someone else make the appointment. Please don't throw me out, I just want a few minutes of your time."

"You're a lawyer, you represent—"

"—the man charged with killing Rae Malone."

"What do you want from me?"

The brusque tone could have meant anger or disappointment. Whichever it was, it was exacerbated by the fact that Hanna had found her attractive and now felt gulled. He was too honest to pretend otherwise.

"A short course on psychopaths," she replied.

Despite himself, he laughed. He still wanted to like her.

"If you're looking for a self-help book, Ms. Flowers, I could recommend—"

"You said on TV the killer was hollow. What did you mean?"

"That interview last May? I'm impressed. But if you'd really done your homework, you'd know I don't testify for defendants."

"A mind is a terrible thing to close."

"What if what I say implicates your client?"

"In the next fifty minutes? I'll take that chance."

Hanna seemed to be waiting for something. After a moment he said, "Most people who come to me for information take notes."

"I listen. Besides, notes have a nasty habit of being discoverable."

As he rose and walked to his desk, Jackie braced herself for a request to leave; instead, to her surprise, he gestured to the chair across from him. "Fire away, counselor."

"You specialize in psychopaths. What are they like?"

"Thoroughly engaging, sincere, at ease with themselves. They're energetic, playful, have a wide range of interests— the kind of men you'd like to sit with at a dinner party."

Was he mocking her? "How do you know anything's wrong?"

"You don't at first. Their strength is their image. In fact, they often make a striking physical impression. They're very alert and expressive; there's a freshness to them, an artlessness that makes them quite attractive to the opposite sex."

Jackie let out her breath. That alone should disqualify Aaron, no matter how much of a Lothario he fancied himself.

"You've examined women too?" she continued.

"Some are stunning, but their careless grooming and posture tell you they don't take their own physical attractiveness into account. Others may be quite ordinary, but they evoke a sexual response a woman with your looks would take for granted."

Just what she deserved for the tight skirt and two-inch heels.

"What's the tip-off?" she persisted.

"When you spend a little time with them, you realize that zest for living, the candor with which they admit mistakes, has very little substance. You wonder why they're so sincere, so at ease in any surroundings. It's because their consciences are untouched. Life leaves no mark on them."

"Are they acting?"

He shook his head. "Not so much that as mimicking. Their problem is they can't distinguish between acting and not. That's why psychopaths are empty suits. Human emotions are their blind spot."

"Can they be treated?"

"I hate to say anyone's a lost cause, but these patients are remarkably resistant to therapy. If you don't feel you need to change, neither peer pressure nor punishment works."

"They must be one in a million."

"Quite the contrary. They come from all walks of life, you probably know one yourself. Perhaps a colleague."

"Oh, come on . . ."

"I'm quite serious. Have you ever met a child who's a little too affectionate and considerate? Bright and articulate, popular with the other students, and when you catch him lying, he cries real tears? He always *seems* to learn his lesson—once he's caught."

"If psychopaths are everywhere, why don't more of them end up in jail or institutionalized?"

"Two reasons: if they commit crimes, they tend to be

petty ones they can talk their way out of, and even those who are most severely disabled present a technical appearance of sanity. Their deviance is sociopathic, but their disguise is a matter of degree. Some succeed in business or professions and 'pass' in their social group, then go off on sprees more harmful to themselves and those who care about them than to strangers. By far the majority of them never kill."

"But we're talking about a killer here." One who was sounding less and less like her tattooed and socially inept client. "Why did you say Rae Malone wasn't his first victim?"

"I shouldn't have shot my mouth off."

"Since you did—"

"I suppose I owe an explanation. Killers tend to start early and small. They abuse pets and playmates, sometimes younger siblings. To work your way up to decapitating an adult takes time and experience, the refinement and acting out of deeply ingrained sadistic fantasies. That's all I meant."

Hanna straightened in his chair. The interview had clearly lasted longer than he'd expected, and though they'd gotten past the initial hurdle, she still hadn't told him the real reason she was there.

"You've already gone on the record with your thoughts about the killer. What do you have to lose by reviewing the DA's file?"

"Murder isn't a game, Ms. Flowers. If your client killed that woman, I have no sympathy—"

"All I'm asking is that you look at the evidence. You don't have to testify."

"Out of the question. My opinion isn't for sale, on the stand or off. Now, if you'll excuse me, I—"

"Afraid to blow your relationship with the DA?"

A cheap shot, but it stopped him cold. At this point she had nothing to lose.

"I couldn't care less about prosecutors, it's the victims who concern me!" Hanna caught himself, and she saw she'd challenged more than his ego. "I'll tell you what, Ms. Flowers. I'll do even better than reviewing that file."

"All I want—"

"I'll review the file and interview your client for the purpose of determining whether I believe he is capable of committing the crime for which he's been charged. If I conclude he is *not*, I will break my perfect record and testify for the defense. On one condition: Your client waives any objection to my testifying for the prosecution if I believe he committed the crime. Take it or leave it."

She rose and Hanna led her to the door on the street side of the room. How had she thought he'd forgiven her duplicity?

"I'll present your offer," she said.

"You do that, Ms. Flowers. His response may tell you more than you're ready to hear."

Chapter | Twenty-one

At the Denver county jail, inmates were sleeping cheek to jowl in blue plastic toboggans. The overcrowding worsened as the temperature rose, and by July the buildings would top out at 110 degrees. The unseasonably warm spring carried the promise of a hot summer, and on this morning one month before Aaron's trial, Jackie was feeling the heat in more ways than one.

Tomorrow was the deadline for notifying Duncan Pratt of Aaron's alibi. Not only did she have to tell her client the price at which Dr. Hanna's participation came, but that alibi had enough holes to sink their defense. According to an insurance adjuster Pilar was dating, the word in the construction industry was that Aaron's father had forced him to fight his brother Mark to inherit the family business.

"Come again?" Jackie had said.

"Aaron was the favorite, and Dad liked to whip up competition. When it came time to retire, he had his boys duke it out for the plumbing company. Just like any red-blooded American father would do."

"They actually had a fistfight over sump pumps and sewage pipes?"

"The winner leveraged the company into a million-dollar gross as of last year and the loser—"

"—became the right-hand man."

"Hind tit to the boss, as a cynic might say. Sure you want to count on Mark for Aaron's alibi?"

As she waited for Aaron to be brought down from his cell block, Jackie pushed a damp curl back from her face. In the next cubicle a guard led in a lanky inmate who, spotting Jackie through the glass, caught her eye and grinned just as Aaron entered.

In his white T-shirt and drawstring pants, Aaron looked like a medical resident who'd been catching a few winks while on call. Jackie was glad he was comfortable, because this interview promised to be tough.

"How are you holding up?" she asked.

"A lot better since the transfer to deuce-deuce."

There was a world of difference between buildings 6 or 8, where two men were crammed into a windowless cold-water cell the size of a broom closet and the only quiet time was between one and three in the morning, and pod 22 with its carpeted day room and game tables. If the felons in 22 were the most dangerous in the system, they were also the smartest, and there was a waiting list to get in. Aaron was evidently behaving himself, but his expression said he still hadn't forgiven her for Pratt revoking his bail. In true passive-aggressive fashion, he was delaying payment of the balance of her retainer.

"Just four weeks to go," Jackie replied.

The skinny prisoner in the next cubicle was staring: she forced her eyes back to her client. Against the pale skin of his forearm, his tattoo seemed to glow.

"What kind of animal is that?" she asked.

"A scorpion." Aaron flexed, and the brightly colored tail whipped.

"Why a scorpion?"

"The sting. And it's my zodiac sign. When I was ten, my brother dared me."

"You always do what Mark says?"

"It wasn't just me, he got one too."

"What's his?"

"A cobra. On his left butt. He'll show you if you ask."

Jurors hated smartasses, especially male on male. Jackie fed him more rope.

"It's a little unusual for brothers eight years apart to be so close. . . ."

"We've always been there for each other."

The same words Mark used before Aaron's bail was revoked, but some families had a peculiar way of sticking together.

"I heard about how you ended up owning the company."

As Aaron threw back his head and laughed, the prisoner in the next booth looked at Jackie with renewed interest. Not the noise or the smell, or even the sallyport, but the sheer barrage of stimulus that bombarded her every time she—

"That old wives' tale still making the rounds?" Aaron replied.

Block out every other sight and sound and *concentrate*.

"Is it true?"

"Depends on what version you heard."

A bead of sweat rolled down Jackie's temple. The cubicle was stifling. She leaned forward to make it more difficult for the other inmate to see. She didn't have to *like* Aaron to do her job; more often than not, that got in the way. And he certainly wasn't the first client she'd wanted to throw out a window.

"Let's just cut the shit. Did you beat up your brother to inherit your father's business?"

"I guess so."

"Didn't you think that was a detail I should know? I mean, we're only relying on Mark for your *alibi*."

"It's not like I've been keeping things from you," Aaron protested.

"How did Best Energy come to audit Rae Malone's home?"

"Floor-to-ceiling glass can make a house pretty cold."

"Why'd she come to *you*?"

"You mean, aside from the fact that we were in all the papers for winning the Entrepreneur of the Year award?" Jackie's face tightened, and he wisely chose to level. "Mark met her in a bar."

"So Mark knew her first. . . ."

"Best damn salesman we have. If he wasn't so valuable on the technical side, I'd just let him roam."

Kinky? A threesome? Or was Mark his brother's procurer?

"You spoke to him," Aaron continued, "what did you think?"

"Who?"

"Mark."

"It was a brief conversation."

"But what did he say?"

"He confirmed the two of you were in Dinosaur."

"If he backed me up, what's the problem?"

Her misgivings about the alibi could not be resolved here, and Jackie moved to the second item on her list.

"Yesterday I met with an expert who might be willing to testify for you." As she filled Aaron in on her meeting with Richard Hanna, he seemed more intrigued than concerned.

"What do you know about this shrink?" he asked.

"He's the top forensic psychiatrist in this part of the country. He did his training at—"

"No, I mean what do you really *know*?"

Was he asking whether Hanna was for sale?

"A straight shooter as far as I can tell . . ."

"I mean, what if he walks in here and decides he doesn't like my looks?"

"He won't do that, Aaron, he's more professional than that."

"Well, what do his other patients say about him?

Jackie could certainly sympathize with his anxiety. Submitting to a psychiatric interview was a roll of the dice—even if you had nothing to hide.

"I don't know who any of his patients are," she replied.

"What does he say about them?"

"Not a word. He's bound by professional ethics, a code of confidentiality."

"Then, how do you know—"

"Look, Aaron. It doesn't matter what you think about Hanna or what he thinks about you. You don't have to *like* each other. The only thing that matters is whether he believes you were psychologically capable of abducting and decapitating Rae Malone."

"How will he decide that?"

"On the basis of the evidence in the DA's file and what he learns by interviewing you. If you're willing to take that risk."

"How come he can't tell you who his patients are but he wants to be able to tell the DA everything I say to him?"

"Because this is a forensic evaluation; you're not seeing him as a *patient*. If Hanna testifies in your favor, the only way the jury will believe him is if he takes the stand and swears nobody tied his hands."

"And if he thinks I did it—"

"That's the risk." It was critical that this be Aaron's decision and not hers. If he thought he had to do it to save face, he'd be sunk; the worst thing was to posture in front of a shrink, particularly one as astute as Richard Hanna, Jr. "If you don't want to take the chance, I understand. If I were in your shoes, I might not—"

"I didn't say no."

"Why don't you take a couple of days to think about it? And call me if you have questions. Don't rush—"

"I *want* him to examine me. I've got nothing to hide."

"Well, do me a favor and at least sleep on it. This is a big decision, maybe the most important one you'll have to make. I want you to be completely—"

"I'm ready now. And tell Dr. Richard Hanna, Jr., to bring that waiver with him. I'll sign any damn piece of paper he wants."

They'd gotten as far as they could for one day. Reaching for her briefcase, Jackie said, "Keep your chin up—"

"—and my mouth shut." He smiled as if that were their song. "By the way, I told Mark to cut a check for the rest of what I owe you."

"Do me one other favor while you're at it."

"You're the boss, *boss*. . . ."

"Wear long sleeves in court."

T he woman typing invoices at the reception desk had one ear glued to the phone but glanced up when Jackie entered.

"Mark Best?" Jackie mouthed.

Another line rang, and the receptionist put the first caller on hold before cocking her thumb over her shoulder at a half-open door. "Best Energy," she snapped into the mouthpiece.

You could learn more in a ten-minute visit to a witness's

workplace than ten hours of interviews in your own office, and Jackie was running out of time to decide whether she could trust Aaron's brother. She knocked on his door and, receiving no answer, looked in.

Mark's office was a mess—paper cups and a wrapper with the logo of a drive-through burger joint on the floor by his chair, hard hat lying on a shelf, work boots stuffed with heavy socks in a corner, and drifts of pink, gold, and green work orders on every surface. Above his desk hung a calendar from an electrical supply company, which featured dogs in cheesecake poses. Mark was hunched over a set of plans at a draftsman's table.

"How do you get anything done in here?" Jackie asked.

"If I'd known you were coming," he replied without looking up, "I would have dumped my coffee cups."

Taking that as an invitation, Jackie entered. Behind the door was a wad of material resembling shredded newsprint. "Is *that* what you guys stuffed into my walls?"

"Beats asbestos. Not that many of our customers would know the difference."

"You certainly look busy. . . ."

"Been going nuts since Aaron's bail was revoked. I can't wait till he gets out." Finally he looked at her. "Are you here for the rest of your retainer? Aaron told our bookkeeper to cut you a—"

"Just in the neighborhood and thought I'd drop by. I have a question or two about that alibi."

"Shoot." He winced.

Clamped to the draftsman's table was a metal tray. One compartment held a half dozen sharpened pencils, another an assortment of pen holders and metal nibs. In a third lay an X-acto knife, a straightedge, and a razor that fit neatly into a wooden handle. The wood had the dull luster of age and there was a light sheen of oil on the blade.

"Is that an antique?" Jackie asked.

Mark shrugged. "Not old enough." Among the drafting tools it seemed out of place, and the X-acto knife would have served the same purpose. "My father liked to whittle; he gave it to me when I was a kid."

She turned her attention to the drawings. As detailed and meticulous as an architectural plan, the one on top depicted a multistory residential complex. It was signed with the initials "MB" and labeled in block letters "Crestwood Park." The project Aaron was meeting on the night Starla McBride was abducted.

"Where'd you learn to draw like that?" she asked. Not just highly skilled, the work was surprisingly artistic. "I thought you studied chemical engineering."

"Does that mean I don't know how to use a pencil?"

Fast on his feet, adept at turning the tables; no matter what Duncan Pratt threw at him, Mark would want to end up on top. Jackie's gaze wandered to the calendar over his desk. One of the dogs was an Afghan with silky blond hair and heart-shaped sunglasses. At least he had a sense of humor. "Why weren't you at the meeting with Aaron that night?"

"When the girl in Black Hawk was killed?" His laugh was spontaneous, the lack of defensiveness disarming. "Aaron's the guy who meets with the brass. For me, the satisfaction's in the details. Besides, I have better things to do on a Saturday night. Is that what you wanted to know?"

"I don't like surprises. How'd you end up at Mines anyway?"

"After four years of military school, digging holes didn't sound half bad."

"Military school?"

"Didn't Aaron tell you? It was that or juvenile hall."

The missing piece?

"I smacked another kid," Mark continued, "and Dad thought I needed a lesson. In his eyes, that's one I never learned. What about you, didn't you ever disappoint your folks?"

"I never got the chance." Fast—and not just on his feet. "Is that why Aaron got the company?"

Mark's shrug said it had happened so long ago, it no longer mattered. "He's done a great job and I'd hate to be tied down with running this operation."

Nothing to prove *or* hide. And that was as close as she would come to an answer. As Jackie tried to think of what to say, he picked up his pencil once again.

"Now, what was it you wanted to know?"

She would tell Pilar to deliver notice of Aaron's alibi to Duncan Pratt first thing in the morning.

Chapter | Twenty-two

Traffic was bumper to bumper all the way back from the preliminary hearing on the date-rape case in Boulder, and by the time Jackie pulled into the lot behind her building she was in a foul mood. Scraping her fender on the cement post that marked the entrance to the lot did nothing to improve her attitude.

Wooing Richard Hanna had been more exhausting than sparring with her client, and as Jackie trudged up the steps to her office she wondered whether putting the two of them together was a mistake. Maybe Hanna would back out . . . and maybe the Hollow Man defense would backfire. But she had to force Pratt's hand. The more she thought about it, the less sense his fanaticism about prosecuting Aaron made. It was political suicide to stick his neck out on a case he couldn't win, which left only two alternatives: he had a smoking gun or he was bluffing. Or else the pressure was coming from—

"How was the prelim?" Pilar asked.

"The judge tossed the case."

"You're kidding!"

"The DA made the mistake of putting Courtney Briggs on the stand." Jackie kicked off her shoes and slumped in her chair. "The rape accusation was like a little girl pinning a dress on a paper doll—she was trying it on for size. It made her feel like an *adult*."

"You stood that case on its head," Pilar said admiringly.

"More like turning the victim's motivation inside out."

The same neurons that scrambled Jackie's letters made up for it in myriad ways. Sometimes they superimposed one image over another in a graphic sequence—like Courtney Briggs trying on her sorority sisters' identities—and on other occasions created entirely new pictures from specks of matter stored in her brain like bytes on a computer disk. Yet try as she might, it was tough to feel proud of the resolution of the date-rape case. Innocence inverted was corruption, but Courtney Briggs was just a child.

"Your old magic . . ." Pilar continued.

"I could sure use some of that now."

"Well, I'm heading off to the dog track with Lenny."

"That guy who told you how Aaron's father tried to beat the inheritance tax?"

"He dropped another interesting tidbit. You'll never guess who's the money behind Crestwood Park."

"Who?"

"Rodger Malone. Small world, ain't it?"

Malone knew Aaron, and not only through Rae.

"Lenny must be mistaken," Jackie replied. "Malone would never have hired—"

"The contract was bid last March."

Before Rae was murdered.

"If the deal was in the works that long, Aaron's meeting the night Starla disappeared must have been coincidence!"

"Who said it was anything but?" Pilar yawned and ran her fingers through her hair. She'd had a touch-up, and her nails wore a fresh coat of crimson. "I could ask Lenny if he has a friend. . . ."

The thought of double-dating with a pair of sixty-year-old insurance adjusters was suddenly too depressing to contemplate. Jackie shook her head but her investigator was not to be deterred.

"When's the last time you spent Friday night with anyone but me or Lily?"

Friday night, whose magic had made adolescence bearable.

"Don't remind me."

"I mean besides that DNA expert from Quantico."

"That was pure sex, and you know it."

"Exactly my point. I'm talking about the guy before him, your heartthrob from the PD's office. How long did that last, six months?"

Living with you is a disaster waiting to happen. You can't manage money, stay within a budget, or run a household; it's a wonder you make it to court on time!

"That control freak?"

"Whatever."

You're either mentally out to lunch or totally immersed in your work. You never let anything go; you memorize every one of our goddamned arguments—is there something you're afraid to miss? And God forbid I should bring up having a baby!

"Lawyers make lousy lovers."

"Before I forget, you had a call from Richard Hanna. . . ."

Jackie tried to snatch the message slip, but Pilar was already dialing for her. As she watched, Pilar punched the button to add Hanna's number to Jackie's speed-dial.

"Don't you have someplace else to be?" Jackie asked while his answering service paged him. The soothing strains of Vivaldi filled the void for patients placed on hold.

"And miss what the good doctor has to say? Not on your life."

"He's going to tell me he changed his mind—he read the file and doesn't want anything to do with the case." Or worse, he'd interviewed Aaron and decided her client was the Hollow Man. The music abruptly ended. "Dr. Hanna, this is—"

"I'm ready to discuss Aaron Best's case, Ms. Flowers. Are you free for dinner tonight?"

Jackie glanced at Pilar. Was there some way she could have put him up to this? But her investigator was a study in wide-eyed innocence.

"—your office," he was saying, "if you prefer."

Her heart sank. Only one way to deliver bad news: quickly and in person.

"No, dinner would be fine. . . . Where shall we meet?"

"Somewhere in the neighborhood. Tosca, seven o'clock?"

Just blocks from her house.

"Fine," she replied, "but I'm picking up the tab."

"I see you haven't lost your touch," Pilar said approvingly when she hung up. "Dig out the mascara. And give him a little cleavage, for God's sake. What are you saving it for?"

Two hours later Jackie was handing her keys to the curbside valet at Tosca. As the valet hopped behind the wheel, she tossed back her hair and entered. On Friday night the place was packed with men in suits that cost more to clean than her share of the office's monthly heating bill, all trying to impress women who earned twice what they did. The maître d' immediately led her to a booth in the rear.

As Richard Hanna rose, she saw he'd already ordered a glass of wine. "I appreciate your meeting me like this," he began.

"I love anything Italian," she replied, plucking a bread stick from a jar at the end of the table. In the low lighting his eyes were soft. The news must be *really* bad. "Do you come here often?"

"Only when I'm with someone I'm trying to impress." In his office he'd been arrogant, pedantic. Was this a peace gesture—or a come-on? "How about a drink?"

"A martini," she said. "It's been a rough week."

She swirled her bread stick in the tapenade as Richard signaled the wine steward.

"Look," he told her, "I'll get right to the point. I was an ass the other day, and—"

"I took you by surprise." She'd almost said *caught you with your pants down*. A pleasing notion . . .

"You were right," he replied, "I did have a closed mind. Maybe I'm getting stale in my work."

"Occupational hazard of experts."

"I like to think of myself as something more than merely a witness." He laughed ruefully. "Or less. It's easy to forget how important it is to have your world turned inside out."

"Careful what you wish for, doctor . . ."

"Richard."

Her drink was served and he lifted his glass for a toast. "To open minds."

"And topsy-turvy universes."

The martini was smooth and cold and slid straight to Jackie's stomach. The waiter brought menus, but the dim lighting and gin said it was hopeless. She passed hers back to Richard.

"Decided so soon?" he asked.

"Turn my world upside down and order for me."

"I didn't know a lawyer could be so trusting. What if it's something you don't like?"

"Not a chance."

He ordered roast duck for them both and a bottle of wine with an intriguing name she forgot the moment he said it.

"I interviewed your client this afternoon," he continued.

"That was quick." She wished she'd been more judicious with the martini. As if reading her mind, Hanna signaled the waiter for another. Getting blitzed would make it easier; her hangover would dull the pain of hearing her case go down in flames. "How much time did you spend together?"

"Three and a half hours."

"And?"

"In layman's terms? Aaron Best's personality structure is weak, somewhat infantile. He's highly suggestible, eager to please. A follower rather than a leader."

That explained Aaron's insistence that Wendy would help him. Richard was right on the money: Aaron Best was a six-year-old expecting Mom to wipe his nose. "Not the Hollow Man, then."

"Hollow Man?"

"One of your psychopaths."

"God, no! Your client's a seducer, not a killer. Aaron wouldn't be capable of so organized a crime, despite the sloppy technique."

That awful moment after Starla McBride's body was found, when she'd wondered whether Aaron did it . . . And when his alibi panned out, she'd thought for *a fraction of a second* that he might have had an accomplice. Jackie was so relieved, she gulped her martini and gasped for breath.

"Technique?"

"Didn't you read the pathologist's report? The killer used

a sawing motion to cut off the Malone woman's head, which generally means lack of familiarity with either the tool or the technique."

"But the bottom line is, Aaron didn't do it."

"That's my professional opinion."

"And you can say that after three hours with him?"

"I'm a quick study, counselor. Almost as fast as you."

But Jackie needed just a little more information. "What *can* you tell me about the man who committed the crime?"

"You want a textbook profile of a serial killer, the kind of generalizations that fly in the face of all my profession holds dear?"

"Dumb it down for me, doc."

"White male, eldest son, family history of psychiatric problems with aggression intertwined, though he himself probably hasn't been in treatment. Unstable residence, biological father leaves home before boy reaches twelve, mother dominates during childhood and adolescence . . . Or so the FBI would have you believe."

"And you disagree?" She should have been paying attention, but she was more intrigued by his mouth. The lips were full but not fleshy. Was it the wine that made them—

"I'm no fan of the cookie-cutter approach. Their so-called profiles are derived from interviewing criminals who were caught, and everyone knows offenders lie. And they *never* cop to the sickest aspects of their crimes."

"But the FBI—"

"—has the lowest conviction rate of any major law enforcement agency in modern times." Richard sighed at her skepticism. "More generalizations? He's sexually competent, normal to superior intelligence, streetwise, and the same race and age range as his victims. Takes good care of himself and his residence, which, except with respect to his first offense, is some distance from the crime scene. He drives a—"

"First offense?" She was registering every sixth word.

"As I said the other day, he's killed before. Probably when he was quite a bit younger, maybe by accident. He kept killing when he realized he enjoyed it. And he most likely works alone."

"Most likely?"

"Reported incidents are rare, but occasionally these killers team up. When they do, they operate symbiotically, each enhancing the other's sense of power. To put it crudely, when you can be both participant and spectator, there's more bang for the buck."

"Where do they find each other?"

"Usually in prison." Now she was thoroughly ashamed of having suspected Aaron. "One tends to dominate the other, and when they're caught, the mastermind often blames the follower. So much for loyalty."

"Are there ever male-female teams?"

"The answer is yes, but it's even more rare."

The waiter brought the duck and made a show of boning Jackie's portion. Fine with her; at that point she couldn't have handled a knife if her life depended on it. She was bombed, the subject matter was sickening, but Richard Hanna fascinated her. Despite his disdain for the feds, he was totally into this; every detail meant something to him. The jury would be eating out of his hand.

"Want to hear more?" he asked. While the waiter fussed with her duck, he'd been cutting his, and she let him take a bite before nodding. "His work record will be sporadic, he'll have a history of walking off the job. If he served in the armed forces, it was the army or marines, and he'll have a disciplinary record that demonstrates contempt for authority. He considers himself a ladies' man. Conscious of style, dates lots of women, likes designer clothes. And he loves to cruise, he's always on the move. That's how he finds his victims."

"According to you or the FBI?"

"On certain of the more obvious points we concur."

She watched the smooth muscles of his jaw tense and his eyes narrow with pleasure at the succulent meat, and realized for the first time why men were turned on by watching her eat. With the right mouth it was nothing short of erotic. Lifting her own fork, she said, "Tell me about the victims."

"No victim is truly random, but your man selects on the basis of opportunity. Oh, he'll start out looking for his ideal, based on a complex matrix of physical details and personal characteristics around which he's constructed his fantasy of abuse, but he's most concerned with gratification at minimal risk. If his ideal eludes him and he's primed to kill, he'll settle for whoever's available."

"Doesn't his desperation tip the victims off?"

"He's much more clever than that. Nothing about his demeanor or dress is menacing, and he strikes up a conversation as a prelude to attack. That's how he begins to assert control. And for him, control is everything. He's a chameleon who compartmentalizes his life. He keeps his work separate from his family, his fantasy life on another plane from both. Like any psychopath, he excels at manipulation. Which brings us to what you really care about, another reason the killer is not Aaron Best."

Under the intensity of Richard's gaze, Jackie's appetite was picking up, but she took her time swirling a large morsel of breast in the sauce before raising it to her lips. Whoever claimed the ultimate turn-on was witnessing your own power over a man had it right. As he refilled their wineglasses she realized she couldn't remember drinking the first.

"—ingratiating but transparent," he continued, apparently unaffected by the wine. "Aaron wants desperately to be liked and doesn't care who knows it."

At this point Richard seemed to be communicating entirely independent of his words. Her hangover would be hellacious, but Jackie didn't care. She hadn't been this horny in months and knew it was reciprocated. By the time the waiter cleared their plates and brought dessert menus, she was afraid to rise to go to the ladies' room.

"—trial?" Richard was saying.

Snap out of it.

"I beg your pardon?"

"When is Aaron's trial? You know, that thing you lawyers do." He smiled; was it that obvious what she'd been thinking?

"It starts four weeks from Monday." And what would he say if he knew she wanted him to opine not only that Aaron was incapable of murdering Rae Malone, but that the man who *was* responsible had killed at least four other women? If she tipped her hand now, Richard might bolt.

"Isn't that awfully quick on a first-degree-murder charge?"

Nothing sobered Jackie faster than talk of a trial date. "With your opinion, our gamble just might pay off."

"How so?"

Another rude reminder of first things first—and not to underestimate her expert. And now she couldn't tell whether the attraction was based on Richard or the booze. If it persisted, there'd be plenty of time to find out. *After* the trial.

"The prosecution has the burden of proof," she replied. "Technically, we don't even have to put on a defense—the DA has to prove his case beyond a reasonable doubt. His forensic work is sketchy and he won't want to rush it to a jury."

"And my opinion—"

"—gives us the edge we need to force the DA's hand."

T hat night Jackie fell asleep to the image of a shiny gourd. Teetering on its axis, it cracked open with a violent shake and out sprang a corn husk. The husk danced a little jig and blew away.

Chapter | Twenty-three

The geometric facade of Richard Hanna's condominium made it seem like a twenty-story piece of art, but its lines were softened and made inviting by the color of the stone. As Jackie walked there from her house the Sunday before the final pretrial hearing in Aaron's case, she reminded herself this was anything but a social visit.

The stakes in Worrell's court the next morning were high: when Jackie informed Pratt of her expert's identity he'd filed a voluminous brief in opposition, and on Monday the judge would decide whether the opinion would be admitted. In the week since Richard had agreed to testify that Aaron didn't kill Rae, Pilar had been busy gathering information about the other victims. Jackie's mission that morning was to sound him out on opining that Rae's death was the tip of the iceberg.

The elevators in Richard's lobby were covered with ornate grilles. Waiting for the doorman to ring his unit, Jackie crossed the marble floor for a closer look. Flute-shaped blossoms nature never intended to climb wound and stretched to the top of the grate, as fantastical as pigs with wings. As Jackie reached to touch one, the door to the penthouse elevator whispered open and Richard stepped out.

"I was expecting the butler," she said.

"Don't be fooled," he replied, "it's Styrofoam and tinfoil.

But I didn't have you pegged as a woman who would be intimidated by beauty."

"I suppose I could get used to it if I really tried."

He escorted her onto the elevator. The key-operated control pad displayed three buttons: Penthouse, Lobby, Garage. With his key in the lock he pressed Penthouse.

"I guess you value privacy." The ride was so smooth, she thought they were standing still. "Is there something about your sources of income I should know?"

"Dad made investments at the right time, and I inherited everything but his financial sense."

"A Carnegie-Mellon, I presume."

"Humble general practitioner back in New York."

The doors glided open and Jackie heard water. They were in an atrium. Lit by a skylight two stories above, a marble sphinx spouted a sparkling stream into a series of oval basins filled with water lilies and koi. The floor was Chinese slate veined pink and gold and moss, and the glossy foliage and mirrored walls surrounding the fountain gave it the effect of a sumptuous garden. She turned to Richard.

"Did you design this yourself?"

"I was on the waiting list when the building went up. The architect let me be a pest."

"I'll say." The repeating images were overwhelming. "Where do you hang coats?"

"Those mirrors are doors." He pointed at a panel to the left of the elevator. "That one's a closet."

"Ever get lost?"

"It's not as confusing as it looks." He led her to the mirror directly behind the fountain, and for an instant Jackie felt like a refugee from the Mad Hatter's tea party. Door after door . . . "Cup of coffee before we start?"

"Sure." The corridor they were in was paved in black granite polished to a high gloss. The sheer expanse of sky reminded Jackie they were twenty stories above the ground.

"Take a look," Richard said.

"Maybe later," she replied, wondering if he'd laugh at her reaction to heights. "I'm dying to see your kitchen. Do you have a moss rock hearth?"

But the kitchen was a study in stainless steel and stone

with countertops four inches thick and glass cabinets built into the walls. In the center stood a gleaming contraption the size of a sports car.

"Let me guess," she said. "You like to cook on the highway."

"It's a Viking, the gas burners fire up to sixteen thousand BTUs."

She shook her head in mock resignation. "Where's that cup of joe?"

He busied himself grinding beans and setting up the coffee machine. As a rich aroma filled the air, he turned back to her. "What are you thinking—conspicuous consumption?"

"Not at all. I'm just wondering where's Mrs. Richard Hanna, Jr. This is a kitchen any woman would kill for."

"Cream or sugar?" he replied.

"Black."

He handed her a mug of French roast and leaned against a counter. "I got married my first year of medical school. She didn't even give me time to run off with the obligatory nurse."

"Poor baby."

He took a careful sip. "I'm the one who was lousy company, I'm afraid. When I'm interested in something, I tend to block the rest of the world out."

"So the nurse came later . . ."

"I went straight into a psych residency, and by the time I was done licking my wounds, there weren't many of them left. Since we're getting personal, what about—"

"What made you choose Denver?"

"Back then the university's program was oriented toward analysis—talking therapy, not drugs. Except for a few pockets of resistance, nowadays you might as well be a pharmacologist."

"I thought psychopaths were untreatable. How does a shrink who believes in therapy end up in a specialty like yours?"

Instead of answering, he said, "Follow me."

As he led her back to the hallway and they approached the panel of sky, Jackie breathed deeply and kept a firm grip on her coffee mug.

"—straight down on the Japanese garden," he said. "You can even see the pond—"

Don't look.

But infinity beckoned and without warning she was suddenly seven years old, snaking up the side of a hotel in San Francisco in a glass elevator. Clutching her aunt's hand and then beginning to scream— Closing her eyes, Jackie stumbled; coffee splashed on the polished floor.

Richard grasped her elbow. "Okay?"

She nodded gratefully. "Sometimes I'm just—"

"—goosey around heights." A left turn and she spotted an oasis of green at the end of the corridor. Solid ground. Richard's touch was firm but gentle, and her panic began to recede. "Tell you the truth, I picked the penthouse for the light and not the view. You'll see why in a moment."

First she felt it.

A delicate scent wrapped itself around Jackie's face like a silk scarf. She was stepping into a forest, the perfume of pine and spruce intensifying as she crushed needles under her feet. Richard let go of her hand and she entered the greenhouse.

The morning had been overcast and now the sun was breaking through. Small clouds with mounded tops were brilliant against the vivid sky, and below them were banks of miniature trees. Shelf after shelf of plants, none higher than three feet tall. Evergreens and ficus, a crabapple whose curved trunk and outstretched limbs reminded Jackie of a one-legged Balinese dancer. The silver trunk of a juniper rose like a serpent before its foliage cascaded over the rim of the pot.

"—time of intense growth. Most prefer to be outside when the danger of frost is past, so I move them to the balcony." The floor of the greenhouse was pebbled and the soaring glass no longer made her dizzy. "Best time of year to graft and transplant conifers," he added behind her shoulder. "Don't mind the mess. . . ."

"Mess? This is heaven!"

"I wanted to show you so you'll understand."

She turned to face him. "I knew you were a gardener, but I never realized—"

"It's not just a hobby. Five years ago I started a program

at the Botanic Gardens. A nursery donates seedlings, and I teach at-risk kids and their parents to prune and wire. We call it Healing Hands." Richard's boyish face glowed, and she was ashamed of the way she'd teased him before. "The results are practically instantaneous; kids who never talk suddenly open up."

"How does it work?"

"By tapping into the human need to nurture." Whoever his ex was, the woman must have been nuts to let him go. "When you work so intensely with life, you can't help but develop self-esteem. That in itself is healing."

"But what does it have to do with psychopaths?"

"I told you my dad was a GP, right? Well, he had his office in the ground floor of our house and I got used to seeing his patients go in and out. I always knew I wanted to do what he did, but I was more interested in *why* they felt the way they did than the cure. So I became a shrink."

"Why not specialize in family therapy?"

"By the time a parent consults a psychiatrist, it's usually too late. Nine times out of ten, the kid's already in serious trouble and they're trying to keep him out of court. The die's already cast."

"I still don't see—"

"A professor of mine had a theory about psychopaths. I told you many have great intellects and succeed in business or professions." She nodded. "They make particularly good executives, in fact, until their destructive urges send them off on sprees. Maybe that high degree of emotional and intellectual capacity they demonstrate as kids thrusts them into situations they can't handle. Genius used to be considered a degenerative psychosis; today we expect irrational behavior from artists."

"What are you saying?"

"Certain creative people show signs of personality disorders."

"But you said psychopaths are fakes. If they're unable to tell the difference between acting and genuine emotion, how can they truly create?"

"I'm not suggesting they can, Jackie, or that psychopaths have the discipline to pursue artistic goals. What I *am* saying is that at critical points in their lives, they may have had great potential for positive experiences. If you could isolate the moment when that potential goes awry and appropriately intervene—"

"You're making a huge assumption, aren't you?"

Richard faced the balcony. The clouds had scattered and to the south Pikes Peak loomed. When he spoke again, it was with the muted fervor of conviction.

"Haven't you met a smartass kid who's so precocious he alienates everyone he meets? So above average in all but maturity that he gets himself in situations in which he can't begin to cope? A man of integrity who finds himself in an ethical bind is more likely to take his own life than one who lacks the morality to tell the difference. Why is it so hard to believe that the disintegration of a psychopath is the flip side of an equally great capacity for positive experience?"

"And that's what Healing Hands is about. . . ."

"Intervening before it's too late, before what makes these kids special is lost. Of course, you don't have to be a budding psychopath to be both gifted and cursed. But you know about that, don't you?"

"Actually, I know a little girl who—"

"I meant someone closer to home." Now there was no looking away, no reprieve from the intensity of his gaze. "Look, Jackie, this is none of my business. But it *is* my profession to read between the lines, to listen for what isn't said. I know what you must have gone through as a kid—I know what isolation's all about."

Had he guessed?

"—worst things you can do to a boy is skip him in grades so he's the runt of the class. You feel like—"

"You know nothing about me, Richard." That stung and she smiled to soften it, but her mind raced. What could he know?

"I didn't mean to intrude. I just—"

"There's no need to apologize."

They retraced their steps to the main corridor and crossed to his study opposite the kitchen. The sumptuous room had none of the trappings of a library—maple shelves matched the grain of the paneled ceiling, and the Sumak kilim was bordered with broad bands of geometric shapes representing animals and birds. While Richard fetched fresh coffee, Jackie settled on the leather couch and planned her approach. Tomorrow was Aaron's final hearing, and she needed to convince Hanna to go way out on a limb. Pilar's research could strengthen their defense immeasurably. But only if Richard would go along.

"What's on the agenda tomorrow?" he asked as he handed her a mug.

"The DA wants to bar your opinion as to Aaron's mental state."

"Pratt still hasn't gotten over the shock of me appearing for the defense, has he?" He grinned. "I never imagined switching sides could be such fun. What are his grounds?"

"Junk science."

"Ouch."

"Whether your opinion comes in will be entirely up to the judge. Criminal defendants normally get wider latitude than the DA in establishing their case."

"What's Pratt's argument?"

"Because there are no medical tests to identify disorders, he has to claim the method by which you obtained the data to support your opinion was unreliable."

"My session with Aaron? But that's the way I always—"

"Exactly. Did you record the interview?"

He shook his head. "It changes the dynamics. Sort of like cameras in the courtroom."

"Take any notes?"

"Too distracting. When you write, you miss subtle cues. Besides," he added with an ironic smile, "a certain defense attorney I'm working with never uses them. She says notes are discoverable, so I've gotten in the habit of not relying on them."

Was that the tip-off, or had it been her loss of balance? "Good."

"Will you need me to prepare a report?"

"I'll notify the prosecution of the nature of the defense, but I'd prefer you not put anything in writing. I'm counting on the fact that the DA has offered your opinion on many occasions in the past, based on precisely the same methodology. I'm not asking you to say Aaron snapped from eating too many Twinkies, rather, that he's *free* from a diagnosable defect. The tricky part will be convincing the judge to allow you to testify to characteristics of the actual killer."

"Which would be impossible to do, given that I know next to nothing about him." Richard looked at her more closely. "What *aren't* you telling me?"

"You read about that woman who was kidnapped from the casino in Black Hawk."

"Starla McBride."

"Doesn't her murder bear striking similarities to Rae's killer's MO?"

"Are you asking me to say they were the work of the same man?" Richard's expression was unreadable and Jackie wondered whether she'd gone too far. "But I don't know anything about the McBride case."

"If I got you the file, would you consider it?"

"I don't know."

Remembering what he'd said about challenges, she pressed on. "McBride wasn't the only one."

"What?"

"There are unsolved murders of women dating back fifteen years." To cut off his protest, she quickly added, "But I'm interested only in Starla and the last three. What if I get the police reports?"

"Not good enough. I'd need hard physical evidence."

"But the reports contain the detectives' analyses. . . ."

Richard shook his head again. "I'm amazed at your naïveté. Didn't you know most crimes are 'solved' by beat cops making an arrest? The patrolman is first on the scene; by the time the honchos arrive, things can drastically change. Even under the best of circumstances physical evidence is routinely ignored, and when it's collected it stays on the shelf—especially if it screws up the prosecutor's theory."

"Pratt has criminalists at the police lab, they're experts—"

"The value of most evidence decreases as soon as it's gathered; you have to see it in relation to the crime scene to truly understand its significance. And as far as police reports go, the only ones worth a damn are written by rookies who are too green to know what's 'trivial.' So-called seasoned detectives leave the most important stuff out."

"You sound like you don't have much respect for cops."

"Their main skill is interviewing witnesses and interrogating suspects, and fibers or wound analysis won't give them a *name*. It's a vicious cycle: the evidence that can solve the crime doesn't get processed till they think they know who did it, and then they use it only to secure a confession and ignore the pieces that don't fit. The same ass-backward approach FBI profilers take, which is why I hate to be called one."

"But the FBI has an enormous database—"

"—of criminals dumb or unlucky enough to be caught. The only advantage to their boilerplate 'profiles' is they can be slapped together with zero training or effort. Is it any wonder so few serial killers are caught?"

"So what's the proper approach?"

"You start with the physical evidence and a thorough analysis of the victim, the crime scene, and the behavioral clues. *Then* form a working hypothesis, an initial assessment of offender characteristics based on all the material. You test and modify the hypothesis in light of new evidence that develops; if the characteristics aren't supported by the evidence, out they go. The profile you end up with is valid only to the extent all patterns converge."

"That sounds great in theory, but—"

"It may not be as glamorous as pretending to get inside the killer's head, but it's a hell of a lot more useful."

"So where do we start?"

He looked surprised. "You don't give up, do you?"

All she had to do at the hearing the next day was open the door to the admissibility of the Hollow Man profile; if and when they passed that hurdle, she would have three weeks to gather whatever information Richard needed. And in the process decide for herself whether the Hollow Man was real enough to present to the jury. "Not once I sink my teeth in something."

"Then we'd better give that mouth of yours something to chew on, Ms. Flowers. I can't think on an empty stomach, much less formulate strategy."

"I know a funky café down by the Capitol if you like barbecued tempeh. Or there's that transvestite coffee shop on—"

"Know what I like about you?" He leaned forward. "You let it all hang out, no matter what anyone thinks."

Had she fooled him, did he give up that easily?

"Don't kid yourself . . ."

"I have a better idea. Want to take my stove for a spin?"

"There's something you should know about me, Richard."

"What might that be?" he asked.

"I'm a *really* lousy cook."

He laughed, his relief so palpable she wondered what he'd thought she was going to say. "I love it; yet another opportunity to demonstrate my superiority. Besides, my Viking's a pro. If he couldn't take the heat—"

"—he wouldn't be in your kitchen."

Five minutes later Richard was whipping up hollandaise and Jackie was cracking eggs in his stainless steel poaching pan. Peering into the refrigerator, he emerged with a package of Canadian bacon. "Just stick this in the copper pan on the front burner," he instructed, "and fire that baby up."

"All the way?"

"I promise it won't explode."

"But the hood must be there for something."

"Quit worrying. There's a fire extinguisher under the sink."

Jackie did as she was told.

"How long have you been afraid of heights?" he asked.

She stiffened. "Since I was a kid."

"Something happened to you?"

"It's just the way I was born." She tapped the last egg harder than she'd intended, and when she tried to fish out shards of shell with a fork, the yolk broke. "Now you know my secret," she added brightly.

Not the only one, not even the worst.

"You know, there are fascinating connections between learning disabilities and spatial disorientation. Kids who can't read often have trouble tracking words on the page— they zigzag and scramble and lose their place. Nothing to do with intelligence; in fact, they develop marvelous compensatory tech—"

"A little outside your specialty, aren't you?"

"Maybe . . ."

He set the saucepan of hollandaise on the burner next to the bacon and began stirring with a wooden spoon. "See how you do it?" he said. "Gently."

With his arm around her shoulder, Richard placed the

spoon in her hand and they slowly began to stir. A light scent rose above the bacon. Spicy, an aftershave she didn't recognize. Sandalwood? As his nose grazed her hair she turned, and their lips met. *See?* he seemed to say, *you haven't fooled me, but I want you.* . . . Barely touching, then more insistent, and she let herself fall into it.

They smelled smoke from the pan on the adjacent burner at the same moment, but it was Jackie who pulled away. "I told you I'd ruin it!" She grabbed the spatula.

Taking it from her hands, he expertly flipped the bacon. "You're a much better cook than you think. Law is far from your only talent."

Cheeks flushed, she returned to the hollandaise. "Care for a rematch on my turf after this case is over? I can't promise eggs Benedict, but—"

"I'll look forward to that. You did say something about an *early* trial date, didn't you?"

Walking home an hour later, Jackie mentally reviewed the materials Richard said he would need. Crime scene photos, autopsy reports, time lines establishing the victims' last twenty-four hours . . . But her thoughts kept returning to that moment by the stove. He'd been guessing— *Nothing to do with intelligence* . . . Did she initiate the kiss by turning her face up, or had he leaned in?

She had no excuse for letting it get that far—with an expert witness, no less. Closing her eyes at a stop sign, she smelled sandalwood, felt his soft breath on her mouth and the warmth of his lips on hers. Gentle, more urgent. She certainly hadn't imagined *that*. . . . As she stepped from the curb, a car honked, jolting her from her reverie. Whatever was starting between her and Richard Hanna would just have to wait.

Chapter | Twenty-four

Duncan Pratt rose as if he regretted having to waste the court's time. Given that Courtroom 16 was packed with reporters who could have been tipped only by his office, it was a tough sell, and the number of lawyers at the prosecution table confirmed how crucial this matter was.

"Defense counsel has indicated she intends to introduce an expert as to her client's mental state and the supposed personality traits of Rae Malone's killer. Further, we have every reason to believe Ms. Flowers will argue this same hypothetical creature is not responsible just for Ms. Malone's death but other crimes with which Mr. Best has *not* been charged. We vigorously oppose these tactics on several grounds."

It was Jackie's motion, but she had no objection to the DA going first. Three minutes into his argument, Worrell was tapping his pencil on the mike. Oblivious to the judge's impatience, Pratt tried to round Cape Horn in a canoe.

"First, Mr. Best waived the issue of mental state by failing to plead insanity. As such, any opinion as to his psychological capacity to commit the crime is irrelevant. Second, personality-trait testimony amounts to nothing more than 'junk science.' The validity and reliability of so-called profiling techniques are seriously in doubt—"

"You're not claiming this court lacks the discretion to allow it in, are you?" Worrell interjected.

"No, your honor, simply that because a witness has 'doctor' in front of his name doesn't mean what he says amounts to good science. Or common sense."

The judge turned to Jackie. "Who is this witness?"

As if he didn't know. The day Bertram J. Worrell took the bench without having read a motion they would be carrying him out feetfirst.

"Dr. Richard Hanna, Jr.," she replied.

Worrell's eyes widened, and Jackie made a mental note to ask Richard how often he'd testified in Courtroom 16. "Can't you voir-dire Dr. Hanna on his credentials and methodology at trial?" he asked the DA.

"Uncharged crimes and Best's state of mind are irrelevant to Rae Malone's death! If *we* tried to bring those matters in, Ms. Flowers would be jumping up and—"

"I note she's been remarkably stable." As Worrell turned to Jackie, his eyes glowed with the intensity of a jack-o'-lantern. Challenged by the novelty of the defense? Or inviting her to place her neck in the noose along with her client's? "Ms. Flowers . . . ?"

"I find it absolutely astounding that the DA would attack the credentials of a witness his office has relied upon on more occasions than I can count. And since when isn't the defendant's state of mind at the time of an alleged crime relevant?" Jackie rose, allowing her outrage to soar to the farthest reaches of the court. "As far as Dr. Hanna's methodology goes, the DA has never before claimed an interview by the most renowned forensic psychiatrist in this part of the country is an insufficient basis to state an opinion as to—"

"The methodology I was referring to relates to the profiling defense," Pratt interrupted. "He has no expertise in that; I don't know how anyone—"

"Your honor, I willingly accept responsibility for the witnesses I call and the law I cite, but no defense in the history of jurisprudence has been held accountable for what the prosecutor may or may not *know*. That is a burden too heavy for anyone to bear."

Before the judge covered the mike she thought she heard him mutter "Blistering." Worrell continued in a louder tone.

"The Supreme Court says I'm to be a gatekeeper and

exclude unacceptable testimony before it is even offered. With characteristic omniscience they expect the trial judge to call balls and strikes before the pitch is thrown. The FBI engages in profiling with highly publicized success. What's your position, Ms. Flowers—are profiles admissible?"

One well-placed swing and she could drive the Hollow Man defense home. Taking a gamble on Worrell's views on the federal government in general and the FBI in particular, she stepped closer to the plate.

"I'm in no position to vouch for the workings of the FBI, your honor. Perhaps its methodology can even be *improved*. All I'm asking is that you give Dr. Hanna—" Turning to gesture in Richard's direction, she suddenly locked eyes with Rodger Malone.

Seated in the front row of the gallery, his hostile gaze was as intent as a snake's. Rae's ex-husband wanted to see her client fry as badly as Duncan Pratt did. How his contribution to Aaron's alibi for Starla McBride's murder must have galled him! But could he hate Aaron so much that he was willing to *frame*—

There was a loud crash from the prosecution table. Papers flew across the floor and fluttered halfway to the bench. Red-faced, Pratt's female assistant knelt to retrieve a stack of files that had been balanced at the edge of the table. As Worrell glowered at the interruption, Jackie's mind went blank.

Focus, *focus* . . .

She reached in her suit pocket for her moss agate. A translucent slice of quartz laced with forest green inclusions. *You can get through this, don't think about what happened before.* . . . She ran her thumb across the satiny surface and prayed.

It had happened during her final trial for Legal Aid. She was representing a tenant in an eviction case, an unwed mother whose food stamps had been stolen. She had two defenses to the nonpayment of rent—one technical, based on the landlord's failure to provide notice, the other founded on decency and compassion. Just as she was about to examine the landlord, there was a noise in the corridor. Two lawyers who didn't realize another case was being heard were continuing their argument. Jackie's brain had turned off like a switch.

Tongue-tied and disoriented, she tried desperately to remember her client's name. This was a thousand times worse than not being able to read aloud or the humiliation of asking a stranger to interpret a sign when she got lost two blocks from home. Here someone was depending on *her*. Overwhelmed by frustration and futility, she went mute.

The judge, a kindly man who'd had his share of student lawyers in court, assumed it was a case of the jitters and called her and opposing counsel into chambers. With a strong hint to the landlord's attorney that he was inclined to rule for the tenant on the notice issue—not that he wasn't *appalled* at this lack of compassion for a woman in such dire straits—he pressed them into a settlement. But Jackie wasn't fooled. Her client should have *won*, not been forced to rely on the pity of a stranger because her own lawyer had disintegrated. . . .

"Ms. Flowers?"

Worrell was staring at her.

The agate was weightless in her hand. Feathers floating in ether. *Focus, focus* . . .

She squinted as if she were framing her next words, and suddenly there was light.

"All I ask is that you give Dr. Hanna an opportunity to lend his expertise to the jury in determining whether my client committed this dreadful crime."

"In that case, I'll indulge you." Worrell looked relieved. "Dr. Hanna may offer his learned opinion as to both the mental state of your client and relevant personality traits of the man who killed Rae Malone. Are there any other matters?"

Pratt turned to his brainy assistant, who was trying to redeem herself by tugging on his sleeve.

"Notes," he said, retaking the lectern. "We want whatever notes Hanna took of his interview with Best, including videos, tape recordings, and any other materials memorializing his impressions."

Jackie thought fast. There were no notes. But if she argued against their production, the judge could toss the DA a bone.

"Had the defense filed a plea of insanity," she replied, "those items would certainly be discoverable." Not wanting to mislead the court, she chose her next words with care.

"But the substance of Dr. Hanna's opinion has nothing to do with mental disease; rather, it goes to *identification*. Behavioral characteristics are the mental equivalent of a fingerprint, the issue is patterns of—"

"No go, Ms. Flowers," Worrell cut in, "but credit for trying. I'm ordering you to produce your expert's notes, assuming he has any. . . . And a brief report outlining the substance of his testimony."

Pratt was scarlet to the tips of his ears, and Jackie wondered whether she'd gone too far. An angry DA was like a wounded bear.

Unpredictable and mean.

Chapter | Twenty-five

As Jackie and Richard drove to Colorado Springs in his Volvo, she reached into the paper bag in the backseat and handed him a raspberry bran muffin. Dry as library paste. Richard munched his with the same preoccupation he'd displayed when he swung by her house to pick her up.

"So much for health food," she said.

"Next time remind me to bring my tracheotomy knife."

He softened it with a grin, but Jackie couldn't help wondering whether he resented being roped into accompanying her to the site where Becky Cox's body had been found—or, more accurately, driving her there. No matter how boldly she highlighted maps or how many red arrows Pilar used, getting behind the driver's wheel was always an adventure. But the real reason she wanted Richard to come was to give her a crash course on the Hollow Man's crimes. To convince the jury that Rae Malone's death followed a pattern, Jackie had to experience that truth herself.

"What are you thinking?" Richard asked.

"How lucky I am to have such an accomplished chauffeur."

"And at a bargain rate."

Glancing across the seat only to be met by an innocent gaze, Jackie wondered whether he suspected this jaunt was an excuse to pick his brains. But if resentment underlay the tension between them, she suspected it was frustration in not being able to pursue their attraction. His eyes had lit with pleasure when she greeted him at her door that morning, but the pass at his condo had not been repeated and he'd been impossibly correct all week. Which, to be honest, was another reason she wanted to be alone with him in a car.

"Speaking of time," she began, "why is it important to track each victim's last twenty-four hours? Surely the police—"

"—will already have tried to determine when and where the victims were accosted, though I doubt they analyzed the killer's familiarity with the location and whether his approach depended on routine." Talking about his specialty seemed to loosen him up. "But it's more than looking for witnesses who might recall him. Walking in the victim's shoes is critical to evaluating levels of risk."

"From her point of view?"

"And *his*." They were zipping past Park Meadows, the mall where Rae had eaten her final salade Niçoise. As if reading Jackie's mind, Richard continued. "Take that woman they say Aaron killed. In determining whether a pattern exists, you consider three levels of risk. The first has to do with her lifestyle."

"Affluent. We know that from where she lived."

"That's just the *surface*. Lifestyle risk is a function of personality traits, who Rae Malone was, and how she related to her environment. Some traits increase risk."

"Such as?"

"Aggressiveness, for one. Impulsivity, emotional outbursts—"

"Like, did she invite the mailman in for coffee or assault the paper boy when the *Post* landed in her petunias?" She couldn't help thinking that Rae had invited Aaron in, and it wasn't for coffee.

"On the other end of the spectrum, passivity also increases risk. Predators can always spot the laggards. Take Becky Cox, since we're going to the place where she was left. What was she like?"

An athletic blonde in a navy tank cut snug and low,

freckles dusting her shoulders. In one of the photos Pilar had produced, Becky's hair was swept back from her face, but you could tell it was long and she gloried in it, was used to wearing it loose. Her eyes peeked out from the top of designer sunglasses whose oversized frames complemented the angular planes of her face. The provocativeness of the pose lay in her expression, not the revealing attire.

"Sporty. Comfortable with her own attractiveness, eager to connect . . . no shortage of men, but still alone. You said three levels of risk—what are the others?"

"Incident risk, a combination of Becky's state of mind and hazards when she was abducted. Were other people around, was the location well lit or dark?"

"The last place she was seen was O'Dell's on a Friday night, but she could have met her killer in the bar or outside. She left her car in the lot across the street."

"Do you think she felt safe?"

The second photograph had been taken at a barbecue Becky's law firm gave a month before she was murdered. Becky and three yuppie males saluted the camera with plastic cups emblazoned *Coors,* and Jackie could see a keg on the manicured lawn. From the way the men clustered around, she was obviously popular, or maybe they were more than a little smashed. How many drinks did Becky have that night at O'Dell's?

"*I* would have," she replied. "It was Friday, she was looking for a good time. . . ."

He nodded. "Alcohol lowers inhibitions, and a woman who feels safe acts differently than when she perceives herself at risk. Becky's state of mind undoubtedly made the encounter much riskier for her than a well-lit, crowded bar would otherwise suggest. Which leads us to—"

"—risk from the offender's point of view," Jackie concluded.

They passed the turnoff to Castle Pines, a grove of gated communities designed around a world-class golf course. The term "gentleman farmer" took on new meaning; ranchers hereabouts raised the Rolls-Royces of cattle—Santa Gertrudis and Limousin.

"The classic high-risk MO is a daytime abduction from

a public place with a security camera, where the abductor allows the victim to see his face and survive the attack. If they had a prior relationship, you'd have to wonder whether he *wanted* to be caught. A low-risk offender targets a prostitute who won't immediately be missed, at a location where he's not likely to be identified or noticed. He takes her to a remote site and kills her, then dumps her body where it won't be found. Analyzing MO tells us what the killer knew."

"Becky certainly wasn't a prostitute, and the cops said her killer was a stranger. He kept her for two days. She was raped and strangled before he cut off her head. There were faint red marks around her legs, like she'd been bound." Jackie shook her head to dispel the image. "The point of this exercise is . . . ?"

"To determine the killer's behavioral characteristics and whether there's a pattern to the crimes. That's the payoff for Aaron Best, isn't it?"

Jackie let an enigmatic smile be her reply. But Richard's directness reminded her that this trip posed yet another level of risk, of which trial lawyers were all too aware. Handling an expert was like driving a nitroglycerin wagon—you never knew when it could blow up in your face. What did she really know about Hanna other than the raw data on his CV, that he owned a stove that could qualify for the Indianapolis 500, and he was a refreshing change from the pompous specialists and neurotic colleagues who populated her increasingly isolated existence? Okay, more than a refreshing change, but for all that, he could cheerfully screw her and not in the way Pilar kept hoping. . . .

"—your mother and father still alive?"

"They died when I was three. I don't even remember them. How about yours?"

"Dad died ten years ago, right before I moved to Denver. When Mom had her first stroke not long after, I wanted to bring her out here, but she went downhill too fast. What happened to your parents?"

"Hit by a drunk driver at an intersection two blocks from home."

"Jesus!" Richard looked over with concern. "That must—"

"They were on their way back from dinner and a movie.

Zorba the Greek. My aunt always said she was glad they'd had fun."

"Is she the one who raised you?"

"My mother's older sister, she was great." The woman who'd read her stories every night to make her *want* to read— to overcome her sense of failure. That hadn't exactly worked, but if not for the hours they'd spent practicing letters, she wouldn't be able to skim the paragraphs she managed on a good day.

"I take it she's gone now."

"I was lucky to have her."

"It still must have been difficult. Didn't you wonder what your parents were like?"

Jackie hesitated. "Sometimes I think I remember little things, you know how that goes."

"Like what?"

"It sounds silly, but the smell of dusting powder always gets to me. You know the gardenia-scented kind that came in a round box with a giant velour puff? My aunt never used it." As soon as she'd been old enough to go to a department store alone, she'd looked everywhere for it. When she finally found a box, she bought it and hid it in her bottom drawer. It got lost in her move to college and no one sold it anymore. "I can't tell whether the memory's real or not."

Richard laughed, then reached over and squeezed her hand.

"That good an imagination, eh?"

"So I've been told."

And what trouble it had gotten her into. The daydreams and distractions . . .

"—kids ask questions?" he continued.

"Questions?"

"At school, about your parents."

"God, no!" *Those* kinds of questions would have been a relief. "School was never my favorite place, but being an orphan had nothing to do with it."

"What did?"

"A long story. Let's save it for when you're already bored to tears."

"With you I don't imagine I'll get that chance."

"Once this trial's over and I go back to defending burglars and con artists, you'll see how dull I can really be."

As they neared Colorado Springs, the clouds hung like soot and the terrain was marked by flat-topped mesas with outcroppings of limestone like ancient cities in the hills. The tension between them had evaporated and Jackie wondered whether Richard's moodiness had been in anticipation of the traffic on I-25. With reluctance she returned to the case.

"What should we be looking for at the Garden of the Gods?"

"The first rule is every crime scene is distinct. Environmental influences and the killer's interaction with the victim have a unique effect on the evidence he leaves behind. There are multiple scenes in Becky's murder—O'Dell's, any vehicle she was transported in, the places where she was kept, killed, and beheaded, and the dump site. Each gives insight into the MO."

"Abduction, rape, and beheading." Jackie tried to remember what else Pilar said. "And he washed her body. What more is there to know?"

"That tells us next to nothing," Richard replied.

"You mean about whether he's organized versus disorganized?"

A laugh of genuine amusement. "The hallmark of the FBI approach: a meaningless distinction whose only appeal is brainless certainty. As dumb as saying all serial killers are white males."

"Aren't they?"

"If you can believe what you're told by white males who have been caught. You might legitimately conclude one committed a series of crimes, but only on the basis of such factors as the women being abducted from settings where a nonwhite male would stick out like a sore thumb."

"So, what does a *real* detective look for?"

"Method of approach, amount of force, precautionary acts, items taken . . . All provide a window on the killer's needs, abilities, and obsessions. The fantasies that drive him."

"Precautionary acts?"

"You said he washed Becky's body. He obviously did that to frustrate the investigation. Was her head found?"

"No."

"He might have hidden it to disguise her identity. Were her hands cut off?"

Jackie slammed the door on her imagination. "Unh-uh."

"Fingertips mutilated?"

She shook her head.

"So he didn't care whether she was identified or not. Other killers take the precaution of disguising themselves or using gloves or a condom. The point to keep in mind is that MO is dynamic. Killers evolve and refine their behavior by experience. Prison is postgraduate education."

Just what Pilar had said.

"But overconfidence breeds sloppiness, doesn't it? Maybe Rae's murder is where he started making mistakes."

Richard's smile was grim. "Let's hope so."

The clouds lifted and Pikes Peak zoomed into focus, snow dusting the veins in its granite face. Multifamily developments clotted the foothills like toy towns, and the roadside was littered with discount malls, chain motels, miniature golf. Exiting at Garden of the Gods Road west of the city, they passed low-slung complexes of high-tech companies.

The road narrowed without warning and an outcrop of burnt orange erupted like a giant molar. The asphalt continued to wind and two sheer walls of red rose from the earth to form a gateway, while a white mound with vertical cracks seemed to have sheared off and migrated forward from a gray monolith farther to the south. Horizontal layers of sediments were fractured and thrust upward, torn asunder and flung with the caprice of an overindulged child.

"What makes the rock so red?" Jackie asked.

"Iron oxide."

"How do you know?"

"Ah, the mysteries of chemistry . . ." They passed the mound and circled behind the cliff. "Where did you say Becky's body was found?"

"The Three Graces."

"We'll find it." His tone was reassuring, and when they reached the next parking area, he pulled into a space. "Let's get out and walk."

The sand by the side of the road was soft and warm as a beach, and as it trickled through Jackie's fingers, it left a powder the color of the rouge her aunt had worn. Wind whispered through tall grass, soaring above the susurration of insects until the high-pitched caw of a magpie brought her back.

Richard was standing by the guidepost at the head of the trail.

"The Three Graces is straight ahead," he said.

Jackie took a step forward, then stopped. Did she really want to see?

The breeze fanned the grass like water.

"Coming?" he asked.

The pavement was flanked by mountain mahogany and scrub oak and the sun made the leaves seem wet. At the foot of the path a circular clearing was partially enclosed by a low wall of polished stone. In the center rose three tall spires.

Hands loosely clasped to form a cathedral, fingers rounded and gnarled, the skin flowing from tip to base like wax. Fissures so black they could easily have swallowed a man . . . Jackie blinked, and the photo taken the morning Becky's body had been found three years earlier clicked into focus. She'd been thrust shoulders-first into the deepest crevasse. Arched feet protruded from the crack between the tallest spires, her ankles pressed together as if poised for a swan dive.

The park worker making his rounds at six that morning thought Becky was a mannequin placed there as a prank; it was only when he tugged at those dancer's feet and felt how cold and rigid they were that he radioed for help. Jackie stared at the gravel where they'd laid her on a tarp. Becky's head had been severed cleanly at the throat and her hips were twisted to one side.

"Higher, Susie . . ."

Glancing up, she saw a girl disappear into the crack between the tallest fingers. Just behind her scrambled her younger sister, while a heavyset blonde who had no business wearing shorts was snapping away with a disposable camera.

"One more!" the woman cried as the smaller child vanished from sight.

Get out . . . Fear for their safety or a sense of desecration, Jackie didn't know, but it was no place for—

Misinterpreting her concern, Richard shook his head in disgust.

"Exactly why they ban climbing," he said in a voice loud enough for the woman to hear. "These monuments can take just so much abuse. . . ."

What story did this place tell?

Ignoring him, the woman kept snapping away. The crest of one formation sprouted grass like hair and the texture of the rock was velvety and porous, like the snout of a golden retriever. The sun changed the color of the cliffs from rose to buff to tangerine and the clouds to umber and rust. It was a holy site, enshrined by figures of stone. Suddenly Jackie was struck by the Hollow Man's perversity and rage.

"Seen enough?" Richard asked.

She turned back to the Graces. The children had lost interest and moved on.

"Faith, hope, and love . . ." she said.

"Not much of that here," he agreed, reading her mind.

They headed back up the path.

"Why was she bent?" Jackie asked.

"Who?"

"Becky. Her legs were pressed together when they pulled her out, but her lower body was twisted to the side. That was how they found her and she was still like that when they laid her on the ground."

"Rigor mortis, I suppose. The stiffness tells us her body was found between two and thirty-six hours after she was killed. That's a pretty wide—"

"But I thought the muscles froze in the same position they were in at the time of death. Isn't Becky's posture *odd*?"

"Maybe he killed her an hour or two before she was dumped and twisted her body when he shoved her in the crack."

"But there was no blood at the scene."

"So it happened when he stuffed her in the trunk of his car."

Becky on the slab in the autopsy room, chest unzipped and torn open like a down vest on a warm day. Left breast flopped to one side like so much padding . . . And her legs were perfectly straight. By then the rigor was gone. Coincidence?

"Pontificate all you want about rigor mortis, it still doesn't explain—" She forced herself to slow down. "It looked deliberate."

Richard laughed and her frustration soared.

"And I suppose you think the Three Graces has some special significance, too?" he shot back.

What's the matter with you, Jackie?—it's staring you right in the face.

"Don't you?"

"I'll tell you what I think: shock value and access. A man of normal strength could easily carry or drag a 120-pound woman from the parking area to this spot. It's a tourist attraction, Jackie, he knew she'd be quickly found and whoever stumbled across her would be blown away."

"But you said the dump site gave insight into—"

"I'm not saying it's irrelevant, just that you shouldn't overlook the obvious."

"What's so damned obvious?"

"The fact that he left his victims nude in tourist spots. He wanted to humiliate and degrade them one last time. *That* was the posing—not some incidental twisting which probably occurred when he jammed Becky Cox between the rocks."

We're all captivated by your flights of fancy, Ms. Flowers, but the answer is much simpler. The application of elementary logic— And now she would explode and, like all the others, he would walk away.

"Of course, you could be right," Richard continued, wrapping his arms around her.

"You're one smug—"

"And you've been sniffing too much sandstone. Can we get out of here and find a decent place for lunch, or do you expect me to survive all day on that godawful muffin?"

T hey ate at a Mexican restaurant Richard thought he remembered from a conference he'd attended years before. Jackie's appetite had returned once they'd left the Garden of the Gods, and the smell of lard assailed them as they stepped through the door. They polished off combination plates of guacamole, tacos al carbon, and chilies rellenos with sweaty bottles of Dos Equis, and were still hungry enough to split a basket of grease-drenched sopapillas dipped in honey from the saucer on the table and wash down the entire mess with another round of beer.

"How old was your mother when she had her stroke?" Jackie asked.

"Fifty-five. It was a blessing Dad was already gone, because it robbed her of her speech. She acted in a theater group right up to the stroke. That's how Dad met her; he saw her in a play."

"And whisked her off to a fancy town house where they lived happily ever after."

"Pretty much, I'm afraid." He signaled the waitress for the check. "I guess this dive proves both our points."

"What points are those?"

"Memory plays funny tricks and a little imagination goes a *long* way."

The Volvo had sat in the sun, and they rolled down the windows until the air-conditioning had a chance to work. With the ride back home her last opportunity to pump her expert outside of an office, Jackie struggled to shake off her torpor.

"Speaking of families, when we first spoke, you made it sound like a psychopath could be the boy next door. Is that really true?"

"From the boy's parents' point of view, perhaps. No one wants to see their child as disturbed, but when you look back, there are always warning signs. Those are often reflected in his signature."

"You mean the beheading?"

"That's one small part, but the killer's signature can be more subtle than the MO—a tangle of symbols that are meaningful only to him. If he's in a rush, he may not have time to leave it, and if he's savvy enough, he may conceal it."

"But if we *could* identify the signature, it would be strong evidence that the same man committed all five crimes."

Richard looked sheepish. "Walked right into that, didn't I?"

"You said it, not me."

"Different people exhibit the same behavior for different reasons, which is why it's impossible to say crimes are 'psychologically identical.' The most you can ever say is there are specific similarities among the crimes that suggest the same *type* of person may have committed all five."

But Richard's skepticism had been eroded by intimacies and beer, and they both knew the fantasy was the heart of the defense. Jackie wasn't about to let him off that easily.

"What does he fantasize about?"

"Start from the premise that fantasies about violence are normal. Kids repress or forget what's said or done to them but not how they *feel*. What makes the kind of killer we're talking about different is that at some stage in his development he fuses violence with *pleasure*. As his fantasies evolve, he needs to act them out. When he ultimately does so, the fantasy is fueled rather than sated and evolves still further. By the time he starts committing these crimes, he already has an idealized scene, a victim and script in mind. Which doesn't necessarily mean he's satisfied every time."

"If he goes to all that trouble, why not?"

"Because at a certain point the urge may be so great, he'll be forced to select a victim on the basis of availability. When he departs from his plan, he's most vulnerable to being caught, but that's where the cops are his strongest allies. They overlook his mistakes because they think unless the MO and signature are identical in every case, the crimes couldn't have been committed by the same guy."

"If the signature isn't only the beheading, what else should we look for?"

"Patterns in victimology, sequence of acts, posing, trophies, dump sites."

"Dump sites? Did I hear that right?"

He raised his hands in mock surrender. "Bring me everything you find and we'll go from there."

It was just past three when they reached the turn for the beltway looping west of Denver, but traffic was already backing up.

"Let's skip all this," Richard said abruptly.

"And go where?"

"Red Rocks." The natural amphitheater famed for concerts and Easter sunrise. And—"Isn't that where another victim was left?"

"Carole Wade . . ."

In Pilar's photo she'd been leaning against a stone wall aflame with bougainvillea, fanning the pleats of her ankle-length skirt with one hand while the other extended above her head like a flamenco dancer flourishing castanets. A lacy camisole showed off the firm flesh of her upper arms, while turquoise-and-silver bangles and a matching choker played up her pale eyes. A publicity shot for the travel agency where she'd worked.

"The one who was kidnapped from the parking lot of her son's school?" Richard asked.

"He was at a recital. She went with a friend and slipped out for a cigarette. When the friend went looking for her ten minutes later, Carole was gone."

"Raped?"

Jackie nodded. Before or after she was killed—the pathologist couldn't say. . . .

"Washed?" he continued.

"And beheaded, like Becky Cox. And Rae Malone." Jackie blinked to banish the photo of Carole after she was removed from the cave. Arms outstretched, one higher than the other in a parody of the flamenco pose. Or was it a contorted embrace? "I've seen pictures of the spot, but I'm not sure where it is."

"He can't have dragged her far."

Richard swung west, and the landscape became more rugged. At Morrison they turned onto the winding road leading to the amphitheater. Here the rocks were a darker red, striations of magenta banded with white. High on the hillside Jackie spotted a building the precise color of the stone, visible only by the sun glinting off the glass. "Can we stop a moment and look?" she asked impulsively.

The thick smell of honey filled the air, with an undercurrent of lemon thyme. From the distance came the warble of a meadowlark. The liquid note steadied her head, but still she saw the abrasions on Carole's upper back. A stun gun . . .

Richard came up behind her and put his arm around her shoulders. "Are you all right?"

"That last sopapilla," she evaded.

"Maybe we should head down."

"I'll be fine."

They got back in the car and continued up the road, which wound past a trading post that sold postcards and snacks. "Want to stop?" Richard asked.

"No, it must be right ahead."

Past the entrance to the amphitheater Jackie's temples began to pound. Telling herself to focus on the task at hand, she tried to picture the site where Carole's body had been abandoned. The mouth of a cave, right off the side of the road . . .

Richard pulled onto the wide gravel shoulder.

"Let's stop." He spoke with genuine concern. "You're pale."

"We're here."

"What?"

"Where he left her. I recognize it."

Cold, evil chambers stacked one atop the other. A gaping maw with its upper lip flattened and striated like muscle tissue.

"Want me to come with you?" he asked.

To tell the Hollow Man's story she had to know what he knew, see what he saw. . . .

"No, I'm fine. Just need to stretch."

Jackie's sandals slid and sank in the gravel, and then she was wading knee-high through prickly weeds and pale grass. As she drew to the mouth of the cave, dampness caressed her flushed cheeks before she saw the dark spots in the roof of the upper chamber.

Why here?

Taking another step forward, she felt the yawning hush. The cave was listening. In its quiet coldness it was waiting.

Don't come any closer.

The lower chamber where Carole's body had been found was ten feet high and twenty feet deep, the upper one-half again as high and extending back farther than she could see. What was the killer trying to say?

Get out, now!

Reaching into the mouth of the lower cave, Jackie touched the ledge where Carole's slender leg had protruded. She turned and ran back to the car.

Tomorrow would be a bad day.

Chapter | Twenty-six

Which one did you say she was?" Jackie asked Pilar for the second time.

The woman in the photograph gazed back at her not unkindly, over half-glasses that only seemed to emphasize the youthfulness of her skin. The contrast was heightened by her silver hair and the unlined flesh at her throat. Her age could have been anywhere from thirty to fifty.

"Fern Kaplan," Pilar replied. She'd color-coded that file green. "Did you forget to eat this morning?"

Jackie had been staring at the photos of the Hollow Man's victims for the past half hour and her mind was going in a thousand directions. She'd forwarded her phone to eliminate distractions, but nothing helped—on days like these she couldn't remember what a toaster was called, much less the names of her client's victims. Thank God she didn't have to appear in court. "The one who was dumped at Pioneer Cemetery, right?"

Pilar wasn't fooled. "I'm getting you a cup of yerba buena and we'll start again." She headed for the kitchenette down the hall, her scarlet blouse as brilliant as the stand of poppies against Jackie's neighbor's wrought-iron fence. They'd made a showy mass with the violet penstemons in early June and Jackie pictured a swallowtail butterfly hovering overhead. . . .

As inevitable but not nearly so predictable as the rising moon, every three or four weeks she would awaken in a fog.

Like dry ice it would seep into the fissures of her brain and within two minutes after brushing her teeth or eating breakfast she could not remember whether she had already done so. If nothing demanded her immediate attention, she could sit at her desk for hours with thoughts flitting from one to the next in a parody of Zen, dwelling on all and nothing and following any notion wherever it might lead. Bad days tended to occur in clusters. They could be triggered by a poor night of sleep or a particularly stressful week. This episode had been building since the trip to the Garden of the Gods.

With effort Jackie returned to the photographs on her desk. Exploring the victims' faces was the first step in re-creating their states of mind, and Richard had said no detail about their lives was trivial. She left the woman with the silver hair and focused on the face staring up from the stack to her right.

Raven-haired, forty-something—deep tan and a flinty look. She'd had a makeover but it couldn't quite conceal competence and grit, the vertical groove between her eyes that branded her a worrier. Her most striking feature was those eyes—pale gray, almost colorless, pupils pinpricks of jet. Like a wolf. The cave at Red Rocks.

"Try this." Pilar had materialized at Jackie's side with a king-sized mug of foul-smelling liquid. "The travel consultant snatched from the parking lot," she prompted. The coral label obviously wasn't enough.

"I remember."

It was just the *names* Jackie couldn't recall. Now she saw Carole Wade's leg protruding from the mouth of that cavern, felt the icy dampness on her forearms and heard that sucking sound, an obscene variation of the sea in a pink-lipped conch from a tropical shore . . . She flipped to the next photo in the stack. The bougainvillea shot. Eyes as silver as the bracelets on her wrists.

"Do you think she wore contacts?"

"Contacts?" Pilar echoed.

"Her eye color, it's so extraordinary."

"And what if she did? Lots of women wear them for cosmetic reasons."

"Don't you think changing the color of your eyes is a little extreme?"

Pilar snorted. "*You* could afford to spend a little time—"

"She was at her son's school attending talent night. They found her—"

"—three days later at—"

"—Red Rocks. I know."

Pilar gave a satisfied smile. "Grandma's brew always does the trick." With or without sugar, yerba buena cured everything from colic to PMS.

Jackie thumbed through the blue-tagged file for the photo of Becky Cox at the law firm barbecue. Her eyes were hidden behind a pair of sunglasses. A candle in a net-covered lamp flickered at the center of the table.

"When was this taken?" she asked.

"Spring bash."

"I mean, what time of day?"

The photo had nagged her and she'd tried scanning police reports on the Cox murder when she came in that morning, but on days like this it was useless. The muscles behind her eyes pulsed like strobes and she'd wanted to grab the page with both hands to keep the print from sailing away.

Pilar shrugged.

"What's with the shades?" Jackie continued.

"She looks good in them."

"But they'd already lit the citronella candles, the sun was down."

"So she forgot to take them off because she was loaded. She'd have to be, to let *those* guys paw her like that."

Flipping to another photo, Jackie shook her head. Becky dressed for success in the prim but stylish suit self-help mavens still encouraged secretaries to wear in emulation of the boss. And shades worthy of Marilyn Monroe. She passed it to Pilar. "Look, here they are again."

"What are you suggesting, that Becky Cox was blind? She was a word processor, for Christ's sake!"

"No one wears sunglasses with a suit like that."

"A fashion statement," Pilar insisted.

Jackie reached for the photo of Fern Kaplan. Now the half-glasses winked ominously from their jeweled frame. Wordlessly, she flipped it to her investigator.

"An attractive alternative to bifocals," Pilar claimed, "I've been thinking about getting a pair myself."

"I'm telling you, there's *something* about these women's eyes."

"So what? Show me a forty-year-old broad and she's lucky bad vision's all that's wrong!"

Pilar had a point. But Jackie couldn't help returning to the studio portrait of Carole Wade. Her eyes were more than extraordinary, the gray was *unnatural.* . . .

"—know what your problem is?" Pilar was saying. "You've told so many lies about eye infections and lost glasses to get strangers to read bus signs for you, you're fixated—"

"What's so funny?"

They both turned to see Lily in the doorway, her red nylon backpack trailing on the floor. Jackie had brokered a truce between Lily's parents and the academy whereby the child would be promoted if she could pass a reading test by the end of the summer. Each morning she attended remedial classes and each afternoon the bus dropped her at Jackie's office. As far as Lily was concerned, that's what was in it for *her.*

"Not a thing," Pilar answered. With the practiced motion of a croupier, she swept up the crime-scene shots and slid them into Jackie's top drawer. "Want a can of pop, pet?"

"Sure . . ." As Pilar went down the hall, Lily came to the desk. "Who's she?" She was staring at the studio portrait of Starla McBride.

"Just a woman in a case."

"How come I have to read and you don't?"

"Who says I don't?"

"Pilar reads for you, I've seen her. . . ." She peered at the photo. "What's wrong with her eyes?"

The pounding in Jackie's temples stopped. "What makes you think something's wrong?"

"They're bugged, like she stuck her finger in a socket." So much for the wide-eyed look; Starla's plastic surgeon would have been crushed. "And the left one's bigger than the right. Is that the secret?"

"Detectives never tell." Could there be something to her hunch after all? She pointed to a photo of Carole Wade. "What do you think of this one?"

"She's like a *werewolf* . . ."

Pilar returned with two Cokes and another mug of the

evil-smelling tea. "There's a call for you on line two," she told Jackie. "I think you'll want to take it." Jabbing the proper button, she turned to Lily. "How about a hand of gin?"

Wondering how long it would take to upgrade the girl to poker, Jackie picked up the receiver. "Hello?"

"Ms. Flowers?"

"Speaking."

"This is Aaron." As if she didn't know his voice. "How's it going?"

"Going?"

"Your investigation." They hadn't spoken since the previous week at the final hearing before Worrell. "Into those girls."

"Okay . . ." The last thing she wanted was Aaron knowing details about murders he wasn't charged with committing.

"What did that shrink say?"

"I told you, he's going to testify that you were psychologically incapable of killing Rae Malone."

"But what did he think of *me*?"

Eager to please.

"That you're not a killer. What else matters?"

"So there was more?"

She tried to think of something to add. "He liked you."

"*Liked* me?"

"Yeah." That seemed to satisfy him, and suddenly Jackie couldn't wait to get off the phone.

"What else did the shrink say?" he pressed.

"About what?"

"The other *crimes*."

"Nothing yet." Had to get him off this . . . She reached for the folder with the red label. "But I'm glad you called, because I've been meaning to ask you something."

"What's that?"

Highly suggestible—as easy as switching the channel.

"Did Rae Malone have problems with her eyes?"

"Not that I know of." His confusion sounded genuine.

"Contacts, cosmetic surgery," she continued, "anything like that?"

"Why do you ask?"

"Just a crazy thought."

"Well, that shrink of yours didn't say anything about it."

"Dr. Hanna?"

"I told him Rae was just a classy divorcée looking for action, and he agreed." Aaron backpedaled an inch. "Well, maybe not in so many words, but that was the gist of it. Nothing about eyes."

He *agreed*? "What else did Hanna say?"

"Nothing," Aaron replied. "Keep me posted on that investigation of yours, okay?"

"You can count on that," she lied.

As she drove to Larimer Square, Jackie tried to keep her eye on the ball. She'd asked Pilar to take Lily home because she wanted to play out her hunch. The yerba buena had chased away enough of the fog to navigate, but after circling Larimer twice she gave up and descended into the covered parking.

The Mesa Gallery featured an artist whose palette was strictly pastoral. Cows grazing in tall grass, antelope on a slope lit by the sun. Nodding at the anxious-looking proprietress in the mid-calf deerskin skirt and concha belt, Jackie was relieved to see she was not the only customer. In heavy mascara and silver earrings that stretched her lobes like dinner plates, Carole Wade's former roommate was striving valiantly to make a sale.

"—just perfect for a foyer," she assured the man in cowboy boots. "Such a peaceful feeling, the glow—"

Jackie wandered to the glass cases at the rear of the store. Squash blossom necklaces, turquoise bangles, triple strands of Pueblo fetish beads. Carole must have bought her jewelry here—at a steep discount, judging from the prices. Nothing you couldn't find at the same quality elsewhere for less, and she wondered how much rent Carole's roommate paid for the privilege of the address.

The bell on the door tinkled as the cowboy left too quickly for a sale. Still trying to figure out her approach, Jackie turned to the nearest painting. A docile bovine stared back, silently chewing her cud. Before Jackie was prepared, the concha woman swooped down.

"Do you have a wall large enough? If not, I just happen

to have a couple of smaller pieces in the back. I've been saving them for the right collector."

Jackie didn't have the heart to mislead her. "Actually, I was hoping you could give me some information."

"Information?" Her wariness suggested an inexplicable dread. Perhaps the IRS had caught wind of that double set of books.

"You were with Carole Wade the night she disappeared," Jackie continued.

The sooty lashes twitched like spider legs.

"Who wants to know?" she replied.

"I represent a man charged with a crime similar to your friend's death. He—"

"I saw it in the paper. If he did what they say, I hope he fries."

"I understand your—"

"But I know he had nothing to do with Carole's murder."

"Who do you think killed her?"

"Her ex, but not without help. Todd was a weakling. Carole divorced him because he was a lousy role model for their son, Clayton."

According to the police reports, Todd Wade had a solid alibi for the night Carole disappeared, but Jackie wasn't about to look a gift horse in the mouth.

"What was she like?"

"Absolutely devoted to Clay, always looking for ways to make up for what was missing in Todd. Who could blame her for needing someone else on both fronts? Clay's flute lessons cost a bundle, but she was so proud."

"Did she feel she was in danger?"

"Besides Todd? Unh-uh."

"Was she seeing any particular guy?"

The concha woman's face turned to stone.

"No one special." She hesitated. "Do you have any idea how hard it is for a single mother to attract a decent man?"

"But Carole was so attractive. . . ." That seemed to mollify her. "I've seen a number of photos and I've always been struck by her eyes. Such an unusual color."

"She wore tinted contacts, so what?"

It *was* the eyes.

"—that make her a whore?"

"Whore? Who said—"

"Todd. That creep was watching her, I told the police, but they didn't believe me. And you want to know what the real irony is?"

Jackie was beginning to see why it was so hard for this woman to make a sale.

"What's that?"

"You know who's raising that precious boy now?"

"Who?"

"Todd's parents."

"At least he's not—"

"Don't kid yourself." Carole's friend drew on a bit of Native American wisdom. "If you want to know your man, just look at his mother."

Thank you, Dr. Freud. But if the eyes were the connection, where did Rae Malone fit?

Chapter | Twenty-seven

Pilar's cherry-red Spider had rush hour traffic eating their dust. As she whipped into a carpool lane and whizzed past irate commuters, Lily stared with admiration.

"Is this *legal*?" she asked.

Pilar shrugged. "Sign says 'Two or more.'"

They were on their way to Roxborough Park for a nature tour. According to the *Denver Post*, whatever crawled, flew, scurried, crept, bloomed, or slithered . . . And the place where Starla McBride had been dumped.

"Besides," Pilar continued, "you don't want to be late for Ranger Bob."

"Who's he?" Lily asked suspiciously. You never knew, this might be a trick to get her to the dentist. She'd asked Jackie just the other day if they could *force* her bottom teeth to grow out.

"The guy who's leading the nature tour," Jackie replied. "It's his brother who's the orthodontist."

Lily stuck out her tongue, stained an impressive grape from the golf-ball-sized jawbreaker she'd requested in lieu of dinner.

Turning west, Pilar motored past prime farming and ranching operations, an "equine clinic" for thoroughbred horses, and the sprawling Martin Marietta plant. Straight ahead lay the Dakota hogback, the vertical sandstone ridge black and brooding in the late day sun. As they headed into the hogback, the developments became pricier, culminating in a winding drive with a sign for a golf course just before the park.

"Wouldn't you know," Pilar muttered as they passed a fire station near the turnoff to the links. "Close to the fancy homes."

The wooden guard shack at the entrance to the park was unmanned, and the Spider jounced along the gravel road past the tawny browns and greens of rolling plain into the foothills. Now they were passing through the hogback, where the sandstone was flaky and crumbling. In the distance of two miles they'd traversed a billion years in geologic time and had yet to encounter a living soul.

"Maybe we have the wrong day," Lily said.

"Nope," Pilar replied. "I called this morning to make sure."

"At least we're on time," Jackie pointed out. "They must be waiting at the visitors center."

Pilar pulled over at the clearing where the wooden sign said *Caution—Rattlesnake Country* and Jackie jumped out, tucked four dollars in the provided envelope, and hastily taped the yellow day pass to Pilar's windshield. At the parking area they exited and headed for the visitors center. Lily became uncharacteristically quiet as the eerie scenery overtook them.

Great pinnacles of ruddy tallow, tilted sedimentary slabs—every surface flushed and rounded, molten. Jackie felt as if she were in the earth's intestines, that these fantastic shapes could have been created only by the wavelike motion of digestive tubes. To the east the Dakota hogback was a jagged ridge of softer pink. The only sound was a breeze rustling through a stand of aspen.

Suddenly a pair of black birds swooped above their heads. One gave a deep squawk and its mate responded with a high-pitched caw.

"An opportunistic bird," a voice behind them said. "See that stout beak? Ravens will eat anything from seeds to carrion."

The woman was clad in a ranger's hat and dark brown trousers, a tannish man-tailored shirt and hiking boots greasy with wear. The green patch on her shirt identified her as a representative of the Colorado State Parks Department and her name tag said Roberta Kunze.

"Real territorial," Ranger Bob continued, watching the ravens. "Knock an eagle or hawk clean out of the air. Threw a baby eagle out of its nest once to the rocks twenty feet below."

"Did it die?" Lily asked.

"What do *you* think?" Ranger Bob replied.

"Cool," Lily said, and for the first time the ranger smiled.

" 'Course, an eagle will kill a raven if it can catch him."

"Of *course*," Lily agreed, and Jackie knew the outing would be a success.

They waited five more minutes, and when no one else showed up, the tour officially commenced.

"Roxborough Park is a transition zone," Ranger Bob began, "where the plains meet the mountains. It has seven distinct microclimates, each with its own community of critters and plants."

Lily was bending to examine a woody patch with glossy foliage.

" 'Leaves of three, let it be; berries white, do not bite. . . .' " At the ranger's ominous tone, the girl looked up. "See that sign, sister? Poison ivy."

Lily jerked back her hand. "What does it do?"

"Toxic oil in the leaves can fry your skin. Ranchers breathe it in when they burn patches of the stuff. Now, *this* is the kind of friend you want to make." Ranger Bob stooped to pluck a sprig of tight-capped white flowers. "Yarrow, proper name *Achillea*. Stops the bleeding. Some Greek hero used it to treat his warriors' wounds."

"Achilles!"

"Someone like that."

Over Lily's head Jackie and Pilar exchanged a glance. They had never seen Lily so enthusiastic. If Ranger Bob wasn't careful, she'd have a new addition to the species populating her microclimates. As they continued up the path, Jackie noticed the rocks were speckled lime and yellow. Lichens. None of it resembled the photos of the place where Starla's body was left.

"—oldest rocks are to the west," Ranger Bob said. "Any day now the Front Range will be celebrating its three billionth birthday. The foothills are granite and gneiss, real old and hard. Now, the Fountain Formation—same stuff you see at Red Rocks and Garden of the Gods—is really just an alluvial fan stood up, sand from an old stream bed of the ancestrial Rockies."

Jackie gazed past her to the east. The salmon-colored stone didn't look right either. Maybe she should just enjoy the tour. . . . But the Hollow Man's sites *couldn't* be random. They had to have meaning—and that meaning was the key to connecting his crimes.

"What makes the rocks lean?" Lily asked.

"Originally, they were laid down flat, but when the plates in the earth's crust collided and the modern Rockies were born, the granite peaks caused them to tilt. I'll give you a booklet and you can read all about it yourself. Would you like that?"

Lily nodded with determination, and Jackie could have kissed Ranger Bob's boots. They headed back down the path and the ranger continued her spiel.

"Bobcats, foxes, coyotes, a few dozen elk, big herd of mule deer. For the mountain lions, a trip to Roxborough Park is like going to McDonald's. Prime hunting times are dawn and dusk."

"Have they ever attacked a person?" Pilar asked. If she didn't, Lily would have.

"June of last year, on Carpenter Peak." Ranger Bob pointed to the mountain to the west. "Guy made the mistake of trying to run. A mountain lion's front paws are bigger than their hind feet, so they can grab from behind and rake."

"Did it eat him?" Lily demanded.

"No, he grabbed a rock and hit him as hard as he could in the eye—"

"The *eye*?" Pilar said.

"Yeah, it had a sharp edge and he creamed that lion. Nearly took that eye out."

"What kind of rock?" Lily insisted.

"A nice heavy one. He swung as hard as he could. As I was saying, the mountain lion's goal is dinner. They'll break the neck to stop their prey from struggling and then feast off the kill for days, covering it with sticks and leaves between snacks."

"Did you ever see one do that?" Lily pressed.

Ranger Bob hesitated.

"Well, not so long ago, right about dusk, I did see a doe and her fawns running through the brush. There was this thrashing sound and the smallest fawn disappeared. A moment later it came out and tried to rejoin its mom, but it was dragged back in. Each time it came out it was limping a little worse. Six or seven times, and then I never saw it again."

"What happened?" Lily cried.

"Next day I went looking in the brush and saw tracks. Mountain lion and two cubs. Best I can figure, she was training her cubs to hunt. It's learned behavior."

"Couldn't you do anything to save the fawn?" Jackie asked.

"No, ma'am," Ranger Bob replied stiffly. "Only time we destroy an animal is when it poses a direct threat to our own species. That lion was just doing what comes natural—teaching her cubs to survive. Fawns may be an easy meal, but someone's got to show them how to do it."

Who had taught the Hollow Man to hunt?

They were back on the flat part of the trail and Lily knelt to poke a cigar-shaped lump on the left side of the path. An identical wad lay diagonally across from it, and the pattern was repeated for several feet.

"Coyote scat." Squatting down beside Lily, Ranger Bob picked up a clump and shredded it in her fingers. "See that little bone? It's a femur, and this gray stuff is hair. Must've eaten a vole or a deermouse. Come August, this scat will be full of grasshopper hulls. They're indigestible, like fur. See how he marks his territory?"

Lily tried to slip a lump in her pocket, but Pilar slapped her fingers away.

"Where are the rattlesnakes?" Jackie asked, to distract the child.

"All over the place, they like to sun themselves on the trail."

That explained why the nature hike began shortly before sundown, not to mention the ranger's ankle-high boots. Could the Hollow Man be afraid of snakes? Is that why he hadn't left Starla by the path? But it had to be here, the reports had said Roxborough Park and the landscape looked like the film clip they'd seen on TV.

"—tend to be on the docile side," Ranger Bob was saying, "but if you see one rattling and coiled, remove the threat by stepping back a pace or two. Eighty percent of bites are dry—snakes don't waste their venom on something too big to eat. Now, if the site immediately turns black and blue and starts swelling—"

"Don't rattlers hibernate in winter?" Pilar interrupted.

"Matter of fact, they do. We've never come across a hibernaculum, but they're along the hogback."

"What's a hibernaculum?" Lily asked, not missing a single syllable. Jackie could picture her getting her first library card. If not by the end of the summer, maybe fall.

"Snakes curl up in a gigantic communal ball to sleep. They were doing some digging out by Martin Marietta and tapped into a ball hundreds of snakes thick. Filled an entire dump truck. Carted them off to be burned."

"Jesus!" Pilar cried.

"Of course, there's a thirty percent mortality rate. Outside layer dies from exposure, the inside from suffocation."

The sun was almost gone and they hurried down the trail with the scent of Ponderosa pine tickling their nostrils.

"What's that?" Lily asked, pointing at a perfectly round hole in the rock.

"A pebble gets caught in a crack, and when the water flows through it churns. Eventually it wallows out a hole."

"Just like a pearl," Lily decided, "but the opposite."

"Exactly," agreed Ranger Bob. "You've got quite an eye, sister. Ever considered the Parks Department as a career?"

"What are those stripes?" Lily's cheeks glowed from the praise. She pointed to vertical streaks coursing down the face of the rock.

"Mineral deposits washed out by water. Some people call them desert varnish."

To Jackie they looked like tears.

By the time they reached the visitors center it was dusk. Last chance, Jackie told herself, my last chance to understand *why here*. . . . Yards from the parking lot she stopped.

Two ruddy boulders were cleaved into one. The stone to

the left had a pointed crest twenty feet high, the one to the right a mushroom dome sixteen feet from the ground. The crack that separated them was deep and narrowing. From this angle they looked like nothing so much as an enormous pair of buttocks.

The brush chittered and swelled and Jackie could hear the Hollow Man laugh.

The dump site of Starla McBride.

Chapter | Twenty-eight

Pilar insisted on driving up and back from Black Hawk before dark.

"Those tour-bus drivers tank up more than once before the return trip," she told Jackie as a Doubletree double-decker whizzed past them going west.

It was ten on Thursday morning, five weeks since Starla McBride had disappeared from the Painted Lady casino and only eleven days before Aaron's trial. It was also almost exactly three years since Becky Cox went missing from O'Dell's in LoDo, a fact that Jackie's investigator had brought to her attention that morning while perusing the Rockies schedule.

"We have to go to O'Dell's tonight," Pilar had said. "The Rockies are playing Houston, just like the night the Hollow Man got Becky. When else will the stars be aligned?"

"The Rockies haven't had a star since Becky Cox was snatched," Jackie pointed out. "They haven't even had a winning season since—"

"You just don't like crowds," Pilar growled. She'd worn her purple Rockies cap to the office every day until Andres (the "Cat") Gallaraga became a free agent.

But the doubleheader made sense. Weren't the Hollow Man's hunting grounds just as important as the spots where he'd left his prey? Jackie was developing a sense of him, but vital links were still missing. Richard said the killer's haunts were too diverse, his choice of victims too random to conclude the five crimes were the work of one man. The eyes weren't enough; if she could just get a sense of how the Hollow Man chose them . . . The last trip, she reminded herself; they were almost out of time.

"If I can convince Richard to testify the Hollow Man killed all five women," Jackie said as they slowed for a traffic light, "I'll never have to call Mark Best to the stand."

"And, having won yet another spectacular acquittal, *you* can ride off into the sunset with Dr. Doom. . . ."

"What exactly *is* your problem with Richard?"

"Aside from the fact that he's dedicated his career to being a shill for the DA?"

To their west lay Mount Zion with the "M" whitewashed on its face by freshmen and seniors at the Colorado School of Mines—Jackie still had difficulty picturing Mark graduating from the prestigious engineering school only to become his brother's employee.

"Hanna's like Safeway," Pilar replied. "All those goodies on the shelf and no delivery."

"Because I haven't slept with him, or because he's not willing to prostitute himself by giving an opinion in which he doesn't believe?"

"Touchy, touchy . . ."

"You can't blame him on either score. Both events are in my control, and one has *nothing* to do with the other."

"I get the picture."

Jackie settled back in her seat. The narrow two-lane had no shoulder, and from time to time a sign said *Falling Rock. That* picture she could read. "How'd your meeting with Becky's sister go?"

"Kim's a nasty piece of work. We met at her estate in Greenwood Village. Very posh. Becky's husband, Phil, walked out on her because their kid, Seth, was a handful. Kim resented the hell out of her younger sister."

"Why?"

"Maybe because Kim settled for the stockbroker with the paunch. I got the impression Phil dumped Seth on Kim after Becky died. In fact, just before I left, the school bus dropped him off. Seemed like a nice enough kid to me."

"What did she say about Becky's eyes?"

"You were right, she was photosensitive. Converted a disability to a fashion statement with those designer shades."

"Enemies?"

"Becky worked her way up from the word-processing pool to supervisor on the night shift, and finally secretary to a partner in the litigation department. But her stock at the law firm was heading south."

"How come?"

"She was making Disability Act waves about reasonable accommodations to her eye problems and didn't find the firm's offer to send her back to the night pool so amusing. At the time she disappeared she was threatening to sue."

"Seventeenth Street firms can be rough," Jackie agreed. "Probably some homicidal senior partner trying to protect his retirement . . . Did you file that new demand for Brady materials?"

With an investigator like Pilar, Brady demands were strictly strategic. She had law enforcement sources the DA himself couldn't tap.

"Sure did. We got Pratt's reply yesterday—'all relevant materials previously delivered.' "

"Nothing about Sunny saying Rae saw Aaron Thursday night?"

"I went back over everything and you were right, not a word about it. You'll have fun on cross."

"What were you able to dig up on Starla McBride?"

"Just what you'd expect. Computer programmer with a minor in aerobics and a modest face-lift." Pilar raised her voice to be heard over drilling in the background, which was drowning out the rush of water in the creek. "An 'endobrow' for the forehead and a procedure for fatty tissue and extra skin around the eyes. The tits were real, by the way."

"Social life?"

" 'She gave too much,' according to her friends." Pilar sighed. "Whatever the hell that means."

"All these women were divorced. What about Starla's ex?"

"One of her coworkers said he would have killed to get her back, but I did some nosing around—the guy has a live-in girlfriend and they're well on their way to starting a second family. Sound familiar?"

Emotionally vulnerable single mothers who felt safe right

up to the moment they were snatched. There was more, she could feel it.

"Based on the interviews and investigatory files," Pilar continued, "none of the victims seem to have crossed paths. The pattern becomes clear only when you look at MO and dump sites."

"He certainly planned," Jackie agreed, "and didn't mind taking risks. To take them from public places without anyone noticing, he must have used a con. He moves easily in a wide range of settings—O'Dell's, the casino, the parking lot of that middle school, the salon in Cherry Creek. That means he's sophisticated, physically attractive, charming—"

"—and packs his own tools. If he wasn't such a maniac, I could go for him myself." Pilar continued in a more serious tone. "Both Starla and Carole had abrasions on the chest that could have come from a stun gun, but there was no follow-up with tissue samples. The pathologist who examined Fern saw something similar, but no one was looking for stun guns back then."

"What about the lines on Becky and Fern?" After the trip to Garden of the Gods and Red Rocks, Jackie had re-examined the autopsy photos. The awkward positioning of their legs when they were found had bothered her, and sure enough Carole had faint red coils on her arms.

"He tied them up to restrain or carry them."

"But why bother if he had a stun gun? And the marks were on their hips and upper limbs. Binding wrists and ankles would've been more effective." Jackie shook her head. "I think those women were already unconscious or dead. Richard says smooth transfer marks—not abrasions or contusions—mean they weren't struggling."

Pilar frowned. "What do you think he was doing?"

"Some kind of ritual. If I had to guess, I'd say it's connected to the positioning of their bodies. Becky's and Carole's hips were twisted *before* he jammed them into those rocks. It must have personal meaning to him."

"Which is as good as saying we'll never know."

"Remember, our job isn't to solve these cases, just—"

"—convince Dr. Doom they're related."

The road suddenly widened to accommodate picnickers, and Jackie was reminded that one of the Hollow Man's earliest victims had been dumped there. "When was that actress at the Central City Opera House murdered?"

"Louisa May? August of 'eighty-five."

"While I was recovering from the bar exam. And Duncan Pratt was interning in the Gilpin County DA's office. Do you suppose that's—"

"—why he's so bent out of shape about your resurrecting unsolved crimes?"

"I wonder if he worked on the case."

Pilar chuckled. "Why don't you ask him right before his opening statement? That'll *really* piss him off."

At the city limit an enormous structure resembling the carcass of a steel dinosaur had been dug into the mountainside.

"What's that?" Jackie asked.

"The next multilevel parking structure for the Riviera."

"Riviera?"

"Black Hawk's answer to topless beaches and virgin sand."

The whole town was a strip mine.

As they turned onto the main street, Jackie saw a sixty-foot crane tearing at the sky. Around the corner the face of the mountain had been blasted away to create room for another parking lot. Only wire netting and cement prevented it from falling onto the cars below. Motorcycles, heat, and flies—even the lobelia and petunias spilling from window baskets in rooming-houses-turned-casinos had a garish, synthetic look. The only honest thing about the place was a stand of sweet peas thriving in the dust along the side of the road.

There were so many elderly people on the sidewalks that Black Hawk could have been a freakish retirement community. Like extras from a low-budget horror flick, they stumbled about in fanny packs, sun visors, and orthopedic shoes, and carried plastic cups the size of cottage cheese containers. Finally locating a place to park across from a real estate office, Jackie and Pilar climbed out of the Spider and narrowly avoided being hit by a black and white People's Choice bus careening down the road.

"Seen enough?" Pilar asked in an I-told-you-so voice.

"As I recall, the purpose of this trip was to visit the place where Starla McBride was abducted. You could at least show a little respect."

"It's a damn good thing I'm not a practicing Catholic," Pilar replied tartly, and set off down the street. From the mouth of Shannon's came a rousing Irish jig. Next door stood the Leprechaun Café. At eleven in the morning it was already mobbed, but Jackie had yet to see a single child. Not to mention a dog. "How about here?"

"Do you actually want to *eat*?"

"This is bound to be easier on a full stomach."

The restaurant was packed with grandparents chowing down on chicken-fried steaks the size of dinner plates. The plastic containers they carried were filled with coins for the slots.

"The only people under sixty are waiters and parking lot attendants," Jackie said after the hostess led them to a table barely large enough for two.

"Remember that law they passed a couple of years ago? No one under the age of twenty-one allowed in a gaming area."

"This entire *county* is a slot machine."

The waiter returned for their orders. He was dressed in a green plaid vest and had dark circles under his eyes. Didn't these places ever shut down?

"Prime rib sandwich," Pilar said. "And a cup of clam chowder."

Jackie gave her a questioning look but kept her mouth shut.

"A bowl of chili," she said when the waiter turned to her.

"That portion is grande. You might be more comfortable with a cup," he added tactfully, "and the onions and cheese on the side."

As he moved off, Pilar whispered, "Don't you wish you'd ordered the prime rib?"

"We should have come at night," Jackie replied, "when Starla was here."

"I got news for you, honey. This *is* night."

Judging from the people, it might as well have been. Jackie looked at the place mat to keep from staring. A green and white map of the United States and Ireland, with Black Hawk the epicenter. *Why travel over 5000 miles,* it asked, *when you can come to Black Hawk for lots of good old-fashioned Irish Luck?*

The kind Starla McBride had found?

Jackie sighed. "Seriously, I don't know how we're going to get a reading on Starla's state of mind in broad daylight."

The waiter returned with their food. Pilar's was a slab of beef three-quarters of an inch thick. An enormous mound of potato salad shouldered aside ramekins of horseradish and jus. Under the artificial glare, the cheese accompanying Jackie's chili had an iridescent sheen.

"What's the evening crowd like?" Pilar asked the waiter.

"Younger but no different." Glancing behind him, he lowered his voice. "If you know what I mean."

"See?" Pilar said as he scurried off.

"Well, I'll give the Hollow Man one thing," Jackie replied. "He certainly is versatile. Not to mention determined."

"How so?" Pilar asked.

"He marked his territory the length of the Front Range."

"Shades of Ranger Bob and coyote scat. You think he kept their heads as trophies?"

"Unless he did something he doesn't want us to know with the eyes . . ."

"Jesus!" Pilar exclaimed. Dipping meat in jus, she downed it in one bite. "What do you make of the dump sites?"

"Limited accessibility, chosen carefully in advance. I'd say he grew up here. And got off on the shock value."

"Shock value?"

"He left the bodies where he *knew* they'd be found." Jackie pushed aside her half-eaten plate. "And not just by anyone, but tourists and kids. Almost as if he were warning them."

"Of what?"

"Garden of the Gods, Red Rocks, even Pioneer Cemetery—they're holy places, but he's defiling them, flaunting his power." She shrugged in frustration. "Who knows what kind of god he worships?"

"He may be godless, but he's savvy about the law."

"Why do you say that?"

"Abducts in one county and dumps in another, and smart enough not to leave anything tying him to the crime. Which brings us to an unpleasant subject."

"Rae Malone. You think she's the one who doesn't fit."

"Well, face the facts. Rae's the only one snatched from

home, the only one whose head was found, the only victim where semen was left."

"Her killer could have used a condom *after* the bareback rider."

Pilar shook her head. "If I were Duncan Pratt, I'd have a pretty good argument that you've stuck your client's neck in the noose."

They paid the check and, without kissing the Blarney Stone by the cash register, went in search of the Painted Lady.

T he casino where Starla McBride spent her final quarter featured Reel Deal Poker and Jumbo Jackpot, and as Jackie ascended from the craps tables on the second floor to blackjack on the third, the listless expressions of the patrons began to get to her. She felt as lost as they seemed. Last chance, last chance . . . Dispirited, she stood just outside the rest room where Starla was last seen.

"A wolf would look pretty good," Pilar commented, "after dropping a few hundred bucks at the slots."

"What makes you think she was losing?"

"House always wins. Anyone who comes here is a loser before they plunk down the first coin."

Standing at the threshold to the ladies' room, Jackie could see what Pilar meant about a wolf looking good. These people were not truly alive. The slots were life-support systems operated with the rhythm of a shunt, and she was no closer than ever to identifying the killer's pattern. But the Painted Lady put to rest one doubt.

"At least we know the Hollow Man isn't Aaron," she told Pilar. "With all those lonely housewives looking for affairs, why hit on zombies in Black Hawk?"

L ocated in the century-old Stanford Hotel and within sight of Coors Field, O'Dell's tavern could be described only as eclectic. Stained-glass lamps suspended from the molded tin ceiling sported a columbine motif, and a blue marlin sailed from the top of the bar. From tail to bill it must have been seven feet long.

"That fish is plastic," Jackie said as she and Pilar made their way through the pregame crowd to a table for two.

"Who'd bother making anything that ugly? Some jack-ass caught it down in the Gulf."

The crowd was as mixed as the decor—men in polo shirts and khakis for the ball game, women in everything from business suits to shorts. Hard-core Rockies fans had come equipped with rain gear and were peering out the windows at thunderclouds rolling in from the west. Almost every man Jackie saw wore a wedding ring.

"This is no sniff bar," she said.

Pilar reached for a bar menu. "Maybe thinking Becky was looking for a pickup ain't the only thing the cops got wrong."

"How much could this place have changed since she disappeared?"

"Besides the fact that every Rockies game was sold out then and fans were stacked three deep at the bar? Not much."

"What'll it be, ladies?" The barmaid was young and enthusiastic but hardly Hooters material.

"Pint of Guinness," Pilar replied. "And chicken wings."

Jackie ordered limeade. "They wouldn't have met here," she continued after the barmaid moved off. Though not entirely indifferent to attractive women walking by, the men wore a glazed look. "The only thing these guys have on the brain is sports."

"The bulb in the little head ain't even lit," Pilar agreed.

"So it wasn't a pickup after all, but someone who was waiting for her. Maybe even someone she knew."

"Becky wouldn't have come here for a casual screw either."

"If she wasn't planning to pick up a guy or go to the game, why *did* she come?"

Lighting a cigarillo, Pilar eyed a group of women across the room. Well-groomed secretaries dressed for success. "Probably scouting out her next employer. This place is filthy with downtown lawyers. You don't threaten to sue your boss and expect a promotion."

Jackie's drink had a refreshing tartness and granulated sugar in the bottom of the glass. As she watched a table of men in Rockies caps, two glanced at their watches to make sure they wouldn't miss the opening pitch. "Sports are like slots. They induce stupor, not pheromones. No wonder the police never found him; they made the same wrong assumption they did in Black Hawk."

"You can hardly blame them," Pilar pointed out. "How many Denver cops drink at O'Dell's? All they know is a good-looking divorcée disappears from a bar when the team's in town. Goes off to the john and never comes back. Next morning they find her car in the lot across the street, two days later her body in Garden of the Gods. Denver and El Paso County play footsie over jurisdiction for weeks, the trail goes cold. End of story . . ."

"And here we are, three years later, trying to figure out what he did with her head."

Pilar looked at her over the top of her glass. "You're really enjoying this, aren't you?"

"*Me?*" Jackie set down her drink. "You're the one who wanted a nice, juicy murder—"

"—and you were tired of date rapes. Quite a change, isn't it?"

"Yeah. Now all I have to worry about is whether the guy who's sacking my groceries is sizing me up for a crack in a rock."

Jackie wasn't about to admit the leering fiends and severed heads that haunted her dreams, much less the awful feeling she'd had in her study just the night before. A moment when she'd felt someone was out there, she was not alone. But it was more than that—and more than the challenge of defending a man for first-degree murder when the odds against winning mounted by the minute. There was something about these victims that was driving her on, a sense that they—and *she*—were being toyed with.

"Well, cheer up," Pilar said. "In a couple of weeks this will all be over and you can go back to arsonists and pimps. You'll look back on this and—"

"Speaking of johns, that's the last place Starla was seen too. I think I'll check it out."

The main bar was separated from the hotel lobby by glass doors and a corridor. At the far end of the hallway and to the left of the bar was another lounge called the Cruise Room. With its art deco decor, tight booths, and red lighting, it was like being stuck in the middle of a maraschino cherry. A place where you took a date once you'd picked her up, not where you went cruising . . .

"Can I help you, miss?"

A waiter in a white jacket stood at her elbow.

"I was looking for the ladies' room."

"Just go down the stairs."

The staircase was two short flights with a landing that turned. The rest rooms were at opposite ends of the hallway, and the stalls in the ladies' room were covered by floor-to-ceiling louvered doors. Jackie closed herself in and settled on the seat.

The cubicle was dark, but she could still hear the noise from the bar. Water dripping in a stopped-up sink was suddenly very loud. She was separated from music and laughing voices by a door, an antechamber, a corridor, steps, a landing, more steps, and a high wooden rail. The isolation suddenly overwhelmed her, and she jumped off the seat and rushed out the door. Disoriented, she turned the wrong way and almost ran smack into the wall. Strong hands steadied her.

"Going to the game?"

He was so close, she could smell his aftershave. And another odor, some kind of soap . . . Jackie pulled from his grasp and stepped back.

Mark Best.

"What are *you* doing here?" she asked, and heard the shrillness in her voice.

"Aside from being mowed down by Denver's premier female defense attorney? Actually, I was exiting the john. And I had some crazy idea about watching the Rockies skin the Astros."

"Sorry about that."

"No need to apologize, you saved me a call." His khakis were pressed and he was wearing a polo shirt—just like half the men in the bar. "I've been wanting to ask how your investigation's coming."

"Investigation?" Hadn't she just had this conversation with Aaron?

"He told me about it."

"Aaron?"

"The investigation."

"Just normal trial prep."

"Have you decided whether you're going to call me as a witness?"

Jackie started for the stairs. She didn't like being put on the spot. "I'll make that decision at trial."

"What about Aaron?" Mark continued. "Will he testify?"

She turned. "This really isn't the time or place."

In the dim light his eyes seemed black.

"You call the shots, then. Your time, your place . . ."

"I'll be in touch," Jackie said, and took the stairs two at a time.

Found what you needed?" Pilar had polished off most of the chicken wings and ordered a second round of drinks.

"Mark Best." Jackie glanced over her shoulder, but he was nowhere to be seen.

"What did he want?"

"To pump me about the case." She reached for her drink and downed half of it before realizing it was ale. "But Lily's wrong about him. He's harmless."

"If there was more to that business with the plumbing company, we'd know by now."

"Yeah." The tightness in her chest was beginning to ease. "You know how crazy I get before a trial."

"So what else did you discover on your field trip?"

"He accosted her outside the john and convinced her to step outside."

"Who?"

"The Hollow Man. That's where he picked up Becky Cox." Jackie looked back over her shoulder. Sure enough, you couldn't see the stair rail from the bar, much less the corridor leading to the street. "But it wouldn't have mattered when or where. He came here because he knew this is where *she'd* be, and that she wouldn't be picked up by anyone else. If she had been, he would've taken her another time."

"You sound awfully sure."

"Becky Cox wasn't random any more than Starla McBride or the others. These women weren't kids, Pilar, and they weren't so hard up that they frequented pickup joints. Whether they knew him or not, if the Hollow Man didn't know *them,* he wouldn't have been able to get them to go with him without anyone noticing. He followed them to places where he knew they felt safe. And if he knew the other victims, he must have known Rae Malone."

"I still don't see—"

"Think of the wound patterns. Except for those abrasions, their bodies had no marks."

"If you discount the *decapitations*—"

"He approached with a con that, based on his familiarity with each victim, he knew would work. Once he got them away from their friends, he overpowered them so quickly, they had no time to put up a struggle. That makes him either very strong or technologically proficient. It's all about control."

"Whoa. What about—"

"Compare his latest victims to the earlier ones. Those who weren't decapitated had ligature marks around their necks. Any other injuries occurred after death, because there was little or no bleeding. Even sex was post mortem. He loosened and tightened the ligature to maintain control, and—"

"But this has nothing to do with Rae Malone."

Jackie was silent for a long while.

"I disagree," she said. "The pattern is entirely consistent if you make one important assumption."

"Which is?"

"That because of overconfidence or deteriorating mental state, the killer kept taking greater and greater risks. That's why he snatched Rae from her house and left her head. He'd become so grandiose, he thought he was invincible."

"I buy that all those other murders were the work of one man. But isn't it still easier to assume Rae's was different simply because a different guy committed it?"

"Except for one thing." Jackie paused. "Do you know how many other decapitations have occurred in the metro area in the past five years?"

"Offhand, I can't remember a single one."

"Exactly. Damn few, if any. The odds of Rae's murder being entirely unrelated to the others are slim to none. The reason he's tracked these women to the places where they were accosted and dumped them so far away isn't just to make it difficult for the cops. He's marking his territory. I don't think he'd tolerate competitors. Maybe the audacity of Rae's murder is a warning to *them*."

"He could have tried an ad in the *Post*—"

"What do you think he did after he abducted them?"

"You mean besides cutting off their heads and having sex?"

"I mean, where were they kept?" Jackie persisted. "We know he didn't decapitate them where they were dumped, because no blood was found."

"Let's see." Pilar furrowed her brow. "If I was the Hollow Man, I'd want a quiet place. Nothing *too* fancy, mind you, but—"

"He needed light, skill, and uninterrupted privacy."

"Not to mention time."

"Someplace secluded." Finishing her ale, Jackie pushed back her chair. The sports crowd had departed and the patrons who were left looked like regulars. Older, with a forlorn air . . . Definitely not a sniff bar. "Which is another reason why it couldn't have been Aaron. Where would he have cut off Rae's head—in the back of his brother's SUV on the way to Dinosaur National Monument?"

A s soon as Jackie returned home, she called Richard Hanna.

"We've wrapped up our investigation," she announced. "You'll be getting a carton of materials on all five murders tomorrow. Investigative reports, autopsy photos, the works."

"Don't keep me in suspense," he replied. "Do you think they're related or not?"

"I wouldn't want to influence your opinion."

"I think I deserve more credit than that."

"The same man killed them all. He's gotten away with it because of confidence, sophistication, and skill. His MO is high risk—he takes his victims from public places where they were known or went with friends, and they had steady jobs, so he counted on them being missed. My guess is he tangled with the law before."

"And?" Richard prompted.

"He knew them."

"Knew them?"

"The victims weren't random. They were women he already knew and was stalking."

"How the heck do you know that?" Richard sounded amused—was she trespassing on his turf?

"Because of the spots where they were grabbed. And the abductions were so fast and smooth—"

"I don't mean to prejudge this, Jackie, but the fact that these victims were taken from public places suggests just the opposite. If he knew them, why not wait till they were alone?"

"Because he gets off on knowing they feel safe at the very moment he makes his move. Kind of a one-way intimacy, a means of destroying their security and control."

Richard burst out laughing. "You should have been a novelist, not a lawyer. With your imagination—"

The first doubts crept in. "But I've been to those places, Richard, I've—"

"You've been *where*?"

She was trampling on his expertise, and he definitely didn't like it.

"Black Hawk, O'Dell's." She was starting to sound ridiculous. She should stop before she lost every shred of credibility. But her pride won. "The Painted Lady."

"You've gone way overboard, become too involved with the victims—"

"But that's what you said to do! 'No detail is too trivial . . .' "

"What you need is a good night of sleep," he said sympathetically.

"Aren't you going to read what I'm sending you?"

"Of course," he assured her. "I'll go over all of it carefully and get back to you before the trial. But remember, the goal of profiling is to suggest a specific type of individual who may have committed a crime, with specific psychological and emotional characteristics. No matter how compelling a case your material presents, the most I would ever be able to opine is that there are specific similarities among the crimes, and the same *type* of offender committed all five."

"I understand. . . ."

"Look, Jackie. I want you to know I admire you immensely. I don't know any other lawyer who would go to the lengths you've gone to defend your client."

Now she was completely humiliated.

"But . . . ?"

"But nothing. I think you're great."

Maybe she hadn't made *quite* such a fool of herself.

"Speaking of psychological characteristics," she replied, "I've learned a few more facts about Aaron's past. Did you know his father made him duke it out with his brother over the family business?"

"He mentioned it, yes."

"Why didn't you tell me?"

"Because fostering competition among children—even adults—is all too common, and from the little Aaron said, he and his brother seem to be close. Frankly, I didn't think you'd care."

So he didn't know Mark was Aaron's alibi.

"And I understand you discussed certain details about Rae's murder with him," she continued. Might as well get it all on the table.

"How else could I probe him on his potential involvement?"

What an ass she'd been! "What else did he say about his parents?"

"If anyone's to blame for Aaron's problems with Mark, it was their mother. She stood by and let it get out of hand."

"Is that unusual?"

"In her case it was more than passivity. Mark is quite a bit older, and after he was sent away to school, the mother made Aaron her little man. Mixed messages are always tough for a boy to sort out. I don't want to get too Freudian here, Jackie, but the need to win his father's approval is undoubtedly why Aaron felt compelled to beat Mark."

Now Richard was in his element, their friction a thing of the past.

"We do seem to be having a power struggle," Jackie agreed. "He's distrustful but eager to impress."

"Not surprising in the least. Aaron is still seeking his mother's approval, but he never mastered issues of control stemming from his resentment of her. Undoubtedly, there's transference."

"Transference?"

"How Aaron emotionally views *you*. Look at what you represent to him, Jackie. He's placed his life in your hands in a quite literal sense. He both fears and needs you. Not unlike the position a therapist finds himself in with a patient, and that can be a two-way street."

"What do you mean?"

"If he's doing his job right, a therapist can't help responding emotionally to his patients. So long as it doesn't get in the way of treatment decisions—or, in a lawyer's case, the advice you give—it's perfectly normal. You've probably experienced it with other clients in the form of overidentification."

"But with Aaron—"

"I'm impressed you can identify with him at all. But right now you're his mother figure and his salvation, so don't be surprised if he comes across as ingratiating and confused."

"Great. Just the thought I wanted to sleep on."

Richard laughed again, a delighted sound that somehow made it all right.

"I'll call you as soon as I've reviewed that mountain of stuff. And who knows, I might even agree."

Chapter | Twenty-nine

They had a two o'clock appointment at Rubio Melendez, but Jackie was running late. Pratt's witness list had arrived just after lunch. No surprises, but she had to review it with Pilar, and by the time she finished, she was fifteen minutes behind.

As she drove up the side street to Lily's school, she saw the girl waiting inside the fence. The gaily painted monkey bars and slides might have been guard shacks and a holding cell. Clinging to chain link like a wrongfully accused waiting to be hauled off to death row—*I don't belong here, it's all a mistake!*—Lily's mute appeal would have won a reprieve from the sternest warden. The only problem was she had no audience. Most of the children were gone, and from where Lily stood, rescue was nowhere in sight.

Jackie parked around the corner and waved, but Lily was facing the other way. A girl about her age with flossy yellow pigtails and a mini designer jumpsuit was emerging from the door by the playground. Jackie watched as she approached Lily, swinging her pink nylon book bag.

"Lil-*lee!*" she sang in a voice as innocent as the ribbons in her hair.

A smile broke over Lily's face and she turned in anticipation. Jackie stopped, not wanting to interrupt. A friend, she thought, she's finally made a—

Dropping her book bag, the girl sucked in her breath

and let out the loudest belch Jackie had ever heard. Lily's head whipped back to the fence, a mask of humiliation and outrage. When she spotted Jackie, she recomposed her features in their customary show of disdain.

"What was that about?" Jackie asked, approaching them. Seeing an adult with Lily, the girl's hands flew to her mouth. Jackie ignored her.

"What?" Lily replied.

"That girl . . ."

"I don't know what you're talking about."

At the car Lily tossed her backpack in the rear with a nonchalance worthy of Marlene Dietrich and climbed into the passenger seat. She said nothing about Jackie being late.

"We have just enough time to get to Rubio's," Jackie said. Having her nails done professionally for the first time was Lily's reward for scoring a "very good" on her reading test earlier in the week, and with the trial starting in ten days, Jackie could use a trim and an eyelash tint. Not to mention the other reason for their visiting the ritziest salon in Cherry Creek. "Still interested in that manicure?"

"Whatever." Lily's tone was meant to convey that she was tired, *tired* of it all.

"You know what you need?" Jackie said. "A makeover. A total, complete—"

"They don't do makeovers in China."

"Who said anything about China?"

"When I'm big enough, I'm going back there." She was staring straight ahead through the windshield, biting the inside of her lower lip to keep it from trembling.

"Why?" Jackie asked.

"My babies are there."

When Lily's parents first brought her home, she would respond only to the name Meimei. *Little sister.* Britt said that in China the older girls took care of the babies at the orphanage as soon they were able; with virtually no chance of marriage, such girls often stayed until they were adults and worked there the rest of their lives.

"Well, in the meantime you're never too young for a makeover."

Lily turned, the first signs of interest stirring in her flat features.

"No gunk on my skin . . ."

"So skip the facial."

"Will they cut my hair any way I want?"

That much less to coat with Vaseline. Jackie would deal with Britt later.

"I'll give you my appointment with Lalo."

At the salon Lalo greeted Jackie with an overblown display of affection while surreptitiously examining her roots to assess whether she'd jumped to a competitor or merely been negligent. Apparently mollified by what he saw, he turned to Lily.

"And what does the little lady want?"

"The works!" she cried.

Lalo eyed her shrewdly, then glanced over her head to Jackie.

"Nothing *too* extreme," she mouthed, but he was already leading Lily to the room where they kept the smocks. Returning to the front desk, Jackie asked if Phylicia was available. She'd been counting on early Friday afternoon being a slow time, and sure enough Phylicia was in back on break.

"What can I do for you, dear?" A foot taller than Lalo, Phylicia was every inch the professional. "Looks like you could use a tint."

Was it that obvious?

Surrendering to Phylicia's reassuring hands, Jackie soon found herself tilted back in a sink for a shampoo.

"You have great body," Phylicia said, expertly adjusting the water so it wasn't too hot. "Love that natural wave. Just a little honey on the roots to scare off the gray."

"You know," Jackie began, "I always wondered what it would be like to let yourself go. Wake up one morning and your hair would be silver . . ."

Phylicia's laugh traveled down the strong fingers massaging rosemary-scented shampoo into Jackie's scalp. "Don't we *wish*."

"I knew a woman who had the most gorgeous hair. She grayed early and I always suspected she used a rinse, but I could never get her to admit it."

"If the color went when she was young and she managed to look good, it must be in the genes. I had a client with silver hair and a fabulous complexion, and the combo was a knockout."

Go for broke.

"This woman wore half-glasses on a gold chain and it drove the guys nuts. They could never figure out how old—"

Phylicia's fingers paused. "You don't mean Fern Kaplan. . . ."

Jackie swiveled in the chair, sending a warm stream of suds into her left eye.

"Did *you* know Fern?" she asked.

"Honey, that ain't no rinse. She used a permanent chemical dye."

"Just awful, what happened to her."

Adjusting the water to a cooler temperature, Phylicia washed away the shampoo. "Would you believe *I* was the last one who saw Fern alive?"

So the police report had said.

"You're kidding!"

Phylicia finished with the rinse and began toweling Jackie's hair. "The things I could tell you . . ."

But Lily was at Jackie's elbow in a maroon smock that reached to her ankles. Her face was covered with green mud that smelled like mint.

"Lalo says if I keep it on long enough, when they take it off, it'll be hard as rock. He says I can hang it on the wall like a mask!" Lily's newfound friend would charge her parents a bundle, but they could afford it. "And he thinks I'd look good in punk."

"*Punk?*" Jackie asked.

"Nothing too funky," Lily reassured her blithely. "Just shorter for the summer."

To hell with Britt.

"I guess it's okay, then." Jackie watched as Lalo led her to the manicurist. An acolyte to the goddess of beauty. Or, as Pilar would say, the patron saint of beauty salons. She returned her attention to Phylicia.

"I knew she disappeared from Cherry Creek, but I had no idea—"

"They think it was right in front of our shop, because she never made it to her car. She was parked around the corner."

"Just like any other time . . ."

"Uh-huh. She was all excited about a party she was going to that night. It was Valentine's Day. You know, a costume thing. Lalo did an incredible job with her hair. It was thick as rope, so he had a lot to work with. Coils and twists, piled on her head in the shape of a heart. She was going as the Red Queen. And her next stop was Pioneer Cemetery."

"I'll bet you knew her better than just about anyone else did. . . ."

"Her day job may have been librarian, but at night Fern liked to trot."

"Trot?"

"Country-western bars were her thing." Phylicia tilted Jackie back and started mixing eyebrow tint in a doll-sized cup. "She had a great bod, that was part of her thing about keeping men guessing. You want to go copper or wheat?"

"Copper, I guess. What about her family?"

"Early marriage, divorce. I think there was a kid. She never talked much about it." Phylicia began brushing colorant into Jackie's eyebrows. "I'm going just a half shade darker. Makes your eyes bigger."

"Any particular man in her life?"

"I doubt it. She would've had to tell him her age."

Lily tugged at the sleeve of Jackie's smock. "Look!"

The manicurist had worked a small miracle with her nails. The ends had been filed smooth and her cuticles pared back with an orange stick. But it was the color that was most striking: a metallic bronze that cast sparks under Phylicia's light.

"Gorgeous," Jackie said, and meant it.

"And Lalo's doing my hair."

"What did you decide?"

"You'll see. . . ." She danced off.

"Cute kid," Phylicia said. "Not the mom, are you?"

An hour later they were back in the car. Lalo had sworn the purple would wash out and the Statue of Liberty spikes were nothing more than mousse. But Jackie's dismay was halfhearted; she was still picturing Fern Kaplan with silver hair piled high, visions of a night as the Red Queen dancing to a cowboy beat in her head.

"Where to now?" Lily asked, preening as she strode down the sidewalk. The afternoon was young, and she *owned* Cherry Creek.

"Don't you have homework?" Fern with the silver hair and half-glasses that drove men crazy . . .

"Just a stupid assignment. I have to bring in something with words, but it doesn't matter what they say. It's part of this dumb idea about making *friends* with the alphabet."

"What are the other kids doing?" Strangled, raped, body cleansed . . . Head sliced clean from the shoulders and never found.

"One kid's dad's giving him a rubbing of the sign on the door of the place where he works. It says the year the building was made. You take a piece of paper and lay it against the sign, then color it in with pencil. The words show up on the paper like invisible ink."

"You could do something like that. . . ." But Fern wasn't dumped at a park. Did that mean she didn't fit the pattern?

"The teacher said find something old. They're trying to trick us into learning numbers." Her voice was fierce with longing. "I have to show them, Jackie. . . ."

Where was her head? Suddenly she had to see.

"How about a gravestone? Would that work?"

"Does it say how old it is?"

"*Two* dates: not just the year the person was born, but when he died."

"Cool!"

Pioneer Cemetery was bounded by the Platte River to the north and elevated gravel-filled railroad tracks to the south, and on the left side of the entrance stood a mailbox.

"Special delivery," Jackie whispered in a spectral tone as they drove past, and Lily giggled.

That they were the only visitors was unsurprising; the cemetery's heyday had been decades earlier. They continued on the paved path until they came to the oldest part, where granite and sandstone crypts faced a dirt road leading down to the Platte. Jackie parked and Lily jumped out of the car with pad and pencil in hand.

"Jackie, look!" she cried.

The gravestones were marked Yee and Wong, and beside them lay an Ahlskog born in 1820. Garlands of stone decked wrought iron hoops in the shape of peony trellises, and Lily ran from one burial site to the next, carefully laying paper over dates and scribbling with her pencil. With one eye on her, Jackie went to explore the vaults dug into the hillside at the north end.

Where had Fern's body been left?

Location, location, location. Occupying the prime spot in their inhabitants' day, these vaults now overlooked a polluted stretch of the Platte. Not here . . .

Fern crouched, kneeling. Hands loosely clasped behind her back, what should have been her chin touching the earth. Had he uncoiled her hair and left her head, the silver tresses would have cascaded like water. . . .

Closing her eyes, Jackie pictured the setting. A marble base, the lower parts of two granite pedestals. As she turned east toward the highway, she spotted a riderless stone horse. Ten feet high, surrounded by granite obelisks that hovered like temple guards. Slowly, she made her way to them. And then she was standing at Fern's final resting spot.

The Red Queen, on her way to the ball.

Off with her head!

What in God's name had he done with it?

Chapter | Thirty

As the man circled the eleven hundred block of Gaylord, he noted the front porch was experiencing a revival. On this decidedly middle-class street of Denver Squares, one or two had been enclosed for sunrooms, but the balance were decked out with wicker chairs and small tables in a grass-roots effort to return to the village green. The exception was a spacious model two doors in from the corner that not only spanned the front of the structure on Gaylord but wrapped to offer a surprisingly intimate view of the house next door. Which was a problem, because that home belonged to Aaron's lawyer.

The house with the porch stood out from its neighbors in two ways: excessive ornamentation and the neglected condition of the front lawn. Festoons of beribboned forget-me-nots and egg-and-dart trim had been painted cranberry and green to match the balustrade, establishing once and for all that taste and money did not go hand in hand. Marching up shellacked steps to the front door with its welcome mat and cheery wreath of dried lavender and roses was a family of plaster geese.

Circling the block once more, he resisted the impulse to wave at the man rocking gently on the swing. On his first pass the seamed face and stooped shoulders had raised a warning in his mind. The last thing he needed was an elderly snoop with nothing but time on his hands. When the figure hadn't budged by the second time around, he realized it was a mannequin. Aaron's lawyer had some *very* peculiar neighbors. . . . Parking was tight, restricted to residents with permits during Botanic Gardens concerts, but this time he found a place catercorner from her house. Opening his window, he settled back in his seat.

For a Friday night the street was almost too quiet. Judging from the tricycles on the sidewalk and the Hondas and Subarus at the curb, many of her neighbors were couples with small children. Too exhausted by the end of the week and too impoverished to spring for a sitter and evening out, they could be counted on to go to bed early and sleep through anything but the baby screaming. The only dogs a pair of arthritic old setters way up the street, streetlamps spaced a comfortable distance apart . . . From the middle of the block came low laughter and the clink of glass. Enjoying their privacy, not the sort to intervene.

The house was dark, and he wondered what was keeping her. He knew she parked her car in the garage and entered from the back, flipping on lights as she moved through the first floor. Perhaps she'd gone grocery shopping; sometimes she did that at odd hours, though he'd noticed she avoided driving after dark. For someone so intent on exposing secrets, what a mystery she was!

Her abode differed from the others in subtle but telling ways. Neat and trim, attempting not to stand out but with the closed-off feel that said its owner observed much and revealed little. Planted in a front flower bed was a discreet sign from a home security company that had long since gone out of business—a sham. The blind on the window behind her porch was angled to permit light while obstructing the view from the street, but the tall pane of glass overlooking the strip of garden to the south was bare. Oddly enough, that was the window facing the hideous porch. Peep show for the neighbors?

He immediately rejected that thought. It wasn't her style and, from what he could tell, the couple next door were almost never home. Glancing at their porch now, he thought he detected a small movement just beyond the arc of light. He decided it was the glider. His thoughts returned to Aaron's lawyer.

He *knew* Rae. This woman was still a stranger.

In the distance a siren wailed and died. He shifted in his seat. Porch lights were winking out, and the breeze carried the velvety scent of pink and lavender night-blooming stock. The wooden man halfway up the block rocked silently beneath a bare bulb. And suddenly her porch window was bright.

Craning his neck, he followed the progression of lights—front hallway up the oak staircase to the landing, onward to the second floor. As the upstairs fixture flashed on, he pictured her slipping off her clothes in the bedroom and padding naked to the bathroom at the rear of the house. First a shower, then towel-dry her hair . . .

The light in the hallway flicked off, and he imagined her walking down the stairs in her robe, coppery hair damp and loose around her shoulders. She never ate after bathing—so fastidious!—but might fix herself a cup of tea before bed. When he saw her shadow cross the window in the front room, he knew she was in her study.

He climbed out of his car, closing the door with a soft thunk. He kept it unlocked, key in the ignition. Ducking his head, he crossed the street in a loose-limbed gait that said he had nothing to hide. When he reached the sidewalk, he slipped into her yard. The light on the porch next door had been extinguished, and he slipped between the houses to the narrow patch of garden by her window. Kneeling in soft earth beneath the sill, he listened. One by one he absorbed the sounds of night.

Crickets, a faint hum overhead, and the timeless drone of cicadas. A sitcom played in a second-floor bedroom two doors down. A mosquito tickled his left ear, but he ignored the impulse to swat it. Next door, still nothing . . . Slowly, he rose on the balls of his feet and looked inside.

She sat in the brocade armchair across from the shelf of minerals. Her eyes were closed and her head was thrown back so her hair flowed over the headrest. In her bare feet and embroidered green robe she seemed defenseless.

He'd seen this room before. It was excessively orderly, almost like the home of a blind man. More orderly even than the exterior of the house, a fact she would not like to have become known. Though the narrow table built into the

wall below the shelf was designed as a desk, its surface was
bare. The space had the contemplative feel of a study, a
refuge in which to read or compose. Except for the mineral
collection, the walls were bare. There were no books, nor
paper of any kind.

She crossed to the minerals and selected one. Returning to her chair, she held the rock to the lamp and gazed
into its depths. As she raised her hand, the sleeve of her silk
robe unfolded like the wing of a butterfly. Just as the light
passed through the cloth and illuminated the outline of her
arm, he saw through her facade.

She was clearing her mind so she could think.

At the faint rustling he froze.

Dropping back on his heels, he shrank into the shad-
ows. Every cell in his body focused on the external threat. As
his eyes adjusted to the blackness, he saw a child staring at
him from the balustrade of the house next door. For a full
minute they silently watched each other.

"Who *are* you?" the child whispered.

He made no reply.

A little girl was peering at him through the rail of the
porch. In the dark all he could see was short, spiky hair, eyes
like coals . . .

"Lily?" a voice called.

The girl stared like a cat assessing its prey. She knew he
was there.

The door behind her opened and a woman emerged.

"Lily?" she said again. "It's bedtime, time to come in."

When the girl didn't respond, the woman came to her
side of the porch.

"You know you shouldn't be looking in Jackie's window!"
she scolded.

Gazing into the darkness one last time, the girl followed
her in.

Chapter | Thirty-one

Nine days before Aaron Best's trial was to start, Jackie had more on her mind than the fact that it was the second week in July and she had yet to plant her annuals. She was on her way to the Botanic Gardens to watch Richard's bonsai class. He hadn't called about his opinion, and she hoped showing up would be a reminder. More than that, she wanted to see how he performed before a live audience.

Expert witnesses came in two brands, hard and soft. The ideal "hard" expert was Mr. Rogers, a high-school science teacher in horn-rimmed glasses and tweed coat whose job was to convince a jury of what could be measured or shown. "Soft" experts like Richard were dicier because their opinions were based on intuition and reason. For the jury to give credence to his testimony, he would have to tap into shared experiences, connect with each juror on an emotional level. Could there be any tougher sell than a bonsai class of kids Lily's age?

Rounding the corner onto York, Jackie passed the low bed of annuals leading to the entrance to the gardens. Carmine verbena, silver and purple salvia, flaming zinnias—designed to catch the eye of motorists on the busy thoroughfare and not please discriminating horticulturists like her aunt, who would have been aghast at the gaudy display. Once again she was reminded that she was a month late on her promise to take Lily to the garden supply center to spruce up her own beds. Tomorrow, if there was time.

The woman at the desk in the lobby said Healing Hands met in Classroom B at Mitchell Hall. The stairs to the basement under the exhibition room opened onto a windowless hallway brightened only by gleaming linoleum. Rounding the corner, Jackie saw a lit room at the end of the corridor.

"—allow us to get closer to nature. But what we really learn is to be patient, and that nature itself may prevent us from carrying out our plans."

Richard stood before a room filled with children and adults. Directly behind him was a counter with a sink, and Jackie could see a line of faces turned expectantly toward him. His soft voice continued.

"Bonsai is, above all else, a tree. But our goal is to create an appearance that reminds the viewer of something other than the tree itself—a scene, perhaps a forest or seascape, a rocky outcrop on a windswept hill. . . ."

Spotting Jackie out of the corner of his eye, Richard winked at her. Not wanting to interrupt, she moved down the hall.

Classroom B was furnished with Formica-topped tables and filled to capacity with boys and girls aged seven to twelve, each accompanied by a parent. On one side of the sink stood a dozen small junipers in plastic nursery containers, on the other a stack of rectangular glazed pots. Reaching for a juniper, Richard sharply rapped the side of the container and carefully removed the plant. The roots were snarled in a tight ball.

"We start by freeing the roots . . ."

With a three-pronged miniature rake he began teasing them out and with infinite patience isolated the tap root.

"Now, this may come as a shock, but the big guy's got to go." With a decisive snip Richard removed it. "That will enable these side ones to grow." He fanned out the remaining roots. "Before we talk about pruning, I want each of you to pick out your own plant and try to imagine its final shape."

There was a rush to Richard's end of the room, and he stepped into the hallway to speak to Jackie.

"I haven't had time to review—" he began apologetically.

"That isn't why I came. I wanted to watch your class. You don't mind a visitor, do you?"

"The lecture was a little truncated." He winced at his pun. "I try not to load them down with too much philosophy."

"It's fascinating. How do you determine the final shape?"

"If you're really interested, I'll give you a private lesson." They glanced through the door, and Jackie saw most of the students had returned to their seats. "Stay tuned."

Richard circled the tables, stooping on occasion to communicate with youngsters at eye level. Though initially reluctant to get their hands dirty, with a little encouragement their parents soon joined in.

"Now let's talk about shaping the trunk and branches. Remember what I said before about bonsai beginning with an image in your head?" This time even the smallest child nodded. "There are certain traditions that guide our vision. One is asymmetry." Richard pointed to a specimen he'd brought, a grouping of spruce planted on the left side of a shallow tray. "Doesn't look very balanced, does it?"

A studious-looking boy raised his hand.

"Yes, it does!" he cried.

"Why's that?" Richard asked.

"I don't know." The boy struggled to articulate, turning to his father in frustration. Finding no help from that quarter, he soldiered on. "I guess because all the trees are on one side but there's the same amount of empty space on the other."

"Exactly." Beaming, Richard turned to a second specimen. "Who can tell me what you like about this?"

"There's nothing extra."

"Great! Discarding excess and leaving what counts is extremely important to bonsai. Now I'm going to show you one more." He reached into a large grocery sack. "Can anyone tell me what's special about this?"

A ten-inch grotto of rhododendron and pines nestled in a moss-covered rock. The pines had been pruned so the needles at the top resembled palm fronds.

"No takers?" he continued. "This bonsai illustrates freedom from tradition. I included it to show you not to be afraid to follow your own vision." He left it on the counter and picked up the juniper whose roots he'd trimmed. Turning its plastic container upside down, he mounted the plant on the bottom of the pot.

"Now for some basic rules to get you started. The first thing we do is remove one of each opposing pair of branches. Think of climbing a telephone pole, using hand grips on alternating sides." Starting from the bottom and traveling up, he made decisive cuts flush to the trunk. "Now let's take off the ones that point down."

When he was finished, he handed out branch cutters and scissors and returned to Jackie.

"What did you call that last aesthetic principle?" she asked.

"The grotto? Abandonment of convention, freedom from orthodoxy. In simpler terms, imagination." Looking over her shoulder, his smile faded. "Without which none of us can survive."

She turned to see a pudgy boy on the verge of tears. In his zeal to prune, the child had clipped both opposing branches instead of just one, and his mother was tersely berating him. Richard excused himself and went over. As Jackie watched, he gave the mother's arm a comforting squeeze and suggested she take a break. She stepped into the hallway and he knelt at the boy's side.

"The wonderful thing about plants," Jackie heard him say, "is you always get a second chance. We have a bunch of alternatives. If you don't want to wait for that branch to grow back"—the child gave a teary grin—"we can either graft a new one on or you can change your vision for the final product. Now, what shape did you want your juniper to have?"

Suddenly she wanted Lily to meet him. "That boy will probably remember what you did for the rest of his life," she said when he rejoined her.

"What?" he replied. "An adult standing up for him instead of making him feel even worse?"

"I'm thinking of signing Lily up for your next course."

"The Chinese girl you told me about?"

"She's a budding naturalist. The ranger at Roxborough Park said she had quite an eye."

"Don't tell me you went there too?" He shook his head

and laughed. "I'll never underestimate you again. Or your formidable legal prowess."

"Speaking of which—"

"If you want to know the truth," he replied in a voice that was suddenly serious, "I've been putting off my opinion. I guess I'm delaying it because I'm afraid that when this case is over, our relationship will end. . . . Come over with her tomorrow." He was so intent, Jackie wondered if she'd missed something.

"Who?"

"Your helper. We'll show Lily my collection, see if she's really interested."

There went the trip to the garden center. But this was more important.

"What time?" she asked. He would be wonderful on the stand, and afterward . . .

"Brunch." He looked over his shoulder. "I'd better get back to the class. We're supposed to get into the basics of wiring."

She lingered a moment longer.

"Wiring is what gives your tree its shape," he was saying. "But it's a clumsy method, which should be practiced only when absolutely necessary to encourage growth in a classic style. . . ."

Chapter Thirty-two

The girl wandered over to the elevators in Richard's lobby and frowned at the vines on the brass grille.

"Lilies don't climb," she said.

"Maybe it's a trumpet vine," Jackie replied.

"The leaves are wrong."

"Since when do you know so much about plants?"

The look Jackie received was tolerant if not pitying. "You know, there are such things as *libraries*."

Richard's appearance spared Jackie the necessity of a reply.

"So this is Lily!"

As he greeted the girl, he gave Jackie a light kiss on the cheek. The gesture was not lost on Lily, whose eyes instantly narrowed. Jackie completed the introductions and kept her fingers crossed as the elevator ascended. The storm-cloud face had not made an appearance since Lily's haircut, but the humidity was rising. They stepped into the skylit atrium.

Richard's pond shimmered in the morning sun and gaudy shapes twisted below the surface. A fish with silver scales and a scarlet cap emerged, its mouth working like an infant's. Lily knelt and reached out, but it darted off. Rather than being discouraged, she patiently waited for the next. Ink-colored and pugnacious, this one's eyes protruded on conical supports and its fins were as gossamer as tissue paper.

"Why do they run away?" she asked.

"They're looking for food," Richard explained. "When you hold your fingers like that, they think—"

"Can I feed them?" she cried.

Saved by the koi.

While Richard got the fish food and showed Lily how to use it, Jackie smelled coffee in the kitchen. With relief that the two of them had found common ground came a ravenous hunger. She knelt beside them and watched as Lily delightedly cast flakes of dehydrated protein like bread on the water.

"I'm starving," she announced. "What was that about brunch?"

Richard had prepared waffles with pats of strawberry butter molded in the form of roses. As he poured orange juice, Jackie noticed he'd put the maple syrup in individual pitchers. The size a child could handle.

"Do you know the story of the sphinx?" Lily asked. She'd recognized the statue spouting water in Richard's pond.

"Lion's body but the face of a woman," Richard replied. "As I recall, she tore apart anyone who couldn't answer her riddle."

"Who slew her?"

"Oedipus."

"Where?"

"Um, Athens."

"*Thebes.*" Lily took a sip of juice. "Who were the Titans?"

Not about to be wrong twice, Richard took his time answering.

"The sons of Uranus and Gaia." He looked at Jackie and winked. "For the uninitiated, that's heaven and earth."

"How many were there?" asked Lily, miffed at his attempt at levity.

"Hmnn." Richard took his time spreading butter on his waffle and dousing it with syrup. "Six."

"Good guess." Picking up her pitcher, Lily poured a drop of syrup on a corner of waffle and cut a piece no bigger than four holes in the grid. "Who—"

"But they had six sisters," he continued.

Frowning, Lily pushed back her plate. "Who was Andromache?"

"Wife of Hector, prince of Troy." He offered breakfast sausages to Jackie before spearing two of his own.

"These are delicious," Jackie said.

Richard held out the platter to Lily, but she shook her head.

"I'm a vegetarian," she replied.

Vegetarian?

"You need animal protein," Jackie told Lily. "Maybe in a few years—"

"She looks pretty healthy to me," Richard said.

"Teiresias?" Lily continued without missing a beat.

"The blind seer . . ."

On and on they went, in a Hellenic version of *Hollywood Squares.* Each time Richard provided a correct answer, Lily would take a sip of juice or a tiny bite of waffle. Just as Pilar predicted, the girl feared being usurped. It was exhausting to watch, but as the meal progressed, Lily began to display a grudging respect.

"Would you like to see my greenhouse?" Richard asked her.

"Does it have fish?"

"Something you might like even better."

She jumped from her seat. She'd finished her juice but eaten less than a quarter of her waffle, and her butter rose remained untouched. Jackie started to gather plates, but Richard intervened.

"I'll get those later," he said.

"You guys go ahead. This will only take a moment."

As they left the kitchen together, Jackie heard the game resume.

"What was Heracles' sixth labor?"

"Cleaning the Augean stables."

"What was the *eighth*?"

With their footsteps clattering down the hall, Jackie took her first real look around. In addition to the restaurant-quality refrigerator and stove, Richard's microwave could accommodate a Thanksgiving turkey, and there were at least two machines that might have been the dishwasher. Washing the dishes by hand would give Richard and Lily more time together, and she was relieved to be alone.

In the cabinet below the sink she found soap and a sponge. As she transferred the sausages to a bowl from the cupboard, she couldn't resist peeking in the refrigerator. It held half a dozen jars of olives, capers, pickles, and pimientos and two bottles of Dos Equis. Limp celery in the crisper and a head of rusty iceberg told the rest of the story. No woman, and he cooked only to entertain.

Returning to the sink, Jackie soaked the pans and washed and dried the dishes. Someone must come in to clean at least twice a week, the floor was spotless. . . . She had run out of excuses for joining them.

Behind the ten-foot pane of glass at the end of the corridor, blue sky beckoned, and in the park below, the sunbathers would be out in full force, their brightly colored towels spread across the grass like so much wash. She listened for Lily and Richard but heard nothing. It wasn't as if the wall would suddenly *open*. . . . Retracing her steps, she entered the room opposite the kitchen.

The study was just as she remembered it but more so. Peaceful, luxurious—Jackie sank into the leather couch across from the desk. This she could get used to. The rich colors of the rug brought out the red in the maple bookshelves and the very walls were permeated with the faintly spicy aroma she associated with Richard. Sandalwood . . . But she was there because of Lily. And Aaron's trial began in eight days.

Directly across from her sat Richard's desk. Immaculate on her first visit, its surface was now covered with neat stacks of paper. She rose from the couch. At the threshold she listened again for voices in the corridor. Hearing nothing, she stepped behind the desk.

Six stacks—one for each victim, the chronology and analysis she and Pilar had prepared set aside. Jackie skimmed the material on Rae Malone. First the investigative report, highlighted in yellow by Pilar with check marks and notes in a hand that must have been Richard's. Settling in his chair, she tried to read them. The cursive was neat but hopeless, but the meticulous annotations confirmed he was as singleminded as she. Next came news clippings on the case—Pilar's penchant for thoroughness.

Halfway through the material on Carole Wade was a news item she didn't recognize. The blurry photo was clearly

Carole and the headline looked like the *Post*, but the story was a couple of paragraphs longer than the one Pilar had pulled. A later edition? Next came a toxicology report Jackie was certain she'd never seen before—an indecipherable string of numbers, none highlighted or otherwise marked. On the back was scrawled, "FYI, but keep it on the QT," and the initials of one of the pathologists in the medical examiner's office. Richard had done his own research into the crimes. Coming out against Pratt scared him more than he was willing to admit, but he was willing to give the defense a fair shot. . . . Where were the crime-scene photos?

The banker's box was under the desk. It held an accordion file for each crime with an index in Pilar's enviable script, and the manila envelope with the crime-scene pictures. As Jackie straightened, the chair swiveled, and she came face-to-face with a series of framed eight-by-ten-inch photographs on the wall directly behind her head. Group shots taken with an inexpensive camera.

At first she thought they were all the same. Smiling children in a semicircle with Richard in the middle, holding out potted junipers like offerings. His classes at Healing Hands. Then she realized they'd been taken in different years. She glanced around the room. With all his honors and awards, no diplomas or plaques were displayed. Just these.

Hearing voices in the corridor, she jumped from the chair and made it to the couch as feet clattered down the hall.

"Medusa was a *heroine*," Lily was saying.

"If she was a heroine," Richard countered in an eminently reasonable tone, "why did Perseus slay her?"

"She lived on," Lily insisted, "not even his curved sword could stop her. Perseus put her head on his shield and she kept turning his enemies to stone. . . ."

For better or worse Richard and Lily seemed to have bonded.

Can I use the bathroom before we go?" Lily asked, with a meaningful glance at Jackie. She'd had enough of this— they were supposed to leave right after brunch.

"She's very important to you, isn't she?" Richard said

when he returned from showing Lily the way. In the library's soft glow his face was suddenly naked.

"Yes," Jackie replied, "and I don't know exactly how that happened."

"Lily's quite adult for her age."

"She puts on a good front."

"You must spend a lot of time together. What about her parents?"

"Britt and Randy have been great. They've done nothing but encourage—"

"She models herself on you."

"You're giving me too much credit," she said lightly. "I thought the Titans were a bunch of missiles, not gods."

"Speaking of which, her command of mythology is awesome."

Did this have more to do with *them* than Lily?

"We've considered entering her in the Homeric trivia bowl. Is there something wrong—"

"Not at all. Mythological creatures can be great friends. They seldom make the demands real people do."

In his eyes she saw challenge—and *desire*.

"Jackie?" Lily had returned. "Can't we go?"

"Of course," she replied, her gaze still on Richard. "But Dr. Hanna will have to allow us to reciprocate."

"I'll bone up on my Greek."

"What'd you think of the bonsai?" Jackie asked Lily on their way home.

The girl shrugged.

"Okay, I guess . . ." Still peeved about the disagreement over Medusa?

"Want to sign up for Richard's class?"

"Frankly, Jackie, I don't understand why he doesn't just let those plants *grow*."

So much for enrolling her in Healing Hands.

"But wasn't that pond spectacular? I know you liked his fish. . . ."

Long silence.

"They were okay, I guess."

"Is something wrong?"

"No."

Jackie glanced at Lily. She'd arranged her features in inscrutable expression number two, the one that meant she really *didn't* want to talk. "Did something happen in the greenhouse?"

"He just showed me his plants. It was when—"

Jackie stopped. Taking Lily by the shoulders, she forced the girl to meet her eyes.

"What did he do?"

"I told you, *nothing*." She looked away and Jackie released her. "It was what I found." Reaching into the back pocket of her shorts, she withdrew a small velvet bag. Midnight blue, with a silken drawstring. She handed it to Jackie. "Look inside."

Jackie opened the bag and shook its contents into her hand. A garnet drop earring with antique filigree. Elegant, from another era. There was only one.

"Where on earth did you find this?" Jackie asked.

"In the table next to his bed."

"What?"

"He said I could use the bathroom. . . ."

"Did he also say you could snoop through his drawers? What did I tell you about asking first?"

"He wants us to think he likes you, but—"

She certainly couldn't fault Lily for loyalty. And if Richard was already involved with another woman, what was all that business a moment ago?

"That's no reason to go through his personal things!"

Lily's only response was an appraising look, wiser than her years. Jackie dropped the earring back in the pouch and slipped them in her pocket. They resumed walking.

"Was the other earring there?"

"Nope. Just that one."

She would *not* ask what else Lily saw. She had no right to be jealous, no claim on him. If some woman had left it there after spending the night, what business was it of hers? They were almost home, and this was as good a time as any for a heart-to-heart about the mysteries of the opposite sex.

"Honey, let's stop for a minute." Jackie sat on the edge of the low stone wall in front of the house with the wooden mannequin on the swing. The few neighbors out on the street were mowing their lawns or tending their yards, and no one was paying them any attention. "We need to talk."

"What about?" Lily perched on the wall beside her, looking at Jackie with guileless eyes.

"Boys—*men*—say all sorts of things, some of which they don't mean." Where was Pilar when she needed her? "What I mean is, dating is a slow process of learning about each other. When you finally fall in love, it will be after you've gotten to know lots of boys and—"she ignored the grimace—"decided *that* person is the one you really like. But up to that point—"

"Is that why he lied to you?"

"Richard never said he wasn't seeing anyone else." Not in so many words, but if kissing a woman over a saucepan of hollandaise wasn't a basis for thinking a man was interested, much less inviting her to a fancy brunch and practically daring her to . . . Of course, *she* was the one who'd put the brakes on it. "And besides, who said I was interested in him?"

"What are you going to do with the earring?" Lily asked.

Maybe I'll just make him sweat.

"Return it, I guess," Jackie replied.

Lily raised one eyebrow, and Jackie suddenly knew she hadn't fooled her one bit.

"Anonymously, of course." Jackie poked her playfully in the ribs. "Can't you just see his face when he opens his mailbox and finds that velvet pouch?"

They giggled the rest of the way home.

Chapter | Thirty-three

The pouch looked newer than the earring.

Seated at the desk in her study Monday night, Jackie examined it and the garnet earring under her lamp. Although the velvet was worn at the seam, the silken string was shiny and looked like it had never been knotted. The screw-back fastener and filigree made the bauble either a real antique or a clever imitation, but the stone didn't look like glass.

All day long Jackie had been trying not to think. She wasn't about to mention the earring to Pilar and risk an I-told-you-so; her investigator had had nothing but disdain for Richard since he'd waffled on the Hollow Man defense, but at the same time thought Jackie was nuts for deflecting his pass. She probably would have applauded Lily's audacity—but all that was beside the point.

To whom did the earring belong?

If the earring was left by an old girlfriend, why hadn't he returned it? Real or costume, it looked valuable. Of course, it could have belonged to his mother or his ex-wife. She could conjure up any number of scenarios, but the one thing she couldn't get past was the fact that there was only *one*.

Jackie opened her briefcase and then stopped.

Distrusting a client was par for the course—they were never what they seemed once you accepted the initial retainer—but no matter what she thought about Aaron, no defense attorney could afford to question her expert on the eve of trial. So why was she even thinking about doing this?

Stop now, before you discover something you really don't want to know. . . .

Wasn't it ridiculous to think she could identify the earring's owner on the basis of a single picture? I don't care who she is, she decided, I just want to know who she *isn't*.

With that, Jackie reached into her briefcase for the manila envelope and spread the photographs across her desk.

Carole Wade standing against the stone wall with bougainvillea. Silver and turquoise at her throat, setting off her extraordinary eyes. Jackie mentally superimposed the garnet earring onto Carole's image. The bloodred stone was striking, but a dainty drop was not her style. She turned to the next photograph.

Oversized sunglasses were Becky Cox's signature, and everything else had been selected to match. In the photograph she was wearing gold button earrings. Jackie visualized the garnet against Becky's cheek. The filigree could never have held its own against glitzy dark lenses, and the shape was all wrong. Her face was too long for a drop.

Fern Kaplan—would the Red Queen have worn garnets? Not on your life. The half-glasses were a throwback to an earlier era, but Fern's calling cards were her flawless complexion and—bottle job or not—her silver tresses. The intensity of the stone would have washed out her skin, the gold setting been unflattering to her hair.

Starla McBride was another story. With her raven hair and dark eyes she had the right coloring for garnets. In her mind, Jackie pinned the drop on Starla's ear. But Starla favored large hoops, and the surgical improvements that gave her a look of exaggerated innocence seemed designed to call attention to the size of her bust. The delicacy of the filigree would have been lost.

Finally, Rae Malone. What redhead wore garnets? And Rodger Malone, to whom every brick of that mausoleum in Castle Pines was a monument to his power and his impotence, would have filled Rae's jewelry box with emeralds and sapphires. With relief, Jackie returned the photographs to her briefcase.

See, she told herself, *it isn't him.* Her paranoia had made her suspect every man involved in this case, from Rae's cuckolded ex-spouse to poor old doughnut-loving Duncan Pratt, whom she'd known for eighteen years! The thought had even crossed her mind that Aaron could have had an accomplice.

No, the earring surely belonged to a woman with small features and dark hair, a woman with a taste for a bygone era. Unless, of course, it went with a *costume* . . . Jesus, would she ever stop? Shaking her head again at her own foolishness, Jackie slipped the earring back into its pouch. Now her only problem was what to do with it. She couldn't just keep—

The doorbell rang, and she tucked the pouch in the pocket of her robe as she rose to answer it. Her caller was Mark Best.

"I'm sorry to barge in on you," he said, "but I wanted to give you this." He handed Jackie a cashier's check for the balance of her retainer.

"A company check would have been fine. And you certainly didn't have to deliver it in person."

But he stepped past her into the front hall, and she belted the robe more securely.

"Actually, I had an ulterior motive. I always like to see for myself whether our insulation really works."

"Considering the fact that it's the middle of July, I wish you the best of luck."

"I remember this house really well. Does that window still leak?"

Was that why he came? But his manner was so inoffensive that Jackie felt her guard begin to drop.

"I'll let you in on a little secret," he continued. "People think we use infrared sensors to gauge heat loss, but I use a piece of higher-tech equipment—my hand."

"Like you said last September, my heating bill dropped ten percent."

"This place looks so different at night." Mark glanced into her study. "Do you bring work home?"

"Sometimes."

Seeing the shelf of minerals, he crossed the threshold

and Jackie helplessly followed. "I didn't know you were a collector. . . ."

"Strictly amateur," she replied.

"Nice pyrite," he said, hefting the bronze-colored stone in one hand. "Where'd you pick it up?"

"It was a gift. Look, Mark—"

He put down the rock and turned to face her.

"When you came to my office the other day, I had the feeling you were interested in something more than my scholastic record."

"I never put a witness on the stand until I see where he lives or works."

"You had doubts about me?"

"Nothing personal. But if we go with alibi, Aaron's putting himself in your hands."

"*If?*"

"That's a decision I'll make at trial. If all goes well, I may never call you."

"But—"

"—you want to help your brother, I know. But let's face it, Mark, if the jury hears Aaron was gunning down horses in a canyon, we'll be fighting on two fronts. I can't afford any surprises."

His eyes met hers and in them she read attraction—and regret. Over what happened in Dinosaur, or that she believed him capable of firing too? It *had* been just Aaron with the rifle, and Mark was too loyal to let his younger brother shoulder the blame.

"Well, I've taken enough of your evening."

"Thanks for bringing me that check."

He followed her to the hall. "Now's the time to take advantage of me. Sure you don't have any cold spots?"

She'd misjudged him and here he was being *nice* about it. "Not unless you count the front closet."

"Exterior walls and dead air spaces are a bad combination."

Opening the door, he reached in.

Hangers scraped on the metal rod, and suddenly Mark pitched forward. There was a thrashing sound and a sharp yelp.

"Jesus H. Christ!"

He backed out of the closet with a struggling figure in tow. Arms flailed, and when he let go, Lily crashed to the floor.

"Do you know this kid?" His thumb was starting to bleed. "She bit me!"

"This is Lily." As if it were the most natural thing in the world to reach into a closet and get your hand nipped. "She lives next door. But you've already met. Don't you remember?"

Brushing furiously at her sleeve to erase the memory of his touch, Lily got to her feet. From her expression, Jackie could see her only injury was to her pride.

"Does she attack often?"

"You're the first—"

"I guess I really have outstayed my welcome." Finally recognizing her, he gave the girl a pained smile. Lily ignored him. "Next time, how about saying hi?"

Jackie waited until Mark reached the sidewalk before turning to the girl.

"What were you doing in that closet?"

"I was trying not to make noise. If he hadn't pulled my hair, I wouldn't have bit him."

"How long were you hiding?"

"Since he came. I was watching from my porch."

"Watching? *Why?*"

"He lied to you, Jackie."

"We talked about this before, Lily. Just because a guy acts like he's interested in me doesn't mean—When did he lie?"

"Remember that time he came to your office?"

"Yes."

"You asked him if he had receipts, remember?"

"And he gave me one."

"But there was another." Lily's face was lit with excitement. "I followed him to the corner. He took out his wallet, ripped it up, and threw it out."

"Ripped *what* up and threw *what* out?"

"Aren't you listening? The other receipt!"

"How do you know it was a receipt?"

"Because—"

"Why didn't you tell me before?"

"I wanted it to be secret." The hurt in her eyes was real. "Don't you believe me?"

"Of course I do, it's just—"

But Lily was already reaching into the pocket of her denim shorts. Slowly, she withdrew a slip of yellow paper that had been mended with Scotch tape. With a triumphant smile she handed it to Jackie.

The receipt was from a Chevron station in Black Hawk.

Chapter | Thirty-four

From across the street he watched the children at recess. Only a dozen of them, but the pecking order was clear.

The boys gathered around their tallest peer, the one with the sturdiest build. He'd staked out the jungle gym as his territory and guarded its entrance with feet apart and hands on hips, the classic bully pose. The girls were more mobile. In twos and threes they orbited around a child whose hair was skinned back from her face in twisty yellow ponytails secured with pink ribbons that matched her shorts and shirt. Seated on one of the swings, she favored first a girl from one group and then another with her toothy smile. Occasionally, she threw back her head and laughed, a theatrical, high-pitched sound the other girls emulated with varying degrees of success.

Except for one.

That child stood alone, at the far end of the asphalt by the slides. Her spiky black hair glistened as she bent to kick a pebble with her sneaker, a red canvas hightop with stars at the ankle in contrast to the platform sandals and lug-soled athletic shoes her schoolmates wore. Her scarlet backpack lay at the foot of the slide, and all her attention was directed to that pebble. Even from this distance he could tell she was counting the minutes until the teacher's aide summoned them inside. Then she would hang back from the others—not a straggler, but as if she couldn't bear the physical proximity of the other children and was savoring those last moments of solitude and freedom. She was always the last to go in. He was banking on that now.

At a burst of laughter from the boys, she looked up. The leader gave one of the smaller ones a shove in her direction, but the boy vehemently shook his head and sidled back. With a confident swagger the second-in-command detached himself from the group and crossed to the slides. Sensing a confrontation, the girls at the swings fell silent.

The man crossed the street for a closer look.

"Hey, Lily!" the boy called out. "Wanna play catch?"

She shook her head and resumed kicking the pebble with small, precise motions. With a graceful dart the boy swooped and seized her backpack. Before she could respond, he was swinging it over his head by the strap. He let it fly and another boy stepped forward to catch it.

"Give that back!" she cried.

The girls began to giggle. "*Lill*-ee!" one chanted, and that was the signal for the boys to fan out, surrounding their target. The two women by the entrance to the school glanced over, then resumed their chatter.

"*Lill*-ee, *Lill*-ee!" The red backpack flew back and forth over her head. As she unclenched her fists and spread her fingers, her nails glittered in the sun. Testing, testing . . . Ignoring the fate of her backpack, she stepped right up to the leader. The children fell silent.

"*Hhssss . . .*"

The sound originated deep in her throat, and the man could see the tension in her neck as she expelled it. The boy took a step back. She drew a deeper breath and he stopped in his tracks. This time the hiss was louder and had a rattle at the end.

"*HHSsss . . . sss . . . sss . . .*"

The boy seemed to shrink. As she reared back her head once more, he beat a hasty retreat to the monkey bars. Retrieving her backpack, she calmly dusted it off and within moments an uneasy peace reigned.

Standing on the other side of the fence in aviator glasses, a Rockies jacket and ball cap, the man was confident he would not be recognized, nor would anyone be able to describe him later. He ignored the sweat soaking the crown of his cap and glanced at his watch. Three more minutes and they would be going in. When he looked up, Lily was staring at him from five yards away. From where he stood he could see the metallic polish on her nails was chipped, the spikes in her head nothing more than gelled strands of hair.

She's just a little girl. . . .

The scowl began at her brow and traveled straight to her jaw, deadening her features in its wake. For fifteen seconds she stared at him through gleaming slits.

He froze. *Don't move a muscle, don't let her see—*

Wasn't that the game?

Her eyes widened with recognition. Resisting the impulse to draw back, he met her gaze. She took a step closer. The gate was ten feet away.

Two could play.

"Lily!" one of the women called out. "Two more minutes!"

The girl waved, signaling that she'd heard. The other children were bunching up, and the woman who'd called mounted the steps and went inside. The other went to the water fountain. The man blinked and a drop of sweat beaded his lens. Reaching for his sunglasses without thinking, he stopped himself just in time. The girl turned back to him with an inquiring look.

She took another step closer, edging toward the gate. Nothing childlike about that look—its boldness, the invitation.

Did she want him to take her?

She gave a little nod, and the raven spikes seemed to writhe. In a matter of seconds he could have her out that gate and into his car, and no one would see. As he moved in the direction of the gate, she reached out and her nails flashed. Bronze, like talons . . .

Take her now!

They were two feet apart and she pressed her palm against the chain link, inviting his touch. Suddenly she recoiled and he jerked his hand back, only to realize he hadn't extended it at all. Had he been mistaken about her flinch? He was slipping, slipping. . . . *Or was it his imagination?*

Her black eyes shone, not guileless like the Korean girl's at All-Star Cleaners, but with a terrible knowledge. *I see you,* they said, *I know.* She reached through the fence, and when he finally felt the smooth, hard sheaths of those monstrous claws, it was he who recoiled.

With a look of utter delight she danced away.

I know who you are, you don't fool me!

A whistle shrilled and she scampered off to join her schoolmates.

Chapter | Thirty-five

How's that opinion coming?" Jackie asked.

"I knew you had a reason for inviting me to lunch," Richard replied. "You weren't kidding when you said you and Pilar dug up a mountain of facts."

At noon on Friday, Sprouts was packed with staff from the nearby medical center, blissed-out retirees, and self-important entrepreneurs yakking in loud voices on cellular phones. A back booth was the perfect spot for this encounter.

"So, what's the verdict?" She tried to give it a light touch. "For the price of a tempeh burger, did the same guy kill all five women or not?"

"I doubt he was thinking about tempeh at all." The waitress refilled their glasses of spiced iced tea, and Richard took a sip before continuing. "You have every right to want an answer before the trial starts on Monday. I should have gotten back to you by now. The problem is—"

Her heart skipped a beat.

"You haven't changed your mind about Aaron, have you?"

"No, of course not. I'm fully prepared to testify that he lacks the characteristics of the man who killed Rae Malone. I'm just not sure yet about those other women."

"But the murders are so similar—" Jackie stopped. The last thing she needed was to strong-arm her expert. And she had to learn what he knew about Mark—the man who had better things to do on a Saturday night than work. The receipt from Black Hawk was dated the Saturday before Starla was murdered; could Mark have been stalking her? She backpedaled. "Is there any other information you need?"

Richard shook his head, and she waited for him to tell her about his research. Or would he not want her to know he'd risked impairing his objectivity?

"It's just a matter of digesting it. There are so many factors, and you know how I feel about cookie-cutter approaches. Preconceptions are dangerous. They create blind spots. And right now I can't afford to overlook—"

Blind spots?

"I certainly appreciate—"

"Don't get me wrong, Jackie. It's just that this case is a challenge and I need to be sure I'm right." He softened it with a smile and she tried to relax. She still had to find out about Mark without tipping Richard off in a way that might jeopardize his testimony. As for the earring—"Next time the tempeh burger's on me."

"On top of my eggs Benedict and Belgian waffle debt?" she replied.

"Speaking of the other day, how did Lily enjoy the visit?"

"She's fallen in love with your koi."

Richard's face fell. "The bonsai didn't grab her?"

"Maybe next spring. At the moment her true passion seems to be rocks." The toddler in the next booth threw his muffin to the floor and started to wail, and Jackie and Richard exchanged a sympathetic glance. "You know how girls Lily's age are. One minute they want to be ballerinas and the next they're going to win the Nobel Prize."

"I was impressed by her inquisitiveness. . . ."

Was he referring to the earring? But Richard's expression was sincere and Jackie hastened to change the subject. "And *I'm* curious about what Aaron was like as a kid. Did he talk about that?"

"As I said before, he was torn between wanting his father's approval and having to please his mother."

"But with his only sibling so much older, it must have been especially tough. What did he say about his brother?"

"Frankly, not much. When they were boys, he looked up to Mark. With parents like theirs, his older brother leaving home would have subjected Aaron to even more pressure. The wonder is they're able to work so well together now."

"Is it unusual for siblings who spent years apart to reconnect later?"

"Not necessarily, but Aaron told me his brother works for him. That's quite a reversal in roles. Assuming they truly *are* reversed."

"What do you mean?"

"Just because Aaron's the nominal boss doesn't mean he calls the shots." He paused. "It's only speculation, of course, but I wouldn't be surprised if Mark still led and Aaron followed."

Speculation or paranoia? She knew better than to travel either of those paths on the eve of a trial—two weeks earlier she'd been prepared to indict Duncan Pratt! It was time to quit playing games, put to rest any lingering doubts. As the waitress cleared their plates, she reached into her briefcase. "By the way, I have something for you."

Jackie set the velvet pouch in the center of the table.

Richard began to reach for it, then hesitated. As his eyes bored into Jackie's, the wailing in the next booth abruptly stopped.

Did he think *she* stole it?

"It must belong to a friend of yours," she continued.

For two full beats the silence stretched. Then his fingers closed over the pouch and, without opening it, he tucked it inside his jacket.

"As a matter of fact, it does."

Wasn't he going to ask how she got it? If he expected her to blame Lily—

Richard was smiling. Not with defensiveness or surprise, but *amusement*. As he signaled for the check, Jackie felt her cheeks flush. Once again she'd made a complete *ass*—

"I guess that's one more item for our raincheck," was his final word on the subject.

Chapter | Thirty-six

Jackie pulled into the lot behind her building and un-locked the back door. She was counting on no inter-ruptions as she attended to last-minute matters this Saturday afternoon. At the top of her list was one last Brady demand to tighten the noose around Pratt's neck. After that she would try to put the trial out of her mind until Monday. The trip she'd promised Lily to the garden center, for what was left of the season's bedding plants, could no longer be delayed, and Britt was dropping the girl off in an hour.

The reception area was cool and dim, and as she climbed the stairs to her office she left the outer door unlocked for Lily. She reached for the microcassette recorder to dictate the demand, but her thoughts returned to lunch the day be-fore with Richard. Aside from the humiliation of having come off like a jealous lover, his comment about blind spots had hit uncomfortably close to home.

As a child Jackie had always missed the obvious—a sneaker in the middle of the carpet when she cleaned her room, a spill left on an otherwise spotless kitchen counter. This occurred with such regularity that she and her aunt had made a joke of it. But as she grew older, it stopped being a joke. Like focusing on the space beneath a chair and over-looking the chair itself, Jackie had the constant sense that answers were staring her in the face. She'd compensated for the tricks her mind played with numbers and words by having Pilar read for her, but how did you make up for what you *could not see*? As perceptive as Richard was—

Maybe she should forget about her love life and concentrate on the case. With a sigh she reached for her microcassette recorder and began dictating the Brady demand.

"Comes now the defendant, Aaron Best, by and through his lawyer, Jacqueline C. Flowers . . ."

What was it Richard had said? *The MO changes but the signature remains the same.* Like an itch you never knew was there until you began scratching it, those dump sites tickled her brain. Despite Richard's skepticism, she thought she understood how the killer operated—but not *why*. Switching off her recorder, she foraged in the credenza for the duplicate set of the files.

As she laid the photos across her desk in a gruesome collage of rock and limb, Jackie saw again that Becky, Carole, and Starla had been thrust into their resting spots headfirst. Or what would have been headfirst had each not been decapitated. Fern, too, was kneeling at the foot of the riderless horse. Did it amuse the Hollow Man to leave his victims with their ankles primly crossed and buttocks high in the air?

Digging through a second batch, she found the one of Carole after her body was removed from the cave at Red Rocks. Arms raised in an off-kilter embrace frozen in death . . . Wasn't this supposed to be her strength, the "gift" her disability conferred—to recognize patterns where others saw only parts? So why did she see nothing but the space beneath the chair? With mounting frustration she switched on her recorder.

"Comes now the defendant, Aaron Best, by and through his lawyer, Jacqueline C. Flowers, pursuant to Rule 16 of the Colorado Rules of Criminal Procedure . . ."

Pilar edited out the anachronisms, but Jackie didn't care. Apart from scrawling her signature at the bottom, it wasn't as if she ever *saw* her motions in print. She closed her eyes to help her concentrate. When she opened them, Fern's butt was still wagging as if she were genuflecting before that damn horse. Kicking off her sandals and propping her feet on her desk, Jackie continued her dictation.

"—and renews his demand of the district attorney for all materials or information within his possession or control, including without limitation the possession or control of members of his staff and any others who have participated in the investigation or evaluation of the case and who either regularly report, or with reference to the particular case have reported, to his office . . ."

Times like these she'd just as soon be illiterate. Who wanted to clutter their head with gobbledygook? Having memorized the code of criminal procedure during her first month at the public defender's office, she could rattle it off without a moment's thought; that and most of the law she needed were embedded in her cortex like the codes she'd used to memorize material in school. How many adversaries had she seen trip over their own convoluted syntax in court instead of watching the jury? A lot of good that did her *now*.

"—which tends to negate the guilt of the accused . . ."

Becky's body was twisted to one side. He'd *screwed* her into the Three Graces. Her inspiration was getting farther away, she never should have pushed it—

"Aren't you going to finish that motion?"

Jackie jerked upright, sending Becky's photo flying. Mark Best stood in her doorway and she had no idea how long he'd been there. She quickly stooped to retrieve the picture.

"Don't you ever knock?" she replied.

"I did. But you left the door downstairs unlocked and I guess you didn't hear. I wanted to apologize for barging in on you at home the other night. Not to mention manhandling your little friend."

The credit slip from the Chevron in Black Hawk was in the top drawer of Jackie's desk. She'd considered showing it to Pilar, asking her to try to find out whether Starla had been in Black Hawk the Saturday before she was abducted. But what would she *do* with that information even if it panned out? Thousands of men patronized those casinos, and implicating Aaron's brother in the Hollow Man's crimes on the eve of trial would point the finger straight at her client. A *team*—hadn't Richard suggested that too? *More bang for the buck when you can be both spectator and participant.*

"I'm the one who should apologize to you. How's your thumb?"

Crossing to her desk, Mark bent and handed her another photo that had fallen to the floor. Starla crammed into
the cleft at Roxborough Park. As he straightened, she saw
his eyes scan her office, taking in everything from the bookshelves to her uncluttered credenza.

"I've never seen a lawyer with so little paper," he said.

"How many lawyers do you know?"

"Some better than others." He reached for the snapshot
of Becky at the barbecue. Was it delicacy that made him select the only one of her clothed? "Does she have anything to
do with my brother's case?"

"Maybe, maybe not." She had to get him out of there
before Lily came. "Look, I'm just about to leave. I'll give you
a call once I decide—"

"Yesterday I met with the DA. I thought you should
know."

"And?"

"He wanted to know the details of the Dinosaur trip."

"What did you tell him?"

"He asked if I could prove where we'd been, so I gave
him a copy of the gas receipt."

Which one? she felt like saying.

"Did you tell him the two of you shot horses?"

She was gratified by Mark's wince. She'd wanted so
badly to believe the best—

"No."

"Are you telling me you lied to the DA?"

"Didn't have to." Now it was easy to picture him in a bar,
picking up Rae Malone. He was so much smoother, more
sophisticated than Aaron. "I answered all his questions, like
you said. Is it my fault your friend Pratt was more interested
in going to lunch than getting the full story?"

"Then you also remember me telling you I don't call
witnesses who intend to lie."

"If you ask me the right questions, I won't."

And what if Mark was just who he'd said he was, and
Aaron's alibi was on the up and up? Could she afford to
blow off that defense on the basis of a torn credit slip?

"Is she another one of the killer's victims?" Mark was
holding the photo of Fern Kaplan. And if he *was* the Hollow

Man, what did he have to gain by screwing his brother on the stand?

She'd had Pilar check out Best Energy. Aaron's wife was vice president and had the right to buy him out at a nominal price if he was incapacitated from running it. Given Wendy's poisonous antipathy toward Mark, if Aaron went down, Mark was out of a job. And hadn't Richard said fraternal conflicts were all too common? She was overreacting, being paranoid. . . . She knew *nothing*. And come Monday, she would want to know even less.

"I plan to argue they were all victims of the same man."

"Including Rae Malone?"

"That's the point."

Mark leaned forward in his chair. "Do you know who the killer is?"

"I haven't a clue," she admitted bluntly, "nor do I care. My job is to get Aaron acquitted, not clear unsolved crimes."

"Aren't you concerned that if this serial killer really *does* exist, your making him the focus of attention may make him crawl out from under his rock?"

Was this a test?

She rose, signaling the interview was over.

"Look, Mark. I'll spare you the song and dance about being Aaron's lawyer and not his judge or jury. Unless I believed in his defense, I wouldn't waste my time or jeopardize your brother's future by defending him."

"Then you're either an idiot or a saint." He, too, got to his feet. "I'll be looking forward to seeing you face off against the DA. That should be quite a match."

Kohler's garden center was in the midsummer doldrums. By mid-July the plants and salespeople wore the same bedraggled look, and the only chipper note was the man with the hot dog wagon. He was doing a brisk business despite the half-empty parking lot. Six weeks earlier the cars had been lined up almost to the highway.

While Jackie found a shopping cart, Lily ran to the vendor. "What have you got today?" she asked.

"Elk, venison, and buffalo," he replied. "Two kinds of Polish, hot and not. Cured the meat myself."

"What's venison?"

"Deer."

She turned to Jackie. "Like at Roxborough Park?"

"Afraid so," Jackie replied.

"Venison," she ordered in a resolute tone. "And hold the mustard."

"I thought you were a vegetarian?" Jackie whispered as the man in the apron earned his $1.25.

"Looks pretty healthy to me," Lily replied, treating him to a mini–storm cloud just as he was about to hand over her dog. "Don't forget the chips."

Kohler's was trying its best, but the annuals were either leggy enough to run marathons or had been pinched back to pygmy size for their second growth. In early spring the greenhouse was an airplane hanger, with row after row of impossibly healthy specimens that withered the moment they hit Capitol Hill clay.

Now the choices were nicotiana, the flowering tobacco that promised more than it delivered, zinnias that mildewed the first time the sprinkler came on, and marigolds bred for uniformity. But it was her own fault for putting off her garden for so long.

As she wandered through the aisles, Jackie felt increasingly glum. Venison dog in hand, Lily had raced ahead to the water garden in search of koi. Maybe she should skip the whole thing, hope for an early frost. . . . But the thought of disappointing Ranger Bob's budding naturalist kept her going through table after table of verbena, cosmos, and stock.

The snapdragons weren't half bad. Cut back so they would be lean and mean in late-season heat. More troubling were the specks of rust on the underside of their leaves, but snaps could be counted on to flower again and sometimes self-seeded. A wise investment, her aunt would say, any time of year . . . When she turned to consult Lily, Jackie realized she hadn't seen her for several minutes.

Stay calm, she's here somewhere.

Abandoning the snapdragons, she wheeled her cart past the checkout stands on the main floor. Lily was nowhere to be seen.

Through the glass doors, past the hot dog man, down the boulevard of perennials and xeriscopic plants. Wherever she went, asking people if they'd seen a little girl with spiked hair.

If anything had happened, someone would know.

Rounding the corner on the northeast side of the mammoth garden center, Jackie ran all the way to the west end of the lot without finding a trace of her.

She's too smart to go with a stranger . . .

Acres of roses, spirea, and dogwood, through the grounds marked *No Customers Allowed,* all the way back to the entrance to the store. Just on the other side of where she began, her heart thudding with panic, Jackie finally found her.

"Where have you been?" she demanded.

"Right here," Lily replied. "Aren't these neat?"

They were in the statuary section, a land of cement gnomes with peaked caps and rabbits bigger than life.

"Do you know how *frantic* I've been?"

"But, Jackie, look. It's like Medusa was here."

"Don't you understand—"

"She glared at them and turned them to stone. Like the horse in Pioneer Cemetery."

And the Three Muses and Red Rocks and those monstrous buttocks in Roxborough Park. The key to the dump sites! Not just popular spots where the bodies would be quickly found—the Hollow Man had turned live women to stone.

But for whom?

Chapter | Thirty-seven

From his vantage point in the parking lot, the man watched the girl bound from the Corolla and run to the hot dog wagon. The stainless steel cart with the red-and-white-striped umbrella apparently exerted the pull of the Pied Piper's flute.

Fashioning his own sausage from buffalo and game rather than pork, curing the meat and selling the product himself—dealing in his customers' curiosity, the fellow in the butcher apron enticed them to a place they otherwise dared not go. And all with the jovial but worldwise demeanor of a carnival barker. As the man watched him dispense his wares, he wondered what was really in those sausages for a buck and a quarter a throw. One part buffalo, two parts dachshund?

While the girl was waiting in line, the woman had emerged from her car and retrieved a shopping cart from the lot. He'd followed them to the garden center and had no trouble keeping her in sight; she handled her Corolla like someone forty years her senior, staying in the slow lane and driving everyone nuts. Wheeling her cart to the vendor with the same tentative precision, she paid for the hot dog and they passed through the gate. He followed as far as the chain-link fence and waited while she examined a flat of pansies fertilized to frightening proportions, had a brief conversation with an attendant in a Kohler's shirt, and turned toward the greenhouse, where more chemically induced wonders lay. When she pushed her cart through the glass doors, he took his first step into the enclosure.

Outside the checkout stand a boy was feeding aluminum cans to a contraption with a sliding vise that crushed them with enviable dispatch. The man could feel the crunch, the boy reveling in the sheer destructiveness of his enterprise as he worked the machine with both hands. Three feet away a little helper collected empty pop cans from the hot dog vendor's patrons. Production, consumption, elimination of waste—a seamless operation, though he was willing to bet the vendor and boy were strangers to each other.

Peering through the glass, he saw the woman and the girl bent over a display of dahlias. Reassured, he turned to the stands ringing the greenhouse. Prices were based on the size of the plastic pot, five colors and shapes with volume discounts. Elevation of quantity over quality, another step toward a world of homogeneity and the death of art. In plastic swaddling these nursery plants were like fetuses waiting for someone to breathe life into them. He reached for a three-inch pot of Shasta daisies and raised it to his nose. No fragrance. Such a contrast to the heady abundance of real gardens, the fermented scent that characterized the approach of August.

The woman had moved down the aisle past the geraniums, and the girl was scampering off to the houseplants in the main part of the store. He would be forced to choose—unless he moved fast he would risk losing them both. Dropping the daisies, he entered the greenhouse.

From behind tall shelves he watched the woman examine one flat of snapdragons and then another. Having zeroed in on her target, she would be looking for the most orderly ones—still some bloom left, in relatively good shape, a dependable if not showy return to demonstrate to neighbors that her tardiness in conforming to their standards resulted from the pressures of work and not a failure to *care*. Certain her mission would anchor her to the snapdragons for the next several minutes, he moved to a more central location.

Following the girl was like tailing a bumblebee. First she zigzagged from orchids to planters, lingering over a cement trough with molded cherubs and a pair of faux Grecian urns. Then she scooted across the floor to the glass doors and outside to the hill of alpine plants. Which posed the greater threat, she who listens or the one who *sees*?

The child. His business with her was unfinished. And this time he would not falter.

By the time he reached the stalls of shade perennials she was staring into the rock pond. Surrounded by ponderosa pine, yucca, and yarrow, deep enough for water lilies and fish. She leaned down until her chin was almost touching the surface, then suddenly stopped. A glance over the shoulder— to tell him she knew he was there? Slowly, she straightened. Then an abrupt about-face and she was off again, following her instincts like a tracking dog. Sniffing out a scent, not knowing where it would lead. Or did she?

Patience, *patience* . . .

She doubled back to the main entrance but instead of returning to the greenhouse continued past the door to an area by the parking lot that sheltered the tackiest selection of garden statuary he'd ever seen. A cart pulled by a donkey, cement geese and ducks, and a rogue's gallery of Christian hagiography—everyone from St. Francis reaching for birds to St. Fiacre in friar garb with beard, gladioli, and pointed spade. Touching all spiritual bases, Kohler's had thrown in half a dozen chubby Buddhas and a pair of dejected-looking gargoyles.

This was her destination, and now he knew he'd been right. She had lured *him*.

Taking her time, the girl scrutinized each statue. A family of deer painted brown and white with long eyelashes and happy faces received close attention. As he watched, she smoothed the brow of a spotted fawn who was gazing up at its mother. She treated them with respect, almost reverence. As if she understood their magical quality. How they got that way . . .

Not a child—not by any means. She'd led him to the parking lot as a tease.

St. Fiacre received short shrift, but when she reached the first Buddha, she peered into his eyes.

Wait until no one could see—

Now she was stooping, placing her mouth to Buddha's ear. She couldn't possibly understand, couldn't possibly *know* . . .

But she did. And that meant she would embrace her fate. He would take her *now*, before—

"Lily!"

At the sound of the woman's voice, he froze. Anger masking fear, shopping cart abandoned in her haste to find the irresponsible child. An intimacy no man shared.

"Jackie, look!" Such excitement, such certainty as she pointed to the Buddha. "Like Medusa was here."

The woman paused. He was hidden from view, but the recognition in her eyes was unmistakable.

"She glared at them and turned them to stone," the girl prattled. But it was hardly necessary. She'd brought those statues to life and now, finally, the woman *knew*.

Once again *she* had won.

Aaron's lawyer had tumbled to the meaning of his dump sites.

Chapter | Thirty-eight

wo children, did you say? Miss, er—"

Fumbling with notes and seating chart, Duncan Pratt looked reproachfully at the assistant who'd fed him the wrong page. Jurors filled out questionnaires before being summoned to the box, but his staff's review had gone for naught. The cases Pratt didn't settle were normally delegated to deputies who could keep a dozen names straight.

Jackie doodled in the boxes on her chart: a fruit with pebbled skin and two pits for the mother of twins; for the electrician employed by the sub who wired Coors Stadium, a lightbulb inside a pennant.

"—Lemons," Pratt finished. "Are you married, ma'am?"

The woman's smile vanished and her shoulders stiffened. Forgetting her name was bad enough, but bastardizing her children was unforgivable. Now Pratt would have to waste one of his free strikes bouncing her off the jury. As Jackie watched the DA maul juror after juror in an attempt to ferret out bright, liberal thinkers—otherwise known as kooks—from those who believed the seven deadly sins were interchangeable, she kept her face impassive. Pratt might be a bumbler, but he was far from stupid, and trials were a ball game: once the opening pitch was thrown, the outcome was anyone's guess.

Seated beside Aaron in a simple blue suit that skimmed her knees, a silk blouse in warm cream, and mid-heel pumps,

Jackie waited for Pratt to repair his blunder by asking the woman her children's age and sex. With a smile that said anyone can make a mistake, he moved on to the next juror, leaving his victim invisible in addition to humiliated. It would be a slow morning, but Jackie was fortified. During trial she risked as little as possible to chance.

Each night she left her toothbrush dabbed with paste beside the bathroom sink, a fresh towel and washcloth on the counter by the shower. Makeup arranged in the precise order in which it would be applied the following morning to the right of her toothbrush. As soon as they were used, she put away each compact and jar so she knew she'd completed the task. The wristwatch she never consulted, her earrings, and an ambiguous gold band she wore on her right hand in court sat on the other side of the sink, the next day's suit or dress hung at the front of her closet with coordinated pumps below them on the floor. Lipstick beside her purse on the kitchen counter so they would be the last thing she saw before she walked out the door.

"—work outside the home?" Pratt was asking a lady with a neat gray perm who was leaning forward in her chair.

Like his demographic inquiries, Jackie knew this had already been answered on the questionnaire. The woman had a mail order business, but Pratt wanted to establish rapport by allowing her to lead with her strength. The Avuncular Guidance Counselor school of jury selection. An improvement over his performance in moot court, where he'd fatally offended the dean's wife by asking if she believed in an eye-for-an-eye in a worker's compensation case.

"—precautions when you're home alone?" Pratt had moved on to a blonde in a black velvet headband and sleeveless cashmere turtleneck. The HVAC in Worrell's court was pumping enough air to draw goose bumps, but it failed to warm that one up. If the DA was fishing for a juror to tap into women's deepest fears, he'd landed the coldest one in the pond.

"Nooo . . . Just the alarm and my Belgian Malinois."

"Belgian . . . ?"

She flashed two rows of perfect teeth. "A German shepherd, but meaner."

With a nervous smile Pratt skittered off to a bald man in

a business suit three jurors to her left. "Now, Mr. Wiest, you noted on your questionnaire that you work at Trident Cable. How many years have you been employed there?"

"Twelve."

"And your current position is?"

"Executive Vice President for Strategic Planning and Finance."

"And you've been married fifteen years?"

"To the same wife." That drew a chuckle, and the ice began to thaw.

Pratt had finally drawn a live one. DAs wanted the same jurors whom defendants sought in a civil case—white collar males who respected the chain of command but prided themselves on rational thinking. No going back on your word or screwing around on the wife. Above all he needed unanimity, a dynamic that relied as much on social lubricators like Wiest as those capable of applying a formula to matters of the heart. Jackie, on the other hand, preferred them a little rough around the edges—people who'd made a few mistakes of their own. As she listened to her old classmate stroke the man earmarked for foreman heedless of the fact that he was ensuring Jackie's first strike, her mind wandered to other members of the panel.

The beautician with two-inch nails whose husband drove a cab—did she, like the majority of her peers, think victims blamed others for their own lack of caution and lawsuits caused higher prices at the grocery store? Fatal for a plaintiff's lawyer in a personal injury suit but not so bad if the woman could be persuaded that Aaron was an average Joe dragged into court through no fault of his own. How would the elementary-school teacher react to Richard's unorthodox views on psychopaths? And would the man at the end of the second row who sat with his arms crossed and left half the questions on the survey blank ignore the judge's instructions in order to reach a "just" result? Jackie had not yet decided whether Aaron should take the stand, but a strategy had taken shape in her mind.

Which women on the panel had the most in common with the Hollow Man's victims? That Jackie was willing to sit at the defense table beside Aaron said more about her belief in his innocence than any argument she could make. And female jurors were *death* to their gender on the stand; when a woman cried, the average male's brain shut down, but a member of her own sex looked to see if the tears were authentic. With Wendy Best and Rae's friend Sunny poised to plunge the knife in Aaron's back, discrediting both would be crucial.

As Pratt rushed through the remaining panel members so none would feel left out, Jackie squeezed her client's arm. Even that small gesture transferred credibility. Every nuance counted, because Aaron's demeanor and dress might be the only way he testified.

In his long-sleeved shirt with subdued pattern, navy knit tie, and pressed work pants, Aaron struck the proper chord. Neat and respectful, not pretending to be anything more than who he was—a hardworking member of the building trades who'd skipped college for sixteen-hour days to make his company a success. Values these good people shared. Someone who might have an extramarital fling but who was utterly incapable of the brutality inflicted on Rae Malone.

"—again thank you for your candor." Pratt surrendered the lectern to Jackie.

Leaving her yellow pad at the counsel table, Jackie strode to the center of the courtroom. With one hand draped over the wooden ledge, she waited until the whispers in the gallery subsided and the last juror had stopped squirming in his seat. When she owned the space, she began.

"Ms. Lemons, tell me the names and ages of your two children."

While the woman Pratt had offended seized the opportunity to redeem herself in her fellow jurors' eyes, Jackie focused on themes. Like all human beings, these people wanted to know who to blame and had to be conditioned from the very start.

"As the mother of ten-year-old twins," Jackie continued, "you know there's two sides to every story. Right?"

"Absolutely." Pratt had made her nervous, and she kept running her hand through her hair as if it had once been longer.

"And the first to say his version may not tell you all the facts. . . ."

"There's always more than meets the eye," she agreed.

"In fact, that first version may not resemble what

happened at all. Sometimes the one who cries loudest does so because deep down he knows he's to blame."

Lemons sighed theatrically. "You got *that* right."

The beautician and the teacher gave sympathetic smiles. A pity Pratt would strike Lemons, but the other two would not forget Jackie's gallantry. As she watched, the research chemist from Beller Labs glanced from the seating chart still on the defense table to her empty hands. Having redeemed Lemons in their eyes and elicited her agreement to the crux of the defense, she could have moved on, but she had a final point to make.

"And when one twin tells one story, and your other boy another, how do you decide which to believe?"

"I look at the one that fits all the facts."

"Exactly."

With one hand still on the lectern, Jackie moved a half-step to the left. Negotiating that wooden stand was an art in itself—Worrell required lawyers to remain behind it, and jurors feared above all else being touched. But Jackie sensed the jury could now tolerate the smallest invasion of their space. She turned to the chemist, whose hair was a half-inch too long around the ears—an eccentric? Pratt would want him because of his profession, but there might be something in it for the defense.

"Dr. Faatz, when you test a product for Beller Labs, do you start with a hypothesis?"

"Some notion of what I expect to prove or disprove," he allowed.

"And if as a result of your tests you find a piece that doesn't fit, what do you do?"

"Change my hypothesis." He turned to the judge, not above cashing in on the relaxed mood. "Beller's not real big on fudging data."

He received the expected laugh. Jackie was all for it; acting as the jurors' straight man gave her credit for humor without risking a joke that fell flat.

"So if the district attorney tried to tell you the same person left his tracks all over a crime scene but took the trouble to scrape under the victim's nails, what would you think of his hypothesis?"

Behind her, Pratt began to object but thought the better

of it. Faatz was looking straight at Aaron, and his answer could go either way.

"I'd say he'd better retest his data or consider other alternatives."

"The simple answer isn't necessarily right?"

"Unless you're lazy."

Thank you, Mr. Wizard.

As Jackie ran through the panel, never missing a name and building on answers they'd given Pratt or divulged in their questionnaires, she began to get a sense of each juror as an individual. Slowly, she moved from the lectern, keeping her fingers on the edge like a ballplayer preparing to steal a base. One or two of the women who'd been afraid to look at Aaron were glancing at him now with curiosity. The first step in leading him back to the campfire . . . She turned to the cable executive.

"Mr. Wiest, does your job require you to review financial statements?"

"On occasion." From his pained expression Jackie knew he already considered himself on the DA's team. Not surprising—with his rotund physique, he could have been Pratt's body double.

"Is it fair to say what's *not* on a statement can be more important than what is?"

"I don't understand."

His self-righteous tone was a warning.

"Not financial statements *your* company might generate, of course. But have you had occasion to review balance sheets of a competitor, or someone else in your industry, where certain assets or liabilities may not be reflected?"

"Well, yes. I can't go into details—"

"I understand. But if you later discovered that *was* the case, would those line items be more likely to have been significant or not?"

"If you're asking whether I'd be more prone to make a decision based on what's missing, I'd have to say yes."

From balance sheets to bedsheets—Wiest had no idea at that moment that Jackie was alluding to the absence of blood on Rae Malone's linen, but he'd be the first to make the connection when the proper time arose. Having neutralized her worst threat, she devoted her attention to the other jurors. Although her strategy varied with the facts of the case, she adhered to certain principles as idiosyncratic as the Grape-Nuts, sliced banana, and orange juice she set out for breakfast each day she was in trial.

Growing up with computer games made it easy to inflict brutality at a remove—jam a quarter in a slot and grease an alien. Was that why Generation X was more callous than its predecessors? At the other end of the spectrum, women over age seventy, no matter how self-sufficient or accomplished, were fatal to female attorneys. Jackie never forgot the first case she lost at the public defender's office. After the trial two of them approached her and said she'd done a darn good job, but did she have to be quite so *aggressive*? College kids and grandmothers were the first to go.

"—families from all walks of life," she said to the teacher. "Every marriage has its problems, doesn't it?"

As she continued planting themes and establishing rapport, Jackie tried to gauge how the jurors were reacting to Aaron. She'd given him three instructions: rise immediately and remain standing whenever the judge or jury entered or left, note any jurors who would not look him in the eye, and not under any circumstances interrupt her concentration. Ceding him custody and control of the legal pad gave him something to do with his hands and relieved her of the annoyance of dealing with what was to most other attorneys an appendage but to her a useless prop. When all was said and done and it was time to exercise peremptory challenges, she would base her selections on gut instinct—eye contact, openness, and above all else, people who had not outgrown the ability to suspend their disbelief.

By the time Worrell recessed for lunch, the jury had been selected. Eight women and four men, including the teacher and the beautician. Knowing she would have to break Pratt's forensic expert, Jackie kept the chemist and a math instructor from Metro State. Pratt struck the mother of twins and the woman with the fancy dog. Neither wanted the mystery man at the end of the jury box, whose responses to oral questions were as unrevealing as those he refused to answer in ink, but with Aaron's approval at the last minute, Jackie kept him and threw out a kid who looked barely old enough to shave. She also tossed Wiest, the financial whiz.

She would rely on Mr. Wizard to get the point about the missing evidence.

As Pratt left the courtroom flanked by his assistants, Jackie saw one of them shake his hand. The DA himself seemed surprised but pleased with the makeup of the jury; he obviously thought women were fungible and couldn't understand why Jackie rejected those she did and kept precisely the ones who could be expected to fear her client. How could she ever have suspected her old friend of anything more sinister than a lack of smarts? The deputies snapped on Aaron's cuffs and chain and returned him to the lockup.

Alone for the first time that day, Jackie closed her eyes and pictured the impression she wanted to leave with the jury. Channel surfers accustomed to sound bites. How did the old-timers in the public defender's office describe them? *Not cruel, just used to things.*

The opening statement would be too soon to hit them with the Hollow Man defense. She had to draw blood before they would be willing to believe Pratt was callous enough to ignore a pattern that led away from her client, much less to a killer responsible for raping and decapitating women up and down the Front Range. And she was still unsure how far Richard would go. It was suicide to promise more than you could deliver.

What she needed was to turn the prosecution's case inside out. Convert Pratt's blind spots into her theory of the case.

What you see is not what you get . . . ?
What's missing from this picture?

Pratt prided himself on presenting his case in segments that fit neatly into a whole, with inconvenient facts pared like scraps from the crust of a perfectly round pie. When the jurors filed into the courtroom at the end of the noon recess, his table was stacked with loose-leaf notebooks and the dolly by the jury box was loaded with banker boxes. A file for each witness and topic, subfiles for direct and cross examinations, and every speck of physical evidence his investigators had amassed. Far from abstractions, he measured the weight of evidence and burden of proof by ream and pound.

Clearing his throat as he stepped to the lectern, Pratt shuffled his notes and made check marks with his pen. When he began to speak, he did so in a voice a trifle too loud for the room. He lowered it and gave the jury an abashed grin. Once again Jackie reminded herself not to underestimate him: that folksiness was the product of hard experience on the campaign trail.

"The district attorney's office wishes to take this opportunity to thank you all in advance for the attention we know you will devote to this case. . . ." On and on he went, five minutes of praise for their willingness to undergo an involuntary duty and ending with a promise that this would be the greatest civic experience of their lives. The chemist shifted in his chair but never blinked.

Pratt moved his top three sheets to the bottom of the stack. He glanced over his shoulder, and one of his assistants retrieved a three-by-six-foot piece of pasteboard that had been leaning against a wall and set it on the easel by the witness stand. A diagram of Rae Malone's house in Castle Pines.

"April 30 of this year began as a day much like any other. . . ."

Pratt was off and running with a chronology of Rae Malone's last hours. In excruciating detail he outlined her lunch with Sunny Abbot, building Sunny up as the witness who would fill in the gaps, and cautiously picked his way around the minefield of the victim's character.

"A woman who loved life and lived it to the hilt. In the wake of an unhappy separation from her husband—"

No mention of divorce.

"—Rae Malone had embarked on an impetuous relationship with a man she trusted to allow into her home." He pointed theatrically at Aaron, who calmly met his gaze. The beautician was rapt; the math instructor stifled a yawn. "It was an affair she came to regret long before she was killed."

He paused to let that sink in, and the teacher gave Aaron a hard look.

"Indeed, immediately before Aaron Best murdered her,

Rae Malone told him she wanted to break their liaison off. Her hope was to reconcile with her husband, whom she dearly loved."

That was a surprise. Jackie didn't need to look to know Rodger Malone was there. Was the DA blowing smoke? Or trying to salve the massive, jilted ego of one of the governor's closest friends?

Pratt's pause confirmed he'd been baiting her. Jackie maintained an impassive smile. Even if what he'd just said *was* true, it was hearsay, but the jury didn't know her yet and objections almost always cost more than they were worth. At least until you established your adversary or his witness were slimeballs.

As Pratt continued with an outline of his forensic expert's best guess as to when Rae was murdered and the postmortem sequence of events, Jackie watched the math instructor. He was squinting in the distance, as if imagining a blackboard. Pratt moved on to the physical evidence against Aaron. She listened for a description of the trip to Dinosaur National Monument and was surprised when Pratt didn't bring it up. Curious, if not *ominous* . . .

"Best's marriage was on the rocks. There had been at least one incident of violence." She could hardly blame Pratt for detonating *that* bomb; the privilege belonged to the side who went first, and in his place she would have done the same. But he made no mention of the fact that Aaron's marital troubles *preceded* the fling with Rae. "At the time of the murder his wife had filed for divorce and custody of their son."

The teacher frowned. She knew what broken homes did to kids.

"Best was between a rock and a hard place. He wanted his son and he wanted Rae Malone and couldn't have both. In fact, he had just learned he could have neither."

Jackie wrinkled her nose—not so overtly as to draw a reprimand from Worrell but enough to tip the jury that something smelled. If Pratt was implying that custody of his son required Aaron to give up his squeeze, Rae had handed him that. Why kill if she was ready to walk?

Pratt turned once again, this time to his female assistant. She reached under the table and withdrew a large brown bag. Pratt reshuffled his notes and continued with his remarks, feigning obliviousness to the fact that all eyes were on the girl. As she slowly reached into the bag and removed a folded length of percale, her distaste was visible. The gallery was silent as she walked to the lectern and handed it to Pratt. Holding the bulky square of flowered cloth by his fingertips, he dramatically turned to the jury.

"Physical evidence never lies. Aaron Best left his signature all over it!"

The smoking sheet.

For the first time, the chemist's eyes were alive. As Pratt returned the exhibit to his associate, who set it on the edge of the table, where it sat in mute accusation, Jackie registered the juror's disappointment. He wanted to see *more*.

"—returned from Park Meadows Mall, Aaron Best was waiting. He had sex with Rae and there was an altercation. Best was the last person to see Rae Malone alive."

A creative fudging of events that heightened Pratt's reliance on witnesses to fill in the blanks. But men had been convicted on speculation and circumstantial evidence more times than Jackie could count. On this note of high drama Pratt yielded the lectern.

Before he was back in his seat, Jackie rose and stepped to his table. Seizing the sheet with both hands, she strode to the jury box.

"Take a closer look," she invited them, unfurling the sheet for the jury to see.

We have nothing to hide.

"And think about what you *don't* see. What's missing from this picture?"

The chemist leaned forward in his chair.

"Where's the blood?"

The print was busy but the colors light enough that blood would have been apparent. The infamous stain itself was so minute, she could barely see it.

"See any rips or tears?"

Jackie gave them a moment longer, then wadded up the sheet in disgust.

"That must have been *some* altercation. And what was it the district attorney said about the killer scraping under Ms. Malone's fingernails? What's missing from *that* picture? If

Aaron Best had already left the stain we've heard so much about, would that make any sense?"

Jackie walked back to Pratt and dropped the sheet in the center of his table. He'd been too startled to object, and now it was too late. By invading his territory for a second time and stealing his flag, she'd sealed her control of the courtroom. She caught Pilar's eye, and her investigator gave a small nod.

From the whiteness of his knuckles on the microphone, she could tell Worrell was furious. In his court you got one free pass, and that was only if the other side was too dumb to call it. She hadn't just put her toe on the line; she'd crossed it. The next time he would chop off her foot. And tricks went only so far. These jurors wanted to back a winner. The sooner they decided who it should be, the quicker they'd reach for facts to support it.

"This case is about a horrific crime and the impulse to point the finger at the most convenient target. Haste and pressure cause mistakes."

Detecting cynicism in the curve of the math instructor's lips, Jackie stepped to the side of the lectern. The barrier impeded communication, and if Pratt objected, she would use her size as an excuse. It was time to cut to the chase.

"Aaron Best had an affair with Rae Malone. We don't for one minute dispute that. They had sex at her home at some point before her death. But that is all the evidence will show. What's missing from this picture is a single shred of proof that Aaron is the man who killed her."

Her gut said to steer clear of the alibi. The fact that Pratt hadn't mentioned it suggested he'd found no way to refute Mark's story, but he might be setting her up for a sucker punch. That left her with damn little at this stage except to direct the jury to the key weakness in the prosecution's case.

"Mr. Pratt outlined some of the evidence. When his witnesses testify, let's see if they can answer the questions their own evidence poses. Listen carefully to what they're *not* saying."

The easel still held the diagram of the estate in Castle Pines. Pratt had left it there as a mute witness, and now Jackie would turn it to her advantage. Out of the corner of her eye she saw Pratt's assistant had returned the soiled sheet to its place of ignominy under the table.

"Mr. Pratt says he'll call police officers to testify to the condition of Rae Malone's home. According to him, the scene of her abduction by Aaron Best." On the chart she pointed to the living room, kitchen, and master bedroom. "You've already heard the house was in disarray." She turned and caught the teacher's eye. "We all know the difference between pandemonium and disorder. What's missing from this picture is *anything* that suggests a violent abduction occurred."

No sense tipping the DA to Sunny's cross.

"Mr. Pratt also speculated about motive. You'll hear from a witness who has studied the dynamics of real criminals and will offer his opinion on their personality traits." As much as she dared say about Richard. "We all know there are two sides to every story. When both sides have had their say, you'll see very clearly that what's missing from the picture is the guilt of Aaron Best."

With that Jackie returned to her seat. She had not once looked at the gallery, because what those people thought she didn't care. The interest on the jurors' faces told her all she needed to know. She and Aaron were in the game.

Chapter | Thirty-nine

And you were responsible for the evidence at the crime scene?"

Pratt's witness's wash-and-wear jacket and trousers were already rumpled at nine in the morning, but their droopiness had an endearing quality that was more dangerous than a three-piece suit. With a world-weary sigh Lieutenant Harry Himes replied to Pratt's question.

"I supervised the collection of certain materials from Ms. Malone's house in Castle Pines and from her body, yes."

The DA couldn't have found a better forensic expert if he'd ordered him from central casting. Himes's thinning hair attested to his thirty years of experience and his pouchy eyes to the gravity of the crime. But as Pratt led the lieutenant from his credentials to the crime scene to the findings of the lab, his shoulders were bowing from carrying the prosecution's entire case. Using one expert to do all was a temptation for both of them to overreach.

"—what you discovered when you arrived at Castle Pines."

"Disarray in Ms. Malone's bedroom and other locations in the home." Himes's apologetic smile said he regretted subjecting the jurors to this. "We collected a sample of organic material that proved to be semen from the bottom sheet of her bed."

Pratt turned to the jury box, one fist at the small of his

back like a portly Napoleon, and Jackie noticed he was
wearing the rep tie he usually reserved for TV appearances.
If there was one thing Pratt understood, it was how to wring
every ounce of drama from the mundane. He would delay
the obvious—whose semen was it?—until the last possible
moment. "What other evidence did you find, lieutenant?"

"Drops of blood in the driveway by the victim's Lexus."

"Were you also summoned to the scene where Ms.
Malone's body was found?"

"Yes."

"And you supervised the technicians who examined her
body for trace evidence before it was removed?"

"I did."

"Was any such evidence found?"

With a reproachful look at Aaron, Himes shook his
head. "No. The body appeared to have been washed."

"Did your technicians check her bodily orifices?"

"Yes, and further examination was conducted at the
autopsy."

"What about her nails?"

"They appeared to have been clipped."

The beautician's eyes widened. Her first sign of interest
since the gore in Pratt's opening.

"Clipped?" Pratt echoed.

"The pathologist scraped under her nails, but no evidence was found."

Evidence. A vague word. Jackie leaned forward. Experts
rarely lied outright, but misleading the jury was another
matter.

"—contents of her stomach?"

"The pathologist said her last meal was salad."

As Pratt's direct continued, Jackie watched for other signs
of hesitation. She detected none. Pratt ended on a strong
note, with Himes describing how and where Rae Malone's
head was found and confirming that the blood in the driveway belonged to her and the semen was Aaron Best's. With a
tight nod the DA tendered his expert to Jackie.

Dress was one advantage female lawyers had in court.
Required to appear in a suit because jurors expected them
to be clothed in solemnity of purpose, Jackie's male counter-
parts could compete only through choice of tie while she was

free to tailor her outfits to the task at hand. The simple collar and three-quarter-length sleeves of her silk dress only enhanced its color, which was the precise shade of her violet suede pumps. During cross-examination the thrust was in the question, not the answer. When she tore into a witness, she wanted all eyes on *her*. Nodding courteously, she began with an area in which the detective would have no choice but to agree.

"Lieutenant Himes, you take great care in collecting and preserving evidence at a crime scene. Am I correct?"

"I certainly do."

"And the men under your supervision are also careful."

"Yes, they are."

"Let's turn to Rae Malone's home. You said the house was in disarray. . . ."

With short statements posed in a respectful tone, Jackie inquired about the physical status of every room in the house. She didn't have to inflict a scratch to get Himes to admit there were no signs of an altercation except for the blood in the driveway. After her stunt with the sheet, she owed the jury that.

"And you found the sheet on the bed," she said.

"Yes."

"The killer hadn't taken it with him?"

"No."

"And it would have been a simple matter to remove it."

"I suppose so." Himes's reluctance felt contrived; these questions weren't the ones he feared.

"There's no way to tell precisely when the semen was left."

"It wasn't old."

"But you can't say Friday morning versus, oh—say, Thursday night."

"That's correct."

"And there was no semen found on or in Ms. Malone's body."

"I said it was washed."

"And her nails clipped."

"Yes."

The chair creaked, but Jackie wasn't ready to spring the trap. Let him relax once more before tightening the noose.

"From the blunt manner in which her nails were cut, you assumed the killer clipped them to eliminate trace evidence?"

"Yes. Her manicurist did them earlier that week and—"

"The killer scraped beneath them."

"*Yes.*" He appealed to the jury; hadn't he just gone through all this?

"And scrubbed her body with commercial soap . . ."

"That's what the pathologist said."

"Does that make sense to you?"

"Beg your pardon?" he replied.

"That the killer would leave DNA in the victim's bed but scrub her body and scrape beneath her nails to destroy trace evidence?"

"Objection!" Pratt lumbered to his feet. "Calls for speculation. This witness was not inside the killer's mind."

"Sustained," the judge ruled. Worrell's tone was mild, and Jackie wondered whether he suspected her line of questioning was a smoke screen.

"You said earlier that when the pathologist looked under Ms. Malone's nails, no evidence was found."

"Yes."

"By evidence, what precisely did you mean?"

Himes's guileless gaze said he knew exactly what she was after.

"Evidence? I guess I don't understand."

"What sort of material were you looking for?"

"Fibers, or something with the perp's DNA. Hair, blood, skin."

The beautician's mouth was slack with fascination. Entranced by the possibilities of what could have gotten stuck there.

"And you found . . . ?"

"No usable DNA."

Bingo.

"No usable DNA," Jackie repeated. "Then you found some material after all."

"Well"—Himes glanced at Pratt—"hardly any."

She took a step closer, as if she weren't sure she'd heard correctly. "Hardly any?"

"Just the tiniest sample."

"Of organic material."

The chair creaked. Now he didn't dare look at Pratt.

"Yeah."

"Was this organic material submitted to the lab for testing?"

"Yeah."

"Did it contain human DNA?"

"Um-hmnn. But it was too contaminated to get a read." The chemist was leaning forward in the jury box. "For all we knew, there could have been two—" Himes broke off.

An unidentified killer. *A forensic basis for the Hollow Man defense.*

"Two men who abducted and killed Rae Malone?" she pressed.

"Who knows? Like I said, we—" Again Himes stopped.

The teacher was watching Aaron, and in her face Jackie saw relief. She read *Cinderella* to her class, wanted to believe Aaron could have patched up his marriage for the sake of his son. Of course she would seize upon the notion of two killers, neither of whom was present in court. From there the Hollow Man was a short jump.

"To your knowledge, was that sample of DNA turned over to the defense so Mr. Best could conduct his own tests?"

"Wasn't my call," Himes mumbled.

"Not your call." She could afford to be righteous, but Harry Himes wasn't her target. "Whose call was it?"

"District attorney's."

"The district attorney's . . ." She turned to Worrell. "May the record reflect that despite *four* Brady demands, no such sample was received by the defense."

"Is that so, Mr. Pratt?" the judge asked in the mild tone with which he'd sustained the DA's objection.

Pratt rose. "May we approach?"

"No, Mr. Pratt. You may not." Worrell's bushy brows obscured his eyelids, but his palm covered the mike. Did he know what she was really after? "You may speak your piece without moving one step closer."

The jury would hear it all.

"That sample wouldn't have done Ms. Flowers or her client any good because it was too contaminated to test. For all we knew, it could've been Best's!"

"Or come from two men," Jackie replied. She wanted them to hear, had been counting on Worrell's distaste for sidebars that kept the jury in the dark. "Neither of whom the prosecution has identified."

"Absurd!" Pratt shook with fury either because he'd been caught with his pants down or because his expert had suggested the first alternative theory Jackie could ride to the bank. "She's taking a speck of nothing and requiring us to prove it wasn't Best's!"

The mathematician was waiting to see how Jackie would respond. His thousand-yard stare had been reduced to ten feet, and in it she read points for exposing misconduct his common sense said was irrelevant. How would he react if she upped the ante?

She turned to her client. Aaron was leaning back with his arms crossed, but she could see the excitement in his eyes. Hyped by the unexpected turn of events, as if his own life weren't hanging in the balance. He seemed to take an acquittal for granted. . . . Jackie went for broke.

"Your honor, I move for a mistrial. The district attorney's failure to comply with Rule 16 of the Colorado Rules of Criminal Procedure has irreparably harmed Mr. Best's constitutional right to a fair trial. Without giving us the opportunity to test the sample, Mr. Pratt can hardly deny its exculpatory potential. The possibility clearly exists that it's the DNA of at least one unidentified person. If not more."

"Is it my fault if the lab was unable—"

"Mr. Pratt." Worrell had heard enough.

And so had the chemist. Bad enough not to get a read on material you admitted was organic, but to blame your staff for your own dishonesty—and a *lab*, no less . . .

Worrell continued. "Mr. Pratt, much as I find your conduct distasteful"—*his* conduct, not that of his office "—it is not sufficient grounds for a mistrial. I am denying Ms. Flowers's motion." As he turned to Jackie, the judge's face was unreadable. He'd played right into her hands. "If you disagree, Ms. Flowers, take it up with a higher power."

Chapter | Forty

From inside Aaron's lawyer's head he watched her eviscerate the prosecution's case. As she roamed from defense table to lectern to witness stand in her tawny hair and violet dress, he saw the well of the court was her hunting ground. So skillful was her attack that the witness never knew he was being stalked.

"You said the house was in disarray . . ."

Addressing her lines to the rumpled sack on the stand but calibrating her voice to the jury, she knew precisely when and where to turn to expose her prey. Such intimacy.

"Nothing out of order in the kitchen . . ."

No script, no notes. Hands free and defenses forged to slash and thrust.

"No stains on the rug or floor . . ."

Her rules, her game.

"And you found the sheet on her bed . . ."

The primitive beat of a drum.

"He had not taken it with him . . ."

Her rhythm, her beat.

"And her nails were clipped . . ."

On and on she went, forcing Pratt's expert to adapt to her tempo and respond to her terse assertions with monosyllabic utterances of his own. As she accelerated and slowed, she turned ever so slightly to this juror or that, subtly validating their reactions to the testimony. Pratt was too busy

staring down his witness or whispering to his assistants to
realize how she'd co-opted them. But *he* knew, because he
was seeing through her eyes.

"No semen found on or in . . ."

Control was better than sex. *Now* he could stop—anytime
he wanted.

"Scrubbed her body with commercial soap . . ."

Power *was* sex.

"Does that make sense?"

Pratt was objecting, but she didn't seem to mind. She
should be putting up a fight. . . . Instead, she veered off and
sprung what he suddenly realized was a trap.

"By evidence, what precisely did you mean?"

He saw fear in the witness's eyes. An aphrodisiac like no
other.

"What material were you looking for?"

The jaws slammed shut, trapping the Columbo wanna-be
in his own private hell. Himes had said one word too many:
and it would cost him his head.

"Just the tiniest sample," he protested.

As the witness sought a last reprieve, the man shifted
his attention to the jurors. The woman two from the end of
the second row had abandoned her gum. He couldn't remember what she claimed to do for a living, but from the size of
her nails and hair she was no stranger to the dance. You'd be
surprised at what gets trapped under there, she'd been thinking as the witness said blood or skin.

The instructor from Metro State was devouring Aaron's
lawyer with his eyes. Give up math altogether to see her
naked . . . Didn't he realize she *was* naked, padding around
the well of the court, tearing the witness to shreds without
raising so much as a welt, and in the process exposing her
innermost nature? All but the secret that mattered most. *He*
held that in his hands.

"Two men abducted and killed Rae Malone?" she asked.
He and Jackie were two of a kind.

The teacher was jumping for it like a scrap of bloody
meat. Woman like that, flaming red hair and fancy spread
in Castle Pines, *of course* there would be two men . . . And
then the hammer dropped.

"I move for a mistrial."

Pratt's bluster, flabby and feeble, the chemist's glare when the DA only made matters worse by blaming his subordinates. That juror thought he was smarter than anyone else—*knew* he was smarter than the DA—and imagined himself marching off to the jury room and pleading her case to his peers. As if she needed a surrogate. Then they would ride off together on his hobbyhorse. . . . And the *he* would be free to wreak his own justice. Set the world aright.

As she turned to the defense table and placed her hand on Aaron's shoulder in a gesture of solidarity and comfort, he felt the acid rise in his throat.

That mewling, contemptible excuse for a—

He swallowed his resentment. Aaron was, after all, her *client*. She had to win this case or all would be for naught. But Worrell was peering at her now with hooded eyes.

"—denying Ms. Flowers's motion."

What?

She accepted the ruling without a word of protest. Nor trace of disappointment.

She hadn't expected the judge to rule in her favor—she'd made that motion knowing damn well he wouldn't grant it. A mistrial wasn't what she wanted.

She wanted to *win*. And her ambition matched his.

Her game, her rules. But his turn was coming.

And when it did, she would understand.

Chapter | Forty-one

Ms. Abbott, how long did you know the victim?"

Rae's best friend Sunny stared up as if the answer could be found in the scallops on the molded ceiling. She tapped her scarlet nails on the wooden railing of the witness box.

"Three years," she finally replied.

It was half past four on Wednesday afternoon, and a yawn rippled through the courtroom like wind through a field of parched grass. On and on Pratt went, oblivious to the torpor and malaise.

The trial was in its third day. Pratt had wasted the past two days on a parade of cops, lab technicians, and pathologists, none of whom added anything of substance to what Harry Himes had said. In another court the recitation would have taken a week, but Worrell had whipped the prosecution on like mushers in the Iditarod. The jurors' eyes were glazed and the bailiffs were shifting on their feet.

Jackie had cross-examined none of these witnesses. She'd already proved with Himes she could tear an expert to shreds, and each time Pratt offered up one of his men in blue, she shrugged away the opportunity as if it were not worth her time. "No questions, your honor" in a tone that said *nothing in this man's testimony concerns me.* She wanted to get her defense to the jury before it or she collapsed. As if sensing her fatigue, Pratt sprang his own surprise.

"Did you and Ms. Malone discuss her relationship with Mr. Best?"

The use of Aaron's formal title was an exaggerated courtesy that enabled Pratt to flare his nostrils in distaste. Jackie pinched her thigh to force herself to focus. Of more immediate concern, he was about to elicit hearsay.

"Yes," Sunny replied. She stared past Pratt to the left side of the gallery, and Jackie turned and saw Rodger Malone. At the thought that Rae's ex might be pulling the DA's star witness's strings, Jackie leaned forward in her chair.

"What did she say?"

"Rae told Aaron she wanted to break up."

Past tense. Not *planning* to tell him, but already had . . . A wise decision not to object. With a grin to the jury that said see, I deliver on my promises, Pratt surrendered the witness.

Jackie gave Sunny a disarming smile. Old friends from the bistro, comrades in arms over salades niçoises. She hoped Sunny didn't remember their conversation as well as she did.

"I take it you and Rae Malone were quite close," she began.

Sunny folded her arms across her chest. In striped espadrilles and a watermelon-pink sweater set, she looked as toothsome as a piece of hard candy.

"We certainly were."

"You said a moment ago that Rae wanted to end the relationship with Aaron Best." Break her testimony into bite-sized bits.

"Yes."

"And she told Aaron that."

"Yes."

"When did she do that?"

"Do what?"

The courtroom abruptly tilted, and without warning Jackie was back in law school. She gripped the lectern with one hand and fixed the witness with an inquisitive smile. With the other she reached in her pocket for the moss agate. She should have known this would happen. Sunny was slippery.

"Do *what*?" A touch of belligerence in the repetition.

Sunny thought she had the upper hand. In another moment the jury would be wondering what was wrong.

Deep breath, don't force it. The agate was smooth, silky. . . .

Unnerved by Jackie's silence, Sunny shifted on the stand. On her face Jackie saw her own confusion.

Snap out of it.

"Could you read the last question?" Jackie asked the court reporter. Voice firm, in control.

" 'When did she do that?' " the reporter recited.

When, *when* . . .

"When did Rae tell Aaron she wanted to break up?" Jackie continued as if there had been no interruption.

"I—I'm not sure."

She slipped the agate back in her pocket.

"Well, it must have been before she died." The jury was looking at Sunny as if she deserved the rebuke. If she hadn't pretended not to understand Jackie's question—"Wasn't it?"

"I suppose."

"When did she tell *you* that she told Aaron she wanted to break up?"

"The last time I saw her."

The courtroom had stopped spinning and Jackie stepped away from the lectern.

"Which was?"

"Lunch that Friday."

She hadn't eaten yet, that's what it was. The price of abandoning her routine during the stress of trial. "So Rae must have told him it was over before she had lunch with you that Friday."

"I guess . . . It was the last time she saw him."

"When was that?"

"Thursday night."

"Did they have sex on that occasion?"

Risky—but given Sunny's claim to the confidences she'd already disclosed, she could hardly pretend not to know the answer.

"Yes."

Even if Rae were horny or narcissistic enough for a last roll in the hay with a man who was history, Pratt's theory of motive defied common sense. If Rae's breaking up with him had driven Aaron to kill in a fit of rage, wouldn't he have done that Thursday night? Why wait until the next day? With a confused frown, Jackie drove the point home.

"Let's see if I've got this straight. Rae saw Aaron Thursday evening, the night before your lunch on Friday, and told you she'd already told Aaron she was ending their relationship."

"That's what she said."

"She didn't say, I'm *going* to tell him."

"No, it was a *fait accompli.*"

So much for motive.

"Thank you, Ms. Abbott."

The rest she would save for closing, when there was no witness to contradict her.

T ell us about the time your husband broke your wrist, Mrs. Best."

It was past five, but at the last break Pratt had informed the court he had one more witness to call and Worrell liked to start each day fresh. Sunny's cross had been a tonic for the jury and Jackie's confidence was restored. As Pratt wound to a close with Aaron's wife reiterating that at the time of Rae's death she'd filed for divorce and sole custody of their son, Jackie focused on damage control.

"What did the two of you fight about?" she began. A gamble, but Wendy wouldn't be able to resist sticking in the knife.

"Other women."

"Were you surprised to learn Aaron was having an affair with Rae Malone?"

"No."

The contrary would have made her a fool.

"But Aaron always came back?"

"*I'm* the one who left."

"But after the argument at your home, you stayed."

Wendy glanced at Pratt, who looked away. No help from that quarter.

"For a short time."

"Short?"

"Six months," she grudgingly admitted.

"And you dropped the charges."

"It was the best thing for my son."

Like testifying here today . . . Jackie paused to let the jury consider that.

"Who owns Best Energy?" she asked.

"Objection!" Pratt's voice rang through the room. "Relevancy."

"It goes to this witness's motive for testifying," Jackie replied.

Worrell cocked his pendulous head at Pratt. "You've been spending an awful lot of time trying to establish motive on the defendant's account, haven't you, Mr. Pratt?" Jackie's point hadn't been lost. "Overruled."

"Who owns Best Energy?" she repeated.

"My husband and I."

"What will happen to the company if Aaron is convicted?"

"Control goes to me. But—"

"How do you plan to run it?"

Wendy shrugged. "I'll keep the employees."

Jackie let that sink in as long as she dared. Times like these, she could really *use* a yellow pad—shuffling through pages underscored the point.

"Is Aaron a good father?"

Another risk, but any answer except *yes* would reflect poorly on Wendy.

"I want custody."

From the teacher's frown Jackie knew Wendy had just crossed the line from wronged wife to vindictive witch. And caring fathers were poor candidates for psychopathic killers.

"Did Aaron ever strike Trevor?"

"No."

"Is he a loving father, will you give him just *that*?"

No answer to the rhetorical question, which was precisely how Jackie wanted to end.

As the courtroom cleared, Jackie saw Aaron's brother slink out the back. She swallowed her irritation. Mark had ignored her instructions to stay away, but she couldn't afford to stew over that now. She needed all her wits about her, because she was about to deliver the advice her client least wanted to hear.

It was halftime and they were ahead on points. A good thing—because if the defense wasn't winning by the time the prosecution rested, the case was most likely lost. Signaling to the deputy that she needed a moment to speak with Aaron alone, she steeled herself for the confrontation.

"I don't want you taking the stand," she began.

"But we're *winning*. You just massacred Sunny and Wendy—"

"That's exactly why."

The conventional wisdom was keep your client off the stand unless you were doing so badly, you had nothing to lose. Defendants inevitably shot themselves in the foot, and objecting made it look like you had something to hide. Better that Aaron vent here than in front of the jury.

"If I don't tell my story, they'll think I'm guilty. Whose side are you *on*?"

It wasn't that Aaron was unpresentable, or that his story lacked credibility. Nor even that he'd lied to her once too often. It was something far less tangible and more dangerous than that—her sense that he was malleable, saw his existence controlled entirely by others. Because he liked being the center of attention but was eager to please, Aaron would be putty in Pratt's hands. And for some unfathomable reason he was absolutely certain he would be acquitted. She couldn't let the jury see *that*.

"Look, Aaron. We've done a pretty good job with the prosecution's witnesses, and I don't want to give Pratt ammunition for cross. Tomorrow morning I'm opening with Richard Hanna—"

"What about Mark?"

She didn't *need* this now, not when she was stretched to the limit. She kept her voice low, trying to mollify her client.

"I haven't decided whether to call Mark or not."

"I see what you're doing." Aaron's voice rose, and the deputy by the door started forward. Jackie waved him back. "You're rolling over on me!"

"You said it yourself, Aaron—we're ahead of the game. Why would I—"

Fists clenched, he stood. "You didn't fight for me when

Pratt threw me back in the can, and now you won't let me fight for myself!"

Two deputies came to his side. One pulled Aaron's wrists behind his back and the other expertly snapped on the cuffs. That seemed only to enrage him more.

"I knew I should have fired—"

They wrestled him out of the courtroom.

It was past six o'clock when Jackie paid the parking attendant at the lot across the street from the side entrance to the City and County Building. Catering to attorneys not lucky enough to find a meter or unwilling to run outside every fifteen minutes to plug another quarter, the lot was stacked four cars deep during the day but almost empty by the time Jackie left. As she pulled out and prepared to turn right, she saw a solitary figure on the corner.

Wendy Best.

Traffic was light and there was no one behind Jackie trying to exit the lot. A red light, then a green. Colfax and Broadway, on every major bus route, was two blocks away, and the bus terminal one block farther north, but Wendy made no move to cross. The light turned for the third time.

She was waiting for someone to pick her up.

A friend, maybe the mother who lived in Pueblo. Someone had to be looking after Trevor. . . . Five minutes passed and a green Explorer coasted down Delaware. It looked vaguely familiar, but Denver had more SUVs than voters in the last election, and they were all the same to Jackie. Pulling to a stop in front of Wendy, the driver leaned over and cracked open the passenger door. Wendy didn't move. After a moment he obligingly hopped out.

Mark Best.

He held the door as Wendy climbed in, then circled to the driver's side. Wendy slid to the center and Mark wrapped his arms around her. After a passionate embrace, they sped off.

A gray haze hovered over the conference table in Jackie's office and the ashtray overflowed with cigarillo butts.

"Where've you been?" Pilar demanded. "Worrell's clerk said court let out half an hour ago."

"Took me a while to get out of the lot."

Pilar glanced at her quizzically, then slid the pizza box across the table. "Forget to eat lunch again?"

Jackie helped herself to a slice. For the first time since the trial began three days earlier, she felt hungry. And she was just as glad she hadn't told Pilar about that credit card slip. "So what's the word in the ladies' room?"

Judges can hurt you, but clerks can kill you. The best way to monitor the impact of the evidence was by listening to what bailiffs, reporters, and the retirees who spent their afternoons in court said during recess.

"They hate Wendy," Pilar replied.

"Great."

"And *love* your outfits. Especially that scarlet number you wore Tuesday."

Jackie bit off the end of her slice and slowly chewed. Sausage, anchovies . . . And diet Coke. Pilar was trying to buck her up. There must be something she hadn't told her.

"How's Pratt doing?" she asked.

"Boring them to tears." Pilar hadn't touched her pizza. Something was definitely wrong. "And you made mincemeat of his motive."

"Guess who I saw on the way home?"

"Who?"

"Mark Best."

"You don't say." Pilar didn't sound surprised. "I thought you told him to steer clear of the courthouse until you decided whether to call him."

"He was in the courtroom too." Jackie took another bite, then pushed the pizza away. "But you can tell Lily to quit worrying about him hitting on me. He was with a date."

"Oh?"

"Wendy Best."

"No shit!" Pilar was genuinely shocked. "What were they doing?"

"Smooching."

"Jeez." She took her time selecting a slice even though they were all the same. "What are you thinking?"

"I can't call him to the stand. If he's screwing his brother's wife, he'd have no compunction about screwing him out of his company. *And* an acquittal. I always thought that alibi was too good to be true."

"Well, it makes this a little easier. . . ." Reaching in the folder by the ashtray, Pilar handed Jackie a fax.

Confidential—File Sealed.

"What's that?" Jackie asked. She didn't want to touch it.

"Mark's juvenile record. There was more to that idyllic childhood than father-knows-best."

"What'd he do, bust a few windows?"

"Another kid's head. Brained him with a baseball bat when he was eleven."

"Christ!"

" 'Fraid so. Papa put in the fix and shipped Mark to a military academy in Georgia. Next time he set foot in Colorado was to attend the School of Mines."

"Did the authorities do any follow-up?"

"Periodic mental status assessments. When he graduated from the academy he got a clean bill of health."

"Pratt must know about it."

"A sealed file?" Pilar's brows soared in mock surprise. "You're such a cynic."

"That's why he doesn't give a damn about the alibi. He's just waiting for me to call Mark so he can shove Mark's record up our collective butt."

"Another defense bites the dust. . . . What about Aaron?"

"I delivered the bad news to him at the end of the day."

"How'd he take it?"

Jackie was too exhausted to laugh. "He thinks I'm throwing the case."

"It's the right decision," Pilar assured her. "No matter how well you dress 'em, on the stand they always revert."

"I don't need Aaron to explain how and when the sheet was stained. Sunny Abbott took care of that. And I've got to get this case to the jury before anything goes wrong."

"So you roll the dice with Hanna. . . ."

"I guess so." Jackie balled up her napkin and dropped it in the pizza box.

"How far will he go?"

"Profile of the killer, which Aaron doesn't fit. Whether

he'll be willing to link Starla and the other three to Rae, I don't know." Richard hadn't returned the messages she'd left the last two nights, and she was trying not to think about what that meant. The fact that Pilar hadn't said she'd told her so was even more depressing. "We're meeting tomorrow morning, before I put him on the stand."

"You think he knows?" Pilar asked.

"That business about Mark? How could he?" Jackie thought back to their conversation after she learned how Aaron inherited his company. "He said it was normal sibling rivalry, with a mother more passive than most. No wonder Aaron was the favorite." She couldn't tell him Mark's history now, not if he was waffling on his opinion. "Besides, Mark's record has nothing to do with Aaron. Why should he care?"

"No time to rock the boat . . ."

At least she didn't say the ship was sinking.

Pilar pushed back her chair. "Sounds like tomorrow will be a big day. Let's go pick out your war paint."

Jackie smiled grimly. "Afraid I'll forget to wear my undies?"

"Something like that."

"Just don't spike Mr. Coffee with yerba buena."

"That's a deal."

Chapter | Forty-two

merican Board of Forensic Psychiatry."

Richard Hanna's clear voice filled the well of the court. Pratt had offered to stipulate to his credentials, but Jackie would have none of that. With a client accused of brutally beheading a woman, she needed an expert who walked on water. Or at least arrived on time.

In his lightweight tweed sport coat and paisley tie, Richard had breezed into court three minutes before the morning session convened, apologizing for missing their meeting. He said he'd been tied up with an emergency. Jackie had advised him only to dress for comfort, but his instincts were unerring: every woman on the jury wanted to redress him, and the men sympathized with his having to wear a tie. Liking him was the first step to accepting his opinion, and she concealed her anxiety.

"Do you belong to any professional organizations?" she asked.

Using the pointer, Richard gestured to the curriculum vitae Jackie had projected on a screen. "The American Medical Association, American Psychiatric Association, American Academy of Forensic Sciences . . ."

Although Jackie used visual aids to vary her tempo and keep the jury awake, she was no fan of technology in the courtroom. If Pratt's job was to banish her client from the campfire, hers was to bring Aaron back to civilization by demonstrating that the accused's humanity was no different from their own. Mechanical apparatus tended to interfere with that, plus she didn't know how to operate them. The one exception she made was in the case of an expert with an impeccable list of credentials.

Pilar had set up the projector just before the jurors were led in, and when Richard took the stand they were anticipating a break in the Q&A. Citing her own ineptitude, Jackie asked Worrell to let Richard step down from the box and walk the jury through his CV—allowing them to observe him without barriers. The fact that he needed something to jog his recollection of his achievements made him less intimidating, and since he hadn't taken notes of his interview with Aaron, she didn't want him consulting written materials on the stand.

"Do you accept private patients?" she asked as Richard relinquished the pointer and returned to the witness box. Today she was wearing a fawn-colored suit with a silk blouse in a blush tone—neutrals, but with a nod to her fans in the ladies' room. Unlike in cross, on direct examination her *witness* took center stage.

"A small number, most of them through court referrals."

"Speaking of courts, have you testified before?"

"On more than a hundred occasions. Civil and criminal cases."

Stepping away from the lectern, Jackie positioned herself by the jury box so Richard could remain in their line of sight while answering.

"Let's stick with criminal. In what areas have you rendered opinions?"

"Mainly regarding a defendant's fitness to stand trial, or the appropriateness of an insanity defense." As he responded, Richard scanned the jury, missing none. He hadn't needed to be told.

"Has Mr. Pratt's office ever retained you in either regard?"

"On fitness for trial, at least a dozen times."

"And your opinion was . . . ?"

"Each of those defendants was fit."

"Has Mr. Pratt ever retained you to render an opinion as to sanity?"

"Yes. On more of those occasions than any other."

"And you opined . . . ?"

"None of the defendants was insane."

Jackie paused, as if perplexed.

"Dr. Hanna, how many times in your career have you agreed to testify for the *defense*?"

"This is the first." He shrugged diffidently. "With my record, maybe they're afraid to ask."

Two jurors laughed aloud and the bus driver suppressed a chuckle. Richard's modesty played well: the bigger challenge would be selling the jury on the substance of his testimony.

"And when I asked if you were willing to examine Mr. Best for purposes of this case, did you attach any conditions?"

"I certainly did." Richard faced the jurors head-on. "I required both you and your client to waive any objection you might have to my testifying in favor of the prosecution if I believed your client was guilty. And anything he said in the course of my evaluation I was free to reveal to the district attorney. In fact, my testimony has no strings attached."

The chemist gave a slight nod. The teacher kept looking at Richard's hands, probably trying to see whether he was single.

"Under what circumstances might the DA have sought your opinion?"

"If Mr. Best subsequently claimed he was unfit to stand trial, or if he changed his plea to not guilty by reason of insanity."

"Neither of which has occurred."

"That's correct."

"So, if you concluded he indeed *was* capable of that brutal crime, would you be sitting here today?"

"Not unless the DA called me."

"The bottom line is . . . ?"

"Your client took a real risk in allowing me to evaluate him for trial, because my opinion's not for sale."

That should do it for even the most die-hard of Pratt's fans, if there were any left.

"Well, let's get down to it." Standing as close as she dared to the jury box, Jackie laid it on the line. "Does Aaron Best possess the psychological and emotional characteristics of the type of person who murdered and decapitated Rae Malone?"

"In a word, no."

Pratt was leaning forward, scribbling furiously as his female assistant whispered in his ear.

"On what do you base your opinion, Dr. Hanna?"

"My personal evaluation of Mr. Best and a review of the crime-scene file."

"When you perform an evaluation, do you take what the subject says at face value?"

"Certainly not. If the information is objectively verifiable, I check other sources. And my experience and training as a forensic psychiatrist play a large role in how I assess what I hear. In this case I was provided with extensive materials regarding the crimes."

A slip, or was Richard signaling his willingness to testify to more than just the murder of Rae Malone? But he'd already gone out on a limb with his opinion, and Jackie didn't want to risk chopping it off.

"The same methodology and materials you've used every time you testified for Mr. Pratt?"

"Correct."

It was time to talk details, and here they had to be sensitive. If it made the jurors queasy, she would get him off the stand before he broadened his opinion to the other murders.

"Tell us the characteristics of the man you believe *is* capable of this crime."

"First of all, he's almost certainly a psychopath." Richard's voice took on new animation. Some experts dreaded testifying and were utterly incompetent in court. Those who relished the opportunity as a vehicle for professional mastery were much rarer. "In layman's terms, he's a social predator who charms and manipulates his way through life."

"How does he get that way?"

"As a result of many factors." He gave an apologetic look at the chemist and then glanced ruefully at the mathematician a row up and two over—how did he *know*?—before continuing. "Psychiatry is a matter of judgment and insight—we're not dealing with something that can be quantitatively measured or drawn. With that caveat, psychopathic behavior seems to be a product of psychological, biological, social, and genetic forces, as well as early life experiences. These traits exist in varying degrees across the larger population. If the child commits no violent acts by his late teens, his potential for violence later is drastically reduced."

"Those characteristics are . . . ?"

"Lack of empathy, failure to accept responsibility, poor impulse control. If they marry at all, their marriages tend to be short-lived. Psychopaths have a shallow affect"—he turned helpfully to the beautician—"which means they're glib and superficial, the emotions don't run deep. Lacking insight and true affinity for others, their stimulation comes almost entirely from without. To them rules are an imposition, normal people either a source of gratification or in the way."

Jackie took a deep breath. "What are the specific factors in Rae Malone's murder that lead you to believe it was committed by a psychopath?" With this question she might lose some of the women but gain every one of the men.

"For one, the crime was particularly brutal and remorseless. Ms. Malone seems to have been taken from her home and kept alive for a considerable period of time at some unknown spot before she was killed. After she was murdered, her body was mutilated. The fact that there was very little disarray in her home suggests she was somehow conned into leaving with her killer." He hesitated. "By that, I certainly don't mean to suggest she *knew* him. He could have been someone who came to her door with a compelling story. And bathing her body and clipping her nails after he murdered her certainly suggests he's familiar with the criminal justice system."

"Meaning . . . ?"

"Those precautionary acts are specifically designed to thwart law enforcement from solving the crime. The entire MO suggests Ms. Malone was not his first victim. He may even have served time for a previous crime or crimes. These guys tend to start young."

Jackie risked a peek at the jury. They seemed to be holding up, but an older woman was looking green. Could she have her cake and eat it too—argue the possibility that the Hollow Man could be *two killers*? Wiser to wait and see what Pratt had up his sleeve.

"And you believe Aaron Best lacks those characteristics?"

Impatiently, Richard shook his head. "Bearing in mind that psychiatry is not a 'hard' science like math or physics"—another nod to the chemist and the instructor from Metro

State—"Mr. Best's emotional makeup is all wrong." As he smiled apologetically at Jackie, she realized he had not once looked in Aaron's direction. "Is it okay if I talk in terms lay people can understand?"

"Please do."

"Mr. Best has an enormous need to please those in authority. And when he fails to do so, he demonstrates genuine remorse. He's almost *too* focused on what others think of him. Those qualities alone strongly militate against the commission of this sort of homicide. It's virtually inconceivable that a person with no significant history of interpersonal violence at a young age would be capable of beheading a woman. The police should be looking for someone with a short fuse, someone who may have done this sort of thing before."

"Not Mr. Best?"

"In my professional opinion, *no*."

Dr. Hanna, you testified you based your opinion on interviewing Mr. Best."

"In part."

Pratt had begun his cross-examination cautiously, almost as if he were afraid to offend the witness. He'd made the mistake of having Richard review his CV again just to establish there were no standard practices or supervisory agencies in the field of profiling—a matter with which Richard readily agreed. Jackie was finding it difficult to concentrate. She knew where Pratt was going. He'd finished laying the groundwork for the argument that Richard's access to Aaron was insufficient to plumb the depths of his psyche with a long series of questions about how many minutes were in the therapeutic hour, the number of visits per week, and the average length of time patients spent in treatment. Now he was preparing to deliver his coup de grâce.

"And how many hours did you spend with Mr. Best? Two? Two and a half?"

"Approximately fourteen months."

Jackie's stomach flipped, but she told herself to remain calm. Not even blink. Beside her, she felt Aaron's quick intake of breath.

"Fourteen hours, did you say?"

"Months."

"Fourteen months?"

Pratt looked like a grenade had been stuffed down his trousers and he was waiting to be told whether to pull the pin. One of his assistants was digging through a file while the other desperately tried to get his attention. Jackie herself was having trouble breathing. Richard, on the other hand, seemed unperturbed. He fixed Pratt with a steady gaze, waiting for the next question.

"But doesn't your report say you visited with him on"—Pratt glanced at the paper his subordinate thrust at him—"June 17 at the county jail?"

"Yes."

"A visit that lasted just a few hours?"

"Three and a half, to be exact."

"Then where did the other fourteen months come in?"

"Aaron Best was my patient."

"Your *patient*?"

"Aaron was initially referred to me by the court for a custody evaluation. He continued to see me as a therapist to deal with issues surrounding his impending divorce."

Jackie dared not look at Aaron. Although her relationship with her client had hit a new low when she'd told him not to take the stand, he'd been even more furious at Richard's description of him as a man obsessed with what others thought. Now she understood why.

"—think that was something the DA's office was entitled to know?"

"Until this morning Mr. Best hadn't waived his doctor-patient privilege of confidentiality with respect to our therapy."

"Now, hold on just a minute, Dr. Hanna. You told this jury Mr. Best *waived*—"

"Any rights with respect to my evaluation of him *for purposes of this trial*. Therapy in connection with his marital difficulties was another matter."

Pratt shook his head vigorously. "And you don't think you and Ms. Flowers have *misled this court*—"

"Ms. Flowers had no knowledge of the therapeutic relationship. Until Mr. Best elected to waive confidentiality this morning, I was under an ethical obligation not to disclose it."

Pratt turned to the judge. "I move that Dr. Hanna's entire testimony be stricken."

"On what grounds?"

"Defense counsel's misconduct. She deliberately misled—"

"Dr. Hanna testified Ms. Flowers was kept in the dark."

"But he—"

With a bob of his head, Worrell cut him off. "That's what cross-examination's for, Mr. Pratt. Motion denied."

Pratt stepped back to the prosecution table to confer with his assistants. The girl was jabbering in his ear, but Jackie could tell he was incapable of assimilating anything she said. Glowering, he returned to the lectern.

"Don't you have a conflict of interest, Dr. Hanna?" he demanded. "As the defendant's psychotherapist, you can't possibly be as objective as a clinical evaluator."

"To the contrary. I've had the opportunity to observe Mr. Best over an extended period of time, to get to know him in a way an evaluator can't. There's always a risk of the subject displaying only what he wants you to see, but a facade that can be maintained for four hours cannot be sustained for fourteen months. I understand what makes Aaron tick."

"What *exactly* did Ms. Flowers retain you to do?"

"To examine her client and review evidence to determine whether Mr. Best was psychologically capable of committing the crime for which he was charged."

"Is that all?"

Pratt was fishing in dangerous waters, but even if Jackie had had a basis to object, she wouldn't have dared: her personal credibility had never been in greater doubt. For an instant her eyes met Richard's. His were impenetrable.

"Ms. Flowers also asked me to examine evidence of four other crimes in the Denver area in order to determine whether the same type of offender who murdered Ms. Malone might have committed those four murders as well."

Pratt took the bait.

"And your opinion was?"

"Based on the great number of specific similarities

among the crimes, I believe the same type of offender committed all five."

Jackie exhaled. The Hollow Man defense was on the table, and it would make or break her case.

"But you have no idea *who* that offender is, do you?"

"That's true." Richard looked straight at Aaron. "But I have a very good idea who he *isn't*."

Pratt was so rattled, he forgot to inquire about Richard's fee before returning to his seat.

"Redirect, Ms. Flowers?"

"Yes, your honor. I think I will."

"Perhaps we should take a brief recess." Offering a break so close to lunch was unprecedented for him. "Five minutes."

All rose as the bailiff led the jury out. Pratt and his assistants exited by the door to the right of the bench and the deputy snapped on Aaron's handcuffs for a trip to the men's room. Signaling Richard to join her, Jackie stepped into the corridor. When he followed, she pulled him into an empty room across the hall.

"What the hell did you think you were doing with that stunt?" she raged.

"Stunt?"

"Why didn't you tell me you knew Aaron before you took this case?"

"When you came to my office I didn't realize it was Aaron. I hadn't been following the case—I didn't even know he'd been arrested. When I met with him at the jail I told him he owed it to you to come clean—"

"Not good enough. I trusted you, you should have *withdrawn*—"

"You're damn right. I should have walked out that door." Suddenly, he was as furious as she was. "You know why I didn't? I've risked my professional reputation because I'm so goddamned *enamoured* with you that—"

"—you were willing to jeopardize my whole case?"

"You've got to be kidding, Jackie. I just *handed* you an acquittal."

"How can you say that? The jury will never believe I didn't—"

"You should have seen your face."

"What?"

He grabbed her arm, forcing her to look at him.

"When I said I was Aaron's therapist. You were so surprised, your jaw almost hit the table. You think Pratt can argue I was a hired gun when the person who hired me learned the score the same moment the jury did?"

Was that supposed to make her grateful?

"Not only was your credibility boosted by that thing you call a *stunt*," Richard continued, "but now they'll have even more reason to believe me when I say Aaron isn't the Hollow Man."

There was a knock on the door, and the bailiff poked his head in.

"Miss Flowers? The judge is ready to take the bench."

When he left, she pivoted toward Richard.

"This better work. If it doesn't, it's Aaron's neck."

W hat was the condition of Starla McBride's body when it was found?"

"Decapitated, like Ms. Malone and the others."

Over Pratt's repeated objections, Jackie had led Richard through the basic facts of the four other murders. As Worrell was pleased to remind the DA, he'd opened the door and there was no turning back. They'd recessed for a short lunch and were at it again.

"And when was Ms. McBride murdered?" she continued.

"Late May."

"Do you know where Mr. Best was the night she disappeared?"

"I've seen an affidavit by Tom Morrissey, the owner of Morrissey Construction, that he and two other men were with—"

"Objection, hearsay!" Pratt was slow on the draw but right on the mark.

"Sustained," snapped the judge.

Jackie paused, as if gathering her thoughts. The chemist shot a hard glance at Pratt. Even men of science weren't above the need to find a person to blame for an investigation that had so obviously gone wrong. First the lab, then impugning the expert's integrity, now *this* . . .

"You told Mr. Pratt"—a reminder that it was her opponent who'd elicited the crucial opinion, and not her—"that the same type of offender committed all five crimes, based on certain similarities. Tell us what those were."

Richard turned to the jury. "The victims were all divorcées in their late thirties or early forties, with medium-risk lifestyles. By that I mean they had stable jobs but were actively seeking relationships. All were abducted from places in which they perceived little personal risk. For the most part, these were crowded, well-lit social settings that posed a fairly high level of risk for the offender. The killer probably approached each woman openly, in a friendly manner, and convinced her to leave with him. A 'con.' "

"How did he control them?" Jackie asked.

"Binding or stun gun. Whatever force he used was sudden, designed to ensure compliance. We know that because there's no evidence any of these women had time to resist. He took them to a secluded location where he would be in control."

"What do we know about how and when they were killed?"

"In all likelihood they were strangled. Do you want me to go on?"

"Please."

"No DNA was found in or on their bodies, but the killer appears to have subjected them to certain sexual acts."

"Forgive me for asking, Dr. Hanna, but was that before or after they were killed?"

"Before." Was he sparing the jury, or had Pilar misread the pathologists' reports? "And we can't overlook the fact that they were left nude, in outdoor spots where they would quickly be found."

"Why no DNA?"

"He bathed their bodies with antibacterial soap before disposing of them. He may also have used a condom, which brings me to another point of similarity. This is a killer who takes great pains not to be caught. By abducting a woman from one county and leaving her in another—with no clothing or artifacts that might be a source of trace evidence—he did everything he could to obscure links. Needless to say, his ultimate precautions were to kill his victims and leave no witnesses."

"We've all heard the phrase 'serial murder.' Is that what these crimes were?"

Richard sighed. The notion seemed to sadden him.

"So-called 'serial crimes' are usually committed against strangers, with a low-risk MO because the killer wants to repeat without being caught. He selects dump sites far from contact points and generally tries to prevent the bodies from being found. How does that square with what we know of these crimes?" He poured a cup of water from the carafe at his elbow. He'd been testifying for three hours now, after spending the entire morning on the stand. The pause seemed only to whet the jurors' interest.

"There are no known connections between the victims," he continued. "From the killer's perspective, these women were risky targets because, although they perceived themselves to be in safe environments when they were accosted, they were likely to be missed within forty-eight hours. I suspect the increased risk made them all the more attractive. A challenge." The air-conditioning in the courtroom was audible as he took another sip. "The fact that the bodies were left at 'destination spots' suggests familiarity with those places but not necessarily a local resident. He may have kept some of their clothing or jewelry as trophies or souvenirs. Serial killers do that to relive the experience later in fantasy."

She had to wrap this up before Pratt woke up or the jury became numb to the gore. The roller coaster of a day was affecting her concentration.

"Based on the five crime scenes, what are the offender's personality traits?"

"As I said before, he's glib, manipulative, dominant, and possessive. He may have law-enforcement training or previous arrests. Even if he has no adult record, he might have demonstrated violence at a young age, causing death or severe injury to animals or a smaller child. . . ."

Confidential—File Sealed.

". . . intelligent, college education, high level of skill with tools . . ."

Maybe even an engineer.

". . . disciplined and patient, so he's steadily employed. His use of a con and ability to assess risk says he thinks on his feet. Because he left the bodies in somewhat rugged nature spots, he's physically fit, maybe works outdoors at least part of the time . . ."

Construction or a related field. Like green energy.

". . . comfortable around women, likes to flirt, thinks of himself as a ladies' man . . ."

Lily would have no problem picking him out of a crowd.

". . . a leader, not a follower . . ."

From tattoos to bar fights to a trip to Dinosaur National Monument—of which there was no real proof.

"And an accomplished liar who has no difficulty deceiving law enforcement and mental health professionals."

She'd even had the credit slip—*how had she let Mark Best fool her?*

Jackie glanced over her shoulder. Aaron sat at the defense table doodling on her legal pad, his expression oddly docile. There was no trace of his earlier anger—no guilt or anxiety marred his features. If the killer were two men and one was Mark, the other could be only— She shook her head to clear it. This was absolutely crazy. She was letting her imagination run away with her when she needed most to focus. Aaron was *innocent.*

"Dr. Hanna, this morning you said the offender's characteristics don't fit Aaron Best. Having told us Aaron was in therapy with you for fourteen months, is there anything you want to add?"

As Richard's gaze finally turned to his patient, Jackie saw only compassion.

"People who are capable of committing the sort of violence inflicted on Rae Malone and those four other women are psychologically damaged in the extreme. Without going into whether they are clinically insane—which is another issue entirely—these killers often reenact abuse they suffered as children. Nothing in Mr. Best's personal history suggests such abuse." He seemed reluctant to continue, but the jury was watching intently. They, too, sensed there was more.

"And?"

Richard's discomfort was palpable.

"Mr. Best has an active fantasy life, one which he freely shared in therapy. . . ."

A follower, not a leader. Highly suggestible—participant and spectator? Nothing Richard had said precluded *two* men acting in concert.

"Though his fantasies are sexually aggressive"—*more bang for the buck?*—"it would be fair to say that the crimes we're discussing here would be so foreign to Aaron's character as to be virtually unimaginable."

Jackie drove directly home from court and went straight to bed. As she fell asleep without taking off her shoes, she saw a corn husk wearing wingtips break into a jig and then split in two.

Chapter | Forty-three

uite a performance."

Duncan Pratt stepped to the lectern, which had been moved directly in front of the jury box.

"Yes, sir," he continued. "That was quite a performance. I hardly know where to start. With the shrink who isn't really a shrink—well, maybe just sorta—or the phantom of defense counsel's opera?"

After Richard had left the stand late Thursday afternoon and the jurors were dismissed for the night, Jackie announced she was resting her defense. In addition to catching Pratt off guard, she wanted to get the case to the jury before the weekend. One rule would never change: the less time a jury deliberated, the better it was for the underdog. The last thing she needed was them mulling about the defense for two days and coming back clear-eyed on Monday.

"Unfair!" Pratt had cried. "She gave notice of an alibi and didn't put one on."

"Ms. Flowers made no mention of alibi in her opening statement, as I recall," Worrell replied. "And if you were so entranced with her witness, you could have endorsed him yourself."

That would be the day. Nor could Pratt complain about Jackie's refusal to call her client to the stand, but he wasn't finished.

"She sandbagged us with red herrings!"

"How many of those herrings do you suppose would fit in a bag of sand?" Worrell mused.

"But I have rebuttal witnesses. . . ."

"That's what sandbagging's all about, Mr. Pratt. Saving your best for last. You're too late. Unless you want to call a profiling expert to rebut Dr. Hanna's learned testimony."

Jackie argued the standard motion for acquittal on the basis of the prosecution's failure to make its case. The judge had promptly denied it and set closing arguments for the following morning, right after he delivered his instructions.

"I want to have them in the jury room by noon," Worrell told them. "Perhaps they, like I, will have more interesting things to do over the weekend than return here."

Pratt was obviously still smarting from having his rebuttal cut out from under his feet, but anger had dangerously sharpened his rhetoric. It confirmed what Jackie always suspected—too much time to prepare was more often a curse than a blessing. As he continued his opening statement in his dark blue suit, snowy shirt, and boldly striped tie, Pratt breathed authority and rectitude.

"To call the nonsense Dr. Hanna spun for you 'junk science' would be damning it with faint praise." Vitriolic but vague. A full-fledged attack on profiling—a word Pratt took pains not to use—could come back to haunt him in a case where the prosecution might want to use it. And having endorsed Richard as an expert countless times in the past, Dunc could hardly attack his credentials now. "He himself admitted the field has never been subjected to rigorous analysis or accountability. . . .

"But setting his gobbledygook aside, what are we to make of a witness who takes the stand wearing one hat and leaves in another? Thursday morning Dr. Hanna was an evaluator retained by Ms. Flowers to interview her client for the sole purpose of this trial. Lunchtime comes and—presto, change-o!—he's a psychotherapist who's known the guy for more than a year. Are we really to believe his mumbo-jumbo about confidentiality and waiver, or was that just another trick in the magician's bag? We'll never know, because—"

"Mr. Pratt."

That was all Worrell needed to say. The DA had come perilously close to commenting on Aaron's failure to take the stand, which would have been grounds for Jackie to seek a mistrial. The last thing she wanted.

"And now we come to the centerpiece of the good doctor's testimony," Pratt continued without missing a beat. "The mystery man no one can identify because he simply doesn't exist. If you think he's real, then no woman on the Front Range is safe."

A shrewd risk. Pratt was tapping into every citizen's fear—that law enforcement agencies didn't have the faintest idea what they were doing—while spreading the blame for Denver's shoddy police work to Gilpin and El Paso counties, with Douglas, Arapahoe, and JeffCo thrown in for good measure.

"Ladies and gentlemen, you've heard from no fewer than twelve forensic experts. They have described in intimate detail their investigation into the disappearance of Rae Malone which culminated in the tragic discovery of her mutilated body. Aaron Best was the last man known to have seen her alive."

Unless you counted the busboy who cleared away her salade niçoise.

"What *do* we know about the defendant?"

Pratt held up a pudgy left hand. Under the fluorescent light the red stone in his class ring winked. Starting with the pinkie, he began ticking off his points.

"First, we know he and the victim were having a torrid affair. Second, we know he was going through a tumultuous divorce involving a nasty custody dispute. Aaron Best had a history of domestic violence, and the situation was so stressful, he sought psychiatric help. Third, we know Rae Malone was planning to end the affair. She told her best friend she wanted to reconcile with her husband. Fourth, we know he had sex with her right about the time she disappeared. And fifth"—he turned to Aaron, jabbing his thumb straight at him—"*no one saw her alive again. Ever.*"

With a nod to the need to protect society's most vulnerable members regardless of how affluent they were or where they might choose to reside, Pratt thanked the jury in advance for reaching a result he had no doubt would be just. It was the only time Jackie had seen him argue without a pad full of notes.

Deliberately, she rose. In royal blue with touches of gold at her ears and throat, she wanted to project power and strength. Were the crime not so violent, or she planned to throw herself and her client at the mercy of the jurors, she might have chosen summer white and pearls. But she had to confront Rae Malone's murder head-on, and there was nothing to apologize for.

As she stepped to the lectern, Jackie took the time to make eye contact with each juror. They'd entered the courtroom that first day with two expectations: the lawyers knew what really happened, and someone was about to lie. After opening statements, both expectations were generally met—and then the question was which side to believe. Denial was never enough; the winner showed them how and why. Because the simplest explanation was most believable and occasionally correct, she began there.

"Cops make mistakes. And the more pressure they're under to make a fast arrest, the more likely they are to pick the most convenient target."

An easier sell than cops were crooks, and Lieutenant Himes had taken enough abuse from Duncan Pratt. Off came the gloves.

"The DA has offered five so-called reasons to convict Aaron Best. I'll give you five reasons to acquit."

She cocked her pinkie. "First, Becky Cox. Abducted from LoDo in July 1993. Found decapitated in the Garden of the Gods two days later. No connection whatsoever to Aaron Best.

"Second, Carole Wade. Abducted from the parking lot of Harland Middle School in June 1997. Found decapitated in Red Rocks three days later. No connection whatsoever to Aaron Best.

"Third, Fern Kaplan. Abducted from Cherry Creek in February 1998. Found decapitated in Pioneer Cemetery four days later. No connection whatsoever to Aaron Best.

"Fourth, Starla McBride. Abducted from a casino in Black Hawk in late May of this year. Found five days later decapitated in Roxborough Park. No connection whatsoever to Aaron Best—he was with business associates." Pratt rose to object, then contented himself with a look of disgust. "Is Mr. Pratt the only one who can't see the pattern?"

Finally the thumb. "Fifth, Rae Malone. Abducted from her home in Castle Pines in April. Found decapitated behind Coors Stadium six days later. But Rae Malone deserves five more reasons of her own, so let's take the DA's 'facts' one by one."

"First, were Rae Malone and Aaron Best having a torrid affair? Aaron was separated from his wife and Rae was already divorced. Despite Mr. Pratt's attempts to make their relationship sound illegitimate, the plain fact is both were free to enter into it.

"Second, was Aaron Best going through a tumultuous divorce? Mr. Pratt's inference is, of course, that Aaron feared his wife would discover his relationship with Rae and killed to keep her quiet. But Wendy Best said the affair was no surprise." She paused. "The sad fact is, in a marriage which *one* of the parties had already decided was over, Aaron's relationship with Rae was simply a nonevent."

"Now we come to the heart of the DA's case. Rae told her best friend, Sunny, she'd told Aaron she wanted to end the affair. The last time Sunny saw Rae, *she already had*. What did Sunny call it—a fait accompli? And there Rae was the next day, none the worse for having delivered the news. If Aaron Best was the volatile, vindictive monster Mr. Pratt would have you believe, *why did Rae Malone live to tell the tale*?

"Fourth, the liaison that left DNA on Rae Malone's sheet. We all know when that happened, because Sunny told us. Not 'right about the time Rae disappeared,' but Thursday night—at least twelve hours before Sunny last saw her, and an untold period of time *before* Rae was abducted."

"Last but not least, the DA's biggest stretch of all—that no one ever saw Rae after her final meeting with Aaron Best. Mr. Pratt must not believe his own witnesses. Rae's friend had lunch with her the next day. And, according to Lieutenant Himes, *for all they know the killer could have been two men.*"

She'd planted the two-man seed without contradicting Richard's thesis, but there was one thing left to say.

"Rae Malone's killer is a twisted monster whose entire life is deceit. He is incapable of enjoying a healthy relationship with a woman, so he targets and stalks strangers for kicks. His goals are to control and degrade women, not to exact revenge for a failed love affair. And he's been doing it for a very long time." She gestured to her client. "Is Mr. Best capable of that?"

She waited until all eyes were on Aaron.

"You've heard from the man who knows him better than anyone else in this room, but that's for you to decide. All I ask is one thing. When you enter that jury room, ask yourselves whether Rae Malone—and Becky Cox, Carole Wade, Fern Kaplan, and Starla McBride—deserve more than speculation. Whether these five victims—these five women—deserve to have the law enforcement agencies of this state take their deaths seriously enough to try to find the real killers."

A fter closing arguments Pilar wanted a late lunch, but Jackie wasn't hungry. She never was, sweating out a verdict. They compromised on a Mexican restaurant not far from the courthouse where Pilar ignored her and ordered for them both. She would have gotten food into Jackie if she had to jerk her head back and pour it down her throat. Then they returned to the office to await the call that the jury had returned.

Dispirited, Jackie flopped in a chair at the dining room table. It was still littered with stale food, scraps of paper, and Pilar's endless legal pads.

"Who are you calling?" Jackie asked as Pilar reached for the phone.

"Worrell's clerk."

"Are you nuts?"

"Shush. She's cool. . . ." Turning away, Pilar spoke softly, waited two minutes, and hung up.

"What did they order for lunch?" Jackie asked.

"Pizza. Three pies, all the same."

"They *agreed*?"

"As soon as the bailiff brought them the menus. They could have had deli."

Deli was a much better sign. The assertion of choice in something as mundane as ham versus roast beef augured well for debate, the disagreement that was the lifeblood of a successful defense. The thought of twenty-four identical slices of pizza was enough to make Jackie positively ill.

She stared at the mess on the table. "Might as well start cleaning up."

"Maybe the jury will hang," Pilar said loyally.

"After ordering the same pizza? Not a chance."

Pilar emptied an ashtray in the wastebasket, then sank back in her chair. She was a great believer in nothing being over until the fat ladies on the court of appeals sang. "Big plans tonight?"

"Richard wants to celebrate. His place, of course."

"Cocky little feller, ain't he?"

"I prefer to think of it as an appealing innocence." Jackie winced. "Sorry—I've got just one thing on my mind."

"I'm sure the doctor will have something to fix you up."

"It better be champagne or vodka, because either way, I'm getting smashed."

Lighting a cigarillo, Pilar blew a perfect ring. "First-date jitters, eh?"

"It's not as if we just met," Jackie replied.

"You can't tell much from a peck on the lips. But I said from the beginning you needed to get—"

"I thought you couldn't stand him."

"The doc? As of the moment he said those murders were related, we kissed and made up. All I care about is he came through for you in the end."

"He certainly did."

"You might as well go for it," Pilar said with resignation. "One day that brass ring's bound to turn gold."

"Such a romantic!"

"Might as well be someone who can support you in style . . ."

The phone rang.

Pilar answered and immediately hung up.

"Grab your lipstick, the jury just came back."

Chapter | Forty-four

Would the defendant please rise?"

As Jackie and Aaron stood, Worrell leaned forward in his chair.

Beside her, she could feel Aaron trembling. In those seconds before the verdict, how quickly fury and resentment fled! Now there was only need—and nothing more she could do. Whatever mistakes she'd made, *he* would pay the price. And the traditional signs were bad.

Avoiding eye contact with either side, the jurors had filed in wearing the impassive stares they'd learned from the judge. None had the jazzed look that came from advocating the underdog. Even Worrell seemed a little too nonchalant as he refolded the verdict slip and passed it back to the foreman to read.

"—charge of murder in the first degree, we find the defendant, Aaron Best, not guilty."

That fraction of a second when she thought she'd heard it wrong, and then Aaron exhaled and hung his head. Why did they always do that when they *won*?

Cheated death once more.

As the courtroom erupted, Jackie turned to Aaron and hugged him. Pilar was there, pounding her on the shoulder, and Jackie crossed the aisle to shake Pratt's hand. Behind him stood a stricken and disbelieving Rodger Malone. At that moment she had never envied her old classmate less.

"Until next time," she told Pratt.

"There won't be a next time for him," Malone replied. "Not if I have anything to say . . ."

Aaron was surrounded by reporters and there was no sign of Richard. Or Mark, for that matter. Signaling Pilar, Jackie slipped out through the jury room. Nothing Aaron said could hurt him now.

They were at the rear door of the City and County Building before either spoke.

"*That* was close," Jackie murmured.

"Two hours was barely long enough to polish off their pizza."

"Trust me, it could have gone either way. If not for Richard . . ."

"You'd better tell the doc to chill that champagne. He'll want to celebrate in style."

R ush hour on Friday afternoon had already begun, and as they exited the parking lot into heavy traffic, Jackie shielded her eyes from the glare. Thunderclouds were moving in from the west, bringing monsoon moisture. With Pilar driving, she could finally relax.

"How about a nip with me first?" Pilar offered.

"What, you want to serve me up to my expert bombed?" Jackie laughed, but she was exhausted. Immersion in a trial was like being pickled. All she really wanted was to sleep for a week. "I may just cancel—"

"Don't you dare!"

"Aren't I entitled—"

"You've kept that fish on the hook long enough. He's earned his worm."

They pulled into the gravel lot and climbed out of Pilar's car. Jackie's Corolla was the only other vehicle there; everyone else had left for the weekend.

"Sure you won't come with me for a drink?" Pilar asked.

"I'm going in to call Richard. Maybe file a few things . . ."

The postverdict mind dump.

"Well, don't be too long. And I want *every* detail on Monday."

Two whole days of peace and quiet. No Aaron Best, no

telephones . . . And the Hollow Man could crawl back under whatever rock he came from.

Jackie kicked off her shoes and speed-dialed Richard's number. No answer. Wait and surprise him. Maybe by then her throbbing headache would be gone. There was nothing like the stress of a trial to bring on the mother of all bad days. Leaning back in her chair, she planted her feet on her desk.

Postmortem.

Not just the Hollow Man's preferred mode of sex, but all the loose ends and should-have-dones that dogged her after every trial.

First mistake: not reading Aaron's damn custody file. She should never have been blindsided by his relationship with Richard. Not Richard's fault, or even her client's, but her own. No matter how good she was on her feet, she could never fully compensate.

Reaching for her briefcase, Jackie dumped the contents on her desk. The compulsive Pilar would be in first thing in the morning to file everything away. Order out of chaos. Where would she be without Pilar?

Second mistake: not knowing the score with Mark. She should have sent Pilar to Dinosaur the minute Mark called her back in May, had her search the juvenile records the next day. And given her that credit slip. Too close a call.

Her desk was awash with paper and she hated that; the disorder was as jarring as the roar of a jackhammer. She began stacking Pilar's color-coded files on the carpet. Might as well make her job easier tomorrow.

Third mistake: trusting Aaron to level with her when she *knew* from day one he was a flake. In that first phone call she'd allowed herself to be suckered by the memory of his devotion to his son and the fact that he'd treated her fairly when he'd insulated her house. How tickled he must have been when she told him their expert was Richard Hanna! Of course he'd known they'd win.

She tossed a pile of unread briefs on the floor. The best thing about an acquittal was that the case was over. No appeals, never having to see the client again . . . Why didn't this *feel* like the end?

Reaching for the phone, she punched the button with Richard's number. Still no answer. Probably tied up with a patient. Irritated, she jerked the cord out of the headset. At least the phone wouldn't ring. Her yellow pad was covered with Aaron's doodles, bull's-eyes and cones and a surprisingly good likeness of Sunny Abbot. His next conquest? She flipped the page.

Rae Malone in a diaphanous gown that left nothing to the imagination—the Goddess of Castle Pines. And a cartoon of Aaron lying on a couch with a bemused Richard holding his patient's head in his hands. "What's next, doc?" the head was saying. Artistic talent ran in the family. Jackie tore out the sheets, crumpled them, and tossed them in the trash. Now her desk was bare except for the envelope of photographs. Undoing the clasp, she pulled them out.

First the victims. Dealing the portraits across her desk in a faceup version of solitaire, she arranged them in five stacks.

Designer shades and a citronella lamp. Half-glasses on a golden chain. Eyes like a wolf's, the worry cleft in Carole's brow . . . Of course it was the eyes. But there had to be another connection. She shuffled the pictures again and sorted them by topics.

Cheesecake shots. Plunging neckline, freckled shoulders, gauzy skirt, and lace camisole. Flowing hair. Beguiling, but so what? Now the family photos. Becky with the boy her sister resented, Carole with the budding musician, Starla with husband and child in happier days. Divorcées all. Big deal . . . She pushed them to one side and reached for the rest.

A valley with gnarled fingers thrusting through the earth. Garden of the Gods. A tighter shot from the ground looking up, three spires with Becky's elegant feet protruding from a crack. What story did the Three Graces tell?

Massive red stones at a forty-five-degree angle. The mouth of a cave whose gums were scabbed with lichen. Sage and gray, a sickly yellow fungus. The yawning became sucking and the resting place of Carole Wade convulsed.

Starla stuffed between an enormous pair of stone buttocks

while the cliff behind her wept mineral tears. Fern's headless body crouched in supplication before a riderless horse. Come-hither eyes, decapitation, colossal figures of stone . . . What would Lily say?

Jackie, look! It's like Medusa was here.

The island of the Gorgons, fields littered with creatures Medusa had frozen with a killing glance. But what was missing from this picture?

"You left too fast for me to buy you a drink."

In her doorway stood Aaron Best.

"Don't tell me you don't drink with clients." He took a swig from his bottle of Johnnie Walker Black, wiped the neck, and held it out to her. Not the first defendant who'd gotten bombed after she snatched victory from the muck. "Why don't we pretend I'm the expert?"

"Look, Aaron—"

"I know you've got a thing going with Hanna." As he sank into the opposite chair, she swept the photos into her briefcase and cursed herself for not locking the door. "What do I care? My team *won*."

"Maybe I should call you a cab." She reached for the phone, but the cord was unplugged. Stupid, stup—

"And I have a surprise for the coach." He took another swig. "Or are you the quarterback? Not much of a sports fan—quarterback, bareback, all the same to me . . ."

Stinking drunk. What had Richard said about Aaron's fantasies? *Sexually aggressive but ultimately harmless.* She'd handled her share of drunks: the trick was not to antagonize.

"—not with a ribbon or a bow," he was saying, "it's bigger than that." Suddenly, he realized she wasn't paying attention. "Don't you want to know what your surprise is?"

"What's my surprise, Aaron?" Now that they'd won, he was trying to make up for accusing her of rolling over. Two more minutes and she would send him on his way.

"If you could meet anyone in the world, who would you want it to be?"

"I don't know what—"

"The Hollow Man, right?"

That was enough.

"The Hollow Man doesn't exist," she replied.

"That's not what you told the jury. Even Hanna thinks he's real."

"That doesn't mean—"

"Only one way to find out . . ." Rising unsteadily, he leaned over her desk. "Come with me."

"Where?"

"To meet the Hollow Man."

Jackie reached for the receiver and blindly punched a button. No ring, but he wouldn't—Aaron grabbed the unplugged phone and flung it against the wall.

"Just us," he said.

She shot to her feet. "Get out. Right now."

He straightened in surprise. "I always knew you were a ballsy little—"

"I mean it. Leave now or I'm calling the cops."

Aaron shrugged. "I just wanted—"

"*Out.*"

Jackie held her breath as Aaron clattered down the stairs. When the front door slammed, she sank back in her chair, trembling. What if he came back? She had to get out of here. . . . She walked to her window and looked down. He was staring at the outer door with the bottle in his hand. After a moment he turned and strode toward his pickup truck. As he climbed in, her fear turned to curiosity. Did he go home after the trial for it? Or did Mark bring it to him? And had he really expected her to go with him? Another fantasy.

Aaron's tires spun on the gravel and his engine stalled. He shouldn't be driving in that condition. The case was over, but where did her responsibility to him end? The last thing he needed was to get busted for DUI while celebrating his acquittal. She glanced at the clock on her wall. Quarter past six, too early to meet Richard. She'd planned to go home and change. . . . What did Aaron *mean* about meeting the Hollow Man?

As his engine turned again without catching, she thought about calling him a cab. Or at least— Grabbing her briefcase, she slipped on her shoes and ran out the door.

Chapter | Forty-five

Aaron was heading south, weaving in and out of traffic at thirty miles an hour. As they approached Washington Park, Jackie saw flocks of yuppies in jog bras and Nikes and cyclists in helmets and tight shorts hoping to get their exercise before it rained. Friday evening, the man of her dreams waiting, and here she was, tailing a drunken client God knew where. . . .

Aaron made a right without signaling and continued west. Two blocks later he turned left onto a street of neatly tended bungalows. Jackie sighed with relief. All a bluff. He was going home. Pulling to a stop at the curb, he jumped out and mounted the steps to his front door. He fumbled with the lock and let himself in.

Jackie circled the block and parked across the street, where she had an unobstructed view of Aaron's bungalow. It started to rain. He was probably already on the couch, sleeping it off. He'd have a hell of a hangover in the morning. Did he know Mark had taken up with his wife?

A light blinked on in the front room.

Why now?

The clock on the dashboard said five minutes had passed. Behind the blinds Jackie saw movement. Was someone else there? She hadn't seen anyone enter. The rain was coming in her window, but she dared not close it for fear it would fog. What was Aaron doing?

She thought back to the photos of the crime scenes. From day one something about them had nagged her, and back at her office she'd almost had it. Fields littered with figures of stone . . . *What was missing from this picture?*

Rae Malone.

Body left under the viaduct, head pitched behind center field. The only victim whose head was found, the only dump site that didn't fit. And the only woman connected with Aaron Best—and his brother, Mark. Unidentified tissue under Rae's nail. Was the Hollow Man really two?

Nothing in Mr. Best's personal history suggests abuse.

But what about Mark's? When Aaron's brother was sent away, Richard said their mother made Aaron her little man.

I don't want to get too Freudian.

Had big brother occupied that spot before, had it driven him to the rage that resulted in bashing another boy's brains with a bat?

These guys tend to start young.

Aaron followed where Mark led. Tattoos, mustangs, women . . . Richard had identified Mark all but by name. And if he was playing with Aaron's wife behind his brother's back and she stood to inherit the company, maybe Mark wouldn't want Aaron to walk. Maybe he killed Starla to reduce those odds.

Jackie opened the door and stepped into the rain. She should find a phone, call *someone*. Or was her paranoia out of control once again? The light was still on, but nothing moved behind the blinds.

Just walk up those steps and ring the bell. If Aaron's alone, tell him you were worried about him and then leave.

And if he isn't?

One step at a time.

The flower beds were choked with weeds and the paint on the porch was pocked and chipped. Jackie remembered the freshly painted garage when she visited Wendy in May, the gleaming linoleum in the kitchen. Since then nobody had cared for the place. . . . With her finger an inch from the doorbell, she hesitated.

What if he wasn't alone? What if he really was meeting the Hollow Man—was she prepared for what she might find? *Sexually aggressive but infantile, passive and eager to please.*

Maybe the Hollow Man was *Aaron's* fantasy. She punched the doorbell.

No movement from inside, the only sound rain drumming the gabled roof. She knocked on the door.

"Aaron?"

Her fist made a feeble sound against the solid oak, barely louder than the rain. She reached for the knob. The door was unlocked. She opened it and stood at the threshold.

"Aaron?" she called again.

The light came from a lamp on the table by the window. Its arc reached from the couch to the fireplace. She took another step forward and listened.

No drips or creaks. In the air an acrid odor. Like a match, but stronger.

On the table beside the lamp stood the Johnnie Walker and an empty glass. At her office Aaron had been drinking straight from the bottle; the glass showed he was expecting a visitor. The couch faced the fireplace, and as Jackie took another step forward, she looked over the back of the cushions to the rug. Where Aaron's body lay.

Faceup, eyes open, mouth gaping. A ragged wound in the shape of a star by his right temple. Blood seeping into the braided rags beneath his head. She knelt to touch his outstretched arm. It was warm. The smell was overpowering.

Rising, she took a step back. Aaron stared up, ghostly pale. The fingers of his right hand were spread, proclaiming innocence one last time. At their tips lay a .38 revolver with a two-inch barrel and a wooden grip.

Jackie turned and ran down the rain-slick steps.

From the 7-Eleven three blocks away, she called 911. She was waiting for them in front of the bungalow when they arrived minutes later. Two patrol cars, followed by an ambulance. Neighbors clustered on lawns and porches. The rain had stopped and the air smelled clean.

"Any reason why your client wanted to kill himself, Ms. Flowers?"

The detective had his notebook out but kept his pen in his pocket. He cared more about her legs than the answer.

"This afternoon he was acquitted of murder."

"Maybe he disagreed with the verdict."

"Aaron Best didn't kill himself, lieutenant. He was—"

"Look, Ms. Flowers." He was trying to be kind, but he'd made up his mind. "These things happen. Guy gets away with murder but his conscience won't let him live with it. It's not your—"

"I'm telling you, he was planning to meet someone!" She forced herself to slow down. Hysterical women—not to mention criminal defense lawyers—had zero credibility with men in blue. And even less with plainclothes detectives. "My client had *no* reason to take his life."

"Was he drunk?"

He'd seen the Johnnie Walker, surely smelled it on Aaron.

"He came to my office with a bottle. He'd been celebrating and wanted me to join him."

His eyes traveled from her sodden shoes to her rain-soaked blouse. "Why'd you follow him home?"

"I was concerned because he'd been drinking."

"The two of you fight?"

"*What?*"

"Passions run high in a trial, especially toward the end. And when you represent killers . . ."

Lady lawyer, you deserve what you got.

"I told you, he—"

"Who was he planning to meet?"

The Hollow Man. If she said that, how he would *laugh*.

"You should be looking for a green Explorer. It wasn't a suicide: Aaron Best was killed by his brother Mark."

Chapter Forty-six

As she mounted her staircase, Jackie wriggled out of her skirt. At the landing she stripped off her blouse. The rain had ruined the silk but she could still smell Aaron. She continued to the second floor, pausing only to flip on the light in the upstairs hallway. Upon arriving home she'd called Richard to tell him she wasn't coming. That Aaron was dead.

"Suicide?" he'd asked.

"Mark."

"Why would Mark—"

"Mark's the Hollow Man. And he's been sleeping with Aaron's wife."

"If he was the Hollow Man, why—"

"Maybe he wanted a fresh start, without his brother tagging along. Doing stupid things like leaving DNA behind. Mark must have been furious when I didn't call him to the stand—or maybe he didn't like his little brother finally being on top."

"That's nuts!" Richard paused, and she braced herself for the linear logic she so envied. "You said the gun was right by Aaron's hand, that he'd been drinking and sounded delusional. Suicide is anger turned inward, Jackie, the product of rage and frustration, fear of rejection. . . . Maybe justice was served."

"Justice?"

"Hasn't it occurred to you that Aaron may have killed Rae Malone?"

"But you said—"

"Killers reenact what they themselves suffered, remember me telling you that? A suicide is the ultimate victim."

"But he showed no remorse. And why did he ask me to—"

"Maybe he wanted you to witness his punishment."

Jackie's head was spinning and her clothes stank. She had to get out of them and into a hot shower. "I'm too tired to think."

"Things will be clearer in the morning." He hesitated. "Look, why don't I come over? We'll get in my car and drive to the mountains. There's a fabulous inn near Estes Park. We could spend the weekend. You need to get away."

A brass bed and pancakes for breakfast. Place herself entirely in someone else's hands . . . "Tomorrow."

"Are you sure you'll be okay? I could—"

"No, I just need a good night's sleep."

"I'll pick you up at nine."

Jackie stood under the spray until the heat burned her skin. She wanted to steam every pore, rid herself of the memory of that star-shaped wound in Aaron's temple, the ragged edges and blackened flesh. Her clothes were wadded in a corner of the bathroom, her shoes already in the trash. She was too exhausted even to call Pilar.

Aaron's trial seemed a hundred years ago. What was that joke—the operation was a success but the patient died? Maybe it *was* suicide. Or the two of them all along. She'd never know whether Mark was planning to screw his brother on the stand, but that alibi would have been a small price for him to pay.

With a thick towel she began drying her hair. Couple of months in an honor camp to spring your accomplice, then permanently shut him up. The follower who did his dirty work . . . and contributed to his sense of *power*. Richard had been right—just because Aaron was the boss didn't mean he called the shots. She should never have let him meet Mark alone.

In bare feet and robe Jackie padded downstairs to the kitchen. Tea would steady her, its warmth cleanse her from the inside out. Then perhaps she could sleep. She filled the kettle all the way and set it on the stove. Toweling her hair, she went to the study.

Her briefcase leaned against the threshold.

Stow it under the desk, out of sight. The tea would be ready soon, she couldn't bear those faces. . . . They were staring right at her.

Why couldn't she see the connection?

The first set of photographs was the bodies. The killer's most private fantasy.

Becky with ankles primly touching, her lower limbs aligned but hips rotated to the side. Carole's arms outstretched, one higher than the other. Fern on her knees, upper body arched forward so that her uncoiled silver hair would have flowed like water. She'd thought they were prostrated at altars, but it was something more. The next set of photos was the dump sites.

The Three Graces—muses defiled. Granite obelisks and a riderless horse. The monstrous maw at Red Rocks, ruddy buttocks at Roxborough Park. Figures larger than life, turned to statues but animated by a twisted mind. Did it empower him to debase his victims so? Or had they debased *him*? Her eyes traveled to the minerals above her head.

What was it about stone?

One by one Jackie arranged the family portraits at eye level below the minerals. Starla with a dark-haired boy squirming in her lap, Carole's son with his flute. Becky's sister said her child was a handful and they'd enrolled him in a special education program. Aaron's mother made him her little man, creating resentment and frustration. Did it spiral out of control?

Innocence turned inside out is corruption—*was that how he targeted his victims?*

"Jackie?"

Richard was standing at her door. Had she left it unlocked?

"I rang the bell, but you didn't hear."

The kettle was starting to sing. That must be why.

"With Mark on the loose, I didn't want you to be alone." Stepping to her chair, he stooped to kiss her on the forehead. Her hair lay damp at her shoulders, the towel abandoned in her lap. He picked it up and began rubbing her scalp. "You smell wonderful."

"Shampoo . . ."

"I couldn't wait until morning." He continued drying her hair. "I don't remember seeing those."

"More photos of the victims."

Pinning cutouts on a paper doll, a garnet earring to Fern Kaplan's cheek. Not her *cheek*—something about the curve of her back as she crouched before that stone horse. Her hair would have cascaded. . . .

Richard dropped the towel and began massaging Jackie's neck. "You thought there was someone else because of that earring. I liked your possessiveness."

"Who was she?"

"An actress I knew."

"I'll bet she's gorgeous."

"She certainly thought so." Strong thumbs kneaded the knobs at the base of her skull, fingertips feathered the crown. As Jackie closed her eyes and leaned into it, images collided— a Kabuki dancer on a wall of bougainvillea—rock and limb— flesh on stone. "Not easy, is it?"

"Hmnn?"

"Opening up. Trusting a man. It's so much safer to be alone. Until you find the one who understands, and suddenly you risk it all."

"You make it sound simple."

"With you, it is. You're different from any woman I've known."

Now those soothing fingers were probing the tendons at her collarbones. So good, so safe . . . An angry mother berating her son for not following instructions, Richard comforting him. Healing Hands was about intervening before it was too late. Knowing what to do to make it right.

"Not so different," she replied.

"But you are. You *see*."

"Not well enough, apparently. Because I still can't—"

"Sshh. Just relax and let yourself go. Your secrets are safe with me."

Healing hands radiating warmth. When you work so intensely with life you can't help but—*Why doesn't he let those plants grow?*

Because children repress what's said and done but not how it *feels*, and killers reenact their own suffering. Did the Hollow Man stunt his victims because he himself was not allowed to grow?

The kettle wailed and Jackie's eyes flew open.

"I'll turn that off," Richard said, and his footsteps echoed softly down the hall toward the kitchen while she stared at the family portraits. There were none of Rae. Abruptly the whistling stopped.

Kitchen, kitchen. Not a kitchen, but—Richard's library? Maybe she'd been focusing on the wrong set of photographs. *What did these remind her of?*

She felt Richard's presence before she heard him.

"Did Aaron ever talk about Rae?" she asked.

"Rae?"

"In therapy."

"Of course he did."

"You think he killed her."

Richard's palms were resting lightly on her shoulders, his fingertips pulsing against her skin. "You've known all along that was a possibility, Jackie. And with Aaron's suicide—"

"Rae's the one who never fit."

"Those women were killed for the same reason. Isn't that what I said in court?"

Not quite. "But she was the only victim Aaron knew."

And suddenly Jackie *saw*. The photos of grinning children behind Richard's desk, junipers proudly held aloft. And Becky's twisted trunk, Carole's limbs off-kilter, Fern a cascade . . . He'd wired their bodies like bonsai. What they had in common was their sons.

"Healing Hands—is that where you met them?"

"Met whom?"

"Those women went with you because they knew you. But Rae was different." Richard's hands tensed, then released her. As he stepped back and she rose from the chair, his clear gaze neither admitted nor denied. "Why Rae?"

"I told you. Aaron was referred to me. At first his problems were his marriage, then the affair. Rae turned him on and off, it was so familiar . . . She was a master at the game. The way she looked, how she played him—"

Shared intimacies potent enough to transcend every boundary, obliterate all judgment. Empathy, control, rage—Aaron's fantasies had aroused the Hollow Man. And when his patient took them a step too far and jeopardized all by killing Rae, how furious Richard must have been!

"—did what he had to do. Rae gave him no choice. But you're not like any of those women, Jackie." For one crazy moment Richard's facade slipped and his eyes were alight—with *hope*? She had to get out of here. "—safer to walk away, but I couldn't. Do you know what I risked by getting involved in your case?"

Keep him talking, get closer to the door . . . "Why did you?"

"Because Aaron took what was private and defiled it! He made it all about sex, but that was *their* game. I had to be the one—"

"Richard, listen to me. We'll—"

"—dead now and I'm ready to stop. I always knew I could, but now I *want* to. With you—"

"Richard, it's over. But you need help."

As his hope died, Jackie knew her only chance to reach him was lost. And out of the corner of her eye she saw scarlet.

Lily.

Frantically, she gestured for the child to leave before he saw her. But Lily stood her ground and Richard turned.

"I knew you would come," he said evenly.

He reached out and Lily took a step closer.

"She's just a child," Jackie pleaded. "She doesn't know anything."

"It's not what she knows," he chided. "It's what she *is*. And she knows exactly what this is about. She sets the rules." He turned back to Lily. "You were watching, weren't you? For me to come."

Lily nodded, mesmerized.

"We're old friends, aren't we?" Richard continued, his voice infinitely patient. He was holding a black plastic device the size of a TV remote, with metal teeth on the outer edges and fangs in between. "I know all about you, Lily. I know you like snakes. . . ."

"Get out," Jackie cried. *"Run!"*

He pointed the device at Jackie.

"Forty thousand volts. Ever wonder how long three seconds can last?"

A blue-white light arced across the fangs to the sound of two sharp cracks.

Pop-pop

The stink of ozone.

Jackie shoved the chair as hard as she could, and the edge of the seat caught Richard in the knees. He pitched forward but steadied himself on the desk, his face spasming with rage.

"She wants me!"

Lily leaped toward Jackie, but Richard grabbed her red windbreaker. Yanking her close, he pressed the toggle switch again.

Pop-pop pop-pop

A chemical odor pierced the room and Jackie jerked the child to her. Lily had peeled out of her jacket and was clutching her chest.

"Okay, baby?" Jackie whispered into her hair.

"He missed."

Richard's hand had tangled in her hood. He freed himself from the windbreaker and flung it to the floor.

"When I hit him I want you to run, okay?"

"No . . ."

"I mean it, Lily, this is no time to—"

Richard was advancing on them with the stun gun in his right hand. The fangs spat twice.

Pop-pop, pop-pop

She would rush him as hard as she could and take it in the chest. Lily might have a chance. . . .

"Come to me, Lily." His voice was soft, seductive. "I'd never hurt you, you know that."

Jackie grabbed Lily's shoulders with both hands.

"On the count of three," she whispered, *"you run."*

He took a step forward.

"Come to me. . . ."

One.

Another step. He pointed the gun at Lily.

"Don't be afraid. . . ."

Two.

Now at Jackie.

"You're the only one who understands. . . ."

Three.

Jackie shoved Lily to Richard's right and leaped for the stun gun. As Lily ran, he tried to grab her, but Jackie had the arm with the gun.

Lily froze.

"Run!" Jackie screamed. Richard was too strong, she was losing her grip. . . .

His left hand was wrapped around Jackie's wrist and a shattering pain shot to her elbow. He twisted and she felt herself falling to the floor. Just past his shoulder Lily pivoted and lifted both hands high over her head. As he leaned forward with the stun gun, Jackie saw a flash and Lily's fists came crashing down. Once, then again.

Richard fell on top of her and Jackie braced for forty thousand volts.

Three seconds passed and nothing happened. Cautiously, she rolled out from under him.

"Did I kill him?"

Lily stood over Richard like a big-game hunter, with the pyrite in both hands. The rock's sharp edges glittered red. Jackie grabbed the stun gun.

"I tried to get him in the eye like the mountain lion," the girl continued, "but I couldn't get him to turn."

The skin above Richard's left temple was torn and bleeding, and he gave a little moan. Jackie fumbled for the toggle switch. If she had to, she'd zap him. As often as it took.

"Call the police," she told Lily, who was still clutching the rock. "Nine one one. Top button on the left, bottom button on—"

"I *know* my numbers."

Jackie pulled Lily to her and kissed her.

"Then make that call."

Chapter | Forty-seven

I wouldn't be caught dead in that," Lily declared.

It was the Saturday before Labor Day and they were shopping for school clothes at the Cherry Creek Mall. Lily's spikes had grown long enough for fluorescent butterfly clips, and she'd been promoted to second grade.

"I thought vests were in." Jackie replied. "You wore one last year."

"Not with *embroidery*. I wish I had a cast." She gazed with longing at the plaster sleeve on Jackie's arm, then skipped to a rack of vests with more pockets than Jackie could count. "Now, *that's* cool."

"What are the pockets for?" Jackie asked. "Your mobile phone or the pager?"

Although Pratt's office was investigating the death of Aaron Best, no law enforcement agency was willing to admit the Hollow Man existed and Richard had been charged only with assaulting Jackie. He was behind the walls of the county jail, but Lily would be a star witness and her parents were taking no chances with her safety.

"My 'brainer.' Can you believe that creep thought I'd go *anywhere* with him?" Lily reached in her backpack and felt for the pyrite. Having written its story herself, she'd chosen it over the Chinese fluorite as her prize. And there'd been no further talk of returning to her homeland. "You really liked him, didn't you?"

"But you saw through him."

A cloud crossed Lily's face. "You think he'll get out?"

"Are you scared?"

"Naah . . ." She clutched the pyrite and Jackie drew her closer. "Not with you to protect me. I'm more worried about school."

"This year's going to be different," Jackie promised. They'd already been to the library for Lily's card. "But you don't have to carry rocks in your pocket."

"*You* do. . . . Now that I can read, maybe I'll go to law school."

"Since when do you want to be like me?"

"Since always."

Arms about each other's waists, they went in search of cargo pants.

About the Author

STEPHANIE KANE has practiced law since 1981. She was a corporate partner in the largest law firm in Colorado and then became a criminal defense attorney. She has lectured on money laundering and white collar crime in Eastern Europe. She has a black belt in karate and lives in Denver with her husband, a federal judge.

If you enjoyed Stephanie Kane's
debut novel, BLIND SPOT, you won't want
to miss her next novel of suspense!

Look for

QUIET TIME

by Stephanie Kane

Coming soon from Bantam Books!